I0818133

THE HEART YOU KEPT

BY T L SWAN

STANDALONE BOOKS

The Bonus

MR. SERIES

Mr. Masters
Mr. Spencer
Mr. Garcia

THE MILES HIGH CLUB SERIES

The Stopover
The Takeover
The Casanova
The Do-Over
Miles Ever After

KINGS OF THE RIVIERA SERIES

The Heart You Kept

KINGS OF THE RIVIERA

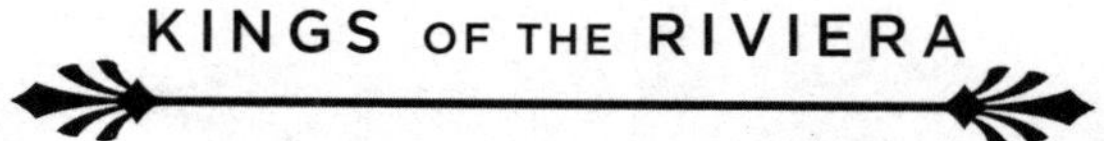

THE HEART YOU KEPT

T L SWAN

Arndell

THE HEART YOU KEPT
Copyright © T L Swan 2026
Published by Arndell, an imprint of Keeperton in 2026
1527 New Hampshire Ave. NW
Washington, D.C. 20036

10 9 8 7 6 5 4 3 2 1

ISBN: 978-1-923232-04-4 Paperback

This novel is a work of fiction. Any reference to names, characters, businesses, places, events and incidents are products of the author's imagination or are used in a fictitious manner. Any resemblance to real persons, living or dead, is entirely coincidental.

All rights are reserved. No part of this book may be reproduced or transmitted in any form or by any means, graphic, electronic, or mechanical, including photocopying, recording, taping, or by any information storage retrieval system such as AI, without the express written permission of the Publisher.

Library of Congress Control Number: 2025943227

Printed in China

Formatted by Kirby Jones
Cover Design by Alex Ross Creative

Sydney | Washington D.C. | London
www.keeperton.com/arndell

I would like to dedicate this book to the alphabet,
for those twenty-six letters have changed my life.

Within those twenty-six letters I have found myself,
and now I live my dream.

Next time you say the alphabet,
remember its power.

I do every day.

Gratitude

The quality of being thankful;
readiness to show appreciation for,
and to return kindness.

CHAPTER ONE

ALORA.

"What next?"

I cannot believe that I'm searching for this.

Setting the letter to the side, I open my computer. I know I promised that I would do every single last thing on this bucket list and I want to…but honestly?

This?

Nerves dance in my stomach.

I tip my head back to the ceiling. "Are you laughing up there, bitch?"

I type into Google.

Anonymous sex club for kinks.

I read through the results.

First one…. No. Again…no…no.

I read on to the next page.

THE ESTABLISHMENT

The Establishment is a private facility five-star resort in Switzerland.

Explore your needs, wants, and kinks in a safe and anonymous environment.

How does it work?

We at the Establishment believe that everyone should live their life to its full potential and leave no stone unturned.

Many people have sexual desires or interests that are not cohesive with their lifestyle, current relationships, or religious beliefs.

We help you move past this without barriers in a clinical and safe environment.

One weekend.
Total confidentiality.
Names and personal information are never shared between clients.

How do I apply?
Submit your application with what experience you would like to explore.

If successful, we match you with a person or people of your desired sex with the same needs and wants as yours.

What can I expect?
Day One Arrive at the resort and enjoy one night in your private room alone.

If desired, all patrons have access to a sexual psychologist for a consultation.

Day Two You will be introduced to your partner or partners as Jane or John Doe, under no circumstances are names ever exchanged.

There are no names or data kept on the in-house database. A security breach or cyberattack is impossible.

You will then spend the next twenty-four hours in a private suite with them living out and enjoying your every fantasy.

All suites are equipped with a private swimming pool, Jacuzzi, steam room, gymnasium, bondage and playroom, swings, and the appropriate benches. All equipment such as toys and lubricant are supplied.

Day Three You part ways with your partner/partners and spend a night in your own private suite to recover.

Day Four Satisfied...you return home to your life without the risk of anyone ever finding out.

Your secrets and health are 100% safe.

CONFIDENTIALITY IS WHAT SETS US APART.

The cost to visit **THE ESTABLISHMENT**
is €70,000.

Don't live life wondering what if.
Apply for your dreams to come true today.

APPLY NOW.

"Seventy thousand euros…what the hell?" I click out of it in disgust, that was sounding so perfect too. Ughh…I knew it was too good to be true.

I flop back onto my couch. I guess at least at that price you know people are definitely going to be discreet.

I mean…I do have the money she left me….

No.

My mind goes back to the hospital, so clear in my mind that it's like it was yesterday. I pick the letter back up and read Misty's bucket list for the ten thousandth time.

I promised that if she didn't make it that I would do it for her, every last thing.

I get a vision of how sick she was and how hard she fought and all the things on her wish list that she should have gotten to do herself.

My eyes well with tears, no matter how much time goes past…. Her loss is something that I'll never recover from. Best friends are supposed to grow old together; it's the unwritten law.

Her words from the hospital echo through my mind: *If I don't get to do these things, Alora, promise me that you'll do them for me.* You will, I told her…. But even then, deep down, I knew she wouldn't. And I was right, because that's how it ended.

I'm living my life for the two of us now.

My eyes skim the letter. I have one thing left to do.

Number Nine...Peg a guy.

I smirk, Misty was a such a dirty bird. How the hell was an eighteen-year-old girl so deviant?

I don't want to do this one, *how can I do this one?* It's so far from anything I have ever ventured into. I click into Pornhub and type into the search bar.

Pegging.

I peruse through the options and finally find one that I like.

I hit play and watch….

I begin to perspire.

It's weird and wrong and…*hot.*

Fuck.

No, it's a hard no.

EDWARD.

Paul looks over the top of his glasses across his desk at me. "Hello, Edward." He smiles.

I run my tongue over my teeth, this guy pisses me off. "Hello."

"How are you today?"

I flick my hands up. "I'm here."

"And have you had a chance for any reflection on our last visit?"

"Yes." I glance at my watch. "I don't have long today."

He smiles calmly as he folds his hands on his lap. "Let's recap, shall we?"

I exhale heavily. "Do you have to say the same thing every visit? Don't you get fucking bored?"

Paul smiles and I imagine myself punching him out of his chair.

He reads his notes. "You are here because you have control issues."

"No."

Paul looks up at me. "Why are you here, Edward?"

"Because I promised my sister, Charlotte, that I would see a psychologist."

He runs his finger up his temple as he watches me. "Charlotte is important to you?"

I pinch the bridge of my nose. "This is a waste of time, this is my sixth visit and I'm not getting anywhere with you. Of course she's fucking important to me, why else would I be here?"

"You can't fix a problem until you admit it, Edward."

I sit forward in my chair. "I don't have a problem. I like control, I like to take it from people...I like to assert mine. That's not a problem...it's an asset."

His eyes hold mine. "How is that working out for you relationship wise?"

I run my hand through my hair.

He keeps reading his notes. "Take your time."

Fuck off.

I glance at my watch.

"On our second visit you told me that you have had a string of broken relationships. That you like strong women but they can only take your need to control for so long before they leave."

"I leave them," I reply, angered.

"Do you leave them because you want to, or do you leave them because you begin to feel out of control yourself?"

I roll my lips.

"You see, I think that you know you have an issue, and that you hide behind Charlotte making you come here. That deep down you want to see me and you want to correct this."

I stay silent.

"Am I right?"

I feel adrenaline scream through my body. "Maybe."

"Tell me this, Edward, have you ever thought of tackling control head-on?"

"Isn't that what we're doing?" I roll my eyes. "Can you hear the things you say sometimes? How am I paying for this bullshit?"

"You are here because I'm left field and I get success. Regardless of how unorthodox my suggestions, there's no denying I do."

I exhale, it's true, he is supposed to be the best.

"You've told me that you're a highly sexed individual," he says.

"Yes."

"How often do you like to have sex?"

"Daily."

"And if you don't have sex?"

"I fuck my hand," I reply coldly. "Get to the point."

"What would you consider the ultimate handover of power to a sexual partner?"

"A woman?" I ask.

"Is that your sexual preference?"

"That's my only preference."

"Okay...let's run with that. How far would you let a woman dominate you in the bedroom?"

"I wouldn't."

He sits back in his chair and smiles. "Not at all? Not even in the moment?"

"Where are you going with this?"

"You came to me because I get results and we are getting nowhere in this office. Let's explore other possibilities."

He digs through his drawer and slides a card over the desk to me.

THE ESTABLISHMENT

"What's this?" I ask.

"It's a private facility in Switzerland, I think it would be very beneficial for you to visit."

"Why?"

He folds his hands in front of him. "I would like you to explore the possibility of handing your power over to a woman. Give yourself completely over to the experiment."

I frown as his words roll around in my head. "Meaning what?"

"Have you ever thought of visiting a dominatrix?"

"Nobody is fucking me with a strap-on cock," I spit.

He smiles, clearly amused by my horror. "It doesn't have to come to that, but I think it would be good for you to explore other ways to hand over your sexuality and vulnerability and to learn trust."

"No." I shake my head. "No fucking way in hell."

"You might like it." He smirks.

"Absolutely know I won't."

"It's one weekend. Confidentiality is assured and you will be anonymously matched with a woman who has the same needs as you."

"What woman would need this?"

He smiles. "I'd like you to find out."

"No."

"If you go and you can't go through with it...at least you'll know."

"Know what?"

"That there *is* a control issue and that way we have a good place to start moving forward."

"What in the hell is letting a woman dominate me in bed going to do?"

"It's going to free you from fear."

"I'm not scared."

"Prove it."

SIX MONTHS LATER.

ALORA.

"Is there anything else I can help you with, Miss Doe?" the bellboy asks.

Like what…?

Wait…do the bellboys give out sexual favors here too?

Oh dear god, I want to run far, far away.

What the hell am I doing here?

"No." I force a smile. "I'm good." I close the door of my suite and sit on the bed and look around. I'm at the Establishment, the kink hotel in Switzerland.

I flop back onto the bed and look up at the ceiling as I search for divine guidance. After going round and round for months I knew if I didn't do this now…that the wish list wouldn't be completed. I have no idea if my future boyfriend or husband is going to be into it and if he isn't, I can't do it with someone else.

It will be too late.

I'm using my inheritance to do this, and I'm terrified and creeped out and I hate to admit it…a little excited.

I get up and turn on the taps as I run myself a deep bath. I sit on the edge as I wait for it to fill.

Tomorrow I meet him, Misty's stranger. I smile as I think how proud she would be of me and even I have to admit, I'm a little proud of me too.

I pace back and forth in my room.

This was a bad, bad idea, what on earth was I thinking? There's no way in hell that I can go through with this. I want to leave; I want to leave now.

He's due any minute…my eyes dart to the door, if I just leave now nobody would be any the wiser….

I'm wearing a black fitted dress and heels; my dark hair and makeup is done.

I'm even wearing lingerie and suspenders.

All I know about my date for the weekend is that he's between twenty-five and thirty-seven, he's heterosexual and that he wants to be pegged by a heterosexual woman.

Who is supposed to be me….

No names or personal information are going to be exchanged and this is the only time we will ever see each other.

I swallow the nervous lump in my throat.

I glance over to the black box that was delivered an hour ago. The equipment we need for the assignment.

Fuck…. I can't even bring myself to open the box and look at it.

*Bang, bang, bang…*goes my heart.

"Shit, shit, shit." I hold my temples as I imagine how horrifically bad this could be.

Knock, knock.

He's here.

I glance to the window, wondering if I can jump out of it and escape.

Oh no, it's too late to leave. I've wasted all my money on paying for something that I'm unsure if I'll be able to go through with.

I open the door and am greeted by another bellboy wearing a white uniform.

"Good evening, Miss Doe."

"Hello."

He steps to the side to reveal the man standing behind him, our eyes meet and the air leaves my lungs.

Tall, dark hair, and handsome, with the biggest blue eyes I've ever seen.

Utterly gorgeous.

We stare at each other as electricity crackles in the air between us.

"May I present Mr. Doe."

CHAPTER TWO

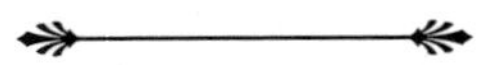

"Hello." He holds out his hand to shake mine.

Oh, he's English.

"Hello."

A weird sense of déjà vu falls over me.

Wait…have we met before?

Mr. Doe's eyes hold mine. "Leave us."

I glance around as I suddenly realize the bellboy is still here.

"Yes, sir." The bellboy turns to me and nods. "Dial nine if you need anything, Miss Doe."

"Thank you." I can't even look the poor bellboy in the eye. Does he know the perverted shit we're here to do?

Of course he does.

I just want the earth to swallow me whole, I'm very vanilla usually…I promise. What must he see working in a place like this?

The door closes as he leaves and we are left alone, I'm so nervous that I can hardly breathe.

Mr. Doe has a dominant power about him, why the hell would he be paying for sex?

He walks to the bar. "Would you like a drink?"

"Yes please?" I say timidly.

"What would you like?"

Cyanide sounds good.

"Umm…." I can't even think, let alone string two words together. "Whatever will be fine."

He stands with his back to me and as he pours our drinks my eyes roam over him. He's tall, standing over six foot three with dark hair, and well built. His suit is perfectly fitted and something about his aura and the way he holds himself tells me he's wealthy.

He turns and walks toward me with a crystal tumbler of amber fluid and ice. My heart somersaults in my chest as I take it from him.

He gestures to the table and chairs and we sit down opposite each other.

Just being close to this specimen of a man is unnerving.

"Thank you." I take a sip and wince.

Fuck.

Tastes like gasoline, only stronger.

He sits back in his chair and sips his drink as his eyes hold mine.

Thump.

Thump.

Thump goes my poor panicked heart.

What's he thinking?

An awkward silence hangs in the air between us and I just need to break the ice.

"You're not what I expected," I say softly.

"What did you expect?"

His piercing gaze has some sort of intimidation superpower, I want to crawl under the table and hide.

"I'm not sure."

His eyebrow flicks up as if unimpressed with my answer.

Fuck...why did I say that?

"Am I what you expected?" I try to sound confident but my question comes out as barely a whisper.

"No."

"Why not?"

"Because you're submissive."

No I'm not...am I?

"You don't like submissive?" I frown.

"I love submissive." His dark eyes hold mine and he lifts the drink to his lips and takes a slow sip. "Very much."

His approval excites me and I feel my face flush.

I nervously sip my drink. *What will I say next?*

Okay...what the fuck is going on here?

I'm supposed to be hating every moment of this and getting something ticked off a to-do list. Having a visceral physical reaction to this man was not in my plan.

"Do you always fidget when you're nervous?" he asks.

"What?"

"Your leg."

I glance down to see my leg bouncing and I put my hand on my thigh to stop it.

What the hell is wrong with me?

"Oh...sorry, I didn't realize." I look around for an excuse for my kindergarten behavior. "You're...." I shrug as I search for the right wording. "Intimidating."

A trace of a smile flashes across his face and he takes a slow sip again. "What are you doing here?"

"I...." I swallow the lump in my throat. "I...."

He raises an impatient eyebrow.

Fuck it. Just tell him the truth.

"I'm living out a bucket list for my best friend."

"A what?"

"My best friend wrote me a list before she passed of the ten things that she wanted to do in her life." I take a sip of my drink, feeling braver. "This is me fulfilling wish number nine. I promised her I would do each and every last one."

"This isn't even something that you want to do?"

"It wasn't...but, now that...you're...." My mouth is so dry I can't even talk.

The truth is you're gorgeous and the thought of fucking you in any shape or form excites me.

He frowns as he thinks for a moment. "What else was on the list?"

"Lots of things." I shrug. "Travel. A sex show in Amsterdam." My brain has gone completely blank under his scrutiny. "Umm.... A tattoo. And ballooning in Cappadocia."

"Anything else sexual?"

"Umm...." Oh god, why did I openly admit this? "A threesome."

His fascinated eyes hold mine and he sips his drink.

"And I did that.... A few years ago now, actually."

"And?"

"I...." I shrug, embarrassed. "I couldn't bring myself to do two men so I thought I would add another woman and...." My voice trails off.

"And what?"

"I learned that I don't like to share," I blurt out in a rush.

A trace of a smile crosses his face. "I don't share either."

"Right? I think it's weird that people do." I smirk, feeling a little more of my equilibrium return.

We fall silent and he sips his drink as if in deep in thought. "I'll have your money refunded. I apologize for wasting your time."

Disappointment runs through me.

"What?" I frown. "Why?"

"I'm...." He gives a subtle shrug as he tries to articulate himself. "This will not be advancing to the next stage."

"Why not?"

He gestures to the air that is crackling between us.

"What does that mean?"

"The physical attraction between us is too strong."

He feels it too.

I fight the goofy smile that is threatening to cover my face. "Isn't that the point?"

"From your perspective perhaps, from mine most definitely not."

What's he doing here?

"Do you think you're gay?" I ask.

"Absolutely not."

"It's okay if you are."

He stands as if outraged and walks toward the door.

He's leaving.

"What are you doing?" I splutter in a panic.

"This is not working."

"Stop." I stand too. "We've gone to all this trouble to get here and we are obviously attracted to each other so what's the point of not seeing where it goes?"

"I know where it goes and it doesn't go there," he spits angrily.

It suddenly dawns on me, he's nervous. This is out of the normal for him too.

"So show me where it does go." I gesture to the couch. "Sit down and...try and relax." I take the glass out of his hand and go to the bar; I refill it and hand it back over. "Drink this one hundred percent alcohol," I instruct him. "Although I think it's illegal to drink this in most countries." I take a shaky sip and I feel it burn all the way down. "But in a Swiss sex kink club I guess anything goes."

His eyes hold mine and I know he's only seconds from leaving.

"Sit down please, Mr. Doe," I whisper. "Don't go."

He hesitates before finally taking a seat on the couch and we fall silent again.

I have no idea what's going through his head.

"I don't like that you're doing this only because you are being forced," he says.

"I'm not being forced. I wanted to fulfill my friend's wishes, and to be honest now that I've met you—" I sip my drink as I try to muster up my courage, "—I think it will be very enjoyable to spend some time naked with you."

He gives me a slow sexy smile and sits back in his chair. "I'm a lot to take on."

There is no air in my lungs.

None.

I shrug, feeling like he's warning me.

"You said you were attracted to me?" I whisper.

"Don't act like you can't feel it."

We stare at each other, the magnetic pull toward him is so strong that I can hardly fight it.

Suddenly I just want the awkward fear gone. I want to get this over with.

Whatever *this* is.

"What happens now in a place like this?" I ask nervously.

His eyes hold mine.

"I've never been in a situation like this." I begin to babble on. "Do we date? Do we small talk? Do we eat dinner?" My eyes search his as I beg him to take control. "What do I do?"

"You take your clothes off," he says.

"What?"

"You said you want me to show you where it does go?"

"I did."

"Then do as I say. Take. Your. Clothes. Off."

My eyes widen.

"Now."

What the hell?

We didn't even kiss and he expects me to undress in front of him?

Wait…do we kiss?

I tip my head back and drain my glass, I cough as the poison burns my throat.

I go to walk into the bathroom.

"There," he demands.

"What?"

"You undress right there."

My heart is hammering in my chest and I glance toward the door, perhaps his idea of running was a better one. Screw this, I'm out of here.

"Look me in the eye and take your fucking clothes off," he growls.

Gulp…. I swallow the lump in my throat. Oh hell…what am I doing?

I take one stiletto off and throw it to the side.

Satisfaction flashes across his face and he sits back.

I take the other stiletto off with a shaky hand.

I'm literally about to have a heart attack.

I go to the bar and pour myself another glass of Dutch courage and take a huge gulp.

I predict copious amounts of therapy coming in my very near future. I hesitate for a moment…. Fuck it, what have I got to lose. I'm here now.

I slowly undo the zipper at the side of my dress.

"Eyes on me," he demands.

I glance up and see him sitting there with his hand on his crotch through his pants.

Oh…. Not what I expected…. I swallow the lump in my throat.

Is this really happening?

No wonder I was nervous, I had a very good reason to be.

With his dark eyes locked on mine I take my dress down over one shoulder and then the other.

"Take it off," he mouths.

Oh hell on a cracker, once he sees my body he really will run for the hills.

Can't we at least dim the lights or something?

With my heart in my throat I slowly slide the dress down and step out of it.

I stand before him in a black lace bra and G-string with a black ribbon suspender belt.

Satisfaction crosses his face as his eyes hungrily roam down over my body.

"Turn around."

"What?" I frown.

"Turn. Around."

He wants to look at my ass.

I nervously turn around.

"Touch your toes."

"What?" I squeak.

"Touch. Your. Toes."

I didn't drink enough alcohol for this.

Oh…this is mortifying…and on some perverted level strangely arousing.

I bend and touch my toes and he inhales sharply. I close my eyes as I hear my heartbeat in my ears.

Help!

I hear the couch creak as if he's stood up, what is it about this man that has me in a puddle?

I see his feet as he comes to stand behind me and I hold my breath as I wait for his next instruction.

His hand runs over my behind and then down to my sex, he pulls my G-string to the side and slides his fingers through the lips of my sex.

"Very nice," he hums in a deep throaty voice; his finger circles through my sex and I see stars. "Very nice indeed."

Hanging upside down with all the blood rushing to my head with his fingers doing that while 100 percent alcohol is rushing through my bloodstream is a heady combination.

I could pass out any second…wouldn't be surprised actually.

I hope he knows mouth-to-mouth resuscitation.

He slowly slides my panties down over my hips and drops them to the ground and he pulls my cheeks apart.

Thump.

Thump.

Thump.

I feel his tongue and my legs nearly buckle out from beneath me.

What the….

He licks me; I feel his stubble burn my skin and I see the huge bulge in his suit pants through my legs.

Oh no…stop that.

Every cell in my body gets a goose bump as electricity from his touch sends me into overdrive. I don't know what alternate universe this is in…but I do know it's fucking perverted.

He slides two thick fingers deep into my sex and my knees collapse

Slap.

Owww….

His slap sends a sharp sting through my skin.

"Stand up," he growls.

CHAPTER THREE

I stand up, not because he told me to but because I'm infuriated. I turn toward him like the devil. "That's the first and last time you ever hit me."

Confusion crosses his face as my words roll around in his head. "It wasn't a hit, it was a sexual slap."

"It was out of fucking line, that's what it was." I don't know what to say next without acting psychotic so I storm from the room, I find myself marching up the hallway to the bedroom. My blood is pumping hard through my body, is it arousal, is it rage, or is it sheer petrifaction…who knows?

Too much, too fast and way too much chemistry.

This is totally out of my depth and I'm freaking the hell out. I bust through the bedroom door, throw the robe on and begin to pace.

What am I doing here?

What the actual fuck am I doing here?

Getting my ass eaten by a god who wants to discipline me… that's what?

I didn't sign up for ass eating.

That's…too in my regions…especially on a first date.

Only this isn't a first date, it's a kink club where anything goes and somewhere I paid a shit ton of money to be.

Ugh…what was I thinking?

I hear the front door click closed….

Wait.

Did he just leave?

I put my head into my hands, damn it.

Alora…what are you doing you idiot?

Can you not even be adventurous for just one weekend?

I drop my robe and walk to the mirror and turn to look at my behind. A large red handprint marks my skin.

How fucking dare he?

I drag my robe back on and I hit the button to open the heavy drapes.

It's blatantly obvious that I'm not cut out for this type of thing. No wonder he left.

Damn it, disappointment runs through me. Especially now I know how gorgeous he is.

As the drapes slowly open they reveal a large sunken spa in the balcony overlooking the beautiful valley down below. It's hot and bubbling, steam is rising into the air, and I give a weak smile. A hot spa bath in the freezing cold in Switzerland...who would have thunk it? This place is a complete mindfuck.

I get a vision of him on his knees behind me...and his tongue.... I feel a throb deep down below

Hot.

Why did I blow up like that? Maybe I overreacted...not maybe, probably.

Ugh....

To be fair, I don't think I would have survived having sex with that god anyway.

Probably a good thing he's gone.

I walk out to the balcony and put my hand into the water of the spa bath, it's hot and inviting.

I look left and I look right, screw it, nobody's here. I drop my robe, peel off my underwear and get in. I sink back into the water and rest my head on the side.

"Hmm." The hot water tickles my senses and I smile.

For a long time I soak but the more relaxed I get, the more I see him.

"Look me in the eye and take your fucking clothes off."

Arousal beats through my bloodstream at the way he was looking at me while I was undressing.

"Eyes on me."

I get a vision of him sitting there with his hand on his cock.

What I wouldn't have given to have just one night with a man like him.

Not in the way he wanted me though…. Just in the way that I wanted him.

Although something tells me that Mr. Doe's version of vanilla wouldn't be anywhere close to mine.

Deflated, I drop my head back against the side of the tub and close my eyes.

Oh well, it is what it is. Sorry, Misty, I tried.

All waxed up and nowhere to go.

"Room for one more?"

The voice startles me and I jump, Mr. Doe is standing beside the spa.

"I thought you left?"

"I did."

"And?"

"I came back."

"Why?"

"We have unfinished business."

I stare at him.

"Can I get in or not?" he says impatiently.

"I have a giant handprint on my ass, I want to hear an apology."

He looks at me deadpan.

I raise an eyebrow.

"Miss Doe, I apologize for getting aroused and slapping you in what I believed was a playful sexual act. I forget that not everyone is playful."

Hmm, that's a passive-aggressive apology if ever I heard one.

"Okay," I say.

"Okay what?"

"Okay you can get in."

"The question is." He glares at me. "Do I want to now?"

"Not sure." I shrug. "But please know I'm naked in here."

"As annoying as you are, that's an excellent incentive."

"You should stop talking," I huff. "I know who the annoying one is."

He takes his suit jacket off and puts it onto the chair as he kicks his shoes off.

Is he going to undress in front of me?

He undoes his shirt buttons and he tears his shirt off over his shoulders. His broad muscular chest comes into view, it has a scattering of dark hair and his shoulders are ripped and buff. I feel my face flush as I sit in the front row to watch the strip show.

Yes…yes, he is undressing.

Hallelujah the world is saved.

I look around as I try to pretend not to ogle, but once he slides his pants down and his large cock springs free…all bets are off and I can't help but look.

Oh my….

Thick quad muscles, well-kept pubic hair, and the biggest dick I ever saw.

The man is a god…or a porn star, but honestly who cares, either works for me.

He sinks into the water beside me and his close proximity steals my breath. There's no denying it, there is some serious sexual chemistry here.

We stare at each other as the air crackles between us.

"You said we have unfinished business. You mean sex?" I ask.

"Isn't that what you're here for?" he replies.

I swipe my hand through the water and it causes a ripple as I try to articulate my thoughts.

"Are you here for sex?" I ask.

"I'm not here for a romantic date if that's what you're asking." He slides his hand up my thigh underneath the water. "Although I must admit I wasn't expecting to find someone as beautiful as you here."

My stomach flutters.

What is it about this guy, even a hint of a compliment sends me weak at the knees.

"Me either."

He pulls me over his lap to straddle him. "You think I'm beautiful?" he asks.

Every cell in my body ignites into a blazing inferno as we stare at each other through the steam.

"Breathtakingly so."

His hand comes up to cup my breast and he dusts his thumb back and forth over my erect nipple. I feel like I can't breathe, his touch is magical, almost otherworldly.

Dominance, reverence, and fire all rolled into one.

He leans up and kisses me, his big lips take mine with a hunger behind them.

Oh....

He pulls me closer to his body and I feel his erection press up against my sex.

Naked and in the water like this there is nothing between us.

He kisses me again and his eyes flutter closed, it's at this moment I realize he's as into this as I am. His tongue swipes through my lips as his hands slide up my back.

Fuck.

The way he kisses....

My legs open wider as my body craves a deeper connection.

He adjusts his dick between us and then sits me down to rest on him.

I can feel every hard vein in his engorged cock.

Oh god....

With his hands on my hips and his tongue deep in my mouth he begins to slowly drag me over him. The feeling of his cock rubbing through my lips and over my clitoris sends waves of pure pleasure through me. So close and yet so far.

Fuck....

The water sloshes around and I moan into his mouth as he kisses me.

His hard body is against mine and my legs are now open wide, my toes begin to curl.

Back...and forth...back...forth.

Harder.

This is too much...too good.

Faster.

Deeper.

Until my entire body is quivering with want.

"I...I need," I whimper.

"You need what?" he whispers into my mouth.

"I need to..." my head throws back in pleasure, "...come."

He smiles against my lips and drags me harder across him and I shudder as an orgasm is ripped right out of my soul.

"Ahhhhh," I cry out as I cling to him.

I see stars.

Before I can even finish I feel my body being lifted out of the spa bath and he lays me down on the deck and opens my legs.

I need this.

But instead of climbing over me like I want him to, he drops his head to between my legs. His fingers spread me open and he licks me deeply, his eyes flutter closed in ecstasy.... Oh.

I grip his hair as his strong hands hold my legs back, he licks me deep and finishes with a flick of his tongue.

He repeats the process, a deep hard lick followed by a flutter.

Oh.

Jeez....

That is soooo good.

Oh god.... How does he know how to do that so well?

I nearly jump out of my skin and my legs close around his head. "Ahh," I cry out as I writhe around. He holds me down as he licks me deep. I thrash beneath him, his strong tongue taking no prisoners as he sucks every last bit of my orgasm from me.

I'm quivering and writhing beneath him like a wild animal. An exorcism of life as I know it.

Because hell, where does a girl go after this?

This man is a god.

I gasp for air as he finishes me off and then he slides up over my body and smiles down at me. "Hi."

"Hi," I pant, struggling for air.

He lies beside me and leans up onto his elbow as he watches me.

"What are you doing?" I frown.

"Watching you." He runs his fingertips over my lips and then as if unable to help it puts four fingers into my mouth then down my throat until I gag, his eyes darken as he watches me struggle to take them. He stands, "Come."

I don't understand. *Doesn't he want to have sex?*

"But aren't we?"

"No." He pulls me up by the hand and wraps my robe around me. "Let's get you in out of the cold." He leads me inside and then through to the bathroom where he turns the shower on, he holds his hand under the water as he adjusts the temperature.

I stand waiting in the oversized robe but I'm so confused.

He's physically aroused, his hard cock hangs heavily between his legs, but he's acting completely in control. Only there's no acting.

He *is* in control.

He turns to me and smiles softly; his big blue eyes have a tender glow. "Let's get you warm, baby."

I nod and step under the hot water and close my eyes as I let the heat sink in. "Are you getting in?"

"I am." He steps in under the water and turns me away from him and soaps up his hands and begins to wash my back. Up over my shoulders and then down lower and lower. Down to between my cheeks, and I hold my breath as I go up onto my toes.

His touch is electric and once again as his fingers nearly penetrate me there the goose bumps start.

Oh....

I'm a weeping hot mess.

"You like me touching you here...don't you?" he murmurs as his finger rims my ass.

Good lord....

I nod, unable to form a single word.

"Is this your favorite place to come, angel?"

I shrug. "I...."

"Answer my question," he says, sterner.

"I've never...."

He turns me back toward him as his eyes flicker with arousal. "You've never taken someone here before?"

My eyes search his.

"Doe?"

"No," I whisper, ashamed. "I'm sorry I'm not more experienced for you."

Unexpectedly, he breaks into a beautiful smile and it makes my heart skip a beat.

Pleasing this man is my new favorite thing.

He puts his finger under my chin and brings my face up to his. "Don't ever apologize for making me happy."

"That makes you happy?"

"Very." He dips his head and kisses me, his lips lingering over mine, before turning me away from him to face the wall. He rearranges my hands up on the tiles above my head before pulling my hips back toward him and spreading my legs wider.

I'm completely at his mercy as he moves me into the position he wants.

I can feel my excited pulse all over.

The chemistry between us is like nothing I've ever felt before.

Does he feel it too?

"Why would that make you happy?" I ask as I act dumb.

"Because I want you here." He slides his finger in my ass to the knuckle and I whimper as my eyes roll back in my head.

He kisses my neck from behind, his teeth grazing my skin as he slowly pumps me with it, and just when my body begins to relax against him he removes it.

Don't stop.

He goes back to washing my back; his soapy hands roam all over me and I reach for his cock and he steps back.

"No."

"No?" I frown.

"No."

"I can't touch you?"

"No."

"Why not?"

He takes my face into his hands as he stares down at me. "I'm waiting."

"For what?"

A sudden disappointing thought flashes through my brain.... Oh.

He doesn't want me like this.

"That's why you're here, isn't it?" I ask. "You want to come with me fucking *you?*"

"No."

"How do you want to come?"

"Patience." His teeth drag my bottom lip out and my eyelids flutter as I hang somewhere between pleasure and pain.

"Good things come to those who wait."

CHAPTER FOUR

Wait…what? I stare up at him as I try to work out what's going on here.

This man is so confusing.

He's hard and ready, obviously aroused, but then doesn't want sex. He's only interested in my orgasms.

I have no idea what's going on. I can't read him at all.

He stands behind me, his teeth grazing up and down my neck as his fingers slide through the wet flesh between my legs. He finds the spot that makes me shudder and I feel him smile up against my skin. "You like that?" he murmurs darkly.

I nod, unable to form a coherent word.

"Just like that, baby." His fingertips flick fast and furiously over my clitoris and I nearly pass out from the pleasure.

"Oh…fuck." My legs go weak beneath me.

He chuckles. "Hold it."

How the hell am I supposed to hold it? He's getting off on making me come.

Don't come, whatever you do don't come.

He grabs my clitoris and pulls it aggressively and I nearly convulse as an orgasm explodes through me.

He pulls and pumps me through it, never have I come by having my clitoris aggressively tugged.

What the actual fuck?

Who does that….

Who knew that that would feel good? I sure as hell didn't and I own a clitoris.

He turns me back toward him, his hand still wedged tightly between my legs.

"You're beautiful when you come, Miss Doe." He smiles as he kisses me, his fingers start again and I step back from him.

"No more."

His face falls.

"I need a break. I can't keep coming again and again."

He chuckles. "I beg to differ." He takes his hand away and wraps me in his arms.

I'm sated and sleepy and I lean up against his broad chest as the hot water runs over us.

There's an elephant in the room, one that I'm not allowed to touch. His huge erection pressing against my stomach.

"Let's go and have some dinner," he murmurs.

Huh?

What about your dick?

I don't like this; it feels like there is an uneven power exchange. He needs to come too.

I slide my hand down through his pubic hair and he steps back. "I said. Not yet," he says sternly; as if annoyed he turns and gets out of the shower.

I stay under the water and let it run over me. My body is throbbing, swollen and wet from his strong fingers and yet I'm not even allowed to touch him.

Huh?

He dries himself and wraps a towel around his waist and then holds a towel out for me. I turn the taps off and step into his arms, he carefully dries me and then wraps the robe around my shoulders. "You need to eat," he says from behind me into my hair.

I'm really not sure what's going on here but fuck, the anticipation is killing me.

Dressed in our robes we go out to the dining room to see the table laden with silver trays with lids.

"I wasn't sure what you wanted so I ordered an assortment of dishes for you to choose from." He begins to lift the silver lids to reveal a delicious selection. There's ravioli pasta and fillet of steak. Sashimi and seafood and then some kind of chicken dish. There's vegetables in some kind of cream sauce and salads.

"Wow," I whisper as I look around. "When did you order this?"

"Before I got into the spa."

I stare at him as my brain misfires; he knew that what just happened was going to happen exactly as it did. In that order and in that timeframe.

"Sit." He gestures to my chair.

"You're very bossy."

"Miss Doe." He smirks. "Now that's a revelation." His eyes have a mischievous glow to them. "Where on earth did you get that idea?"

It's not a revelation, I'm pretty sure it's going to be on his tombstone. I bet he's a real bossy bastard on the outside.

I sit down and look around the choices. "Do you want the pasta?" I ask.

"No." His elbow is leaning on the table and his pointer finger is steepled up over his temple as he watches me. "It's all yours." He passes it over to me.

"Thanks." I pick up my fork and glance up to him, he's still sitting back watching me. "Are you eating?" I ask.

"I'm hungry...but not for food." The air crackles between us as we stare at each other. His tongue slides over his bottom lip and I feel it between my legs.

He's so intense...jeez.

"I'm not eating alone, so either you come over here and eat me or you eat dinner alongside of me."

Amusement flashes across his face and he picks up the fillet steak and puts it in front of him. I watch on as he dishes out some vegetables and then he gets up and fills two glasses of iced water. He puts lemon wedges into both and then sits one down in front of me.

He's very strategic in everything he does, I get the feeling nothing is left to chance with this man.

He picks up his knife and fork.

"Do you like control, Mr. Doe?" I ask.

"Yes," he replies without hesitation, he bites the steak from his fork.

"In everything?"

"Yes." He chews his steak; his eyes dare me to ask more.

"Not having sex.... Is that a control thing?" I ask.

"It's a pleasure thing."

I frown. "I don't understand, how is not having sex pleasurable?"

"Abstinence is my drug of choice." His dark eyes hold mine.

Huh?

Either this guy is supersmart or I'm just super dumb.

"What does that mean?"

He cuts his steak as if he has this type of conversation every day. "You sit there opposite me satisfied and sleepy."

I frown, more confused than ever. "And?"

He chews his steak in slow motion as he watches me.

"If I'm sitting here satisfied and sleepy…what are you doing?" I ask.

"When I spread you wide and tasted you by the spa…you thought it was for you."

Huh?

"If it wasn't for me, who was it for?"

"I was tasting your body to give mine the information it wanted."

"Why would you want information?"

"To calibrate my senses."

I stare at him, confused.

"You see, Miss Doe, when I give my body a taste of the DNA it could possibly have…it performs at a much higher level."

I feel a throb between my legs. *This man is fucking hot.*

"My senses are at an all-time high, working like never before." He continues, "As you sleepily sit there…. The predator in me can smell you." He whispers darkly, "I can feel your pulse as it runs through your body." His tongue swipes over his lips as if tasting something. "I can still taste the beautiful creamy come that came out of your tight little cunt."

Dear god.

"Every single cell in my body is screaming to claim yours."

I feel all of the blood drain out of me, every last drop.

"Eat your dinner now because you're going to need energy later." Our eyes are locked. "My primal instincts are going to use your body well tonight. When I claim you as mine."

I swallow the nervous lump in my throat.

"I'm already sold," I whisper.

He breaks into a breathtaking smile and butterflies dance in my stomach.

Suddenly I desperately want to please him, I want to blow his mind as much as he's blowing mine. It's only fair.

I stand. "You eat your dinner. I'm sucking your cock." I crawl underneath the table and open his robe; his thick length is already hard and weeping with pre-come.

I take him into my mouth and he lets out a deep husky moan.

Fuck.

This is already the best sex of my life and we didn't even do it yet.

I take him deep as I stroke him and he inhales sharply as he leans back in his chair. His hand goes to the back of my head. We get into a rhythm and he begins to fuck my mouth. His behind rises off the chair as he begins to lose control.

The moans and noises his body is making are turning me inside out. I say his body because I honestly believe I'm sucking off his base needs now.

Mr. Doe isn't here anymore; I'm feeding the animal inside of him.

He drags me up from the floor by the arm and bends me over the couch and pushes my head down into the cushions.

I hear a rip of a condom, then he slams into me and holds himself deep and we both cry out in ecstasy.

Oh.

My.

God.

This is too good.

He's huge, stretching me to the hilt, but it's the way my body is rippling around him that's sending us both over the edge.

He's right, this isn't sex between two people.

This is two bodies feeding their most human base needs in the most primal of ways.

He lifts his foot to put it on the couch beside me and pulls out and slams back in.

I cry out, the pressure of his grip almost breaking my spine.

Fuck.

Then he's pumping me at piston pace, our skin slapping together as he takes what he needs.

Oww....

I can't think, I can't breathe, and the position he has me in I can't even move. I'm bent over the couch, my feet not touching the ground.

His hands are spreading me wide and I'm taking his pumps blow by blow.

He's moaning, deep and throaty. The most orgasmic sound I've ever heard in my life.

He's like an animal.

I've never ever been fucked like this before.

"Fuck." He moans. "So...."

Pump.

"Fucking."

Pump.

"Good."

Pump.

Oh....

He holds himself deep and grips me hard.

The sound of his excitement sends me over the edge and I cry out as I come hard.

My vision blacks out and I swear I have an out-of-body experience.

Skin slapping around me, his deep moans and...damn it, I may not survive this kind of sex.

He holds himself deep and I feel his cock jerk violently as he comes deep inside my body.

"Fuck..." he moans. "Oh yeah, fuck yeah." He slowly keeps pumping me to completely empty out his body.

I pant as I desperately try to catch my breath. I stare into space as I try to regain my physical consciousness.

What the hell was that?

I wake as my back arches off the bed.

The bedroom is shrouded in darkness and I feel teeth graze my clitoris.

I look down to see Mr. Doe is going down on me underneath the blankets.

Fuck.

This man is an animal, I've lost count of how many times I've come.

He's been fucking me for hours, every which way, and after the last time I drifted off into an exhausted sleep…only to wake to this.

I actually don't know if I am going to make it through until morning.

His four fingers slowly fuck me as his tongue flicks over my clitoris and I moan.

I can't even act cool anymore, he's ripped any sense of self-awareness right out of my soul.

"Please," I whimper, scared to come again. "I can't…."

"Shh," he whispers. "One more time, baby, and I'll let you sleep." I screw up my hands in his hair as my eyes roll back in my head. "I only have you for one night, Doe." He sucks on me. "I can't get enough."

Don't say that.

With this physical connection, how could we only have one night?

No world is that cruel.

My body begins to convulse and I moan as I come hard on his fingers, he kneels up over me and slides his cock down my throat and comes in my mouth.

I gag and choke as I try to deal with him.

He smiles down at me in the darkness as he tenderly brushes the hair back from my perspiration-clad forehead. "So fucking beautiful, Doe," he whispers, he keeps stroking himself into my mouth.

We stare at each other and something shifts between us. A feeling so tangible that it turns into the physical. A force to be reckoned with.

Whatever his body was searching for, it just got. With his satiety, I can feel the tectonic plates move into place.

But where they're moving to…I have no clue.

Only that I want more.

CHAPTER FIVE

The heavenly scent of freshly percolated coffee wakes me from my slumber and I stretch as I try to focus my eyes.

Where am I?

My body feels heavy, achy, and instantly I'm reminded of last night and the god I went to bed with.

I look over to his empty side of the bed, where is he?

I slowly get out of bed and wince, I'm sore from last night. Every one of my muscles feel stretched and used. I throw my robe on and make my way out in search of my Mr. Doe.

I make my way into the living area and look around; everything from dinner last night has been cleaned up and packed away.

"Miss Doe," he calls from the balcony. "I'm out here."

I walk over to the door and find him sitting at the table, breakfast is laid out and the morning sun is beaming. He smiles broadly and taps his lap.

My heart swells and I float over to him and sit down on his knee.

He kisses me tenderly. "Good morning."

"Hi." I smile shyly, suddenly embarrassed about my whorish behavior last night.

As if he can read my mind he smiles down at me and combs his fingers through my hair. "Your beauty takes my breath away."

I probably look like a racoon.

We kiss, slowly at first and then deeper and our eyes close as we get lost in each other, I wasn't imagining it or lost in the moment last night.

In the light of day it's still here between us.

A blindingly beautiful chemistry, so bright that I can hardly see straight.

"We part today," I say sadly.

"Hmm." He kisses me again. "About that."

"Yes," I say hopefully, please tell me that you want to run away together or something equally as crazy.

"Spend another night with me." He readjusts my robe to protect me from the cold.

This is my chance; I want to know more about him.

Hell, I want to know everything there is to know.

"On one condition," I tell him.

"What's that?"

"I want to leave this place."

"What?" He frowns.

"Not *leave*, leave. I want to…." I shrug. "Explore the village, go for a walk in the sunshine." I smile softly. "Maybe go on a date to a restaurant tonight?"

"Doe…." He sighs, unimpressed that I want to break the rules of the hotel.

"It's just one day." I kiss his big lips as I try to talk him around. "And then we get another night here."

His eyes hold mine.

"We're never going to see each other again," I whisper. "I hate the thought. Give me my one day."

"This was not our arrangement and I really don't…."

"You asked for another night too." I cut him off.

He looks out over the valley below as he thinks this over.

"Or we can just say goodbye now." I stand, annoyed that he even has to think about it.

"No, no." He pulls me back down onto his lap. "One more night."

"And one day."

"Yes." He holds my face in his hands and kisses me, our lips linger over each other's and a warm fuzzy feeling passes between us.

More than just lust, less familiar than love. A whole new ballgame to the one we signed up for.

This goodbye is going to suck.

"Are you ready?" Mr. Doe calls from the living area.

"Uh-huh." I grab my purse and walk out and he frowns as he looks me up and down.

"Where are your coat and hat?"

I glance down at myself. "I don't need them, do I?"

"It's cold outside, you'll freeze half to death."

"Oh." I shrug. "When I was packing I didn't think it would be this cold. I'll be fine, we'll be walking anyway so I'll be able to keep warm."

He rolls his eyes. "Hang on, you can wear something of mine." He walks into the spare room and I follow him. His suitcase is on the luggage rack and he opens it up.

Everything is folded and organized to precision and I frown as I stare into it. "Who packed your bag, a drill sergeant?"

He glances back at me. "What does that mean?"

"Why is it so neat?"

"I like things to be organized like an adult."

"Me too." So not me too, I'm a hot mess and can never find shit in my suitcase or when I'm packing. I roll up onto my toes feeling like a petulant child.

He pulls out a gray beanie and puts it on my head and kisses me quickly before turning back to his suitcase to dig for more.

He's very kissy.

I smile goofily as I wait, doing domestic everyday things with him is my new favorite thing. He holds out a big coat. "Put this on."

"It's huge."

"It's about to snow." He widens his eyes. "And you want to walk around the countryside in a thin cardigan? I don't think so."

"Fine." I sigh as I put my arms into the sleeves, he does up the zipper and pulls the waist cord to tighten it snug. He reaches down and grabs a handful of my sex and gives me a squeeze before turning back to his suitcase. "Now…." He passes me a pair of leather gloves. "These will keep those pretty little hands warm."

I hold out my hands and he puts them on for me. "Can we go now, Boss?" I ask.

"We can go now, Doe."

We've somehow arrived at nicknames for each other, he's Boss and I'm Doe.

I'm wearing my oversized beanie, huge jacket and gloves the size of flippers. "I feel ridiculous." I smile up at him.

"That's because you look ridiculous." He dots the tip of my nose. "Now…where are you taking me on our date?" He breaks into a slow sexy smile and my heart skips a beat; he has the most beautiful face I've ever seen. Big blue eyes and pouty kissable lips. His hair is dark and has a curl to it and his stubble creates a shadow over his square jaw.

Probably the most gorgeous man I have ever seen, but maybe that's just because he's a sex god and I'm still drunk on his pheromones. He's released so much oxytocin into my bloodstream that it's a wonder I've survived the overdose.

We walk to the door and out into the corridor. "At least nobody will be able to recognize me in this abominable snowman outfit," I say as we arrive at the elevator and push the button.

"Lucky you." He twists his lips as if unimpressed.

Oh…shit. I didn't even think when I asked him to leave the resort. If he's seen here, will it have implications for him on the outside? "It is okay if we leave, isn't it?" I ask him.

"Well, too late now, isn't it?" he mutters as we get into the elevator and turn toward the doors.

Does he have someone on the outside?

Shit….

The reason he came here flashes through my mind, we have to do that for him when we get back. I don't want him to go home with regrets.

He came here with a goal and I need to make sure we get it done.

The elevator doors open and we step out into the foyer, he walks slightly in front of me out through the front doors of the resort and down the driveway.

I scamper to keep up, and once at the end of the driveway and out onto the country road he turns to wait for me.

"What's the rush?" I ask.

"We're in a fucking kink club, Doe. Not something I want as common knowledge. What if I know someone in there?"

"Oh…." I hadn't thought of that. "Well, if they're also here, they have a hidden kink too."

He chuckles and I link my arm through his as we walk. When I breathe out, fog comes out of my mouth. "It *is* cold."

"Like I told you."

"Does it snow where you live?" I ask.

"Yes." He glances down at me. "Not from where you're from?"

"No." I think for a moment. "I've only seen snow once before."

"What?" He seems surprised.

"Yeah, it was on a school trip. We went to the Rockies. It was a ski trip, although I didn't ski."

"Why didn't you ski?"

"We couldn't afford the ski rental costs so I just watched my friends."

"How much was the ski rental?"

I shrug as we walk. "I don't know, I think it was like sixty-five dollars. My dad had already taken a second job…third job, actually, so that I could go on the trip at all."

He listens as we walk.

"My mom died when I was young and…." My voice trails off.

He stays quiet as he waits for me to finish.

"My dad had to give up his full-time day job to look after us, he worked night shifts so that we could stay overnight at Grandma's. We just scraped by, so any extra activities were a treat."

He nods once as if acknowledging my story and we walk in silence for a while.

"How many siblings do you have?" he eventually asks.

"I have a sister and a brother." I kiss his shoulder. "Do you have any siblings?"

"I have a sister and a brother too." He smiles as if thinking of them fondly. "They're the light of my life."

"That's nice." I smile. "And your parents?"

"I lost my mother too."

My face falls. "Oh no. How?"

"Car accident."

"Did your family struggle?" I ask as I look up at him.

"Very much so, we still do."

My heart aches for him, what are the chances we share that same grief?

"What do you do for work?" he asks to change the subject.

"I'm a math teacher."

He frowns as if surprised. "Would never have picked that."

"Well." I shrug. "Numbers are my thing, what can I say."

I walk along and I have a question on the tip of my tongue that I've been dying to ask. "Are you wealthy?"

"In some things." He stares out over the rolling green hills as we walk. "What makes you ask that?"

"Your accent. The way you sound."

"My accent?" He smiles as if fascinated. "How do I sound?"

"Like an English nobleman or something."

He chuckles. "How many English noblemen do you know?"

"Well, none." I giggle. "I was confused because I'm pretty sure that English noblemen don't know how to fuck like that."

He throws his head back and laughs out loud.

"I'm being serious." I smile up at him. "I think maybe you're a porn star or something. I've never met anyone before who has sex like you."

"Sex like me, what is sex like me?" He smiles.

"So…." I widen my eyes. "Great."

"Great." He repeats the word. "I don't like the word *great*." He scrunches up his nose. "*Great* sounds very average to me."

"You are anything but average." I laugh. "Believe me."

"Yeah, yeah, keep digging." He smiles as he walks. "This hole is deep, Doe."

I laugh and think for a moment. "Okay, *great* isn't the best word. I would describe our sex last night as…" I narrow my eyes as I try to articulate myself, "…life changing."

"Life changing?" He stops, pulling me back by the arm. "How was it life-changing?"

"Well…." I think for a moment. "I'm pretty vanilla on the outside."

"You are *not* vanilla." He cuts me off.

"No, I am." I smile as I pull him to walk once more. "I've only ever had two boyfriends and…I've never had a one-night stand."

He stares down at me. "How many people have you slept with?"

"Four." I shrug. "Well, five now." I continue to babble on, "Well, six if you count that one time I had a threesome."

He chuckles. "The one you didn't like to share the dick in?"

"Yes." I smile goofily. "That one." I glance back and see two men walking in the distance behind us. "Who are those men?" I ask. "Are they following us?"

He glances back. "Oh…. They're from the resort. It's standard for them to send someone with a client if they leave the hotel." He nudges me with his shoulder. "In case I'm a serial killer or something."

My arm is linked through his and I can feel his hard forearm under my hand. "How many people have you slept with?" I ask him.

"A lot," he replies without hesitation.

"Oh." I nod. I hate that answer, he's probably slept with the most beautiful of people.

Insecurity rears her ugly head, what would he ever see in someone like me?

Then I remember the cold hard facts.

He didn't choose me; he was matched with me. I was just the lucky number that got pulled out of a hat.

We walk for a while as my brain goes into a silent confidence crisis.

"So I have to ask…." He breaks the silence. "For someone as inexperienced as you…. Why would you pay to come to a place like this? I'm sure there are a million men who would give anything to have you peg them."

"I don't know." I think for a moment. "I guess I was searching for something more."

He nods as if processing my words.

"What about you, I'm wondering the same, why did you come here?"

"I honestly don't know." He hesitates. "Maybe I was searching for something more too."

"What a pair of misfits we are." I smile sadly. "I'm vanilla shortbread, you're a chocolate fudge whorebag. You want to be pegged but you don't want to be pegged. I need to do Misty's list, but when push comes to shove I'm not sure I'll actually be able to do it because I'm pretty sure I don't know how to work a prosthetic dick without disemboweling someone. We can't know anything about each other and yet I feel like I already know *everything* about you. And I'm quite sure that long after spending this weekend with you I will mourn your loss while you will probably never think of me again because you are just the most amazing lover of all time and well…I'm just me," I blurt out in a rush.

He stops us and turns me to face him and smiles softly down at me. "You have it mistaken, it is you who is the most amazing lover, why do you think I couldn't stop last night?" He takes my face in his hands and kisses me softly. "Why do you think I need an extra night?"

My eyes search his. "I wish we hadn't met here."

"Doe…." He sighs. "Don't." He pulls me into a hug and holds me tight in his arms.

My heart constricts because I know that's his way of dismissing any chance of a meeting on the outside for us.

He already has someone.

As he holds me, a lump in my throat forms; we're so close but so far.

I'm reminded that we really don't know each other at all.

"Let's just enjoy every minute of our night together, okay?" he whispers into my hair.

"Okay." I smile, feeling stupid.

I knew what I signed up for…*keep it together, fool.*

I pull out of his arms determined to do better. He did not come here to put up with my whiny and needy behavior. I'm not his girlfriend, hell…we don't even know each other.

It is what it is.

I came here to finish Misty's list and that's exactly what I'm going to do.

It's time to put my heart in a box and sharpen my sword to prepare for battle.

Tonight…I'm going to fulfill his deepest and darkest fantasy.

Who knows, it might turn out to be mine too.

If déjà vu had an official day, today would be it.

Mr. Doe and I are on the love boat, we went for a walk around the village this morning, and had a late lunch.

We've talked and laughed and taken a big hot deep bath and then this afternoon we had a nap, well I slept while he lay on his side and watched me.

We're acting like an old couple in love and haven't had sex once today.

Or maybe it's just that he had enough of my body last night.

I crave his touch and yet at the same time I want to prove to myself that we are more than what we came here for.

Does he feel it too?

I stare at my face in the dimly lit bathroom mirror, my dark hair is loose and I'm wearing my tight red dress and strappy stilettos.

Tonight was our date.

We've had dinner and danced; Mr. Doe has wined me and dined me and I can't imagine a more perfect night. We're still at the restaurant and it's 10 p.m. but I don't want to go back to the hotel because then it will be our last night and when I wake up he will be leaving.

And I know it's coming…and I know I can't stop it.

But god, how I want to.

I stare at my reflection. *Go out there and do what you came here to do.*

"You can do this," I whisper as I give myself a pep talk.

The door opens as someone walks in and I force a smile and walk back out into the restaurant.

Mr. Doe's eyes hold mine as I walk toward him, he gives me a slow sexy smile as his eyes drop down to my toes and back up to my face.

"Miss me?" I smile as I take a seat opposite him.

He sips his drink and gives me the look.

"You know…." I smirk. "You shouldn't look at people like that."

"Like what…?" He swirls his red wine around in his glass as his eyes hold mine.

"Like you want to do unspeakable things to them."

Electricity sparks through the air.

"There are no people here." In slow motion he lifts his glass to his lips and takes a sip. "Only you."

And I feel it, like an undercurrent, the pull toward him is so strong.

"Then you should take only me home and do all the unspeakable things."

"I intend to." He raises his eyebrow; our eyes are locked and damn…how is he so freaking hot?

He stands and takes my hand and leads me out of the restaurant, my mouth falls open in wonder as I look up at the sky. "Look, it's snowing."

"I ordered it just for you." Mr. Doe smiles down at me.

"Thank you." I giggle.

Wouldn't surprise me at all if he had that power.

I slide my arm under his overcoat and he puts his arm around me as we walk down the sidewalk toward the car. The hotel security guards are with us again and were loitering around out the front of the hotel while we had dinner.

The Establishment sure does offer great security, no wonder it's so expensive.

One of the security men opens the back door of the black SUV and we climb into the car. Mr. Doe holds my hand in his lap and turns his attention to out the window.

He seems lost in his own thoughts and I wonder if he is dreading saying goodbye tomorrow half as much as I am.

As we drive into the snowy night I know I have to count my blessings; no matter what happens in the future, I'm grateful for the time that we have had together…even if it is limited.

It's been a beautiful day and that was a wonderful dinner date. Probably the best I've ever been on.

My mind wanders to the night we are about to have. I have no idea what is about to unfold and I'm nervous and excited, perhaps even a little terrified.

Let's do this.

CHAPTER SIX

We walk into the suite and Mr. Doe takes off his jacket and hangs it up and I walk to the bar. "Nightcap?" I ask.

"Yeah."

I begin to pour our two drinks and he comes and stands behind me, his lips drop to my neck as his arms wrap around me from behind.

I can feel his body harden against mine. "There it is." I smile. "I wondered where he'd been."

He chuckles and pumps me with his hips. "Waiting." He pumps me again. "To strike."

I turn toward him and pass his drink over; my eyes hold his as I take a long sip. "So?" I smile.

"So…."

There are a million words hanging in the air between us, sexy, dirty and forbidden words.

I set my drink down and go to the black box. "I think it's time we open this."

His eyes hold mine as he sips his drink, the look he gives me could start a fire.

I pull the lid off and peer in. I pull out the first thing I see. "We have massage oil."

He smirks.

"A very large bottle of lubricant." I hold it up and then place it on the counter beside the box. "A blindfold." I pull out a black blindfold, I frown as I see the next item. "Handcuffs."

He breaks into a sexy smile and raises his glass toward me.

"You like handcuffs?" I ask.

"Very much."

"Oh…." Of course he likes handcuffs, he's a fucking deviant. I keep digging through the box. "A butt plug." I pull out a black butt plug and hold it up.

He rolls his lips, seemingly unimpressed with this one.

"Oh look, there are different sizes." I pull out four more butt plugs and set them down on the counter. I frown as I spy something else. "What in the world…?" I pull out a butt plug with a horse tail attached to it and I hold it up.

Mr. Doe breaks into a playful smile. "Giddyup."

I giggle in surprise. "I mean…really?" I keep digging and see a snakelike thing rolled up. "What is…." My mouth falls open as I pull it out. "A whip."

His eyes blaze with fire as they hold mine.

"You like this?" I whisper, slightly horrified.

"We already know this about me," he replies.

"We do?" I frown. "A smack on the behind is not a whole-ass fucking whip."

"And you couldn't even take that." His eyes hold mine as if daring me to say something.

My heart sinks, I hate that I unknowingly failed that test.

"Yeah well." I set the whip down onto the counter. "Nobody gets to hit me."

"It's not about the hit, it's about control."

I begin to get annoyed.

"Nobody gets to control me either," I fire back.

Amused, he smirks and sips his drink as if knowing something that I don't know.

There's no doubt about it, Mr. Doe and I would clash in the real world.

He's controlling, I'm controlling…. Not ideal circumstances for a warm-your-heart love match.

I see three strap-on dildos in the bottom of the box and I purposely get out the largest one. "Here we are." I hold it up. "It's going to feel great fucking you with this." With my eyes locked on his, I put it into my mouth and suck it. I hold it out to him. "Your turn, Mr. Doe."

"I don't suck cock."

"You might surprise yourself." I smirk. "Let me put it on and hold you by the hair and fuck your throat until you gag."

Sound familiar, fucker?

He glares at me as a sudden surge of animosity runs between us.

I put it back in my mouth and close my eyes and moan for added effect.

Screw you and your control bullshit.

I'm wearing the pants tonight...literally.

If he's leaving me tomorrow...and he will...he's going to fucking remember me if it's the last thing I do.

"Get on your knees," I tell him.

"You trying to top from the bottom, angel?" he whispers darkly.

Nerves simmer in my stomach.

"You know what I do to naughty girls who try to pull that shit?"

His dark eyes hold mine and he walks toward me, he pulls the strap-on cock out of my mouth and throws it to the side. He unzips his pants and pulls his hard dick out and slides it down my throat.

With both hands in my hair holding me just how he wants me, he lets me have it.

I struggle to take him, and good god, I've woken the beast.

Like a carbon copy of what I've just threatened to do to him, he does to me, and I gag around him.

He pulls himself out of my mouth and suction releases with a pop, he leans down so that we are face-to-face. "Here's how tonight's going to go," he whispers. "I'm going to oil you up and I'm going to make you see stars through that pretty little ass of yours."

"I'm fucking you tonight," I announce.

He breaks into a sarcastic smile. "We both know that's not happening. Not even close."

"But you wanted—"

"My therapist wanted." He cuts me off. "I want no such thing. The only fantasy I have is to fuck *your* ass, and that's exactly what we're going to do." He pulls me to my feet and in one fell swoop takes my dress off over my head.

"But Misty's list," I stammer.

"I'm not here with Misty. I'm here with you." He grabs my head and kisses me aggressively. "We're doing *our* lists, not the ones others have set for us." His teeth stretch out my bottom lip and I feel a sting of pain.

Yesssss.

Adrenaline screams through my veins as we stare at each other.

He takes off my bra and his teeth drop to my nipple and he bites me there. Hard enough for pain, soft enough for pleasure.

The perfect combination.

Goose bumps scatter up my arms at the dominance of the act.

He slides my panties down my legs and his fingers move to my sex.

"Dripping." He smiles darkly as he slides his fingers deep into my body. "Just like I knew you would be." He pumps me with his fingers. "Admit it, Doe, you like me in charge." He pumps me hard again and I whimper and throw my head back. "Don't you, baby?" His teeth graze my jaw as he brings me undone.

His hand is nearly violent as he fucks me with it.

Fast and hard…deep.

The sound of my arousal sucking him in echoes throughout the room, and I begin to lose all coherent thought.

I shudder and he takes his hand away. "Please…" I whimper, every one of my senses on fire. "I need…."

"I know what you need, angel." He picks up the bottle of massage oil and kisses me, then taking me by the hand he leads me into the bedroom and lays me down on the bed.

He props pillows behind me and half sits me up and then spreads my legs wide open.

I watch him rearrange my body in a detached state, as if I'm floating up above and watching us below.

Never have I been with someone who knows exactly what he wants, and exactly how he wants me. Nothing is left to chance, the master of control.

It melts my brain to know that there are men like this in the world. I mean, you hear of them, but meeting one in the flesh is rare.

With his eyes on me he takes his shirt off over his head, I'm blessed with the view of his broad muscular chest. He slides his jeans down and reveals the *V* of muscles that leads to his large manhood.

His pubic hair is short and well kept, and every muscle on this god's body is in peak condition.

From the very back of my depraved mind I get a fleeting thought….

You are my bucket list.

He kneels on the bed and then drops his mouth to my sex; he licks me there and his eyes close in pleasure.

His fingers spread me wide as he sucks me deep.

Oh…*fuck*.

The way he has me sat up so that I can watch him do this is too much.

My eyes roll back in my head.

I begin to quiver, the need to come so strong.

"Sshh." He stills. "Hold it…."

"I…." I pant. "I…."

"Sshh, angel." He smiles into me. "You need to learn to control this."

There's a plan.

You probably need to teach me…in a three-month full-time training camp in the Swiss Alps.

He licks me again and I nearly bounce off the bed.

"Ahh…. So eager to come." He smiles darkly, flips me over onto my stomach and pushes the pillow away. I feel the hot oil pour onto my back and over my behind.

He spreads my legs wide and pours oil all over my sex and then massages it in with his fingers. He takes his time, slow and steady.

Oh….

Good lord.

I may not survive the night.

He straddles my body and begins at my shoulders, his magical hands rubbing and massaging me into the mattress. He rocks forward and I can feel his hard cock up against my back.

I clench to try and get some kind of traction between my legs.

His hands massage down my body while I hang in ecstasy, and every now and then as he rocks forward I can feel every vein on his hard, weeping cock.

His fingers move lower and he slides off me and sits to the side, pulls me up onto my knees and begins to massage the oil through my lips and over my ass.

His two fingers slide into my sex and he pushes his thumb deep into my other opening.

My head dips as I try to deal with his onslaught.

"Relax," he breathes, he pumps his thumb deeper until my eyes begin to roll back. "That's it, angel…relax."

For a long time he massages me just like this, oil all over, fingers in my pussy, thumb in my ass.

All the stars in my eyes.

"You want me here." His thumb gets rougher. "You want me in this tight little ass, angel?"

I nod, unable to speak.

He shuffles around to behind me and with one hand occupied on my sex he puts his other hand on my shoulder and begins to bring my body back onto his with force.

Oh….

His thumb gets almost violent. "You want more?"

"Yes," I whimper. "Give it to me."

He keeps going and I begin to grab the sheets between my fingers.

I need more.

I feel oil being poured over my sex and he bends and kisses my ass cheek tenderly. "Just a sting," he whispers. "Once I start we don't stop." He kisses me again. "Okay?"

I nod and close my eyes.

I feel the tip of his cock at my entrance and then I feel more oil being poured over us.

He runs his tip through the lips of my sex and I hear him inhale sharply. "Fuck," he whispers.

I smile, he's as lost to this as I am.

He pushes forward and I feel more than a sting. "Argh."

"Sshh," he whispers. "Relax, Doe, let me in."

He moves with force and it burns…and it hurts.

"Argh," I whimper. "Oww."

More oil gets poured over us. "You've got this," he breathes, his hand tenderly runs up my back to calm me.

I'm not sure I do.

He surges forward again and I'm filled with pain.

I wince and screw up my face.

After what feels like eternity my body finally releases and he slides in to the hilt.

An overwhelming sense of dominance fills me.

"Oh my god." I pant at the new sensation.

"Fuck…." He moans. "So good." His fingertips come around to my clitoris and he circles them as he stays deep inside me. His lips are at my ear as he curls over me, his thick quads are either side of mine and cocooning me in.

But it's the possession of his cock as it sits deep inside my body.

Owning me like never before.

This is an out-of-body experience, raw and intimate.

Like nothing I've ever felt.

"Kiss me," he breathes.

I turn my head and we kiss over my shoulder. Deep and different and so fucking perfect.

For a long time we kiss and I know what he's doing. He's letting my body adjust to his size.

But what about my heart, how does she recover from this?

Pleasure starts to build and I move a little, wanting some friction.

"That's it." He smiles into my mouth. "Just like that."

He slowly pulls out and slides back in, once more. Slowly pulls out and then slides back in.

Oh….

He does it again, and then again.

My eyes flutter closed.

This is actually…enjoyable.

He gets rougher, deeper, and I begin to push back on him as I chase the closer connection.

Then we are hard at it, our skin slapping together. The bed is hitting the wall.

His deep moans are all around me as he completely loses control and fuck, this is too good.

He pumps me hard and I scream out as I come hard.

He holds himself deep and I feel the telling jerk of his cock as he orgasms strongly inside of me.

His deep moan echoes through the apartment and I smile into the mattress, now there's a hot sound.

He turns my head and kisses me as he holds my face in his hands.

It's tender and loving.

Intimate, everything I ever dreamed of.

I'm totally and irrevocably forever ruined.

CHAPTER SEVEN

EDWARD.

Hoe walks out with her bag and puts it by the door and she gives me a sad smile.

"Time to say goodbye?" I ask.

"Yep."

Her eyes search mine, and if I were a better person I would say something meaningful and significant. But as I stare at her beautiful face...words fail me, so instead I take her into my arms and kiss her.

Last night was more.

Way more than I had bargained for, much more than I deserved.

My lips tenderly take hers as a million questions I'm unable to ask linger on them. She's perfect, absolutely fucking perfect, and I'm unable to offer her a goddamn thing.

She puts her head on my chest and I stroke her hair as I hold her in my arms.

We both stay silent, lost in our own thoughts.

"It was nice meeting you," she whispers.

"Believe me—" I smile into her hair, "—the pleasure was all mine."

She giggles and it drops my stomach.

"What time does your plane leave?" she asks.

I glance at my watch. "In a few hours."

"Mine too."

She stares up at me and I know she wants me to ask to see her on the outside.

If I could...I would.

"You should get going," I say softly.

She nods and pulls out of my grip and instantly the absence of her warm touch is felt.

She walks around the suite and collects her things and puts them into her carry-on luggage while I stand still on the spot, willing myself to let her leave.

I discreetly take my phone out of my suit pocket and turn my data off. I hit search for wi-fi.

Alora's Phone.

Alora.

Her name is Alora.

She walks back into the room and I quickly stuff my phone into my pocket before she sees.

She comes back to stand in front of me. "Are you sure we can't do what we came here to do?"

"My apologies....I just...." I exhale heavily, disappointed that I can't do this for her.

Why aren't I better with words?

"I'll make sure you receive a credit," I tell her.

"I don't want to do that with anyone else," she whispers.

I stare at her as her words hang between us.

If I were a better person I would tell her to come here again with a new partner, fulfill the list and make her friend proud.

But I can't.

The thought of her touching someone else is not something I can bear to think about.

"Will you remember me?" she asks.

"Yes. Will you remember me?"

"Probably not."

I smile down at her and I press my lips to her forehead as I hold her close. She closes her eyes to my touch. "I love it when you kiss my forehead." She smiles against me.

Enough.

This is getting fucking morbid; I need to cut it short.

"You should get going." I step back from her.

"Okay," she whispers, her nostrils flare as she holds in her tears.

Don't....

Before she can say another word: "Goodbye, Miss Doe." I nod, then I turn and walk out of the suite. The door clicks closed behind me and I hesitate for a moment as I hold the door handle in my hand. I imagine her on the other side of the door.

I can *feel* her on the other side of the door...waiting for me to come back through it.

I close my eyes in regret.

Leaving her was harder than it should have been.

I straighten my tie and calmly walk back to my room.

It's time to go home.

ALORA.

The cab ride to the airport is long, it's snowing now.

And unlike the magical snow of last night in his arms, today it's cold and depressing.

What are the chances that I meet my dream man in a place like this?

I've cried for over an hour.

I know that there's no future for us...hell, he's probably married or something.

Men like him are never single.

With a connection like we had I get the feeling he would have asked to see me on the outside if he didn't already have his life set out in front of him.

He's with someone for sure.

The scenery flies by and I remember the sex and the wild lovemaking, the tender showers and the way he looked after me, and my eyes well with tears anew.

The way he made me feel.

What the fuck is wrong with me?

Such a loser.

I drag my hand down my face in disgust, only I could catch feelings in an anonymous kink club?

Two hours later I sit at the airport bar by the window.

I'm on my second glass of wine, because as the saying goes, if you can't be happy be drunk.

I'm on the very last terminal and I watch a big plane pull out to take off and a sleek black private jet parked on the tarmac comes into view.

Wow.

There must be someone famous in town.

There are people refueling it and a truck is delivering produce. Imagine being that rich that you had your own private jet. I see the captain and the three flight attendants board; it must be leaving soon.

It's the weirdest day, I keep flicking between present time and memories of the weekend. I feel like I'm between worlds, I want to stay back there with him but I'm being forced and dragged to be in the present.

It doesn't seem fathomable that I will never see him again.

My heart aches at the depressing thought.

I sip my wine and look down at my phone and scroll through for a moment. I glance back up to see two black SUVs pull up beside the black jet. I wonder if it's a sportsperson's jet or maybe a pop star or something.

I watch as a bodyguard gets out and opens the back door of the second car.

I knew it was someone famous.

I grab my phone and flick open the camera; nobody is going to believe me when I tell them I saw Taylor Swift if I don't have a photo.

I smile as I wait for the person to get out, and then when they do my face drops.

Dark suit, sunglasses, and perfect posture. Dark just-fucked hair, and I would know that physique anywhere.

My Mr. Doe.

He walks up the stairs of the plane, the pilot is waiting at the top, he shakes his hand as he walks past him. With my heart in my throat I watch on as he disappears inside. The men in suits who I'm assuming are the bodyguards carry the suitcases onto the jet and eventually the door is shut.

My mouth falls open and I glance down at my phone, damn it. I was so gobsmacked that I forgot to take a photo.

The bodyguards from yesterday…they weren't from the resort at all.

They were with him.

I stare at the jet as it slowly pulls out and drives away into the afternoon sunset.

What the fuck….

I sit back, shocked to my core.

I think I just had a dirty weekend with someone rich or famous.

Who are you?

The server walks past my table and puts a fortune cookie down as she hands them out to everyone. "A present for you." She smiles.

"Thanks." She moves on to the next table and with a heavy heart I crack mine open.

Make a wish.

I hold the fortune cookie in my hand as I go over the weekend and all I can feel is the deepest sense of gratitude.

I know that I didn't tick off Misty's wish list.

But I sure as hell ticked off mine.

"Mr. Doe. I don't know how, I don't when…." I smile fondly and close my eyes as I make my wish. "May we meet again."

CHAPTER EIGHT

My phone dances across the table, *buzz, buzz, buzz, buzz*. "Hello," I answer as I watch the swanky plane take off into the sunset.

"Hi, love."

"Hi, Dad." I smile. "How are you?"

"Not great.

"What's wrong?"

"It's Uncle Edgar." I can hear sadness in his voice.

"Is he okay?" I frown.

"No, he's had a heart attack and has passed away."

"Oh my god." My face falls as I get a vision of my beloved uncle being in pain with a heart attack. "Was he alone?" I stammer.

"No, thankfully he was with friends and out to dinner, so he wasn't alone. They've assured me that it was quick and relatively painless."

My eyes well with tears. "I'm so sorry."

"Me too."

Uncle Edgar was my dad's brother, he married a French woman and moved there to be with her over thirty years ago but unfortunately she passed away not long after they were married. He never met anyone else and he never left because France was where he felt closest to her. It's the saddest love story of all time.

"I'm on my way home, I'm at the airport. I'll be there as fast as I can."

"Oh, Alora, there's so much to do…we have to organize the funeral, his house and everything…."

Poor Dad.

"It's okay," I try to reassure him. "I'll take some time off and we'll go to France and figure it out. I'll help, it's okay."

He sniffs and my heart breaks, he was his only sibling and the last person alive in his family. We were all so close with him. "I'll be there soon, okay?"

"Okay."

"Don't cry."

"I'm not," he lies.

My eyes well with tears. "I'll be home soon."

"Sorry to ruin your weekend away."

It was already ruined.

"Don't be silly. See you soon." I hang up as I visualize my beautiful Uncle Edgar, so enigmatic and eccentric, always laughing and the life of the party.

The lump in my throat begins to hurt as I glance at my watch.

I need to get home.

THREE WEEKS LATER.

"To my brother Kelvin Sorenson, who I love with all of my heart, I leave my villa in Paris, my estate in London and my car and jewelry collection." My dad shakes his head in disbelief.

The lawyer looks over the top of his glasses. "To my nephew River, I leave my home in Beverly Hills in Los Angeles." We gasp, oh my god, that is worth millions.

"To my niece Raylyn, I leave my apartment in Manhattan in New York." Our eyes widen.

"And to my niece Alora I leave her my entire antique collection and my terrace house in Mont Boron, Nice, in France."

We all exchange glances, is this for real?

"I leave you all a twenty-five percent share of my home in the Hamptons; it is my hope that you use it as a family vacation haven together. Please know how much I love you all. See you on the other side."

Oh my god.

The car pulls up at an old run-down factory building and my dad, River and Raylyn and I all frown at each other in question. "He must have rented a storage unit inside of it." Dad shrugs.

"Yes, he rented a space," the lawyer replies with a heavy French accent from the driver's seat. He parks the car and we climb out, we wait while he fumbles through the biggest key ring I have ever seen. Eventually he opens a huge, rusty roller door and we all stare in, clueless to what we are even looking at. There's an entire factory packed to the rafters with all kinds of random things and antiques. Stuff is hanging from the ceiling and things are stacked dangerously high on top of each other.

My eyes flick to the lawyer. "What's this?"

"Antiques."

"Yes, but which ones were his?"

He holds his hands up. "All."

"All," Raylyn and I say in unison.

"All?" My father gasps as he looks around. "Surely not."

"Yes." He nods. "He loved his antiques so much."

"All of these are…." I frown.

"Yours."

My eyes widen. "But what the hell am I going to do with all of this?"

"I have no idea."

* * *

It's funny how life turns out.

You think you know how it's going to go and yet somehow the choices are made for you. A higher power orchestrates your true destiny, regardless of what you imagined. No matter how hard you may try to fight it, what is meant to be yours, will always end up being yours.

I know this for certain because although I haven't chosen this life, I feel at peace with where I am and I couldn't imagine a different outcome.

I live in France now, with the need to sell Uncle Edgar's antiques I originally came for a month and opened a market stall. It did so well that I started trading and now find myself the proud owner of a boutique antique store in Nice. Funnily enough, without any prior knowledge of the industry, I apparently take after Uncle Edgar and have a sharp eye for antiques and have carved out a very successful career for myself.

My store is a true piece of my heart, the people who work for me are my close friends, I have a beautiful terrace house in Mont Boron and the most wonderful boyfriend in the world.

Life is.... Blissful and full of joy.

Simple.

I'm laid back and feel at ease with where I am in the world, and although I miss my family in the States, they come to visit often.

My left arm holds out as I turn the corner, weaving between the cars like a pro, I ride my bicycle to work every day. It's baby blue and has a wicker basket on the front, it even has a bell. So French, that some days I hardly recognize myself.

"Morning, Alora."

I ring the bell on the handlebars as I pull up onto the sidewalk. "Morning, Franck," I call back as I dismount my bike.

"Beautiful day."

"It is." I inhale the heavenly scent drifting out of his patisserie. "I will never tire of that smell, Franck."

"My strategy is working, then." He disappears back into his store.

Franck is the best pastry chef in all of France, also a very bad influence.

"Good morning." I check the mailbox on my way through the front door.

"Bonjour," Jonty says as he fills the cash register with money.

"Bonjour." I smile.

"Good morning," Helene calls as she carries the heavy sign out the front and sets it up on the pavement. I'm lucky enough to have the most beautiful people working for me. Jonty is twenty-eight and a budding artist, he was supposed to be here for a month helping us through a busy period but was too amazing to ever let go. He's funny and quirky with long auburn curly hair that he pulls back into a ponytail. He wears little circle gold glasses like John Lennon. Helene is twenty-six and the hardest worker you will ever meet. She's the exact opposite of me but has somehow become my best friend. While I am easygoing and carefree, she is highly strung and wild. Where I have long dark hair, she has a blond bob cut. She dates everyone and anyone, is never home, hates to cook and loves to club. While my favorite place to be is at home, chilling out while cooking or gardening. She says that I am the yang to her yin and somehow even through all our differences, we just work. To be honest, I think that Misty organized our friendship from heaven, she had to. There's no way I would be lucky enough to have two best friends in one lifetime that were so similar unless someone pulled some strings from above.

"Morning, Alora," Jonty says as he powers up the cash register. "You have five messages on the answering machine."

"Thanks," I say as I flick through the letters. Ugh.... Bills. I look around my store and smile, no matter how long I work here, I will never take it for granted. The vivid rich colors of the furnishing and that distinct antique-store scent, I love this place. It's quaint and has an eclectic beauty about it, one person's trash is another's treasure. Luckily for me, my idea of treasure seems to be appreciated by the masses.

Who knew I would turn out to have good taste?

I walk around the store and turn on all of the lamps, they are varied in size, style, and texture but I always put in a warm glow lightbulb to tie them into the ambience.

"Are you ready?" Helene calls.

"Hang on." I quickly straighten my hair up in the mirror and walk over to her. "Let's go."

She holds her phone up and smiles. "And go."

"Good morning." I smile. "I'm Alora from Sorenson Antiques and this is our morning run-through of our store. This arrived yesterday and isn't she beautiful." I run my hand over the double doors, "This is a Baroque armoire, circa early seventeen hundreds." I point to the carved details. "As you can see it has beautiful craftmanship, fully hand-carved cherubs and detailing around the edges."

Helene twirls her finger in the air to symbolize to keep going, ugh...social media, the bane of my existence. Unfortunately though, it's what sets our store apart and why we do so well, many people tune in each day to see our new arrivals.

"This armoire has been in the one family for many generations and is in perfect condition." I open the doors and drawers. "The lock has both solid brass keys still working." Helene walks around the armoire as she films it. I wave to the camera with a smile. "Have a beautiful day everyone, au revoir."

"And that's a wrap." Helene begins to rewatch our video on the phone and posts it. "It's up, now we can open."

I turn the sign on the glass door.

OUVERT — OPEN

Jonty flicks on our playlist and jazz music begins to play, loud and boisterous. "You're feeling energized this morning," I call, we usually start the day off with a calming piano orchestra.

"Let's pretend it's five o clock already."

"First comment." Helene reads from the work phone. "What cardigan are you wearing, Alora?"

I roll my eyes. "Why the hell do they always obsess about what I wear?"

"Because you have great taste, that's why."

The kettle sings and I make us all a cup of coffee and weave through the furnishings to deliver Jonty's. "Merci," he replies as he takes a sip. "Did you give any more thought to the auction?"

"I did and no, I didn't come up with anything." I sigh as I turn on my computer.

"Well…what cardigan are you wearing?" Helene calls. "Everyone is asking."

"Umm." I frown as I think. "It's vintage Chanel, I think it's seventies from the spring collection."

"You know what will be the next question," she calls.

"I got it at a flea market in Paris," I call back as I try to focus on what I'm doing.

"Did you have any thoughts on the auction, Helene?"

"Honestly, what on earth can we donate as a learning scholarship?" she says as she dusts. "What exactly even is a learning scholarship?"

Leaning against the doorjamb, Jonty's forehead creases as he thinks. "I read it as they want something educational to auction off."

"About antiques, though?" I screw up my face. "This is ridiculous. I'm self-taught, what can I possibly donate to an auction that will teach someone what we do?"

"I don't know." He twists his lips.

"Maybe like a book on antiques or something." Helene shrugs.

"This is supposed to be a main auction, a book just isn't going to cut it." I throw my hands up in disgust. "How did we even get roped into this?"

"It's *your* boyfriend's fault, why don't you ask him?" Helene huffs. "It's like he's setting us up to look stupid."

"I'm going to kill him." I hit the computer keys with force.

Pascal Deschanel is on my hit list, and as wonderful as he is, this time he has gone too far.

"He put us forward for this big fancy charity auction in Monaco and said it would be a win-win situation that would bring a wave of new customers to our store. But now that we have to think of a prize to donate I think it's a terrible idea," I huff.

"It has to be good or we're going to be the laughingstock of the auction." Helene rolls her eyes. "This is just so Pascal."

I smirk, Helene doesn't really like my boyfriend. She thinks he's smug and any chance she gets to blame him for something, she will.

"Why don't you call him and try and find out the other prizes so we can get an idea of what to offer?" Jonty suggests.

"Good thinking."

The bell rings over the door, notifying us of our first customer. Jonty disappears out the front. "Bonjour," I hear him greet them.

"Bonjour."

I dial Pascal's office number. "Bonjour, Pascal Deschanel's office," Aila his PA answers.

"Hi, Aila," I reply.

"Good morning, Alora. He's in a meeting, I'll get him to call you as soon as he's finished."

"Merci. Have a nice day."

"You too."

Pascal and I met at a party two years ago and we started out as friends but one thing led to another and we've now been dating for twelve months. We're on opposite ends of the spectrum, I'm easygoing, calm and grounded in small business and live my life surrounded by art and antiques. He's structured and highly strung, on the board of directors for the National Council of Monaco and has two PAs who run his hectic life. While he's making monumental decisions about the future of Monaco, my biggest decision is where can I search for my next vintage treasure and if I like a lamp enough to put into my store.

I open my emails and physically get to work but in the background my mind wanders aimlessly.

Prize, prize…. I need a prize.

PHILIPPE.

The silver McLaren turns into the Monte Carlo Polo Club fields and we pull in after it.

He parks, grabs his things from the trunk before making his way over as his strappers unload his horses from the trailer.

We park the Bentley and take our time; polo is a relatively safe outing where guards usually outnumber the players.

We grab some coffee and make ourselves comfortable and an hour later the umpire throws the ball in the air and the game begins.

The loud echo of horses' hoofs and people yelling. Adrenaline screaming through the air.

Beautiful women are in fold-up chairs along the sidelines. While cars of men line the parking lot to watch over their bosses, we're all here for the same reason.

The Kingsmen, the Monte Carlo polo team, are some of the wealthiest men in the world. And we…we are the bodyguards that keep them safe, and although it's the best job in the world, it's not without its challenges.

"Yah," he calls to his horse as he bumps full speed into another player, nearly knocking him from his horse.

"Fuck you, Prescott," the man yells.

"Your wife already did that." Edward smiles as he flicks the peak of his helmet. "Elizabeth loved every inch of it." He grabs his crotch. "I can still hear her moans."

The other man's face falls. "You're fucking dead," he cries after him.

Prescott laughs as he sprints off, polo stick in the air. The more he pisses them off, the more fun he and his team have.

Everything's a game to them.

"Jesus Christ." Andre drags his hand down his face. "How do you keep that prick alive?"

"It's not easy." I shake my head.

Those challenges I was talking about are greatly enhanced for us, you see, we're the security team for Edward Prescott.

Undoubtedly one of the most hated men on earth.

The ladies love him, the men hate him, and he...well, he doesn't give a fuck about anything or anyone.

Bang.

He hits another player off their horse and they go flying to the ground with a hard *thump.*

"Argh," the player cries.

Prescott laughs as he looks down at him, stick over his shoulder. "Learn how to ride a horse, you fucking gimp."

"I think my arm is broken." The man groans.

Prescott canters off without a care and we all chuckle from the sidelines.

This motherfucker has a death wish.

The elevator rises and we all stand facing the doors. Edward has a business meeting at the Monaco council, his lawyer is with us, which can only mean one thing.

This isn't going to end well.

"Remember to let me do the talking," Louis says.

Edward clenches his jaw as he adjusts his cuff links. "Remember who you fucking work for."

Merrick and I make eye contact. *Here we go.*

"I just know that you...." Louis cuts his sentence short.

"You know what?" Edward snaps.

"You have a way of infuriating people." He holds his hands up in surrender. "There's no denying that you do." He widens his eyes. "I'm just saying that this is...."

"Stop fucking stopping mid-sentence," Edward barks. "Do you know how annoying it is?"

"This is an important meeting and I need you not to piss anyone off today," he blurts out in a rush.

Edward rolls his eyes. "Just you concentrate on *your* job and let me handle mine."

"I am."

"Then secure the extra hours for the casino," he barks. "Why else would I be here with you wasting my fucking time?"

"I need to remind you that your only job here today is to mend fences, put the past in the past. Be charming and friendly," he continues.

Edward gives him the side eye. "Do you know how fucking annoying you are?"

"At times, but...." He exhales. "Just try it for once."

Edward straightens his tie and cracks his neck. "Just going to this imbecile's office winds me up."

"We can't get this deal through without him." He plasters a big fake smile on his face. "Like this."

Edward looks over at him deadpan.

"Try it."

"Fuck. Off."

I drop my head to hide my smile. I'm with Edward on this one, his lawyer really is very annoying.

The elevator doors open and Edward strides out as Louis scurries to walk beside him.

"Bonjour." Louis smiles to the receptionist. "We have a meeting with Pascal Deschanel. I'm Louis Richards and this is Edward Prescott."

"Yes, sir." She smiles. "Nice to meet you both, this way to the conference room." She leads us up a long corridor and into an office with a large round table.

Merrick and I fall in to stand beside the door. "Please, take a seat." She pours two glasses of iced water from a carafe that sits on the table. "Mr. Deschanel is just finishing up his last meeting; he won't be long."

"He has five minutes." Edward looks at his watch.

"Will you relax," Louis replies softly.

"This is me relaxing," he snaps. He glances at his watch again. "Four minutes."

"My apologies, Mr. Prescott," she stammers as she closes the door behind her and scurries up the corridor.

"My god." Louis pinches the bridge of his nose. "Remind me why you're here again."

"Because Deschanel wouldn't have this meeting without me being present." Edward rolls his lips. "He wants me to suck up to him."

"Which you are *going* to oblige."

"I wouldn't count on it." He glances at his watch. "Three minutes."

Deschanel and Edward have a long history filled with heated arguments. He's a do-gooder who hates everything about the casino in Monte Carlo. Edward's a businessman who is sick and tired of him standing in his way.

"Two minutes."

"Listen," Louis whispers. "You will sit there and you *will* play nice. The entire board of directors are counting on you to behave today."

Edward clenches his jaw. "This fuckwit has me over a barrel."

"Exactly. It's fifteen minutes, suck it up."

Merrick and I stand quietly as we disappear into the walls.

The door opens and the familiar face comes into view. "Gentlemen." He smiles as he looks between them. "Sorry to keep you waiting."

"No bother at all." Louis smiles as he shakes his hand. "Thank you for seeing us."

He turns to Edward and outstretches his hand. "Hello, Edward."

"Hello, Pascal." They shake hands and sit down.

"Beautiful day," Pascal continues.

"Yes." Edward forces a smile and then drops it immediately. "Get to the point."

I roll my lips as I stare at the ground, he's such an ass at times that it's hard not to react.

"Your office has been renovated since I was here last time," Louis says as he looks around.

"Yes it has," Pascal replies. "It's lovely isn't it, they did such a good job."

"It is," Louis agrees.

"Such a joy to come to work."

Edward drags his hand down his face and Louis widens his eyes in silent warning.

"So...we're here to have the preliminary meeting regarding the request for operating hours extension for Casino De Monte Carlo." Louis tries to move things along.

"We received your application." He opens the folder and begins to flick through it. "You have requested a daily four-hour extension."

"That's right," Edward replies.

"You are currently open from 2 p.m. until 4 a.m. daily."

"Yes," Louis replies. "We are receiving several requests for extended hours from our patrons, they want to be able to have lunch with us."

He looks up from his folder and smirks as if finding that statement amusing. "I find that very hard to believe."

Edward bites the side of his cheek as if to stop himself.

"You see, if we grant you an extended license we will be in fact giving you a license to close down every restaurant in Monte Carlo."

"Restaurants in Monte Carlo have nothing to do with us," Edward fires back.

He clasps his hands together as he looks across the desk at him. "Edward."

"Mr. Prescott to you."

Louis steps on his foot and Merrick and I exchange subtle glances.

This isn't going to end well.

Pascal's eyebrows shoot up as if surprised. "Alright, Mr. Prescott." He leans forward in his chair. "We are opposed to the extension of hours and will not be accepting your request at this time."

"You said that two years ago."

"And our decision still stands."

"Don't fuck with me, Pascal."

"That's Mr. Deschanel to you."

Animosity bounces between them. "I'll take you to fair trading court," he tells him.

"You won't win."

Edward smiles and sits back in his chair. "We both know that you don't have the funds to fight me." Louis squishes his foot into the ground and he rips it from beneath him. "Stop."

"Just because you are wealthy, Mr. Prescott, doesn't mean you are above the law."

"It's called restriction of trade and it's illegal. It is you who is not above the law."

They glare at each other across the table.

"Now, gentlemen," Louis stammers. "Let's workshop this and try and come to some middle ground."

Edward stands. "I will not be workshopping anything."

"What does that mean?" Pascal asks.

"It means I will see you in court." Edward walks from the office and we walk out after him. As we make our way down the corridor I hear Louis stammering and scrambling, trying to defuse the situation.

Edward hits the elevator button. "What a waste of my time," he mutters under his breath. The door opens and we follow him in and stand at the back. Louis comes running down the corridor and gets in. He nervously glances over to Edward. "That wasn't great."

"Why didn't you just drop to your knees and suck his cock under the table?" He raises an eyebrow in question.

"I'm trying to network."

"You're pathetic," he barks as he adjusts his suit coat. "I presumed lawyers were supposed to have some fucking balls."

"Do you always have to be so aggressive?" Louis fires back.

"Only when my lawyer is a pathetic wimp." The doors open and he strides out and Louis scrambles to walk beside him.

"The next meeting will go better," he promises.

"It will because I'll have a new lawyer. You're fired."

"What?" Louis stammers. "You can't fire me."

"I just did." He strides out of the building and out onto the street. I open the back door of the car for him.

"Well, what am I supposed to do now?" Louis cries from behind him.

"Apply for a job at Grow A Set dot com."

ALORA.

My eyes skim the page but not a word registers. I get all the way to the bottom, I go back to the top of the page and start again. Pascal is brushing his teeth as I pretend to read in bed.

"I don't see the big deal," he murmurs around his toothbrush.

"The big deal is that I don't have anything to donate for this stupid thing, I wish you never suggested it," I call.

He rolls his eyes at my dramatics.

"Don't roll your eyes at me," I huff. "It's being announced everywhere as a major prize."

"That's a great thing." He spits the toothpaste into the sink and finishes up. "This is fantastic publicity." He comes and lies across the bed and leans up on his elbows.

"I have no doubt that this is all true if there *was* a great prize," I scoff. "Why did I agree to this? I've been wracking my brain all week and I've come up with nothing. If I don't think of something substantial this is going to be a publicity nightmare."

He rolls onto his back and looks up at the ceiling as he thinks. "What about an armoire?"

"A cupboard?" I screw up my face. "Seriously? A cupboard is the best you can think of."

"I think an armoire is great."

I let out a deep sigh and go back to pretending to read.

"What about an internship?"

My eyes rise to meet his. "What kind of internship?"

"Well…" He thinks on the fly as he explains it to me. "Whoever purchased it could give it to a young person or someone who wants to enter the antiques world."

"Like a gift?"

"Yes, like a gift. It could be an amazing start for someone. You could show them the ropes, teach them from the inside, and share your knowledge."

"Who's going to pay for that?"

"It's not about how much someone would pay for it, it's what it is worth. The honor of learning from the best, a proven successful antique dealer. These opportunities just don't come up."

I twist my lips as I think it over.

"That is a great prize, and lots of people know someone who would want it. We live in France, everybody loves antiques."

"I mean…." I shrug. "It's better than a cupboard, I guess."

"Armoire," he corrects me.

"Well, how would it work?" I ask, my interest piqued.

He shrugs, still thinking out loud. "You offer an internship of say…fifteen hours a week. They shadow you and work alongside your team for a period of time, like two months or something, and you all share your knowledge and mentor this person. This isn't a monetary prize; this is time with you. A prize that money cannot buy."

My eyes hold his as the idea rolls around in my brain. "I could take them to the Paris market and introduce them to our wholesalers," I think out loud.

"Yes. If they are old enough to travel, you could." He smiles, knowing that he may have just solved our problem.

The more I think about this idea the more I like the sound of it, a broad smile slowly covers my face. "What would I do without you, Monsieur Deschanel?"

"Probably not have to think of prizes for auctions." He lies down on his back and points to his cheek. "You can start here."

Huge bouquets of flowers line the red carpet. Security with earpieces, reporters covering the event, and acrobats walking on stilts with fire, the entrance is every bit as exotic as promised.

"Wow." I smile to Pascal as we climb out of our car, my nerves simmer as the auction approaches. Tonight's the night and if everything goes to plan, my prize will slip between the glamor and the glitz and be just enough to hold a place.

Pascal takes my hand in his and we walk up the large staircase to the flashes of cameras. I feel like a princess and am wearing a red vintage evening gown with my hair and makeup professionally done. I've never gone to so much trouble before, but I figure if I'm going to do it…I may as well try and look the part while I do. "Mr. Deschanel," a reporter calls. "Are you excited for tonight's event?"

"Yes I am." He smiles with a nod and a wave, and leads me in through the front doors and when I see the grand ballroom, my stomach dips and suddenly I feel like throwing up.

"How…. What…where…." My eyes dart around at our surroundings, a catwalk stage is right through the middle of the room, the table and chairs are set around it.

"What's that for?" I stammer.

"I think there's a fashion parade or something later," Pascal replies.

"Oh." I put my hand over my heart to try and stop it beating so fast.

"Will you relax?"

"How can I relax?" I whisper. "This is literally my worst fucking nightmare."

He looks down at me and chuckles as he tucks a piece of hair behind my ear.

"What?" I ask.

"Looking like that and cursing like a sailor."

"Well, this sailor is about to walk the plank and jump overboard."

A waiter walks past us with a silver tray filled with champagne flutes and offers us one.

"Cheers." Pascal smiles as he holds his glass to mine.

"Cheers." I take a sip and the cool bubbles of deliciousness dance on my tongue. "This is good."

"Only have one until the auction is over." He winks.

"Good idea," I agree. "Don't want to be auctioning off the wrong thing."

Pascal's eyes land on something across the room and he clenches his jaw.

"What's wrong?" I frown.

"What is *he* doing here?" he mutters under his breath.

"Who?" I glance around.

"That entitled bastard who owns the casino."

"Oh." I sip my champagne as I zone out, this topic is becoming very old.

"Of course he's here with the prince."

"The prince is here?" My interest reignites, the Prince of Monaco is one hot specimen. "Where are they?"

Pascal tilts his chin in their direction and I subtly glance over to the corner. Prince Theodore Chapelle is wearing a black dinner suit and bow tie; his sandy brown hair has a curl to it and damn.... The man is fine. His bodyguards are by the wall as they watch his every move. It still seems surreal to me that Monaco has a reigning royal family.

Prince Theodore says something to his date and she laughs up at him and cups his face.

Agnes Maras...she's blond and beautiful, a Danish billionaire heiress who often graces the local news on her prince's arm. She's laughing and talking to another woman wearing a white silk gown. I take a sip of my champagne as I pretend not to be interested, but unable to help it my eyes go back to linger on the beautiful people.

The woman in white has long golden hair and a figure to die for. Her date is tall with dark hair, he has his back to me but has his arm firmly around her.

Jeez.

I sip my champagne and drag my eyes away. "Where are we sitting?"

"The seating arrangement is on the wall." He takes my hand and leads me over to it; I glance back at the beautiful people just as the man with the dark hair looks over.

Our eyes lock and the air leaves my lungs.

It's Mr. Doe.

CHAPTER NINE

Our eyes are locked and then his chin tilts to the sky as if angered, he leans down and says something in the woman in the white dress's ear before walking toward us.

Oh no….

My heart beats like a drum and I take a large gulp of my champagne before glancing down at the glass, damn it, it's nearly empty.

Not now, fucker.

Pascal leads me to the seating chart and starts to read through the tables. From my peripheral vision I can see Mr. Doe approaching us.

No…no…no…what *is* he doing here? He's not supposed to exist in the real world. He was the fantasy man I worked hard to forget.

"Here we are, table eight," Pascal tells me. I blink as the words on the seating chart blur. I feel him before I see him; standing beside me, his presence overtakes the room.

Pascal glances up. "Prescott."

"Bonjour," he replies in his swoony English accent, he nods to him and turns to me. "Alora."

He knows my name.

Thump, thump, thump beats my heart.

The familiar scent of his aftershave envelops us, reminding me of a time when he touched me.

"Hello." I force a smile. He bends and kisses my cheek; his lips burn my skin and every cell in my body screams. "Hi," I whisper as the air leaves my lungs.

Oh my god….

Just being this close to him sends goose bumps scattering up my arms.

Thump

Thump… goes my heart.

Pascal looks between us. "You know each other?"

"Alora and I are old friends," he replies calmly, totally unruffled by his lie. "It's lovely to see you again."

My eyes search his, *what is he doing?*

This man has more front than a double-decker bus.

"How do you know each other?" Pascal demands in such a tone it drags my eyes back to him. He's unimpressed and on the defensive.

"Alora is close with my sister, Charlotte." He turns his attention to me and I wither under his gaze. "We're old family friends, aren't we?"

"I…." I swallow the lump in my throat as I process what he's saying "Umm…. Yes."

Why did I just lie?

"Come, I would like you to meet Hermione." He takes my hand in his. "I'm stealing her for a moment," he announces to Pascal before pulling me away.

Oh my god. Oh my god.

My body screams with excitement at his touch.

He pulls me by the hand through the crowd but we don't head toward the beautiful people, we head toward the door. "What are you doing?" I whisper.

"I need a word."

The feel of his big hand around mine sends tingles up my arm and I know full well that this is a disaster of epic proportions. We burst out the side door and land in some kind of reception area. He looks around and spots a staircase. "Here."

"What?" I stammer as he pulls me along. I look around guiltily, what if somebody sees us? "What are you doing?"

"I need a word." He takes the stairs and I'm forced to follow.

Forced isn't the right term…. I could stop this anytime I wanted to, but I want to hear what this word is.

We get to the top of the stairs and he looks left and right and then marches down a hallway until we get to a library; he pulls us in and closes the door behind us.

Suddenly alone, we stare at each other. My eyes roam over every inch of the face that I have dreamed about, cried about, and wished so desperately to see again.

Oh….

"What are you doing here?" he asks, his voice soft and cajoling. Just the sound of his dreamy English accent in that husky tone lights a fire in my memory bank.

"I live in Nice."

He frowns. "You live in Nice?"

I nod.

"All this time you've been in Nice, half an hour away from me?"

What?

"Where do you live?"

"Between London and Monaco."

We stare at each other and the pull I feel to him is otherworldly. Like a rope is tied between us, tightening harder with every word he says.

"It's good to see you," he whispers as he cups my face in his hand, he brushes his thumb over my bottom lip as I stare up at him. "It's still there."

I nod, not because I want to…but because there's no denying the chemistry between us. "Yes."

"I tried to find you," he murmurs.

There's an undercurrent of affection running between us. Wild and strong, unstoppable.

He bends and softly kisses me; our lips linger over each other's as if this is the most natural thing in the world. The earth moves beneath me and just for a moment the planets align into perfect position. A total eclipse of my heart.

Pascal.

What the fuck are you doing?

"I…." I abruptly step back from him. I may be a lot of things, but I am *not* a cheater. "I'm with someone."

"Him?" he asks incredulously.

I nod.

We stare at each other; our chests rise and fall as we struggle to breathe.

"And you're with someone," I remind him.

"I am." He drags his hand through his hair as if only now remembering.

"This…." I put my hands over my eyes in disgust at our behavior. "This can't happen again."

"It can't," he agrees. "I just…. You're hard not to touch."

I nod, but I get the feeling that isn't what he was going to say; he's filtered his words.

"I have to get back; you stay here until I'm long gone," I tell him as I rush off.

"When can I see you again?" he calls after me.

I turn back toward him. "I don't even know your name."

"Edward." His eyes search mine. "Edward Prescott."

My heart drops.

Oh no….

I've heard that name before, heard of the monster who my boyfriend despises with every ounce of his being. Never once could I have imagined who was behind it.

"We can't…." I shake my head, overwhelmed with emotion. It's the weirdest thing, it's like my loyalty lies with him and not the man who I'm currently dating. Why do I feel so close to this stranger?

It was just sex.

Snap out of it.

"We are with other people, Edward; I can't see you again."

"Even though you want to?" His eyes search mine.

For the first time in my life I am in a happy, healthy relationship with a good man, and I cannot throw it away for a sexual connection at a kink club years ago.

I won't.

"I don't want to see you again," I tell him. I turn and on shaking legs I walk down the stairs and back into the ballroom and look around frantically for Pascal.

Where is he?

My heart begins to panic, I just lied to him and kissed someone else, this is not okay.

What the fuck am I even doing?

I see him across the room talking to a friend of ours and I hasten over to him. "There you are." I smile as I put my arm around him.

"I cannot believe you know him," he whispers as he leads me away to talk in private.

"I had no idea he was the man you knew from work. Small world, huh?" I grab another glass of champagne from a passing tray and take a gulp.

Help!

"How can you be friends with someone like that?" he asks. "He's ruthless and will stop at nothing to get what he wants."

My heart is thumping hard in my chest, frazzled from our connection upstairs.

Tingling lips and all.

"I'm friends with his sister," I lie again. "I have no idea about his business affairs. We're family friends, that's it."

Fuck.... Stop lying, stop it right now.

"Let's take our seats." I force a smile. Taking his hand in mine, I turn us both toward our table and I see Edward walk back over to the beautiful people. The gorgeous woman in the white dress slides her arm around his waist as she laughs and says something to him, he says something in return and she laughs again.

My stomach twists with jealousy.

I take a huge gulp of my champagne and puff it into my cheeks as I go over what just happened. My cheeks are on fire and I'm as flustered as all hell.

This is an actual nightmare.

We take a seat at our table; it's round with white linen and adorned with large vases of pretty flowers in the center with silver candelabras. "It's beautiful," I say as I take Pascal's hand into mine onto my lap. He twists his lips, openly angered that I know Edward.

Edward.

His name is Edward.

Another couple sits down at the table, an older man and woman in their fifties. "Hello, Pascal." The woman smiles.

"Ah, Irena." Pascal smiles. "Hello." He turns to her husband. "Hello, Vonte."

"Good to see you, Pascal." They shake hands.

"This is my girlfriend, Alora," Pascal introduces me.

The worst girlfriend that ever did live.

"Hello." I smile, they begin to chat and the tables begin to slowly fill as people take their seats.

Don't look....

I stare at the tablecloth, determined not to look Edward's way. For what reason though I'm just not sure. Is it because I want to be with Pascal or is it that I don't want to see him.... Or is it because I don't want to see him with *her*?

I take another gulp of champagne; this is going down way too well and shit, I've got the auction coming up.

Focus.

I put my champagne down onto the table with a *thud.*

No more.

An hour later the table is deep in conversation, the night has run smoothly and the fish was divine. As always, Pascal has been a dreamy date, the table has laughed and he's been attentive to me. He's a wonderful boyfriend and I've gained some perspective of the situation, just because I'm attracted to Edward doesn't mean a thing. It was a shock to see each other, that's all. It took him by surprise just as much as it took me and we lost our heads for a moment, that kiss means nothing, it will never ever happen again.

Of course we were going to be excited to see each other, we never thought we would.

I tried to find you.

Butterflies swirl in my stomach at the thought.

Did he try to find me...or did he just say that to make himself sound good, because truth be told I tried to find him too.

Why the hell are you thinking about this?

Stop it right now.

The MC gets up onto the stage. "Good evening, ladies and gentlemen, I would like to offer you a warm welcome to the Children's Medical Research Annual Charity Fundraiser."

The crowd claps loudly and my stomach flips, Pascal reads my mind and smiles and squeezes my hand in his. "You'll be fine," he whispers in my ear. I smile and look up into the stare of Edward. He's sitting three tables over and is facing us.

Has he been watching us the entire time?

My god....

I snap my eyes away and try to focus on the MC and what he's saying.

I'm going straight to fucking hell....

"Let's start our charity auction tonight with a surfboard signed by none other than the legend himself, Jérémy Florès."

Everyone has bidding paddles with numbers on them and as the excitement builds, people begin to hold them up to bid.

"One thousand."

"Two thousand."

"Fifty thousand," a man calls, and the crowd cheers.

I take a gulp of champagne, if ever there was a night that I want to drink like a raging alcoholic, tonight's the night.

I'm nervous, I'm flustered. I'm a horny, cheating, lying snake.

"Fifty thousand going once. Fifty thousand going twice. Fifty thousand going three times," the auctioneer calls. "Sold." He slams the hammer down. "A wonderful purchase to the gentleman on table two."

The man stands and takes a bow as the crowd cheers. Okay, that wasn't so bad, maybe I might survive.

"The second item to be auctioned tonight is a week on a superyacht in Saint-Tropez."

The crowd rumbles with excitement.

Pascal picks up my hand and kisses the back of it as the bidding begins.

"Two thousand," someone calls.

"Five thousand." Someone else holds up their paddle.

"Twelve thousand."

"Do I have twenty?" the auctioneer calls.

Someone's paddle goes into the air.

"Thank you, sir, sold. To the man on table ten."

An hour and a dessert break later the auction begins again.

"We are up to auction number twenty-four and this is without a doubt an opportunity of a lifetime," the auctioneer calls. "Tonight we are offering an internship with Alora Sorenson Antiques."

The crowd goes silent and my stomach drops, god help me... here we go.

"This is a once-in-a-lifetime opportunity, people," the auctioneer continues. "You will get to learn from Alora Sorenson herself. She will mentor you for a period of two whole months, you will get to work in her boutique alongside her team and travel to Paris with her for further education. You will be roaming the countryside in her eternal search for the ultimate in lost treasure."

I bite my lip to hide my smile, so dramatic.

"This is a prize that money cannot buy for the aspiring antique dealer," the auctioneer calls as he looks around. "The perfect gift for someone you love. Do we have a first bid?"

"Five hundred thousand euros," a deep English voice calls.

The crowd gasps and I turn to see Edward holding his paddle in the air.

No....

"Good lord," the auctioneer calls. "Do we have a higher bidder?"

What. The. Actual. Fuck.

The room collectively holds their breath and my heart threatens to escape my chest.

What is he doing?

"Going once for five hundred thousand euros."

Silence....

"Five hundred thousand euros twice."

"Third call for five hundred thousand." He slams down his hammer. "Sold to Mr. Edward Prescott."

CHAPTER TEN

EDWARD.

"Third call for five hundred thousand." He slams the hammer down. "Sold to Mr. Edward Prescott."

The crowd cheer and Theodore holds his hand out. "You crazy fucking bastard." He chuckles. "I'm positive you're insane."

I dip my head with a smile.

"What in the world are you going to do with that?" Hermione laughs as she claps in disbelief.

"Donate it to the Royal Scholarship Scheme."

Theodore laughs and shakes his head. "You could have gotten this for forty thousand."

"It's a charity auction." I shrug. "Everyone is a winner this way."

"Auction number twenty-five," the auctioneer calls as the next item comes up. "We have a diamond pendant."

My eyes roam across the room to land on Alora; she tips her head back and drains her glass of champagne, she's clearly rattled and I roll my lips to hide my smile.

I hope that helps her cause.

One of the good things, no...the best thing about having money is being able to help people. Donating this prize will make a difference and hopefully bring some much-needed media attention to the Royal Scholarship Scheme.

I take another sip of my scotch and I feel a tap on my shoulder. I glance up to see Pascal leaning down to speak into my ear. "A word outside," he whispers.

My eyebrows shoot up in surprise, and unable to help it, a broad smile covers my face. "What do you want?"

"Now," he growls before walking off through the crowd and disappearing out of the ballroom.

I chuckle and finish my drink; this will be fun.

Stupid prick.

"I'm going to the bathroom." I excuse myself, stand and begin to walk toward the exit, my two security guards begin to follow me and I subtly shake my head. "No," I mouth. "Stay here."

They exchange looks and then make their way back to take position by the wall.

Walking into the reception hall, I see Pascal pacing, he looks like he's about to have a heart attack.

"What are you doing, you fucking idiot?" I whisper.

A couple walk out of the ballroom and he points to the stairs. "Up here."

"What?" I frown.

"Come up here where we can talk in private," he snaps.

My eyes hold his and I know this visit up the stairs isn't going to be half as enchanting as my last one was. He stomps up the stairs and walks down the hall to the exact library, and I smirk and follow him in.

He turns on me like the devil himself. "How fucking dare you!"

"What are you talking about, you imbecile?"

"I see what you're doing."

"And what is that?" I sigh as I lean my behind against the desk and cross my feet in front of me.

"If you think that Alora's respect can be bought you've got a rude shock coming."

I roll my lips as my eyes hold his.

"I've seen you, watching her all fucking night, and then you make this ridiculous bid on her stupid internship."

"Stupid?" I raise an eyebrow. "Nice."

He's rattled.

"You know what I fucking mean," he stammers. "Alora is with *me*. Alora is in love with *me*."

I smirk at his delusion, that's why she was kissing me in this very room two hours ago.

"Stay away from her, do you hear me?" he growls.

I like this game; my smile gets wider. "Or what?"

"Or you will have *me* to deal with."

"How terrifying." I smile as I put my hands into the pockets of my suit pants.

What is she doing with this loser?

"I know what you're doing and you make me sick," he spits.

"What am I doing?"

"You're going to use her to get back at me."

"I don't need Alora to get back at you."

"Yes you do. You know that I have power over you and your sleazy casino and there's nothing you can do about it."

Our eyes are locked, contempt runs between us like a river.

"Taking innocent people's money through gambling addictions does not make you powerful," he sneers.

I lift my chin, angered. "I was donating that prize to the Royal Charity but...I just changed my mind."

"To what?"

I don't reply.

"Well?" He's panicky and talking fast.

"I'm going to *fuck* your girlfriend so good and so fucking *hard* that she won't even remember your pathetic wimpy little name." I push off the desk and stand and straighten my bow tie. "You can watch me do it if you like."

His face falls, his chest heaves as he struggles for control. "You go near her and see what happens to you," he whispers angrily.

"I believe I just started an internship." I smile with a wink. "The Paris trip is going to be especially fun." I put my hand on his shoulder as I walk past him. "Commiserations, my friend. We both know you've already lost." I walk out of the library and back down the stairs.

I walk in through the ballroom doors and I have to concentrate to keep the smile from my face.

This one is going to be especially fun.

ALORA

FIFTEEN MINUTES EARLIER.

"Sold, to Mr. Edward Prescott."

The crowd cheers and I fake a smile as I feel my heart drip into a puddle under the table.

No, no, no….

This is all wrong, what *is* he doing?

"Oh my god," a lady at our table exclaims. "This is simply incredible. Congratulations, dear." The clapping goes on and on and on.

I glance over to Pascal; he sips his drink and rolls his lips, his eyes straight ahead, the anger radiating out of him is palpable.

Great, now he's pissed at me. This isn't my fault, he's the one who suggested I do this stupid charity event.

The next auction starts and my face is so flushed and damn it I need to get some fresh air before my head explodes. "I'm going to the ladies'," I push my chair out as I whisper to Pascal. He nods but doesn't reply.

You know what…. Fuck you too. How is this my fault?

I weave through the chairs as I make my way to the exit. Okay, so we kissed…. But he doesn't know that…yet. Of course I am going to tell him…. I imagine having that conversation and how it will go.

Argh, I kissed him.

My god, this is the worst night of all time.

I'm a ho.

I make my way out of the ballroom, take my phone from my purse and hold it to my ear as I pretend to take a call as an excuse to leave the party. What I really want to do is get on a plane and get the hell out of here because damn it, in three hours flat my life just got stupidly complicated.

I walk out the front doors and find a chair in the garden and sit in the dark.

Echoes of the party inside float through the air.

Though the sound of my heart beating in my chest does

nothing to comfort me; if anything it just reminds me that a cardiac arrest is near.

In through my nose and out through my mouth…. In through my nose and out through my mouth. I repeat the mantra to try and calm myself down. In through the nose and out through the mouth.

I cannot fight with Pascal tonight, who knows what I will say in the heat of the moment. I need to think this through, and tonight is not the night to tell him what happened in that library.

Especially now after the auction. Five hundred thousand euros….

Fuck.

"You okay, miss?" I hear a voice from behind.

I turn and see a doorman walking toward me. "Yes." I stand. "Just getting some fresh air. I'm going back inside now."

He gives me a kind smile and turns and walks back to the doors with me as a silent escort. I make my way back into the ballroom and as I walk toward my table I see an empty seat.

Where's Pascal?

I look around and I lock eyes with Edward who is sitting at his table, he gives me the best come-fuck-me look of all time and I snap my eyes away.

Don't even….

Your girlfriend is sitting right next to you, you know.

Ugh…why the hell is she so beautiful anyway? I take a seat at the table and pick up my glass of champagne and take another gulp. Yep…. This is turning into an outright disaster.

Where is Pascal?

I subtly look around, what if he knows what we did?

Eventually he appears through the crowd and he takes a seat beside me. "You okay?" I whisper.

He smiles and takes my hand in his. "Just at the bathroom."

"Okay." I squeeze his hand in mine and it's familiar and safe and exactly what I need in my life. Just having him beside me is comforting, and no matter what happens….

I can't ever forget that.

EDWARD.

Glenfiddich Grand, has there ever been a better-tasting drop? Sitting in front of the open fire with my feet up on the ottoman, I sip it slowly and feel it all the way down.

Who is Alora Sorenson? Nice Antiques.

I wait for the answer to come up.

Alora Sorenson is an antique dealer. Owner of Sorenson Antiques in Nice, France.

Although reasonably new on the scene to the antique world, she has already cemented herself as a force to be reckoned with. Known for her impeccable taste and timeless style, she's often referred to as the modern-day Audrey Hepburn. Alora Sorenson has garnered somewhat of an online cult following for her classic beauty and love of vintage designer clothes.

I sip my scotch, well well....

"You coming to bed?" Hermione asks from the hall.

"I'll be there in a minute," I reply without looking up.

"Okay."

I wait for her to leave and then click on images.

A gallery of photographs appears of the enchanting Miss Doe and I click on them all one by one. Long dark hair, perfect posture, the most perfect face, and a beautiful smile.

Angelic.

I get a flashback of her on her knees in front of me, her eyeliner smudged from near choking. Her lips red raw...her big eyes pleading for me to go easy on her.

My cock twinges with excitement and I smile and sip my scotch.

Found you.

ALORA.

The clock ticks over as I watch Pascal's back, he's lying on his side turned away from me and has said all of three words since the auction. "You okay?" I ask softly.

"Just tired."

Although he hasn't said anything, its crystal clear that he's upset about Edward.

Well get in line, motherfucker, because that makes two of us.

I close my eyes and I feel Edward's hand on my cheek, I feel his lips against mine and my heart free-falling from my chest. Every emotion in Technicolor perfection.

The way he looked at me, the fire behind his kiss.

Sadness fills me at the realization that I don't know if I feel like that with anyone else.

Not even the man that I love, and how is that fair?

Why would I be reminded of an attraction so substantial in my life that it changed my DNA. What kind of person am I… feeling like that about another man when I'm with someone so wonderful?

The lump in my throat hurts and the salty hot tears run down my face and drip into my ears.

In the darkness, beside him, I cry alone.

The bed dips as Pascal climbs out and I inhale deeply with my eyes still closed.

Hell, what a night. I feel like I haven't slept at all.

He pulls his pants on at the end of the bed and I lean up onto my elbows. "What are you doing?"

"I have to go."

"Where to?"

"Work."

"It's Sunday." I frown. "I thought we were going out for breakfast this morning?"

"Sorry, something's come up." He leans down and kisses me quickly. "Call you later." But before I even have a chance to reply, he's disappeared down the stairs and gone. I hear the door click as he leaves.

I flop back down and put my hands over my eyes. "Shit." Guilt is the worst feeling in the world. Pascal knows we kissed; he has to. That's the only logical explanation for the way he's acting.

Why did I fucking kiss him, this is not who I am.

My god.

I stare up at the ceiling for a long time, my body too tired to get up and my mind too panicked to sleep.

Forget it.

Forget everything about Edward Prescott, nothing good can come of thinking about him.

Finally I drag myself to the shower. If I'm not going to sleep or relax I may as well make use of myself and go grocery shopping.

I make my bed as I talk out loud to myself, "It's fine…this whole situation is fine, it's just a speed bump. It was a shock to see him, that's all. I was surprised and overwhelmed and it will never happen again. I have a wonderful life and a beautiful boyfriend." I punch the cushions on my bed to get them in the right shape. I punch them again for good measure.

"Everything is going to be just fine."

When someone else lies to you, you get angry, but when you lie to yourself you're actually just an idiot.

It's 4 p.m. and I haven't heard from Pascal all day, which is weird…actually, not weird, it's a disaster, because he calls me and tells me every little detail of his day all of the time. The fact that it's Sunday, which is our day together, only confirms what I suspect.

He knows, and I'm totally fucking screwed.

A whorebag of epic proportions and to make matters worse all I can do is think about Edward fucking Prescott, it's taken every ounce of my strength not to google him today. But all that's going to prove is that I'm an actual asshole.

I dial Pascal's number. *Ring, ring…ring, ring.*

"Bonjour," he answers.

My heart sinks, he had his phone on him but didn't call me. "Hi. Where are you?"

"Just leaving work now."

"Are you coming over?"

He exhales. "Ummm."

"Do you want to go out for dinner." I cut him off. "I think we need to talk."

"We do, that's a good idea."

My eyes widen, *oh my god*...he does know.

"Okay," I reply. "Will you pick me up?"

"About seven."

"See you then."

"Yep." He hangs up without saying another word.

Without a thought, I do what I said I wasn't going to do. I google:

Who is Edward Prescott?

Viscount Edward Prescott is the CEO of Prescott Holdings with an estimated personal worth of 32 billion dollars. The heir to the largest portfolio of casinos in the world.

"Viscount." My eyes widen. "What the hell, he has a title?" I read on....

Known for his striking good looks and sharp wit, he pulls no punches in the workplace and is known for his exceptionally high standards, which are noted to be impossible to uphold.

I read down the article until I get to the part that I'm looking for.

Personal life.

His father, Harold Prescott, is the Earl of Nottingham, his mother Angelique Prescott died in a tragic car accident many years ago. He has two siblings, Lady Charlotte Prescott Jones and Sir William Prescott.

Stringently guarding his privacy, very little is known about Edward Prescott's personal life. Although it is believed that after a string of failed relationships in his twenties he has become somewhat of a recluse over the last six years, preferring to focus on his career and his family.

Hmm, I frown as I keep reading another heading,

Viscount Edward Prescott spotted on luxury yacht with Princess Hermione....

She's a fucking princess?
Oh hell, this is a disaster…I read on.

Princess Hermione of Switzerland has been spotted on the luxury superyacht of Edward Prescott, CEO of Prescott Holdings. No statement has been issued by either party.

I click on the images to see the beautiful blond woman lying on the deck of the yacht in a white string bikini. Edward is lying beside her propped up on his elbow with his hand on her stomach. He's wearing sunglasses and is smiling down at her all gorgeous like. I click through the photos, one of them sunbathing, then another of them kissing in the ocean. I swallow the lump in my throat as I go through the images, there's one of them walking off the yacht on a gangplank with security guards trailing behind them, she's dressed in a sexy evening dress with stilettos, he's wearing a linen shirt with the top buttons undone and casual linen pants that are rolled up on the bottom, he looks all just fucked and casually sexy. I imagine them on an exotic date in Monaco or Saint-Tropez.

Ugh, she's even more beautiful in person if that's possible.

"When was this?" I click on the date…. "Eight months ago." I twist my lips as I go back through the photos, they've been together a while then.

I type into Google:

Princess Hermione of Switzerland.

A barrage of images comes up and damn it, this woman is perfect. Thick long blond hair and the perfect figure. Blue eyes…. Dimples and white teeth. Bodyguards.

Ugh…. Sickening.

I lie on the couch and stare at the images for a while as my mind goes into a million scenarios of his life and my life and all the things that I shouldn't be thinking.

If I were single and he were single…. What would happen?

Nothing, *you're not!*

And he's dating a fucking princess…. Of course he is.

I click out of it and throw my phone down in disgust, I need to get a hold of myself.

This is stupidly stupid.

Tarte Mison is my favorite restaurant, it's romantic, the cocktails are perfect and the food is the best in France, and I don't know what I was thinking coming here tonight. Will it still be my favorite restaurant when I get dumped in it by my boyfriend for kissing another man?

Probably not….

I sip my wine and smile over at Pascal; he's not talking again and I know for certain he's waiting for me to tell him.

"So…." I try to broach the subject. "You've been very quiet since the auction."

"Yep." He sips his wine and rolls his lips as if annoyed.

"And…." *Fuck*. "I…." My god, how do I say this? "You're angry that Edward won the auction of my prize?"

"No." His eyes hold mine.

I take a huge gulp of my wine.

"I'm angry because he told me that he's going to fuck you so deep and so hard that you won't remember my name."

What?

I snort my wine up my nose and cough. "Excuse me?" I splutter as I spiral into a coughing fit. He sits still, watching me, void of any empathy of me choking to death before his eyes.

"What are you talking about?" I squeak.

"When you went to the bathroom last night I went to see him."

Edward told him…. This is worse than I first thought, much worse. My lungs convulse in protest to the wine that has gone down the wrong pipe. "Why?" I splutter and cough as I beat my chest. "I might die here, you know?"

"I wanted to thank him for the kind donation."

The server approaches us. "Are you okay ma'am?"

"Yes." I throw Pascal a dirty look. "Thank you for your concern." I take a sip of water and finally my lungs begin to calm down. "Wait a moment, I'm confused. I don't understand what you mean," I reply. "He said he was going to fuck me?" I ask.

"Until you don't remember my name."

Something about Edward announcing that to Pascal is just so like him and so bastardish that it brings an unwelcome hit to my funny bone.

Arrogant asshole.

I roll my lips to hide my smirk

"You think this is funny?" he snaps.

"No," I stammer. "It's just…." I shake my head in disbelief. "He said this to you at the table in front of everyone? He has a girlfriend, Pascal, are you sure you heard him right?"

"No, we went outside to talk in private and ended up going upstairs to the library."

"The library?" I squeak. *Oh fuck me dead*…the same library we kissed in only an hour before.

There's no doubt about it, I'm going straight to hell on the slut bus.

"I…." I shrug. "I don't know what to say. He's not normally like that, I'm lost for words."

"I know this has nothing to do with you and everything to do with me." He sips his wine casually.

It may have a little bit to do with me.

I need to forget about the other night, telling Pascal what happened is only going to break us up and truth be told, Edward doesn't even care. This is just a game to him. He's not worth it.

"Look." I take Pascal's hand over the table. "Edward Prescott has nothing to do with us."

He gives me a stifled smile.

"He only said that to upset you."

"It worked."

"I'm sorry." I give him a sad smile. "Can we just put the auction and Edward Prescott out of our minds and concentrate on each other, please?"

"I'd like that." He smiles as he squeezes my hand in his.

The server comes back over. "Are you ready to order?"

"Sorry, yes." I open my menu; I stare at the choices but the words are blurred.

He's going to fuck you so deep and so hard that you won't remember my name.

I feel overly heated as the image plays out in my mind.

Dear lord....

MONDAY MORNING.

My bicycle bounces as I mount the curb. "Morning, Franck."

"Morning, Alora. Beautiful day."

"It is." I dismount and walk my bike around to the side of my shop and tie it up.

I'm a little late today, Pascal and I had wonderful makeup sex all night and everything is rosy again.

I push the heavy door open and the bell rings to announce my arrival.

"Hi, Jonty." I smile.

"Bonjour, Alora." He passes me a cup of coffee and widens his eyes. "The auction was successful?"

"It was." I walk to my office and stop on the spot at the door.

Big blue eyes meet mine. "You're late," Edward growls.

CHAPTER ELEVEN

Wearing a charcoal suit and a crisp white shirt, he is sitting behind my desk.

In. My. Chair.

He runs his tongue over his teeth as if annoyed. "I don't like to be kept waiting."

"And I don't like you sitting in my chair," I fire back.

Jonty scuttles to the front of the store, scared for his life.

"What are you doing here?" I whisper angrily.

"Waiting for my internship to begin."

"There is no internship," I spit as I look around. I discreetly close my office door. "You know damn well there isn't."

"Ha." He leans back in my chair. "What the hell did I pay for, then?"

"You paid for the right to be a fucking idiot."

He smirks and raises his chin. "What kind of employer curses at their intern?"

"What kind of a man tells someone that he is going to fuck their girlfriend so hard that she won't remember their name?"

His eyes dance with mischief. "He told you?"

"Yes, he told me," I fume.

"He's even wimpier than I thought."

"How is telling me wimpy?"

"Well, if someone said that to me about my woman—" his dark eyes hold mine, "—they wouldn't live to tell the tale, let alone go running home to Mommy."

"*You* might not live to tell the tale," I spit. "Get out of my chair."

"No." He keeps sitting there. "When I am in this office, this will be my chair."

"Edward." I pinch the bridge of my nose. "I don't know what you're playing at."

"I'm playing at five hundred thousand euros and you…had better start cooperating."

"That was before I knew you were goading my boyfriend," I whisper angrily.

"I do wonder." He spins back and forth on my chair. "What did he say about you kissing me?"

My eyes bulge from their sockets. "Keep your voice down," I whisper as I look around guiltily. "Do not ever speak of that again, and *you*, kissed *me* not the other way around."

He smirks as his eyes hold mine and damn it, why is he so fucking attractive?

It's criminal.

"So…." He steeples his fingers in front of him. "What happens now?"

"What happens now?" I repeat.

"Yes, what happens now?"

Who the hell knows what happens now, not me that's for sure.

I grab a feather duster and hold it out to him. "Go…clean something."

"The only thing I'm going to be cleaning are the cobwebs out of your vagina." His eyes dance with delight. He's playing with me now and honestly, his attempt at humor is way off. I'm on the edge of losing my living shit.

"Edward," I fume. "I mean it."

He stands. "So do I."

"And I do *not* have cobwebs in my vagina."

"I seriously doubt that." He snatches the feather duster from me and walks out into the shop. I flop into the chair and put my head into my hands, this is a literal disaster.

Helene walks in and closes the door behind her, she peeks at Edward through the glass door. "What is happening right now?" she whispers as she cranes her neck to look at him. "Why is he here?"

"He won the auction."

"What?"

"I know." I throw my hands up in disbelief.

"But isn't that…the owner of the casino?"

"Uh-huh."

Jonty walks into the office and closes the door behind him. "What the hell is going on?"

"He's the owner of the casino," Helene whispers as she continues to peer through the blinds at him. "He's like a gazillionaire."

"I'm so confused right now," Jonty whispers. "Why does he want an internship at an antique store when he could afford to buy the whole of fucking France?"

"I don't know," I lie. "Just keep him busy."

"Doing what?" he asks.

"I don't know, teach him stuff," I stammer.

"Like what?" Jonty asks.

"I could teach him a thing or two." Helene smirks as she watches him.

I seriously doubt that.

"What should I teach him?" Jonty asks again.

"I don't know." I hold my hands up. "Go…show him how to use the cash register."

"Okay." He frowns. "Do you think he wants to buy our store?"

"Maybe," I lie.

"Right…." He cranes his neck to watch him. "Are you thinking of selling?"

"Oh my god, Jonty!" I snap. "I need to think in peace for a moment, please go out there and do something useful."

"Fine." He disappears out into the front of the store, leaving the door open, and all is silent for five minutes. "Don't touch that," I hear him say.

"Interns touch everything," I hear Edward's voice fire back. "Isn't that the point of interning?"

"That egg is an ancient artifact."

"That has *dust* on it."

A comeback for everything. I feel my temperature rise even higher.

"God, he's so fucking hot, right?" Helene murmurs as she watches him through the blinds.

That's it!

I can't hold this in for one moment longer.... I have to talk this out.

"I have something to tell you," I whisper. "But you have to swear on your life not to tell a soul."

"It's me." She shrugs. "Who am I going to tell?"

"I know him. I mean I knew him before." I wobble my head around as I search for the right way to put this. "Like *really* knew him if you get my drift."

Her eyes widen. "Oh my god. You slept with him?"

"Sshh," I splutter. "Keep your voice down."

"Well, did you?" She holds her face as she waits for my answer.

I shrug. "Maybe a little bit."

"Was it good?"

"Very."

"I fucking knew it." She throws her hands up in the air. "He has huge, big dick energy. I can smell it a mile off."

Sure does.

"Anyway," I whisper. "He bet on the auction on Saturday night and now he is here to make my life miserable because he and Pascal hate each other."

"Screw Pascal," she whispers. "This guy is way hotter."

"He's got a girlfriend. A princess." I widen my eyes.

"You could totally take her," she huffs as she once again spies on him through the blinds.

"I'm not interested in him like that."

"Oh my god," she murmurs.

"What?" I get up and go to the window to see what she's looking at; Edward has taken off his suit coat and is leaning over a chair. His tight ass and thick quad muscles are on display.

"He is so fucking fine." She sighs dreamily.

Don't I know it....

"He's taken. I'm taken.... This won't be an issue."

"So can I sleep with him?"

"Absolutely not."

For half an hour I have sat at my desk and listened to Jonty and Edward bicker while Helene watches him with love heart eyes, and for the life of me I don't know what to say or do.

His little cleaning-out-vagina comment indicates that he's still in flirt mode, and this has to come to an end once and for all. This is not happening in any shape or form.

Having him around is playing with fire, a fire that could burn my life to the ground.

"And in here is another camera." Jonty opens the office door and gestures up to the camera.

"What are you doing?" I ask.

"Just showing him where all of the security cameras are."

"Why?"

"You know." Jonty widens his eyes. "Interning need-to-know stuff."

"Right." I concentrate on keeping my eyes on my computer screen so that I don't have to look at his fuckable face.

"Out through this back door is the bathroom, it's off this little courtyard, see," I hear Jonty explain. "But there's a camera out here too. See."

"Is this courtyard secure?"

"Well, it has a brick wall around it so nobody can get in," Jonty replies.

"Because nobody ever jumped a brick wall before," I hear Edward mutter under his breath.

Such a smart-ass.

They walk back out the front of the store and I can hear them chatting. Okay, new plan. I'm just going to go out there and act normal.... If he wants to be an intern then fine, let's intern.

I walk out to find Jonty serving someone and Edward is talking to a group of women in the corner. I watch him from across the store; wearing his designer suit and his swanky shoes, he looks so out of place here, the feather duster in his hand doesn't help the matter. I edge closer so I can hear what they are saying.

"This is a nice piece," he tells them as he runs his hand up an armoire.

"Divine," the woman says as her eyes follow his hand. "What year?"

"At a guess, I'd say 1870s."

Hmm, not bad. 1875 to be exact.

"I'll think about it." The woman smiles.

"This piece is sold," he tells her.

"Oh." Her face falls. "It doesn't say sold."

"I know, I hadn't put the sign on it yet. Someone just called and asked to purchase it." He runs his hand up along it again as if admiring it. "Such a beautiful piece."

I roll my eyes at his dramatics, he's a bad actor.

"Well, if the sign isn't on it yet it isn't technically sold," she replies.

"True," he replies. "But If I sold it to you—" he looks left and right, "—you can't tell anyone."

"Alright." She exchanges glances with her friends. "I'll take it. Do you deliver?"

What the hell?

"I don't know, I'll check." He walks over to Jonty and me. "This lovely lady is taking the armoire, help her please." He passes me the feather duster and throws me a wink.

Excuse me?

"Lovely to meet you, ladies." He shakes their hands. "Jonty, clean it up before it goes out, please."

Jonty looks at him deadpan and Edward raises an eyebrow in a silent dare.

"Thank you, Edward," I snap. "I'll take over from here." I smile an over-the-top smile at the ladies. "What a find. I wanted this piece myself."

An hour later I finish serving someone and Edward is nowhere to be seen. Where is he? I walk around the store and check all the alcoves, nope.... He's not here.

"Where did he go?" I mouth to Jonty.

He shrugs. "He left."

"Oh." I frown, odd of him to leave without saying something. I walk to the front door and walk out; I look left and then right and then my eyes land on something inside the café on the opposite side of the street.

Edward is sitting at a table drinking coffee like a king.

Seriously?

"I'm going out for a little bit," I tell Jonty and Helen.

"Okay."

I cross the street and make my way in and sit at the table opposite Edward. He raises an eyebrow in question.

"What are you doing?" I ask.

"Taking a break."

"You didn't do any work yet."

"I sold an armoire." He dusts his suit jacket off. "What exactly did you do?"

"I've been very busy in my office."

"Doing what?"

Having a panic attack.

"Paperwork," I lie.

He nods and casually sips his coffee. "How'd that go?"

"What are you doing, Edward?" I sigh. "We both know you don't want to be my intern."

Amusement flashes across his face as he blows on his coffee. "What gave it away?"

"Why did you bid at the auction?"

"To support you."

My eyes hold his.

"And I was going to donate the internship until your pissy little boyfriend carried on." He frowns. "I still can't believe you're with *him*."

"And you're dating a princess?"

"I am."

We stare at each other as a million unanswered questions swim between us.

"Are you and she serious?" I ask.

"We are."

My heart sinks.

"I...." He cuts himself off.

"What?"

"I know you're not ending up with Pascal, so I'm not even going to bother asking you the same question."

"How do you know that?"

"He's not the man for you, Alora."

"You know nothing about me, now I'm going to ask you again, Edward. What are you doing here?" I repeat.

"I came to say goodbye."

My eyes hold his.

"I'm going to donate the internship to someone who actually wants it."

Oh....

"Thank you."

"I just thought I'd have a bit of fun with you before I left."

"Our ideas of fun must be different."

"We're seeing other people and...." He shrugs. "We need to keep this strictly professional."

"I agree." Relief fills me. "That's exactly what I was thinking." Then I remember something. "So why tell Pascal that you wanted to fuck me if you had no intention of going behind his back?"

"Make no mistake, I do want to fuck you, and I would have no problem taking you from him." He gives a subtle shrug. "The problem comes from my end."

He loves her.

"Well, I don't want to have sex with you anyway," I add.

"Liar," he mouths. "I do have one condition on stepping away."

"A condition?"

"I want you to be my intern."

"What?"

"I have no interest in antiques, but you do need to know business. Which just happens to be my specialty."

"What are you proposing?"

"We meet one afternoon a week and I will mentor you."

I roll my eyes.

"Not that kind of mentoring." He smirks. "Business acumen. Accounting, sales, targets, things like that. Last time we met, you were a math teacher; I read up how you came into this business, and it can't have been an easy transition."

"I was and it hasn't." I think for a moment. "Why would you do this?"

"Because I care what happens to you." He shrugs. "And if I cannot pursue you—"

"Why did you kiss me the other night?" I cut him off.

"Honestly?"

I nod.

"I couldn't stop myself; I was so happy to see you that it overflowed, and before I knew it I had you in my arms."

I get a lump in my throat as I stare at him, a silent message runs between us. A distant memory of a wonderful weekend in each other's arms.

"If things were different…" he murmurs as his eyes hold mine.

"I know." I nod. "Why did you bait Pascal?"

"Because I can." He shrugs. "He's an easy target."

"You're evil."

"Motivated."

"To tell him you're going to fuck me so deep that I won't remember his name."

He smiles sadly. "If only."

We stare at each other as something hangs in the air between us but what that is exactly I just don't know.

"This mentorship, how would it work?" I ask, to change the subject.

"We would meet one afternoon a week and talk business. I could be a sounding board if you need any advice."

"Where would we meet?"

"At your store or at my office."

"What day?"

"Friday afternoons are good for me. I mean when I'm in the country, of course. It wouldn't be every week; my schedule is fully booked most of the time."

I bite my lip as I think it over. I do need training, and this would be a great insight into big business. He could teach me how to grow and expand. This could be really beneficial, actually. Who am I kidding, the masochist in me just wants an excuse to see him.

"But Pascal…." I think out loud.

"Will think that I'm demanding you hold up your end of the deal. He doesn't need to know of this arrangement."

"He's a good man, Edward."

"I have no doubt." He shrugs. "Not quite sure how he managed to pull you, though, but that's another story."

I smile softly over at him. "I'm glad you're happy."

"That Jonty is annoying, isn't he?" He frowns.

"Not in the least." I smile.

"So…Friday?"

I nod. "Friday."

"Your place or mine?" he asks, and the double meaning hangs in the air. "You know what I mean?"

"Let's do your office this week," I offer.

"Okay. I will text you my details."

"You have my number?"

"I got it from the auction sheet."

"Right."

"I should get back to work."

"You should." He sips his coffee.

"See you Friday."

"You will."

I stand and leave and I don't know what I just agreed to, but I can feel his eyes watching me as I walk out of the café, and I'd be lying if I said they didn't feel good.

The doors are heavy as I push through them and the sunshine hits my face, my conscience whispers something silent.

This is a bad idea….

If making a bed were an Olympic sport, we would hold the gold medal.

I'm on one side and Pascal has the other, we grab the corners of the quilt and walk them back to fold down as we get ready for bed. "So…." I swallow the lump in my throat to try and make this sound as casual as I can. "Edward Prescott came into work today."

Pascal looks up from what he's doing.

"And you were completely right," I tell him. "He admitted to saying those horrible things only to bait you because you and he don't get on."

He raises his eyebrow, unimpressed. "What else did he say?"

"That he's donating the internship to someone who needs it and that he only bid so high because it was for charity."

He keeps folding back the blankets back as he listens.

"You have nothing to worry about, he's not going to be an asshole any longer."

"It's Edward Prescott," he mutters. "He can't help himself."

"Well, anyway, we don't need to worry about him anymore."

"Good." He climbs into bed and flicks on his side table lamp and picks up his book and begins to read. I climb in beside him and roll onto my side to watch him.

There's no playing between us, no passion, just this wonderful warm feeling of routine.

And I have to wonder, is it Pascal that I love or the security that he brings me?

For a long time he reads as I watch him, he doesn't even look up.

I roll onto my back and stare at the ceiling, my mind once again goes into overdrive.

Honestly I've never dissected my feelings as much as I am lately, I'm not sure if it's healthy…or constructive.

I glance back over to Pascal; he doesn't ask me what I'm thinking about because he doesn't notice that I am. I get a vision of Edward in my store today and the excitement that came with it. It's like every time he's near every one of my senses is standing to attention.

The only thing I'll be cleaning are the cobwebs from your vagina.

I smirk at the memory and then roll onto my side facing away from Pascal so he doesn't see my face.

Ugh…I need to stop this.

It's stupid, it's pointless and honestly, it's becoming toxic. I'm going to ruin a relationship with a good man over fantasizing about sex with a bad one.

I need to stop.

My phone beeps with a text.

Hi Alora

My car will pick you up from your store at 1 p.m. on Friday.

See you then.

Fine, good.

My mentoring is starting.

This is just a business training method; there is nothing to be excited about. I bite my bottom lip to hide my smile and stuff my phone back into my pocket.

What will I wear?

CHAPTER TWELVE

"With the lamp, that will be two hundred and eighty euros please." I ring up the purchases on the cash register. The bell over the door chimes and I look up to see two men in black suits walking in; they are big and burly and stand to the side as if waiting for something.

Edward's drivers are here and they are waiting for me. After the longest week in history, it's 1 p.m. on Friday.

Nerves dance in my stomach as I finish up the sale. This is just a work transaction, calm, calm, calm, I am *totally* fucking calm.

I walk over to the two men and play dumb. "May I help you?"

"Miss Sorenson?" one man asks.

"Yes."

"We're here on behalf of Mr. Prescott to collect you. My name is Philippe, and this is Merrick."

"Oh." I act surprised like I forgot this was even happening. "I won't be a moment, I'll meet you out the front." I glance back toward Jonty and Helene behind the desk to make sure they aren't listening in. I've decided I'm not telling anyone about this, not even Helene. That way there's no chance of it getting out or misconstrued. "Would you mind driving around the corner and waiting for me please?"

The men glance up at my staff as they connect the dots. "Of course." They leave and I go back to the counter and make myself appear busy as I tidy. I put the pens in the holder and change the cash register receipt roll.

"I have that meeting this afternoon, remember?" I tell them.

"Yes." They tidy alongside of me. "You better go or you're going to be late."

"Okay. I'll see you tomorrow?"

"Sure thing."

I go out the back and run to the bathroom, I quickly take out my compact and fix my makeup, brush my teeth, reapply my red lipstick and try to calm my nerves.

"Bye," I say casually as I walk out the front doors. I make my way around the corner and see the blacked-out Bentley parked to the side.

Of course he has a Bentley.

One of the men is standing by the building, and when he sees me coming he walks forward and opens the back door for me. "Good afternoon, Miss Sorenson." He smiles.

"Good afternoon." I slide into the back seat.

Wow....

The leather interior is a cherry maroon color and the doors are all fancy wood paneling.

Jeez, it doesn't feel like a car, it feels like a step back in time to royalty.

He does have a title....

"What kind of car is this?" I ask as my eyes roam around the luxury.

"A Bentley Mulliner Bacalar," one of them replies casually.

"It's nice." I squirm in my seat as I rub my fingers over the wood trim on the door.

"It is." They keep their eyes to the front and I get the feeling that making light conversation is not high on their priority list.

I subtly take out my phone and type into Google.

Price of Bentley Mulliner Bacalar.

An answer pops up.

Starting at three million euros.

What the....

I stuff my phone back into my purse, that's quite enough googling for today.

I check my bag for the tenth time today, calendar, pen, pencil, eraser…what else would I possibly need?

Lingerie….

Ha, not funny. I take out the pen and click it open and scribble a little on one of the pages, better check it. A perfect blue line shows up, yep, it works. I put it back into my bag and put it back down onto the seat beside me.

The car drives like a dream, so smooth, and when we pull up at the lights people look at it. I don't think they can see me though because of the blacked-out windows.

"You have some iced water in the tray, Miss Sorenson," the man in the front says.

I look down and see a glass of water with ice and lemon in it sitting in the middle.

"Oh…." I frown as I pick it up. "Thanks." I feel obliged to take a sip and with a shaky hand I put it back down. Water and lemon in a glass in a car, ha, what next?

Thirty minutes later we pull into Monaco and then the car heads down to the marina in Monte Carlo.

I crane my neck as I look around, I'm confused.

"Ahh." I think out loud. "I thought we were going to Mr. Prescott's office?"

"Mr. Prescott is working from his yacht today."

"His yacht?" My eyes widen as the car pulls into the dock. I look out the window at a huge black superyacht, five stories tall.

Shit, shit, shit.

This is supposed to be a work meeting, yachting around Monte Carlo with a man in a relationship is not a good look.

I begin to sweat bullets, Pascal is going to freak, that's if I survive his princess having me assassinated by one of her bouncers.

Fucking hell.

Oh god, I knew this was a bad idea.

The car door opens and I gingerly climb out, I look up at the yacht and suddenly feel very insignificant. I pull down my black blazer over my pantsuit, which was perfect for an office, but yet ridiculous for a yacht. At least I'm wearing red lipstick, I guess.

I follow the two men up the dock and we walk over the gangplank. "This way," the man says. I follow him onto the yacht and as I look around my knees nearly buckle out from under me.

What the hell?

Timber parquetry floors and big, plush rugs, the most beautiful couches I have ever seen. A huge bar stocked with more alcohol than an actual bar. Through the glass doors there's a huge deck and swimming pool.

A fucking swimming pool....

This looks like a mansion of epic proportions, not a fucking boat. A grand staircase is in the center leading up to the next level.

"Would you like to take the stairs or the elevator?" the man asks me.

There's an elevator?

"Um...." I'm like a deer in the headlights. "Stairs," I squeak.

"This way." I follow him up the flight of stairs and we get to the next level.

I stop still on the spot in shock.

Floor-to-ceiling windows, a giant dining table with huge vases of fresh flowers on it, giant chandeliers hanging overhead. I count the leather chairs, fifteen each side and one each end. A thirty-two-place dining table.... Are you kidding me right now?

I have no words, none.

We go up to the next level and this floor is different, it's divided with a wall. One end has a beautiful casual living area and we walk through to the other end and there's a huge conference room with a big board table with numerous chairs around it, again with the floor-to-ceiling windows.

"Mr. Prescott is in his office."

A big black door comes into view and he knocks.

"Come in."

He opens the door and sitting behind a big black grand desk is Edward, he looks up from his computer and smiles. "Good afternoon, Miss Sorenson."

"Hi." I fake a smile; this isn't awkward at all.

"Thank you," he tells the driver. "We may leave port now."

"Yes, sir." The man leaves us alone and closes the office door behind us.

"Leave port?" I frown.

"Yes," he says casually as he stands and goes to the bar. "What would you like to drink?"

I swallow the lump in my throat, seeing I'm leaving port with a taken man and I have a boyfriend, ho juice sounds good. "I'll have a Diet Coke please."

"Take a seat." He smiles. "Make yourself comfortable."

I awkwardly sit down at his desk as I look around, there is nothing remotely comfortable about being here. "I thought we were meeting in your office?"

"We are in my office." He passes me my Diet Coke and sits back down behind his desk; he has a glass of amber liquid with ice in a crystal tumbler.

"*This* is your office?"

"Uh-huh." He takes a sip as his eyes hold mine. "One of them, I have many."

"Just how rich are you?" I frown as I look around.

"I do okay." A trace of a smile crosses his face as he leans back in his chair.

"Your version of okay and my okay are not the same okay."

"Okay." He does smile this time; his eyes linger on my face. "You look lovely."

My fingers tighten around my handbag on my lap. "Thanks."

He's wearing a navy suit and a cream shirt; his dark hair has a bit of a curl to it and that damn square jaw is here to taunt me. But it's the big blue eyes that steal my breath. There's no denying he's a beautiful-looking man.

"So...." He traces circles with his finger on the desk. "Where shall we start?"

I shrug. "I'm not sure."

"Hmm." He rolls his lips as he watches me and I would pay good money right now to be able to read his mind. "Tell me about your situation."

"My situation?" I frown.

"Yes. If I'm going to help you grow your business, I need to know everything."

I swallow the lump in my throat as my eyes hold his. *If you must know everything I think I'm in the middle of a midlife crisis.*

"Three years ago my uncle died. Actually, it was the weekend I was with you."

"I'm sorry."

"Me too. He…." I pause as I try to collect my thoughts. "He married a French woman and they settled here. Unfortunately, ten years after they were married she died, and he never remarried. Antiques and Nice were his life."

He listens intently and sips his drink; he sloshes it around in his mouth as if savoring the taste before swallowing it.

"Anyway, when he died he left an entire warehouse of antiques to me in his will and when I came here to try and sort them out, I ended up staying and opening an antique store."

"I see." He smiles as he watches me. "From what I see you have an eye for detail and are doing well. Congratulations."

"Thanks." I feel proud of myself, from the corner of my eye I see something move in the window, I look out to see that we are pulling out of the marina. "Where are we going?" I ask.

"Just out to sea for a little bit."

"Why?"

"Why not?" His eyes hold mine. "It's nice not to be disturbed."

"Right."

This is a bad, bad idea….

"What are your plans moving forward?" he asks, totally undeterred by us going out to sea.

"I would like to build my antique store and perhaps open a second location."

"Whereabouts?"

"Paris."

"Okay." He smiles as he listens. "And what about personally?"

"What?"

"Your personal plans moving forward?"

"I hardly think we need to discuss my personal life."

"If I'm going to mentor you, it's a full-package deal."

"What do you mean?"

"I can't mentor you if your personal goals don't align with your business goals. I need a full picture of everything to become clear on where we are going."

"Oh."

"It makes no difference to me, but I do need to know where you see yourself in five, ten and fifteen years from now."

"Right." I twist my fingers on my lap, unsure if I want to be here anymore.

Mentoring me for business is one thing, opening up about where I want my future to be is going too far.

He takes out a notepad and pen from his top drawer. "Let's break it down. This is always daunting for people when we start this process."

"You've done this before?"

"I've mentored many people," he says as he rules lines on his notepad. "I really enjoy it."

This is not so special then.

"Let's do a list, where do you want to be personally in twelve months?" he asks.

"Happy."

His eyes rise to meet mine as if taken off guard by my answer. "Are you happy now?"

"Yes."

"Why do I feel like…."

"Like what?" I cut him off.

"Why do I get the feeling that you're not happy?"

"I don't know, because I am," I snap.

He writes something down and underlines it. "Where do you want to be in five years?"

"I would like to be settled down and happily married."

He continues taking notes. "Seven years from now?"

"Perhaps starting a family."

He nods and keeps writing. "And in what capacity do you want to keep working if you have children?"

I think for a moment before I reply, "I would like to be active in the business but not tied down working nine-to-five full days."

"Right." He takes more notes. "Do you currently have an online presence for your business?"

"Yes and no. I do a daily product post on socials but my website and marketing skills could definitely be a lot sharper."

Over the next two hours Edward leads me through a series of questions, things I've never considered or given any real thought to about my life before now. I'm beginning to see the value in him mentoring me, he really does have a deeper understanding of the principles of business.

The yacht is turned around and we are heading back to shore. "Surely you can have a glass of wine now?" he asks me.

"I guess I can." I smile, I'm confident that this isn't a sleazy pickup attempt and I now feel the confidence to let my guard down a little.

"What are you doing this weekend?" he asks.

"I'm going to New York to see my brother graduate."

"Ahh…I'd offer you my jet but I'm going to be using it myself."

"Where are you going?" I ask.

"Home to London for the week. It's my sister Charlotte's birthday. You know, your best friend." He winks.

"Oh, yes." I laugh. "Give her my love."

He goes to the bar and pours me a glass of wine and himself another glass of whatever he's drinking and I smile as I take it from him. He holds his glass up as I touch mine to it.

I take a sip and frown as I stare at the glass. "Well, this is delicious."

"It is."

I look around our luxurious surroundings. "I can't actually believe that this is your life."

He looks around as if trying to see it through my eyes. "Me too, some days."

"I'm…" I shrug, "…gobsmacked."

He chuckles. "Do you want the tour?"

"Sure."

He leads me out of the office and past the boardroom. "There's a gym on this floor and three bedrooms." We walk down and see a state-of-the-art gymnasium.

"Jeez." I smile.

"An infrared sauna." He opens a door at the back of the gym to reveal a timber sauna complete with steam.

"Wow." I giggle. "This is unbelievable."

He opens the doors of the bedrooms and shows me them, all huge and beautiful with their own bathrooms.

"How much time do you spend on this yacht?"

"Quite a bit, actually." He leads me up the stairs. "This is the master level." We get to the top and the air leaves my lungs. A huge, beautiful bedroom with glass walls and beautiful modern furnishings. "What size is this bed?" I gasp.

"Big." He laughs with a shrug. "I don't know, more than a king, not sure what comes after that."

"So your sheets and linen are all custom?" I frown.

He shrugs again. "I'm guessing."

I laugh. "Do you know how spoiled you sound right now?"

His eyebrows flick up. "I hate to think." He opens up double doors to reveal a huge bathroom with a round sunken bathtub in the center.

"My god." I gasp. "This is…just beautiful."

He opens up the doors to a giant-sized walk-in wardrobe, his clothes are all lined up neatly. Row after perfect row of suits and swanky shoes.

"Do you wear suits every day?"

He scrunches his nose up as if embarrassed. "Possibly."

"Well…. Wow." I shake my head in disbelief. "This is incredible." I look around the bedroom and a thought comes to me. "What does your girlfriend have to say about you having women on this yacht?"

"Like you?"

"Yeah, like me. If I were her, I would not want you to have women in your bedroom. I'd go postal actually."

"I'm friends with most of my ex-girlfriends."

"But I'm not an ex-girlfriend."

"You would have been if I could have found you back then."

Oh…I think on that for a moment as I look around and turn back to him. "Why couldn't you find me?" I ask. "With this kind of money I would have thought you could have found anyone."

"Not at that club. Believe me, I tried to bribe them and all." He smiles wistfully. "I eventually assumed it wasn't meant to be."

"True." I nod as I continue to look around. "How often do you sleep on here?"

"Probably sixty to seventy percent of the time I'm in Monaco."

"You don't like your home?"

"I do." He shrugs. "I don't know why I spend so much time here, I haven't really thought of it before."

"It's beautiful." I walk to the window and look out over the ocean and he sits on the bed behind me. "And for the record, I think she's utterly crazy letting you entertain women here," I add. "Screw that."

"She feels secure with my work colleagues, I guess." He smirks. "Although I'm thinking that would change if she knew you were my surefire."

"Surefire?" My eyes flick back to him. "What's a surefire?"

"You know, someone who always gets the job done."

Huh?

"You've lost me."

He smiles in surprise. "You don't have a surefire?"

"What the hell is a surefire?" I frown.

"You know this…." His smile is full of mischief. "All men have a surefire."

"They do?"

The yacht begins to pull into the marina and we turn around and begin to reverse.

"Please explain *this*." I laugh. "I'm completely lost."

"You know…. When you're alone and you want to…." His eyes hold mine. "Touch yourself. You have someone that you think of while you do it. Or if you're with someone and it's not happening…. You think of that certain someone, mentally begin to fuck your surefire, and it instantly gets you over the line."

My eyes search his and I begin to hear my heartbeat in my ears. "*I'm* your surefire?"

"Yes."

We stare at each other, the air crackles with electricity and the sexual energy between us is like nothing I've ever felt.

You could cut it with a knife.

"You think of me when you touch yourself?" I whisper.

"I have." His tongue darts out and swipes over his bottom lip and I feel it all the way to my toes. "Remember the spa bath in Switzerland?"

"Maybe," I lie.

Ha, remember it, it rewired my fucking brain.

"Maybe." He repeats my answer and taps the bed beside him. "You in that spa bath was the single hottest sexual experience of my life."

I remain standing as my eyes drop to his lips, the magical chemistry swirls between us.

"I should go," I whisper.

"You should." He stands and we come face-to-face, millimeters away.

"Who's your surefire, Alora?" he murmurs, he's so close that I feel his breath tickle the skin.

"I've never needed one," I lie again, I basically couldn't lie straight in bed now.

Compulsive.

They keep coming, one after the other.

"I...."

I suddenly feel tight chested and I know if I stay here I am one hundred percent committing adultery and I'm going to break that big fuck-off bed of his. "I have to go." I turn and rush down the stairs and down to the next level and I feel him coming after me and I walk faster and faster. I get to the ground floor and head for the door.

"Alora. Stop," he demands.

I stop on the spot as I face the door, my breath hitching as I try to gain some much-needed control over my traitorous body.

"Let me walk you out," he says calmly from behind.

I nod and he walks past me and opens the door. The security are waiting on the end of the gangplank. "Give us a moment please," he says as we walk past them and they stay where they are.

We walk in silence back to the Bentley and he opens the back door and I pause before I get in. "When?"

His eyes hold mine.

"When was the last time you used me as a surefire?"

"Yesterday." His tongue swipes over his bottom lip as he stares at me. "I fucked your mouth and I blew so fucking hard."

I audibly gasp, my heart races.

He leans in and puts his mouth to my ear. "Then I needed more, so I fucked your ass." His breath on my ear sends shivers up my spine. "And you loved every fucking inch of it."

I get a vision of him pulling himself as he pictured us together, the image heats my blood to boiling point. I pull away from him, my scared eyes search his. The hold this man has over me is terrifying.

"Goodbye, Edward."

A trace of a smile crosses his face. "Goodbye, Alora."

I get into the car and he closes the door, and then as if nothing happened he casually turns and walks back to his yacht. I slump back into the seat as if I have just run a marathon.

Dear god.

CHAPTER THIRTEEN

My moral compass has always been a shining light, my ethical standards a cut above the rest. My standards are high, my love is true and I've judged people for less.

What a joke, I don't even know who I am anymore.

I'm definitely not the girl I was this time last week. Last Friday night Pascal and I went to the movies and laughed and ate at our favorite restaurant and everything was normal and controlled and in order as it should be.

This week, I'm on a plane to New York, alone. Carrying an extra-large suitcase of guilt.

Since Mr. Prescott came back I've lied to Pascal, I lied to my friends, I kissed another man, and today without telling a soul where I was, I went to his yacht. Stood in his bedroom and nearly did something that I would never forgive myself for.

This is toxic.

I cannot and I *will* not become someone that I don't recognize. Someone that I'm not proud of.

The guilt is eating me alive.

I'm blocking Edward's number and I'm forgetting all about this stupid internship idea. Nothing good can come of me believing that Edward Prescott and I could be friends when it's blatantly clear that we can't.

The sexual chemistry between us is way too strong.

I will not be that nasty girl. I will respect my beautiful boyfriend and I will push down any attraction I have to Edward Prescott.

You in that spa bath was the single hottest sexual experience of my life.

Unfortunately, his admission has taken me back to a time when we were wet with perspiration, skin slapping and the moans…god, the moans. Over and over and over again until I can't take it anymore and I drag open my tear-filled eyes.

What the hell am I going to do?

"River Sorenson," the dean calls out.

A huge smile covers my face as Dad, Raylyn and I clap ferociously as we watch our beloved brother and son walk up onto the stage. Looking every bit the medical school graduate that he now is, he accepts his honor and turns and smiles over at us.

A knife runs straight through my heart and my eyes fill with tears; I quickly try to wipe them away before anyone sees.

Mom should be here to see this.

I know she would have given anything to be here to celebrate this day. I glance over to see Dad wiping his eyes too and I know he's having the exact same thought as I am. I put my arm around him and kiss his cheek and he puts his hand over mine as we smile up at River through our tears.

We don't talk about Mom all that often, simply because it hurts too much and nobody wants to upset anyone. But some days the emptiness she left is so chasmic that no pretending could ever fill the hole.

My nostrils flare as River's silhouette blurs. *I really need to talk to you today, Mom.*

So you could tell me that I'm not a bad person, that everything's going to be alright.

I've hardly slept since Friday, I feel like I'm on the precipice of a monumental life-changing mistake, one that I won't be able to come back from.

Raylyn is tougher than me, more together. She's older and married to her high school sweetheart. She would never be tempted by the devil, and even if she were, she would never give in to it.

I need to be more like her, more…together. I want to make my mom proud, and thinking and feeling like this isn't the way to do that. My eyes well with tears of disappointment.

As if sensing my current mental state, Dad's arm slinks around my shoulder and he pulls me close and kisses my temple. "It's okay," he whispers. "It's going to be okay."

I nod through tears, the lump in my throat hurts as I try my hardest to hold everything in. "I know." I force a smile.

And I do know.

I'm not the first girl to be confused, and it really isn't that hard, or at least it shouldn't be. But admitting to myself that maybe I'm not in love with Pascal is a hard pill to swallow.

Because I should be.

He's a beautiful man who deserves so much better than being dragged over the coals and lied to. I'm disgusted that his girlfriend has a sexual attraction to a man that he hates. And no matter how much I want to deny it, and push it away, for the life of me I can't stop thinking about Edward.

Mr. Doe.

He's in my every waking thought, starring in my nightmares, and making me ache like never before. He's haunting me…even though we have no future, even though he's with someone else. If that fact alone isn't the biggest red flag in history, I don't know what is.

I fucked your mouth and I blew so fucking hard.

He has a girlfriend and he's saying that to someone else. A woman he once slept with.

This isn't a fairy tale of long-lost eternal love.

My relationship with Edward is nothing more than a carnal attraction that's going to hurt people.

I look up at the stage with renewed determination, this stops now.

"Three cheers for River," Malory, River's housemate calls with a giant beer stein in her hand. The table erupts into laughter as they cheer.

As the night's gone on, I feel better. This isn't who I am and I'm not a victim here, and I don't know why I'm acting like one. It's time for me to pull on my big-girl panties and take control of the narrative.

"I'm just going to the ladies'," I tell them as I push my chair out. I grab my purse and walk outside; I scroll through the numbers on my phone until I get to the one I'm looking for.

Mr. Doe.

I hit call. *Ring, ring…ring, ring.*

EDWARD.

Orange and red flickers across my face, the warmth of the flame matching the scotch as it goes down. I lift the crystal tumbler and take a long sip. It's late and I've been sitting here for hours, staring into space.

Desperately trying to get a hold on this...attraction.

She's all I fucking think about.

I drain my glass and fill it again; I add ice and it sloshes over the sides.

My phone lights up with the name:

Alora

She's calling me, my heart picks up with anticipation. Instinctively, I reach for it before I stop myself midair, no.

Yes.

"Hello."

"Edward, hi. It's Alora."

"I know who it is."

"Right...umm."

I wait on the line. "Yes," I snap, impatient.

"I don't think we should see each other again."

"I agree. I've already donated the prize to the Royal Scholarship Institute," I lie. "They will be in touch with you about the finer details moving forward."

"Oh." She listens for a beat as if unsure what to say.

Time's up.

"Goodbye, Alora, it was nice seeing you again." I hang up the phone and drag my eyes back to the fire.

ALORA.

"A weekend with my favorite people on earth is just what I needed." I smile as I hug River, Raylyn and then Dad.

"Love you, sweetheart."

"Love you too, Dad." I grip him just that bit harder.

Airport farewells are never fun.

With one long wave goodbye I make my way in through security with a spring in my step. This weekend really was just what I needed, being with my people is good for my soul and I don't feel so alone.

Distance gave me perspective.

I walk out of the boarding gate feeling lighter and a deeper sense of who I am.

It's time to face the music.

I don't know much about things but I do know for certain that guilt is not for me and no matter who or what I've done, nothing is worth losing respect for myself over.

I'm going to talk to Pascal and lay everything out on the table, he couldn't pick me up because he was working but he's coming over tonight.

I wait for my luggage by the carousel as I go over the conversation in my head, a practiced speech that I think I've nailed. It's all I've thought about for two days.

I may be a lot of things, but I am not a coward.

I'm not going to see Edward again and I feel so much better for it.

Now, it's time for me.

HOURS LATER.

My heart pounds in my chest, my stomach churns and damn it, sitting at the table across from Pascal I'm not feeling so brave now. I push my pasta around my plate with my fork as I try to find the words.

Just say it.

"I have a surprise for you." Pascal smiles.

"You do?"

He reaches into his inside jacket pocket to get something. "I think it's time."

No....

"Stop," I blurt out. "Whatever you are going to say, I need to say something first, and whatever my surprise is...please keep it in your pocket."

He frowns and pulls his empty hand out. "What is it?"

"I...." I swallow the lump in my throat as my eyes hold his. "I don't know Edward Prescott through his sister. I know him because we briefly dated years ago."

His face falls.

"And...on the night of the auction, Edward and I kissed and I lied to you and I hate myself for it."

Anger flashes across his face.

"And I don't think we can see each other anymore because if I were really in love with you I would never have allowed this to happen in the first place."

His eyes hold mine but he stays silent.

"You're such a good man, Pascal, and you deserve someone who appreciates every single inch of you and I wish it were me. But...." I'm talking fast to try and get this off my chest, trying my hardest to make this sound better. "I've let you down and I don't deserve you."

"You're right, you don't." He folds his napkin and puts it on the table in slow motion as if processing my words. His eyes rise to search mine.

"Don't look at me like that," I whisper.

"Like what, like you're throwing away a real love with me for a fantasy with him. And it *is* just a fantasy Alora, he has a fucking girlfriend and you will never be more to him than a piece of ass on the side. You think he's over there breaking up with his princess for you? Confessing his sins. This is how he operates; this is what he does. You think you're the first woman he's strayed with, please. Don't flatter yourself. You're just one of many, he probably kissed ten women at that auction. He's probably fucked another ten since. You are *nothing* to him."

His silhouette blurs.

Ouch.

"This has nothing to do with him and everything to do with me," I whisper.

He stands. "Keep telling yourself that, and when the challenge of taking my girl is over and he's used you and thrown you in the trash, don't come running back to me." He marches toward the door.

"Pascal, wait."

Slam...goes the door.

I sit as his words echo in the silence. *Don't flatter yourself.* The hot tears break the dam and roll down my cheeks.

Pascal is right, every word he said was spot on. I mean nothing to Edward and maybe I wasn't meant to be with Pascal, but I am definitely not going there with him because, unlike my current relationship, there's one thing I know for certain.

If given the chance, Edward Prescott could break me.

MONDAY MORNING.

I turn the key in the lock.

"So." Helene smiles from beside me. "How did it go?"

"Well...." I push the door open. "Not great. I'm pretty sure he hates me."

Helene and Jonty exchange glances. "Why would your brother hate you?"

"Oh." I remember that a lot has gone on this weekend and they don't know yet. "My brother doesn't hate me. His graduation was great, I meant Pascal."

"Why, what happened?" Helene asks as she hangs her purse up on the hook in the back room.

"We broke up."

"Oh." Jonty's eyes widen. "This is so unexpected."

"Not really." I sigh as I go to the cash register and begin to count out the float.

"Did something happen between the two of you?" he asks all interested.

"Not one thing, I guess a lot of little things combined."

"So you are the one that broke it off?" he asks.

"I guess."

"Was it a big fight or…."

"Why are you suddenly so interested in this?" I sigh.

"I just find it fascinating that you can break off with someone without warning. The evil minds of women fascinate me."

"Well, it wasn't without warning, obviously," Helene answers for me. "She told him that he needed to get better in bed." She begins to dry hump the air.

"I did not." I smile. "You are so bad."

"But so good at it, right?"

Jonty turns the stereo on and a deep beat of jazz livens up the space.

"What day are you interning this week?" Helene asks as she begins to dust.

"I'm not." I shrug as I pick up a vase and move it. "The internship has been transferred back to the Royal Charity Institute." I reshuffle some books and go around and turn all of the lamps on. "So that's great." I force a smile.

The bell over the door rings as the first customers arrive and Jonty and Helene fuss over them, my mind wanders back to the fact that Edward didn't want to see me again either.

I may be his surefire…*but he loves her.*

CHAPTER FOURTEEN

EDWARD.

I step out of the jet and make my way to the car that is waiting on the tarmac, Claude opens the door for me. "Good evening, Mr. Prescott." He smiles.

"Hello, Claude, miss me?" I get into the car.

Amusement flashes across his face. "As always, sir." He gets behind the wheel and we begin to make our way home. Claude has been my driver for eight years, he used to travel with me everywhere until he met a woman here in France and got married. He stays here now and only is with me when I'm back in the country.

We drive through the night and weave through the traffic as I stare out the window. My mind is a whirl of activity, what would happen if I went to Alora's house right now...would she let me in? Would she kiss me and hold me in her arms?

Would she let me taste her...?

I get a visual of her naked and beneath me.

Buried so deep inside her body, I readjust myself in my pants as my erection becomes painful.

I chew my lip as I stare out the window, something's got to give here.

This can't go on.

For every second of every minute of every hour since I saw Alora on Friday, I've been hard, my cock has been throbbing like a broken appendix and begging for attention. She's all I can think about, consuming me like an addiction.

Her face floats through my mind like an apparition, taunting me with things I can't have.

Things that only she can deliver.

There's no denying it, Alora Sorenson has something that feeds the darkness inside of me. Her raw sexuality is like a drug that my body can smell, and the fact that she doesn't want me only makes the hunter in me more desperate to take her.

To own her.

I imagine dragging her down to her knees by her hair.... *Throb...throb....*

I tip my head back against the seat as I ride the wave of arousal.

I've never jerked off so much in my fucking life.

"Miss Hermione is at your place, sir." His eyes flick up to meet mine in the rearview mirror.

What?

"I thought she was in Switzerland."

"She's surprising you, sir." He gives me a stifled smile. "Act surprised."

I exhale heavily and drag my gaze back out the window, fucking great.... This is all I need tonight. I was looking forward to a week on my own.

I have a much-anticipated date with my right hand tonight, a rough hard ride with Alora's open mouth in my mind.

Ughh.... I drag my gaze out the window in disgust, what the fuck is wrong with me? Can you even hear yourself?

I would rather jerk off while thinking about someone that I can't have, rather than have actual sex with a woman who loves me.

A sweet, beautiful woman who worships the ground that I walk on. A woman I wish to god could fuck me the way I need to be fucked. As much as she tries she just can't fill the needs that I have.

What kind of man does that make me?

I drag my hand down my face, just when I think I can't be any more fucked up than I already am.... Alora Sorenson walks back into my life and makes me question everything that I've worked so hard for.

I get a vision of her naked, her legs open wide...calling to me on another level.

I close my eyes as I fight myself over this primal attraction. *She's all I fucking think about.*

Stop.

Stop it right now.

I am well aware that if I'm not careful I'm about to fuck everything up for a woman who I know I couldn't have a relationship with.

We would never work in the real world, I'm too strong... the need to control her is already consuming me in a very unhealthy way.

Rein it in.

THREE DAYS LATER.

I pant, my hips rise from the bed and I moan as I swipe Alora's hair back from her face. Wet with perspiration, my two hands in her hair, I ride her beautiful mouth.

Deeper...harder.

I tip my head back as her teeth slide over the head of my cock and I moan deeply as I come hard down her throat. My cock jerks violently.

"What are you doing?" A voice interrupts me.

My eyes snap open as I pant, disoriented, I look around the room.

Where am I?

My chest is heaving as I struggle to catch my breath, my cock weeping the last of ejaculate as it drips from my body.

"What's wrong?" Hermione asks from beside me in bed.

I close my eyes in disgust.

Fuck....

"Bad dream," I pant as I climb out of bed.

"Are you okay?" she whispers.

"I'm fine." I get up. "Go back to sleep, I'm going downstairs to get a drink."

"Do you need anything?" she asks.

Alora.

She snuggles back into the blankets and closes her eyes and I stare at her in the darkness, disgusted by my thoughts.

If only you were her.

ALORA.

A huge wave of splashing water flies in the wake of the truck. "So." Helene glances over her cocktail at me. "Do you miss Pascal?"

We sit at the window bench, watching the rain come down outside, it's Wednesday and we're drinking on a school night.

"Yeah." I chew my lip as I go over the last two weeks. "Lately, these last few days, I've been wondering if I did the right thing."

"You haven't heard from him at all?"

"No, and—" I shake my head, "—I'm not expecting to anytime soon."

"Hmm." She's listening and deep in thought. "But is it him you miss or just having someone? I mean is it him or the thought of him?"

"Honestly—" I shrug, "—I don't even know anymore."

"Have you heard from Edward?"

"Nope."

"Hmm." She narrows her eyes. "So you broke up with your boyfriend for another guy but then he hasn't even called."

"No." I cut her off. "I broke up with my boyfriend because I realized that my feelings for him weren't what they were supposed to be."

"Because seeing Edward again made you realize that."

"This sounds worse when I hear it out loud." I let out a deep sigh. "God, Helene, why am I such a fuckup?"

"You're not a fuckup."

"He's off and in love with his princess and hasn't thought of me again once."

"Hmm." She sips her drink. "Which obviously sucks."

"Obviously," I agree. "I can't deny, it does."

"Anyway, who cares about men? Fuck them, all I say."

I give a weak smile. "Yeah, sounds like a plan."

"Wait a minute." She frowns. "I thought we're supposed to be talking about what we're filming for socials tomorrow."

"Isn't that what we're doing?" I giggle and sip my cocktail.

"Not quite." We sit in silence for a while and the thought of going home alone tonight is depressing.

The truth is that I'm at a time in my life where I want it all. To be so in love that I can't see straight, to be with someone who sets my heart and body on fire. Who loves me back just as hard.

Edward….

A fleeting vision of him flashes through my mind like a spell.

Not really there but holds the possibility of magic.

Unfortunately, I know that this spell hasn't taken. It's not coming true, just someone sent to test my ideals of reality. A glitch in my moral compass, he's in love with another woman and I can't pretend it doesn't hurt that my feelings for him aren't reciprocated.

"I thought we had something," I murmur.

She nods as she listens. "I'm sorry."

"Meh." I shrug, resigned to my fate. "Fuck them all."

"Yeah, can we actually start doing that?" She sips her drink. "Let's go to a swingers party on Saturday night or something."

I giggle. "Umm…. Let's not."

"Ugh, boring. Are we going home, then?"

"Yes." We drag ourselves up and pay the bill, and arm in arm under an umbrella, toddle down the street to the taxi stand where a long line of cabs is waiting. "Thank you for always listening to my crap." I pull her into a hug. "Love you."

"Crap just happens to be my favorite subject." She squeezes me. "Love you more."

I climb into the back of the cab and wave as it pulls out onto the road. The thought of a cold bed waiting for me is depressing.

Home time…. Alone.

ONE WEEK LATER.

EDWARD.

The office door opens. "Edward."

I stand, walk in, and sit down.

Paul smiles as he looks me over from behind his desk. "You look well. I haven't seen you for a long time."

I nod as I clasp my hands together. I hate this fucking shit, remind me why I come here again?

"So." He swings on his chair as his eyes hold mine. "I'm assuming something is going on."

"What makes you say that?"

"Well." He opens his notepad. "You requested an urgent appointment and flew to London especially to see me." He adjusts his pen so he's ready to write.

"I was already coming to London," I lie.

"Okay." He smiles. "Tell me, how are things progressing in your world?"

"Good." I clench my hands together harder.

"Are you still with your girlfriend?"

I nod.

"You've been with her a while now."

"Yes."

"How long, exactly?"

I shrug. "Over twelve months."

"How is she?"

"*She's* perfect."

"The way you say *she's* perfect makes me think that you are not."

I pick my fingernail to evade his gaze.

"How are things within your relationship?"

"Strained."

"I see. Have you had a fight or an incident?"

"Nothing like that." I sigh. "Actually, you are to blame for this problem."

"Me?" He frowns. "How am I responsible for a problem of yours?"

"Well, you made me go to that stupid club in Switzerland way back."

"Oh." His eyes light up. "Yes, I remember. What about it?"

"I ran into her."

"Ahh." He swings on his chair as if fascinated. "If I remember correctly, you tried to find her after you returned from Switzerland."

"Yes." I roll my lips as uneasiness falls over me.

"How was it, seeing her again?"

I wring my hands together. "Good."

"Just good?"

I exhale, disappointed in myself. "Too good."

"It's still there between you?" He scribbles something down on his notepad. "What is her name?"

"Alora."

"What happened when you and Alora saw each other?"

I puff air into my cheeks. "I stole her for a moment away from her partner and took her upstairs and we kissed."

"Okay." He watches me as he listens. "So she is also in a relationship?"

"Yes."

"Married?"

"No."

"Have you seen her since?"

"I have."

"What happened?"

"I was mentoring her." I shrug. "Strictly professional, of course."

"May I ask, if you wanted to remain strictly professional, why you would offer to mentor someone that you are sexually attracted to?"

I stare at him but remain silent.

"Would you consider entering a relationship with this woman?" he asks.

"No."

"Why not?"

I screw my hands together as I contemplate my answer.

"This is a safe place, Edward; you came to talk this through, so let's talk this through."

"I just don't understand how I can feel more attached to *her* than I do to a woman who I've been with for over twelve months."

"You feel an emotional attachment to Alora?"

I shrug. "It doesn't make sense...." My voice trails off. "It was one weekend of sex. It meant nothing."

"It makes a lot of sense, actually. This is physiology." He

swings on his chair as his eyes hold mine. "Forgotten memories shape our behavior, Edward. Our bodies keep score."

"What do you mean?"

"Your body is just doing its job."

"Speak fucking English," I snap.

"When we as humans have a heightened sexual experience, our brains release a hormone called oxytocin. Have you heard of that before?"

"I've heard of oxytocin but...."

"Do you know what it does?"

"Makes you happy." I shrug. "I guess."

"It's a bonding hormone." He writes something down and underlines it. "When you and Alora spent the weekend together, I'm assuming the sexual compatibility between the two of you was heightened?"

"Yes." I twist my hands as I listen. "Very much so."

"If the orgasms were extremely strong and over an extended period of time, then your body would have released a huge amount of oxytocin into your bloodstream."

"So?"

"Oxytocin, often called the love hormone, plays a crucial role in bonding with a mate by promoting feelings of trust, affection, and attachment. It's released during physical affection like hugging, kissing, and sexual activity, strengthening the emotional connection between partners. Oxytocin also enhances empathy, communication, and positive relationship memories, contributing to the maintenance of long-term bonds."

I sit back, disgusted.

"The interesting thing is that she would have had it released into her bloodstream too."

I frown as my eyes hold his. "What are you saying?"

"I'm saying that whatever confusion you are feeling right now is probably being mirrored in Alora's life."

I begin to hear my heartbeat in my ears.

"I don't care what's going on in her life," I snap. "Why would I?"

"Is that so?" he asks. "Are you sure about that?"

We stare at each other for a moment.

I hate this fucking guy….

"I have to go." I stand.

"Sit down, I haven't finished." He points to the chair.

"Hurry up about it," I snap impatiently as I sit back down. "Because I have."

"Is it true that you have been coming to me for a long time because of your inability to form emotional attachments to the women you spend time with?"

I twist my lips, annoyed. "Yes."

"And now that you have found one, are you really going to walk away from it?"

"My point exactly, I *shouldn't* have one. Do you listen to me at all? That is why I am here; I want you to erase it. This is a huge overreaction; it was three days and a very long time ago."

"And yet she has you completely rattled."

"No she doesn't." I stand. "As usual, I've got nothing from our visit." I walk to the door. "This was pointless."

"Will you be flying to London to see me again next week?" He smirks.

Sarcastic asshole.

"Absolutely not."

He smiles as he writes on his stupid notepad. "We'll see."

I storm out through reception.

"Would you like another appointment?" the receptionist asks.

"No." I march past her and open the door.

"Should I call you later to discuss?"

"Don't bother."

ALORA.

I shuffle through my pile of mail.

Sender…

Royal Scholarship Institute.

What?

I tear it open.

Dearest Alora,

We value your sponsorship and would like to extend an invitation for you and a friend to attend.

THE MOON AND THE SEA

An art exhibition with heart.

Two gold tickets slide out and fall onto the floor and I bend and pick them up.

"What's that?" Helene frowns as she walks into my office.

"Not quite a swingers party." I shrug as I hold up the tickets. "We've been invited to an art exhibition."

"Hmm." She twists her lips. "Sounds extraordinarily dull."

"But it's a night out." I shuffle the gold tickets.

"I guess." She sighs. "But if they serve bad wine we are leaving immediately."

"Deal."

THREE WEEKS LATER.

EDWARD.

I readjust my earphones so I can watch the video on my phone.

"Good morning." She smiles. "I'm Alora from Sorenson Antiques and this is our morning run-through of our store. This arrived yesterday and isn't she beautiful." She runs her hand over the double doors as my breath catches.

"This is a Baroque armoire, circa early seventeen hundreds." She points to the carved details and my eyes drop down her body, even only onscreen every inch of me entranced. "As you can see it has beautiful craftmanship, fully hand-carved cherubs and detailing around the edges."

She smiles and catches her bottom lip in her teeth and I feel it all the way to the tip of my cock.

Fuck....

My heartbeat the only sound I hear.

I sit forward in my chair, mesmerized.

"This armoire has been in the one family for many generations and is in perfect condition." She opens the doors and drawers. "The lock has both solid brass keys still working. Have a beautiful day everyone, au revoir."

"We're about to land in Vegas, sir." The flight attendant interrupts my thoughts as she walks up the aisle of my plane.

"Thank you."

Just one more....

I scroll through her Instagram business page and click on another video.

I'm sick, I know it. But like an addiction I need to feed, I can't stop myself from watching these over and over again.

Hearing Alora Sorenson say good morning is my new obsession.

I'll stop tomorrow....

"Ban him." I turn back to my computer.

"Sir," Belinda stammers. "He's a whale, we can't just ban him."

"I just did." I hit send on my email.

"He spends millions here every year."

"And yet he treats our staff like shit. He's out, I warned him last month, this is it."

She shakes her head. "Let's talk about this tomorrow when we are fresh."

"Let's not." I turn back to my computer.

"Why are you still here?"

I glance up at her. "What do you mean?"

"You've been here since 9 a.m. this morning."

"And?"

"It's 2 a.m. and you're still working?"

I glance at my watch. "Fuck." I look around. "Where are my boys?"

"Outside your office." Belinda folds her arms as if unimpressed. "Like always."

"I work them too hard." I sigh.

"I know."

I stand and call downstairs. "Niall."

"Yes, sir."

"Send your six best girls up to my office, please."

"Yes, of course. For you, sir?"

"For my guards."

"Yes, Mr. Prescott."

I hang up. "I'm leaving now. You go home too, Belinda. Thank you for today."

She gives me a lopsided smile. "You work yourself way too hard too, you know?"

"You don't need to worry about me, I'm fine." I begin to close down my computer.

"How long are you here for?" she asks.

"Until I get everything I need done. Probably until the end of the week."

She watches me for a moment. "Why don't you let off some steam and take those girls for yourself?"

"They have nothing I want."

Knock, knock.

"Come in," I call.

Six beautiful women dressed in evening dresses appear, looking like walking wet dreams, curvy and glamorous. "You called for us, sir?" They smile hopefully.

"Yes, please come in." I smile, my eyes drop down their heavenly bodies as they walk past me.

Delicious.

I open the door on the other side of my office that leads out to reception. "Boys."

They glance up. "Come in here, please."

They walk into my office and their eyes linger on the women. "Hello." They nod politely.

"I lost track of time and I've worked you too hard today." I gesture to the girls.

"Each pick two of these beautiful women and retire for the night. Late start tomorrow."

Their eyes flick to me and then back to the girls.

"Hurry before I take them all myself." I sigh.

"Unnecessary, sir," Philippe replies.

"But enjoyable just the same." I raise my eyebrow.

He smiles, words not needed. "Good night."

I wink. "Have fun."

They disappear out the door with the girls and I smirk as I imagine the night they're going to have.

"Look at you." Belinda smiles as we walk out of the office and lock it behind us. "You make out you're so tough." She tuts. "I see you."

"I just gave my staff blowjobs wrapped in hot flesh, Belinda. Not puppies in wicker baskets," I reply as we walk down the corridor. "I wouldn't get carried away." I get into my private elevator.

"Good night, sir."

"Good night." As the elevator rides up to my penthouse, I take out my phone. Hermione....

9 Missed Calls

I exhale and stuff my phone back into my pocket.

Great....

ALORA.

"Good morning." I walk into the store to find Helene and Jonty already filming content.

"Hi." They keep filming as they walk around.

"Don't forget the lamps," I mouth as I point to the corner.

Jonty nods as he keeps filming.

Helene looks me up and down. "Oh, I love," she mouths as she gestures to my outfit.

"Nice, huh?" I mouth. "Fifty euros." I glance down at myself, I'm wearing a cream cashmere vintage Prada dress, it's fitted with a big cowl neck and long sleeves. I've teamed it with wedged knee-high camel-colored suede boots.

"Why can I never find this good shit in the flea market?" she mouths back.

I flick the kettle on, unwrap my scarf and hang it on the brass wall hook in my office. My hair is loose today with the leftover curls in the ends from last night. I neaten it in the mirror and reapply my red lipstick.

"You ready?" Helene calls.

"Coming." I pour the water into our tea cups and make my way out. "What are we doing?"

"We've already filmed the stock and did the walk-around; you just have to talk about one of the new arrivals and then talk about our market night in two weeks."

"Right." I frown. "It's going to be hell."

"I know, but we have so much new stock coming in and with nowhere to put it we need to get rid of some pieces. You know our market nights always sell out."

"Okay." I tuck my hair behind my ear as I look around the store. "Shall I talk about the lamps?"

"Yep, and go."

"Hi, I'm Alora from Sorenson Antiques. Just popping on to say good morning to you all. Look what arrived yesterday." I walk over and run my hand down the lamps. "Two Ming Dynasty lamps, in perfect condition. Sage green with 22-carat hand-painted gold filigree. These lamps are to die for and are in perfect condition." I smile.

Helene circles her finger. "Keep going," she mouths.

"And just a reminder about our market night that's coming up. Huge discounts, never-seen-before pieces, beautiful art, and as usual we'll have three mystery boxes and some lucky person will walk home with some very valuable items. There will be canapés, wine, and great company. Tickets go on sale this morning at 11 and as there are only a limited number available, they do always sell out within half an hour. I can't wait to meet you all." I smile and wave. "Au revoir."

"And cut," Helene says as she begins to play it back.

Jonty is scrolling through the paper on the front counter. "Oh look. What's his name broke up with that princess."

Helene's and my eyes fly up. "Who?"

"That rich dude that bought the internship."

"Edward?"

"Yeah, that's him, Prescott."

"Let me see." I storm over and snatch the paper and Helene reads over my shoulder.

> The love affair is over between the darlings of Monte Carlo's social set.
>
> Princess Hermione of Switzerland has reportedly broken up with her billionaire beau, casino mogul Edward Prescott.
>
> Sources say Prescott ended it between them last week and she has officially moved back to Switzerland to nurse her broken heart.
>
> No reason for the split has been revealed as yet, stay tuned on this one.
>
> It's sure to be juicy.

"Oh my god." My eyes meet Helene's. "I knew it," she mouths.

"No way," I mouth back.

"What?" Jonty looks between us. "What's going on?"

"Prescott has the hots for Alora," she announces. "I bet he left the princess for her."

"He does not." I roll my eyes. "There's no way."

"The way he looks at you, though."

"He looks at every female like that," I huff, and I walk around the store pretending to be busy. "That's just him and his womanizing ways. He's a raging sexaholic."

"Uh-uh." She shakes her head. "He doesn't look at me like that. Oh how I wish he did."

Jonty rolls his eyes, unimpressed. "If he was broke you two wouldn't even care."

"His big dick energy has nothing to do with money." Helene smiles dreamily. "He could live under a bridge and I'd still fangirl over him."

I get the giggles as I imagine Edward Prescott living under a bridge. "Anyway, who cares about him. We have bigger things to worry about."

"Like what?"

"Getting ready for market night."

"Oh yeah." Helene looks around. "So what are we marking down?"

"Everything."

Darkness.

I type into Google,

The best place to buy high-quality disguises.
Facial prosthetics padded bodysuits.

I read through the results, take my pen and paper and begin to take notes on websites.

I think for a moment. It's imperative that I keep my search history on my devices clear....

Tomorrow I'll buy a burner phone in another name.

ALORA.

We walk up the wide sandstone stairs and I glance up at the painted ornate ceiling. "This museum is so beautiful," I whisper.

"I know, my god, I had no idea, how haven't we been here before?" Helene stops on the steps and tips her head back to really study it for a moment. "I want to live here."

I continue up the stairs as I wonder if I will bump into anyone Edward knows tonight. "Do I look okay?"

"You look hot, I love this sixties vibe you've got going on."

I glance down at myself, I'm wearing high-waisted denim jeans, they have a little pocket on each side at the front with a plaited material detail and the legs are bell bottoms. I've teamed them up with a black turtleneck and a cream vintage handbag and wedges. To top off the look my hair is curled and up in a high ponytail. "These jeans were the find of the century." I run my hand down over my behind.

"I know, I love how the blue is so blue. Why don't they make denim in that color anymore?" Her eyes drop down the length of my body and back up to my face. "You look like a hot Twiggy."

"Mission accomplished." We continue up the stairs. "Because I do love a hot Twiggy." We arrive at the top floor and make our way through the double doors to the ballroom. The walls are adorned with giant paintings of different landscapes. People chatter as they wander around looking. "Oh." I smile, pleasantly surprised. "Look how beautiful these paintings are." There are moon and stars and oceans and cliff faces, all so different but following the same nature theme.

"Let's go to the bar," Helene whispers. "Things look even better after alcohol."

I giggle. "Sounds like a plan." We walk over to the bar. "Can I please have two glasses of white," I ask.

"Of course." She passes me the two glasses of wine.

"Yesssss," Helene whispers as she cranes her neck. "Look who's here."

"Who?"

"Prescott."

"What?" I turn so fast that the wine nearly spills over the sides of the glasses. "Where?"

"In the right corner."

I sip my wine as I casually glance over and I see him straight away, he's talking to three other men, and while the others all blend into mediocrity, there's no hiding when you have that stance. Legs wide, gray suit, perfect posture and dominance oozing from his every cell. Edward Prescott is a beast to behold, beautiful and wild.... But a beast just the same.

Instantly my heart begins to hammer in my chest and damn it, why does he affect me so much? I put my hand on my lower stomach as I try to calm myself down, I can hardly breathe when I'm in his vicinity. It's like I'm orbiting his sun and the power he emits instantly sucks mine away, leaving me powerless, and vulnerable.

Completely at his godlike mercy.

Act cool.

I take in a long, shaky breath and turn my back to him.

"Look at you," Helene whispers with a smile.

"What?" I act oblivious.

"As soon as you see him you get all flustered and red in the face."

"I do not," I scoff, but I know I do and it's becoming embarrassing that I can't hide it.

"He's spotted you," she whispers.

"What?" I gulp my wine and wince as I look at the glass. "What the hell is this?"

"Arsenic, I'm sure." She fakes a smile. "He's coming over."

"What?" I whisper, please don't come over…I can't trust my slutty mouth not to say something inappropriate.

Act. Fucking. Cool.

"Alora," his deep voice purrs from behind me. I turn and act surprised.

"Edward." I smile calmly. "How nice to see you." Seeing this man in the flesh brings out juxtaposed emotions. Bitchy but needy, I should get a T-shirt made with the word *Nitchy* across the chest. It's my newest superpower.

"Likewise." His dark eyes hold mine.

"You remember Helene?" I smile.

"I do, hello," he replies but his eyes stay locked on me.

The air crackles between us, an electric current of epic proportions. From my peripheral vision I see Helene look between us. "Hi, Edward, it's nice to see you again. Please excuse me, I'm going to the bathroom."

Edward sips his drink and then licks his lips and I swallow the nervous lump in my throat. He steps forward and grabs the zipper of my jeans and pulls it up with a sharp snap, he puts his mouth to my ear. "Just helping you get dressed."

His breath tickles my skin, goose bumps scatter at his close vicinity and his cologne dances around me.

"I could smell your pretty white panties from across the room."

CHAPTER FIFTEEN

"I beg your pardon," I whisper, outraged. "You could *not* smell my panties from across the room."

"Oh, my mistake." His eyes dance with mischief as he sips his drink. "I meant see…not smell."

Okay…stop flirting with me.

You may be newly single but I already know I'm not emotionally equipped to be on your rebound roster.

I put my hand down over my zipper to check that it's up…. *Oh, the horror.*

"Is that why you came all the way over here?" I act annoyed. "Just to do up my zipper?"

"I'd prefer to undo it…but it will suffice…for now."

For now.

His words hang in the air between us, bringing with them visions of legs over shoulders and beds being broken.

Focus.

"How are you?" I change the subject.

"I'm well. And you?"

"Never better."

A trace of a smile crosses his face, can he feel my arousal as it pumps through my veins? Who am I kidding, they can feel it downstairs in the parking lot.

"Next time you're in Paris I want you to meet my interior designer," he says matter-of-factly.

"What for?"

"I have a boutique hotel that I want you and my designer to collaborate on. I want eclectic pieces that work with her vibe."

"Oh." That sounds interesting, I would jump at the chance for something like this. I've thought about tackling the commercial market before but hadn't any idea where to start. Maybe if this works out it could lead to future work, at the very least it would be good to have a contact in the industry…hmm. I should do this.

"I'm actually going to Paris next weekend."

"You are?" He frowns.

"Yeah."

"What are you doing there?"

"Umm…." I try to think on my feet. "I have a business meeting."

"On the weekend?"

"Sunday, but thought I would take the weekend to enjoy and do some shopping."

"Okay, well if she can meet you briefly, would you have time?"

"Yes, of course."

He takes out his phone and texts someone and my eyes flick between him and the room. "What's her name?"

"Nel Davenport."

"Nel Davenport?" My eyes widen. "You know Nel Davenport?"

Why did I say that, it made me sound like a five-year-old groupie.

"Yeah, she's great." He puts his phone down and glances over to me. "Do you know of her?"

"Vaguely," I lie. I've got every book she ever wrote, not that I'll ever admit it. "I've heard she's pretty good." I try my hardest to act casual. Nel Davenport is the rock star of the interior design world, and this is the opportunity of a lifetime.

I want to bounce in excitement.

His phone beeps with a text and he reads it. "Is 11 a.m. on the Saturday suitable?"

"Sure." I roll my lips to hide my smile, oh my god…. Is this for real?

He texts her back as my mind runs wild with possibilities.

"All set." He keeps texting. "I'll organize a room for you at the hotel so you can get a feel for the vibe I want."

"Oh." I should say no but in all honesty that's probably a good idea, I guess I could always cancel the hotel I booked. "Okay, if that's not too much trouble."

He reads something on his phone. "All set."

"Thank you."

Ding, my phone sings in my bag and I glance down at it.

"I just sent you the hotel's address."

"Great, thanks."

"Edward." Someone calls his name and he glances over to another man I haven't seen before.

"I have to go; we have another engagement to get to. As always it was pleasurable to see you." He leans in and kisses my cheek before whispering in my ear, "My right hand has been thinking about you a lot."

Before I can even reply he strides off across the ballroom and down the stairs with a group of men.

His right hand.... Are you fucking kidding me?

"Where did he go?" Helene whispers as she walks back over.

"He had another engagement."

"Like what?"

"Who cares." I sip my wine. "Let's look at these stupid paintings and get out of here."

"Can we get some dinner?"

"You bet." I'm all flustered and flushed. "I'm having chocolate cake."

We begin to wander through the paintings. "So what did he say?" she whispers.

"He's all flirty with the sexual innuendo but then does nothing about it. If he wanted to actually talk to me he wouldn't have rushed off."

"Maybe you're misreading it, give me an example of his flirty."

"He did up the zipper on my jeans because it was undone. Said he could smell my white panties from across the room."

Helene's eyes widen. "Hell on a cracker, that man is fucking fire." She thinks for a moment. "But your zipper wasn't even undone."

"Well, that's what I thought, but maybe it was. Honestly, how embarrassing." I let out a deep sigh. "Who walks into an art gallery with their vagina hanging out?"

"Is your underwear white?"

"Huh?"

"What color panties are you wearing?"

I subtly pull the waistband of my jeans out to look. "Black."

"So he was lying."

I stare at her as I connect the dots.

"He just wanted an excuse to touch you."

"Ugh." I sip my wine. "He doesn't like me, he just wants to fuck me."

"What makes you say that?"

"Because there is no conversation, it's all about dick and vagina."

"Which is an excellent topic by the way." She taps her glass with mine. "I, for one, love a man who wants to talk about my vagina with me."

I giggle. "Of course you do."

"I think he has potential."

"I'm twenty-nine years old. I don't want a man with potential, I need a man who is fully potenched."

"Right." She nods. "Good point."

"I'm not going to be a booty call, he either likes me or he doesn't. It doesn't matter regardless because I'm not worried either way."

"Well, that's ridiculous because we both know you are worried both ways plus another spare way."

I giggle again. "Right?"

We keep wandering through the exhibition. "What's going on with Raphael anyway?" I ask.

"Meh." She curls her lip as if disgusted.

"What happened, I thought you liked him?"

"I don't know." She shrugs. "He's not doing it for me now."

"This is becoming a pattern." I frown. "Why do you only like them until you find out that they like you?"

She shrugs. "I guess I'm not interested in someone who has poor judgment."

I throw my head back and laugh. "Liking you is poor judgment?"

"Absolutely." She nods as we stop in front of a giant painting of the sea. "I wouldn't date me. Would you?"

"Probably not."

"I'm a walking red flag," she murmurs as she stares at the painting.

"Like someone else we know," I reply as I stare at the painting too.

"Yeah, but he's a hot, rich, red flag."

"Worse. A hot, rich, red carpet."

She laughs out loud again and I do too.

I love Helene, she always makes everything seem fun.

"I'm just saying," she continues as we keep wandering, "I think you should give him the benefit of the doubt. Maybe he does like you and sex is his way of introducing some sort of contact between the two of you."

"No." I sigh. "I've already slept with him, I already know that I really like him. I can't be his booty call. It will break me."

"So what *do* you want from him?"

"Effort."

"Like how?"

"Like ask me how my day was, go on a dinner date, take me dancing. Call me to say good night. Send me peonies, damn it, he can't even stand here and talk to me without insinuating dirty talk." I shrug. "All I know is that I haven't broken up with a nice guy to be used for sex. I'm at an age where I want more."

"You want the fairy tale," she murmurs, unimpressed.

"Yeah, and damn it, I deserve it. I'm a good catch, and if he doesn't see that then I'm not lowering my standards just to spend one night with him. I've no interest in fucking around with bad boys."

"Fine." She widens her eyes. "More for me, I guess." We keep wandering through the exhibition and she glances over to me. "So are you going to think about him all night?"

"Of course I am."

PHILIPPE.

I rub my hands together to try and warm them up, the morning is fresh on the marina. I glance at my watch as I stand with the two others on shift, we'll be leaving soon.

"Hi." Angelo walks over. "Cold morning."

"Freezing." I smile. Angelo's a guard from a few yachts down. We all know each other and chat while we fill in time.

"I heard about your bonuses." He lights a cigarette. "Is it true?"

"What do you mean?" I glance back at the Prescott yacht, still no sign.

"Word on the street is that your team got a three-hundred-thousand bonus last month. Each." He widens his eyes. "Surely not."

I chuckle. "Who told you that?" We actually got more, not that I'd ever tell.

"Seriously, man." He blows a thin stream of smoke into the air. "I need you to get me a job. My boss is a fucking tight-ass. I get a miserable hourly rate with no extras."

"Our team is full." I shrug, I get hit up for jobs on the hour by every guard we meet. "Everyone wants to be on Prescott's team, you'll need to get in line. Nobody in their right mind would ever give up this gig."

And why would they, we travel the world, our food and accommodation are included, and we get paid a criminal amount of money.

"Who has to die for me to get a job?" he jokes.

"Seriously." I laugh. "It's probably the only way."

"That's it," a woman screams from the deck of a yacht down the marina. "I've had it."

We all glance over to the York yacht. "At it again."

More yelling, more fighting.

"Do they even like each other?" Angelo frowns as we watch on.

"I heard they're getting married." Stefano shrugs.

"Surely not. He can't marry her."

From the corner of my eye I catch sight of Edward walking out onto deck.

"Got to go," I tell Angelo.

"Get me a job," he calls as he walks back to his post.

We meet Edward at the gangplank. "Morning, boss."

"Morning." He nods and walks past us; we fall in and walk behind him toward the waiting car.

More fighting echoes across the marina.

"I'm leaving," she screams.

Edward gives the yacht the side eye. "Please. I beg of you."

We chuckle as we walk.

"I have no idea what to do with you," he calls.

"Tie her to the anchor," Edward mutters.

We laugh again and arrive at the car and I open the back door of the Bentley. "Our flight to Zurich is on schedule, sir."

He gets into the car and I close the door behind him.

Another day, another country....

ALORA.

Market night is always crazy, but this one is intense.

"My god," Helene whispers as I wrap a vase. "Why are they all drinking so much, we're going to run out of wine at this rate."

"There's three more boxes in my office."

"They're hot."

"So go put them on ice." I fake a smile to the customer. "Thank you so much for coming." I pass her the paper bag. "Enjoy your vase."

"Oh, I will." She smiles.

In true market night fashion, this has been a sell-out event. We have every casual staff member working and still we can't keep up.

Helene begins hauling wine out of the office and dumping it in ice buckets. "We're nearly out of cheese as well," she whispers. "This isn't a restaurant, fuckers."

"Pigs," I mouth. "Hi." I smile to the next customer. "How can I help you?"

"I'd like the pair of Ming lamps please?"

"Oh, they're divine." I walk over and put a sold sticker on them. "I'll just run out the back and grab the boxes." I walk out to the back room and begin hunting down the boxes, Helene is on her hands and knees emptying wine bottles.

Jonty comes around the doorway. "Those idiots are here but don't worry, I told them tickets are sold out."

"Who?" I put my hands on my hips. "Have you seen the boxes for the Ming lamps?"

"Prescott and his stupid friends."

"He's here?" My eyes widen.

"With whom?" Helene snaps.

"The prince and whatnot. I told them to leave but Prescott refused, told me to go get Alora."

"Jonty." Helene slaps him hard on the arm. "Are you fucking insane." She marches to the front door. "Hello," I hear her over-the-top gush. "How lovely to see you again, Edward. Come in. Come in."

"She's pathetic." Jonty rolls his eyes.

Boom, boom…boom goes my heart.

What is he doing here?

I take my time as I try to find the boxes for the Ming lamps, which have somehow miraculously vanished into thin air. I hold my fingers to my temples as I inwardly freak out.

Calm down…it's fine. Everything is fucking fine.

"Hello." Edward walks into the back room. He's wearing a perfectly fitted navy suit and a cream shirt; his hair is just-fucked perfection and can we have a moment of silence for the scent of his aftershave, it's dancing around me naked.

Dear lord.

"Hi." I force a smile, suddenly the store feels way too small for his energy. His presence penetrates every inch of space.

"What are you doing here?" I act casual as I concentrate on the shelving.

Where are these fucking boxes?

"I came to say hello." He leans against the shelving with his shoulder, his hands in his suit pant pockets.

"Hello."

"Thought I might pick up one of those mystery boxes."

I glance over at him and he gives me the best come-fuck-me look of all time.

How does he know about them…wait a minute, does he watch my morning videos?

"You don't need to buy a mystery box." I keep looking for another troublesome box, true to its name its designation is a complete fucking mystery.

"You're going to give it to me for free then?" He raises an eyebrow as his eyes hold mine, and the air crackles between us.

Okay, stop.

Everything that comes out of his mouth sounds so sexual.... Or maybe it's just that I really, really want to have sex with this bastard.

"Edward, I'm very busy tonight." I find a pair of boxes, too small for the lamps but who cares at this point, I'll stuff them in if it kills me.

"Too busy for me?"

I look back over to him; his dark eyes hold mine as he leans against the shelving.

Never.

"Umm." I hesitate as his closeness causes every cell in my brain to misfire, not a single coherent thought.

"Well?" He reaches over and tucks a piece of hair behind my ear. "Is there anything I can do to.... Help?"

Tear my clothes off.

I swallow the lump in my throat. "Umm." Again.... No words. Nothing. Just complete and utter deer-in-the-headlights dumbass.

He breaks into a broad smile; the bastard knows he has me flustered.

"I'll go look around the store." With a last long smolder, he walks out the front and I drop my head into my hands.

Fuck.

How is this man so ridiculously hot? It's criminal, no woman on earth could find a box in these conditions.

"Oh my god, oh my god." Helene comes around the corner like a hornet, she peeks through the blinds. "His hot guard is with him."

"Which one?"

"The one that looks like Jason Statham."

"That's Philippe." I pass her the boxes.

"Well, Philippe is delicious and I am totally screwing his

brains out." She shoves them back. "I have my own boxes to look for."

"No you are not," I whisper angrily. "Nobody is screwing anybody."

"What is wrong with you?" she whispers.

"What is wrong with you?" I fire back.

"Where are the boxes?" Jonty sticks his head around the corner and widens his eyes. "What the hell are you two doing? There's a thousand people out here waiting for boxes at the cash register, you know?"

Having a heart attack, if you really must know.

"Sorry." I rush back into the store, crap...he's right. People are everywhere, and from the corner of my eye I catch sight of Edward's friends walking through the aisles as they look around, Theodore, Nicholas, and that other friend of theirs, I forget his name. They are all wearing suits, chatting away while looking all orgasmic.

He brought his friends to my store; do they know anything about me or our history, has he told them...what the hell does this mean?

I feel the blood begin to drain from my body as I realize something. The Prince of Monaco is here... and we have no fucking cheese.

Argh!

"Hello." I smile calmly to the next customer at the front desk. "How can I help you?"

"Hi, I'm interested in the grand piano," a man asks.

"Of course," I reply, my eyes flick over his shoulder to the smolder squad, loitering around like God's gift to women. Not an analogy, these men are literally God's gift to women.

"This way." I briskly walk to the other end of the store with the man trailing behind me. I open the lid. "It's beautiful, isn't it?"

"May I?" He gestures to it.

"Be my guest." I discreetly wipe the perspiration from my brow, this night is a pressure cooker and I am the meat.

He sits down and starts playing a classical tune and the store collectively stops and listens.

He's good….

I look up to the other end of the store to see Edward mutter something under his breath to his friends and they all chuckle, seemingly unimpressed.

Smart-asses.

I'd like to see you play better…actually, these tossers probably all play harps and shit. I don't even know what rich people play, but I'm sure it's not the recorder like normal people learned at school.

I see Jonty hold up wineglasses to Edward and his friends and they nod.

Oh, hell on a cracker…. For the love of god, do not drink that wine!

It's average at best. I widen my eyes to Helene.

Help!

Mr. Piano Man keeps playing and playing and playing and from my peripheral vision I can see Helene's shoulders bouncing up and down as she giggles.

That bitch can read my mind, and this isn't a concert, you giant dickhead.

I don't have time for this.

"Would you like some cheese and crackers?" Jonty calls to them.

Shut up, Jonty. Please. Just shut the hell up.

"Yes, why not," Edward replies.

I discreetly wipe my brow again, it's so fucking hot in here.

Combustible.

Helene ducks into an aisle and loses it, laughing hard as she leans her hands on her knees.

But Mr. Piano Man keeps playing…. On and on and fucking on.

"Excuse me." I fake a smile. I march into the aisle that Helene is hiding in. "Oh my god," I whisper as I pull her farther away out of sight. "That fuckwit won't stop playing the piano and Jonty is poisoning Edward with cheap wine and bad cheese. Do something."

She throws her head back and laughs harder. "That wine is really bad."

I hold my temples. "Get rid of them."

"Who?"

"All of them, especially Piano Man."

"Go talk to them and then they'll leave. I'll handle Piano Man."

"Good thinking." I fan my face. "Are you hot?"

"No, are you?"

"Fucking volcanic." I wipe my forehead with my sleeve and walk out of the aisle, I make my way over to Edward and his friends. "Hello." I act calm. "How are you?"

"Hello, Alora," Prince Theodore says, he leans in and kisses my cheek. "Your store is incredible."

Eeep!

"Thank you."

Nicholas and the other man all kiss my cheek. "Hello."

"Thanks for coming." I smile.

Edward hangs back watching, why he didn't kiss my cheek is what I want to know.

"What brought you all out tonight?" I act interested. "Do you like antiques or…?"

"We had dinner with Prescott around the corner and he wanted to call in on the way home."

"Oh." I smile. I glance between them just to catch Edward bite his lip to stop himself from smiling.

That was a lie.

"We're going soon, though," Theo says. "I'm buying this painting on my way out."

"Okay." This is so awkward. "Thanks for coming, it was nice to see you again."

"You too."

What's the etiquette here, do princes pay full price for stuff or is there a royal discount I don't know about?

Jonty rings up the painting and I serve another customer, though my mind is in overdrive. Why did he bring his friends here?

He seems different tonight, perhaps a little better behaved, but maybe that's just wishful thinking. I mean, coming to my market night is kind of an effort.

Nearly….

I serve a few more people and they wave. "Bye," they call as they leave.

I let out a sigh of relief and turn to see Edward still here, he disappears into an aisle.

What is he doing?

I finish serving and go off in search of him, I find him in the taxidermy aisle. "Hello," I say.

"Hi." He smiles, he picks up a stuffed rat and studies it. "What interesting things you have here."

"Uh-huh." I nod with my hands on my hips.

"I always wanted one of these." His eyes dance with mischief. "Said no one ever."

"I thought your friends left."

"They did." He puts the stuffed rat back onto the shelf. "I thought I could stay and see if you needed my help with anything."

"What would I need your help with?"

His eyes hold mine and he gives me the look. "There must be something you need help with."

Oh…how much temptation can I handle before I crack?

Do I play…. Or do I play hard to get?

No. Short-term pain for long-term gain. He can't just turn up here and get a booty call, as tempting as it is.

"No. I have no idea what you could possibly help me with, Edward."

His eyes hold mine and he steps forward, pinning me to the shelves, his erection digs into my stomach and I feel a rush of arousal run through my body.

Jeez.

I glance over and see the fake eyeballs of the rat staring at me…stop judging me!

"Excuse me, miss," Piano Man interrupts.

Not now, fucker.

"Be there in a minute," I snap.

Edward pushes his body harder against mine. "Are you sure there is nothing I can do for you?" He flexes his dick between us.

Oh….

We stare at each other as I feel myself weakening. It would be so easy….

No!

Does he really think he can not call me, not take me on a date…. Turn up at my place of work and stick his hard dick in my stomach and I'm going to goo and gush how lucky I am that he picked me?

"Yeah, there is, actually." I step back from him. "You can respect me."

"What the fuck is that supposed to mean?"

"Do you really think that you can turn up here in your slutty little suit and get whatever you want?"

A slow, sexy smile crosses his face. "Slutty little suit?"

"That's right." Not an exaggeration, everything about that suit makes me want to be slutty. "E is for Effort, Edward." I put my hands on my hips. "You should try it sometime."

He glares at me and I glare right back.

"I don't have time for this tonight, I'm too busy." I march off back to the stupid concert pianist. "Now, how can I help you?"

FORTY MINUTES LATER.

I wrap the glasses and put them into the bag. "Thank you so much for coming."

"This was the night from hell," Jonty whispers.

"Put the closed sign on the door, for god's sake," Helene mutters under her breath.

The crowd is slowing up with the last of the people loitering around shopping. Jonty and Helene go and finish up serving them.

I stand at the counter and feel a hot body slide snugly in behind me.

"You should probably delete the security tapes," Edward whispers in my ear.

"Huh?" I glance back at him. "I thought you left ages ago."

"Good night, Alora." He leans in and kisses my cheek. "I had a good time."

Without another word he walks out of the store with his two guards trailing behind him.

What? He waited all this time to just leave before we finish.

Helene holds her hands up in question. "What's happening?" she mouths.

I shrug. "He left."

"God, he's so weird."

"Tell me about it," Jonty agrees.

"Shut up, Jonty," Helene scolds him. "You can't say that."

"You said it first," he fires back.

"Yes, but I have questionable opinions and terrible taste in men, everyone knows that."

Darkness.

I slide the blade through the tape holding the large box closed and fold the lid open.

I remove the plastic and look over the contents.

A padded suit, this will add at least forty to fifty pounds to my appearance, making me unrecognizable to the naked eye. I'll be able to come and go without being noticed.

I smile, pleased with my purchase.

I open the second parcel and look over the three wigs and the two prosthetic noses.

How do I attach?

I carefully read the instructions.... Medical-grade adhesive....

Hmm, I type into Google.

Medical-grade adhesive for facial prosthetics.

ALORA.

The night comes to an end but my mind is in overdrive, of course I'm going to delete the security tapes. Nobody needs to see me getting pinned to a shelf of taxidermy.

I smile. Although I might want to.

"You guys get going. I'm going to get some takeout and reconcile the cash register."

"We'll wait."

"No. I insist." I pour myself a glass of wine. "I'm going to wind down a little and take my time, you guys go. Thanks for today, you're amazing."

"Okay. But lock yourself in."

"I will." I walk them to the door and flick the lock, now…I march to my office at double time. I open the security footage link and begin to scroll through, my screen is split into four screens. One of the front shop, one of the aisles, one of the bathroom area out the back and one out the front of the store. I smile as I watch Helene and Jonty navigate the night. As it plays in the background I call my favorite Chinese restaurant.

"Hello, Lucky Charm."

"Hello, can I order some home delivery please?"

"Of course, what would you like?"

"I'll have Chilli king shrimp and fried rice please."

"Sure thing, it will be around twenty minutes."

"Thank you." I pay and give them my address, pour another glass of wine, and go back to watching the security footage. I hit fast-forward and watch as everyone moves at double speed. On the bottom right screen I see Edward and his friends arrive and I click to full screen.

"Hello," Jonty says.

"We're here for the mystery box," Edward says, void of emotion.

"Tickets are sold out. Sorry, bad luck."

Edward looks at him deadpan and his friends chuckle behind him.

I giggle too, Edward's face is priceless.

"Go and get Alora," Edward tells him.

"She's too busy to talk to you."

Theo and the other boys burst out laughing.

Edward leans in and says something that I can't hear and Jonty rolls his eyes and walks inside.

What did he say to him?

I rewind it and watch it again but can't make it out. I sip my wine and fast-forward it again, I watch on as Edward and his friends walk around the store. I can't hear what they're saying but they are chatting and every now and then they laugh as if something funny was said.

I walk past the screen on the left and Edward's eyes drop down to my behind and he says something to his friends and smiles darkly, I hold my breath as I watch on.

What did he say?

I gulp my wine; this is the most fun I've had in months.

I fast-forward and everyone goes into speed mode, every now and then Edward comes onto screen and I slow it back down so I can watch him. The way he overpowers everyone in the room.

He's just so....

I fast-forward again and finally get to us in the taxidermy aisle, I enlarge it and chew my nail as I watch. He says something and tucks a piece of my hair behind my ear.

The air leaves my lungs as I watch us together, the sexual chemistry between us is palpable, I can feel it through the screen.

I can see the erection in his pants and he towers over me, and then he pins me to the shelf as I stare up at him.

I swallow the lump in my throat as I watch, then rewatch and then rewatch our interaction. The way he looks at me...the way he steps forward and pins me.

Jeez....

I'm downloading this, I need to watch this on repeat. Forever.

I feel myself getting hot under the collar, I totally should have been his booty call tonight.

What am I.... A fucking nun?

I keep going forward, I want to see where he comes up to me at the end of the night.

I catch sight of him say something to his guards and then they go and stand by the back door.

Wait...huh?

I rewind and then fast-forward. What are they doing?

Then I notice Edward on the bottom square, he's out in the courtyard out the back that leads to the bathroom.

But....

I frown, confused, and enlarge the screen. There's a speaker with music playing out here, we run it all night for ambience. I can hear it on the footage, the song is 'I Did Something Bad' by Taylor Swift.

He looks up at the camera and smiles darkly. "What is he doing?"

He unzips his suit pants….

My eyes widen.

He spits into his right hand.

Bang, bang, bang, sounds at the front door and I nearly fall off the chair.

The Chinese is here.

Argh!

I pause the video and run to the front door and open it in a rush. "Thank you." I snatch it from him and slam the door in his face. I run back to the office.

Oh my god. Oh my god.

I hit rewind and watch it in slow motion.

Edward looks up at the camera, smiles darkly, and undoes the zipper of his suit pants. His large erection comes into view and my eyes widen.

He spits into his hand.

Spits.

He begins to pull himself, hard and violent.

His head tips back in ecstasy, his body jerks and moves with every stroke.

My eyes widen as my hand flies over my mouth. "What the ever-loving fuck."

I have no words.

None.

He's so bad…*but so fucking good.*

He keeps going and going…arousal seeps into my soul as my ovaries begin to chant for his arrival.

Yes, yes, yes.

He comes hard and his eyes flutter closed.

The air leaves my lungs as I watch on, my heart completely stopped.

He smiles up at the camera, his chest rises and falls as if searching for air.

He mouths something.

Huh?

I rewind it and play it in slow motion.

"E stands for Ejaculation," he mouths. I watch on, entranced. With his dark eyes locked on the camera, he licks the semen off the palm of his hand.

Oh.

My.

Fucking.

God.

CHAPTER SIXTEEN

Arousal heats my blood and I rewind it on double speed until I see him talk to his guards. I slow it down as he says something to them, what did he say?

"Guard the door. Don't let anyone go out there."

"Oh." My hand flies over my mouth. "He knew he was going out there to do that."

Why the hell would he come to my store and wank for me on my security tape?

To turn me on.

Excitement screams through me and I know this makes me as bad as him but damn it he's making it really hard to continue on this good girl act.

I watch as he undoes his zipper, his large erection comes into view and my insides begin to flutter.

*Bang.... Bang...bang...*goes my heart.

He spits into his hand.

Spits.

I feel a rush of arousal down below.

He takes himself into his hand and begins to stroke himself with his dark eyes locked on to the camera and I hold my breath as I watch on.

Dirty innuendo I can resist, but this...this is next level. This is porn where I could fuck the male lead if I wanted to.

And I really do.

Hard.

I watch it until the end and I rewind it and watch it again and then again. He did this for a reaction, he's putting the ball in my court.

What do I do, what do I do?

I get up and walk around the store as I think. I need to be strategic about this, he came here with the specific purpose to bait me.

Any normal woman would cave under these circumstances… hell, I want to so badly.

What would happen next if I played into his hands?

I pace back and forth as I think, I would call him, he would talk dirty and ask if he can come over. We would have wild sex and then he would leave in the morning and because nothing has been established or talked about other than sex I probably will never hear from him again.

I drag my hands through my hair, honestly…. How can I *not* call him?

No woman is this strong.

And he knows it, he's weaponizing my sexual attraction to him. Baiting me into action and trying to force my hand. I already know that I like him too much to be a casual fuck buddy.

But what do I really want from him?

Effort.

It doesn't have to be a marriage proposal, and hell, we probably wouldn't last anyway, but I want to feel respected. I want a real chance of something more.

I continue to pace as I think.

If I was going to do the exact opposite of what he's expecting… what would I do?

Not call him.

Make no contact and pretend I didn't watch the tapes as if unbothered.

I put my head into my hands, I honestly don't think I'm that strong.

Do you want him for one night or do you want a chance of forever?

Okay, determination runs through me.

I haven't come this far with him to only come this far. We already did the fucking thing and it nearly broke me. I'm not doing that again.

I walk back into my office and send the security footage to my email; I check that it arrived and then I resend it again just to be sure.

I can't lose this footage whatever I do, it's my new favorite show.

I screw up my face as I delete it off the security tapes, Ouch… this feels like a crime to humanity.

I flop back into my chair. I'm not calling him. I'm not even acknowledging that I saw it.

I get a vision of him spitting into his hand and I smile, it's going to be a long hard night with my vibrator.

EDWARD.

In the darkness I pace back and forth on the deck of my yacht, I check my phone.

No missed calls.

"Call me, fuck it," I murmur, infuriated.

I glance at my watch, 10:30 p.m.…did she even fucking watch it?

Never have I met a more infuriating woman. My cock is near painful, throbbing with want. She knows I need her.

She's forcing her hand, trying to make me toe the line.

Well, fuck that…because I'm not.

I keep pacing and run my hands through my hair as I think, should I just call her?

No.

"Is everything alright, sir?" Philippe asks as he appears. "Do you need anything?"

"I'm fine," I snap. "Leave me be."

"Yes, sir." He nods and disappears.

I check my phone again.

No missed calls.

ALORA.

"So…." I sip my coffee, should I tell her?

"So what?" Helene asks as she looks around, blissfully oblivious that I have a dirty little secret.

Well…it's more of a big secret, nothing about Edward Prescott is in any way little.

"Can you keep a secret?"

She rolls her eyes. "What do you think?"

"So Edward left a present for me on our security tapes last night."

"He did?" She frowns. "Like what?"

"He may have…." I smirk as I search for the right wording. "Touched himself."

Her eyes widen. "He touched himself?"

I nod.

"Like how?"

"Like…." I smile again, this conversation is unbelievable even to me. "Like…really hard."

Her mouth falls open. "He did not."

"He sure did." I giggle into my coffee. "The best thing I've seen onscreen in my entire life."

"Oh my god," she whispers. "I need to see this."

"No," I scoff. "You are *not* watching it."

"Oh, come on," she moans. "Let me watch it."

"No way."

"So you went over there, right?"

I shake my head. "No."

"*What?*" She screws up her face. "You called him?"

"No."

"Are you fucking serious right now?"

"I want a chance of something more and I know he is trying to force me to make this about sex."

"Everything is about sex, you idiot."

"Not this."

"Oh my god." She puts her head into her hands. "Have I taught you nothing?"

"Too much, actually."

"So did he call you?"

"Nope."

She drags her hand down her face. "Go home right now and FaceTime him naked."

"No way."

"I'm not even joking, he is the hottest male on the planet. Stop playing games with him."

"He's the one playing games," I fire back. "If he wants to see me he has to make more of an effort than jerking off in my back room."

Her mouth falls open as her eyes hold mine. "He jerked off in the back room. Did he come?"

I smile and her eyes widen.

She simulates sliding down her chair. "God…I see what you're doing for others. When is it my turn?"

"It was so hard not calling him, but I have faith that he's going to call me."

"He has to, right?"

"Honestly—" I shrug, "—I don't even know." I think for a moment. "Luckily I'm going to Paris this weekend. It will take my mind off it."

"Why on earth would you ever want to take your mind off seeing Edward Prescott jerk off for you?" She thinks for a moment. "Wait, did he have lube or…."

"He spat in his hand."

Her eyes roll back in her head as she fans her face. "I'm. Dying."

I giggle. "Me and you both."

Paris….

The cure for all. The right to the wrongs, everything is rosy in Paris.

At least it is for me.

I smile into my glass of wine at my tiny table for one as I look around the romantic restaurant. Candles are on the tables and people are chattering away and having a grand old time.

"Can I take your order?" the waiter asks.

"Oui." I smile. "You can."

I check myself out in the elevator mirror, fitted dress, flat ballet shoes and my hair swept up into a ponytail. I think I'm nailing the cute corporate look…well, at least giving it a red-hot crack. I'm excited for today, Nel Davenport is the contact of contacts, and if all I was supposed to reconnect with Edward for was to meet her then so be it. She texted me yesterday about our meeting this morning and I've never been more excited.

The elevator doors open and I stride out into the foyer, I've got this.

Even if I haven't, I'm going to fake it till I make it.

I walk into the restaurant and look around and I see her sitting by the window with her laptop open.

I nearly skip over to her. "Nel Davenport?" I ask.

"Yes, you must be Alora Sorenson?" She smiles as she stands.

"Hi." My voice comes out high and squeaky.

Play it cool

"I mean…hi," I say lower as I hold out my hand to shake hers. "It's nice to meet you." God, she's beautiful. Even more stunning in real life than in photos.

"I hope you drink coffee." She gestures to the table. "I already ordered." A cup of something black as the depths of hell sits in front of me.

Eesh….

"Thank you, I love coffee." I smile, not a lie, I do love coffee, just more the type that doesn't kill you.

"So…." She looks me up and down. "You're a friend of Edward's."

"Oh, well." I act casual. "An old friend, but we reconnected recently at a charity auction." I shrug as the need to elaborate takes over, I'll go with his story, "I went to college with his sister in London and when he found out that I owned an antique store he wanted me to meet you about the refurbishment of the hotel."

"Oh, how fascinating." She smiles all dreamily as she leans on her hand. "You've known Edward for a long time then."

Hmm….

Something tells me that Nel Davenport is interested in more than the refurb.

"I have."

"So were you as shocked as I was?"

"About?"

"Him and Hermione breaking up."

"Did they break up?" I act oblivious.

She looks left and right as if about to commit a crime. "My sister's best friend's cousin is Hermione's personal assistant."

"She has an assistant?"

"Yes, and out of the blue, Edward called it off with her a few weeks ago," she whispers. "Apparently she's devastated."

It's blatantly obvious that she likes him, and I begin to hear my jealous heartbeat in my ears. "When was this?" I ask.

I haven't heard from Edward at all. I have, however, watched the security footage an alarmingly large amount of times and my poor vibrator has been working double time.

"I don't know, apparently he abruptly broke up with her but nobody knows why."

Boom

Boom

Boom goes my heart.

"So when he messaged me yesterday and said he was coming to Paris to see me…." She cuts herself off with a shrug. "I mean…."

I wait for her to finish her sentence….

Wait, what?

"He's coming *here?*" I stammer. "To see *you?*"

What the hell?

"Oh my god," she whispers as she sits back. "Here he comes now."

I look up and see him walking though the restaurant, gray suit and dark hair, looking like he just stepped off the catwalk. He has two bodyguards trailing behind him.

"Ladies…."

"Hello, Mr. Prescott." She swoons.

"You look lovely, Nel." He leans in and kisses her cheek and she blushes on cue. "Hello, Alora," he says, he undoes his suit coat button with one hand as he sits down.

Hmm….

Where's my 'you look lovely'…? *Asshole.*

He sits back, crosses his legs, and brings his eyes to meet mine before raising an eyebrow, arrogance personified. He raises his hand for a server and she comes over. "I'll have an espresso please."

"Yes sir." She disappears into the kitchen.

He seems different today. Cocky or something, pissed even.

Ha, he's pissed that I didn't call him…well, screw you, asshole.

He's here to see Nel and I want to know what the ever-loving fuck is going on here.

"I didn't realize you were coming to Paris," I say, damn this bastard for being so sexy.

"I have business here this weekend."

"And yet you didn't mention it?"

"My calendar is a private matter."

Really?

Like that is it? We glare at each other as animosity bounces between us.

"Alora was just telling me all about how close the two of you are," Nel gushes in an overenthusiastic tone.

"Was she now?" A trace of a smile crosses his face.

Shut up, Nel, you big-mouthed idiot.

"Not how close we are." I feel my lying face begin to blush. "How close I am to your sister."

"Come now." He smirks sarcastically as he takes a sip of water. "We're basically family, Alora. You're like an annoying little sister."

Nel laughs on cue. "Haha, that's hilarious."

The sky turns red….

Okay. Fuck. You.

I don't know anyone who jerks off for their annoying little sister.

"So, Alora, do you have someone special in your life?" Nel asks.

"Recently single," Edward answers before I get a chance.

My eyes flick to him, I'll answer my own questions, asshole.

"I would like to know more about you, Nel," Edward says. "Are you with someone?"

"No, very single." Her eyes light up as she stares at Edward for a beat longer than necessary.

Ugh…this woman is getting annoying.

"I find it hard to believe that someone hasn't snapped you up." Edward smirks into his coffee as his eyes hold hers.

"Just waiting for the right man to show up." She smiles as she runs her hand through her hair.

They're flirting.

I get a vision of myself flipping the table upside down.

"Aren't we here to talk about the refurb?" I open my notepad with a sharp snap.

"Yes, let's do that," Edward replies. "Nel, why don't you run Alora through the brief."

"Sure." She retrieves a folder and begins to flick through the pages while she explains in great detail what the design plan is. And I wish I could tell you I am listening to every word, but I can't even think when I'm this close to him.

His aftershave dances around the table like a tangible force, bringing with it memories of spas in Switzerland and legs over shoulders and pulling himself in my back room…and he's here to see fucking Nel.

"And here in this room…" Nel continues, bringing me back to the present.

I watch the two of them flirt in a detached state. Edward Prescott takes what he wants and to hell with the consequences; if he wants Nel, I'm positive he'll have his wicked way with her.

Not that it's anything to me. I don't care about him, he's made it crystal clear where his interests lie with me.

Wait…. Have they slept together before? My eyes flick between them as I look for evidence, I mean she is beautiful.

"So, Alora…." More muffled voices.

What do I care anyway?

"Are you listening at all?" Edward says. "Alora?"

Huh?

I glance up to see them both looking at me as if waiting for an answer.

"Excuse me?"

Edward puts his hands up in question. "What are you doing?"

"I beg your pardon?"

"Stop wasting my time," he snaps. "You aren't even listening."

"I *am* listening," I fire back. "I am processing."

"Processing what?"

"Don't be rude, Edward," I snap. "I am not in the mood for you today."

"Well, I am not in the mood for you either."

"Oh my." Nel laughs. "You two really are like siblings." She pushes her chair out. "I'm going to the bathroom." She disappears across the restaurant and my eyes come back to Edward.

"What are you doing?" he snaps. "I am giving you the opportunity of a lifetime and you are sitting there daydreaming."

"For your information," I spit, "I am not daydreaming, I am *fuming*."

"Fuming?"

"Why did you bring me here to watch you flirt with your interior decorator?"

Amusement flashes across his face.

"This isn't funny, Edward."

"Jealous?"

"Not one bit," I fume. "Disgusted."

"Disgusted?"

"Yes. You disgust me."

He leans his elbow on the table and steeples his pointer finger up over his cheekbone, his eyes dance with mischief. "So why do you keep thinking about me?"

"I'm. Not. Thinking. About. You."

"So..." His eyebrows flick up. "My cock, then?"

"Listen here, you," I whisper angrily. "Stop talking about your cock to me. Your cock has nothing to do with this."

"Famous last words."

"Of whom?" I fire back. "I never read any famous last words about your dick in the history books."

"That's because you are out of touch with quality literature."

"So..." Nell says.

We both lean back guiltily.

"I think I have enough to start on." I close my notepad that doesn't have one frigging note in it. "I'm going to workshop this and I have to get going because I have a...." I try to think on my feet. "I have a lunch date I have to get to."

Edward's eyes meet mine. "With who?"

I shrug nonchalantly. "The man I came to Paris to meet."

Yes…this is good.

"Really?" Edward's eyes meet mine. "I'd love to meet him."

"Oh…you will." I smile sweetly.

Fuck….

"Great. Let's meet back in the bar at say six."

What?

"Um…. Oh…. Well." I feel my face turn a shade of fuchsia red flustered.

Edward rolls his lips to hide his smile, conceited ass. He knows I'm lying…. Damn it.

"Sounds great," I lie.

"We'll make a double date of it." He gives me a playful wink.

Oh…so he *is* here to take Nel on a date. Of all the bastardly assholes on earth.

Suddenly single and he's chasing fucking Nel.

"Awesome." I smile through gritted teeth, and by awesome, I mean this is a fucking catastrophe. "Nice to meet you, Nel." I shake her hand. "I look forward to working together." I turn and walk back to the elevator at fast pace.

Fuck's sake….

An hour later I'm pacing in my room.

What do I do…. What do I do?

I don't want to cancel tonight and I don't want him to have the upper hand. He thinks I was lying about having a lunch date…. And I was, but he doesn't know that.

He can't know that.

Here I am constantly daydreaming about all things Edward Prescott and trying to force a tiny bit of effort and here he is flying to Paris to spend time with Nel.

Oh god, I'm such an idiot.

He thinks it's all about him…. I need to get the upper hand.

But how the hell do I do that?

I flop back onto the bed, now I'm going to have to go out and find a man in approximately… I look at my watch. Six hours. Which is impossible because you can't find a decent man on earth in an entire lifetime. I don't want some average Joe, I need an expert. Someone really fabulous.

Unless….

No.

Surely not.

I bite my lip as an idea rolls around in my head…. I mean, it could possibly work.

I pick up my phone and google.

MALE ESCORT PARIS

My heart races as I wait for the results.

THOMAS STONE.

Professional and discreet.

With shaky hands I dial the number.

"Hello," a deep sexy voice answers.

"Um…hi. Is this Thomas Stone?"

"It is."

I close my eyes, mortified by what's about to come out of my mouth.

"My name is Alora and this is the lamest thing I've ever done but I have to go out tonight and I need a platonic date to pretend to be on a real date with me," I blurt out in a rush.

"Where are you?" he asks.

"I'm in Paris."

"Okay." He thinks for a moment. "You're in luck, I'm also in Paris this weekend and I don't have anything on tonight."

"You don't?" I frown.

"But I do have a job on tomorrow so I will need to be out early in the morning."

"Oh." I widen my eyes in horror. "You can leave tonight. This isn't a real date." I scrunch my hair in my hand. "Absolutely two hundred percent platonic."

Arghhhhhh!

"We'll see." He chuckles. "Text me the address and time."

"Okay," I whisper. I hold my chest, I'm sure I'm about to have a heart attack at any moment.

"Oh, and Alora."

"Yes."

"Wear something sexy."

My eyes widen and the phone goes dead.

What the hell have I done?

CHAPTER SEVENTEEN

I hold the dress up to myself in the mirror, it's black and fitted and could be cute, although I'm not sure how it's going to look on me. I'm in the middle of a shopping nightmare. I didn't bring anything sexy to wear, I was going to Paris to have a weekend of rest and retreat, never in a million years did I think that I would be hiring a male escort to piss off Edward Prescott.

Honestly…if this isn't the most hairbrained scheme that I've ever had, I'll eat my hat.

"Can I help you?" the sales assistant asks.

"Yes, what does this look like on?"

"Beautiful." She smiles.

You would say that, wouldn't you?

"What are you after?" she asks.

"Well, I don't actually know but something that fits well and makes me look like…" I widen my eyes, "…irresistible."

She smiles. "I have exactly the dress that you need."

"You do?"

"This way, please." I follow her to another part of the shop and I look around nervously, this is the expensive part of the shop, I'm sure of it.

You know what…who cares what the price is. If it gets the job done, then it's worth every pretty penny.

She starts rattling through the racks and passing me things left, right and center. "This red one is fabulous."

"No, I wore a red dress last time I saw him."

"Right." She looks me up and down. "What about this white one?"

"I'm not sure it would be flattering on me."

"Trust me on this, it's perfect on everybody." She passes it over along with another pile of things that are way too overpriced. "The change rooms are this way."

I hurry in and start undressing, I glance at my watch, shit is that the time? Oh my god he's going to be here in three hours and I've still got to do my hair and everything.

I pull on the black dress. It looks okay, I turn around and look at my behind. Not very wow, though.

"What does it look like?" the sales assistant asks me.

I pull open the curtain. "It's okay, I guess."

She twists her lips and looks me up and down. "We can do better."

I give her a half-hearted smile. "What should I try on next?"

"The white. Definitely the white."

I tear the black dress off and step into the white one, no way this is going to work. Probably going to look like a giant polar bear or something. It's fitted and off the shoulder and zips up under one arm, the skirt is tight around my waist but falls nicely over my behind.

"How does it look?" she calls.

"To be honest—" I open the curtain, "—better than I expected."

She smiles as she looks me up and down. "*This* is the dress."

"Really?"

"Do you want this man eating out of your hand?"

I give a half-hearted shrug. "It couldn't hurt the situation, I guess."

"Then this is the dress, here, let me find the shoes." She marches off across the shop and my eyes go back to myself in the mirror and I turn to look at my behind again, it's flattering without being too much. But then white, is that too formal just to go out for dinner?

With a fucking male escort....

Oh my god, this is ridiculous.... I just...what was I thinking? That's the problem: I wasn't thinking at all. I'm going to cancel Thomas Stone.

I'll still go down to meet them at the bar, but I'll just pretend that my date couldn't come.... Why did I even tell that stupid lie, it's just ridiculous.

I keep looking the dress up and down. But I do still want to look good tonight.

The saleswoman reappears with a pair of strappy silver stilettos and puts them on the floor in front of me. "These will match perfectly."

"You don't think they're too much?"

"Ha," she huffs. "Darling, you can never be too much."

Twenty minutes later I am rushing down the street with my shopping bags in tow, and I dial Thomas's number.

Hello, you've reached Thomas Stone. I can't take your call right now.

Leave a message and I'll call you back.

Shit.

"Hello, Thomas, this is Alora Sorenson, I spoke to you earlier today. I would just like to thank you so much for offering to come tonight but my situation has changed and I don't need you anymore. Please send me a bill for your booking fee, I'm happy to still pay. Thanks…and if you could you please text me back when you get this message just so I know that you got it. Goodbye."

I let out a sigh of relief, okay so that's done. I need to find a cab and then to get back to the hotel and do my hair. I glance around and notice a hair salon on the corner, they won't have any appointments but I guess I can try my luck. I push through the front doors. "Hello, I was wondering if you have time for a quick blowout?"

"Now?" the gentleman asks.

"If possible. I'm on a really tight deadline."

"Yes, I have an opening right away, please come through."

"Really?" I smile, very pleased with myself as I follow him, this is all happening so easily, dress, shoes and now hair, maybe it's a good sign. I take a seat in the chair and he comes to stand behind me. "How would you like your hair done today?"

"I have a date tonight and I just want to look…" I shrug, embarrassed, "…better than this."

He laughs as he fiddles with my hair with his hands. "Better than this coming right up."

I hold the phone to my ear as I pace back and forth.

> Hello, you've reached Thomas Stone. I can't take your call right now.
>
> Leave a message and I'll call you back.

"Answer the phone, damn it."

I haven't heard from the elusive Thomas Stone, which means I have no idea if he got my message, which means he could possibly turn up here any minute.

Beep, sounds the answering machine.

"Hi, Thomas, it's Alora, and it's imperative that you call me back urgently please. I have left five messages for you this afternoon and I would just like to reiterate that I don't need your company tonight and I need to know that you got my message. Call me as soon as you get this message please." I hang up and throw my phone onto the bed, how hard is it to have common manners these days? All he had to do was send back a one-word text or even a thumbs-up. Anything would do.

Ring, ring, ring, ring.... The hotel phone bellows through the room.

Huh? I haven't heard one of these things ring in years. "Hello," I answer with a frown.

"Bonjour, Miss Sorenson. This is Annika from the front reception."

My eyes widen in horror, oh no. "Hello."

"We have a Thomas Stone here to see you, can we send him up?"

Fuck, fucking, fuck.

Oh hell, he mustn't have got the message, I can't not let him up. I'll just tell him I don't need him when he gets up here. Shit, what if he's angry that I wasted his time?

"Um...sure."

"Merci." I hang up and jump up and down on the spot in a silent freakout. Oh my god, you idiot Alora. I've had some hairbrained ideas in my life, but this has to take the cake. Five of the slowest minutes later, my worst nightmare comes true.

Knock, knock.

I put my head into my hands, this *cannot* be happening.

Knock, knock, sounds again.

Argh!

I open the door in a rush. "Hello."

"Hello, Alora." He smirks. He's wearing a sports coat and jeans. His hair has a curl to it and he has big blue eyes. "Tried to cancel on me, did you?"

Oh no…he's cute. Like really cute, hot even…and I want the earth to swallow me whole.

Help!

"I'm so sorry to waste your time, but I don't—"

"Yes you do." He cuts me off before walking past me into my room.

"No, really, I honestly don't need you anymore."

"Let me guess." He flops onto my bed. "You are going to a function and someone you know is going to be there and you need to make them sweat."

I open my mouth to reject his claim but nothing comes out.

"I do this for a living, Alora." He smiles. "You have nothing to worry about, and we are going to make whoever it is squirm." He looks me up and down. "You are absolutely gorgeous, by the way."

I puff air into my cheeks as I look him over. "You are not what I expected."

"What did you expect?"

"I don't know."

"More Fabio?"

"Maybe." I smile.

He has this fun playful air about him.

"Well, a little about me. I'm a doctor. American."

"A doctor?" I gasp.

"But I don't practice anymore because I make a shit ton more money dating beautiful women." He raises his eyebrows. "Which is satisfying in many more ways."

I giggle at his front. "I imagine."

"And I'm here to meet a client tomorrow and you're in luck."

"Look, honestly I don't need you anymore. It was a dumb idea."

He gets up and goes to the fridge and grabs a bottle of champagne and two glasses. "Tell me your dumb idea."

"Well, there's this guy."

"There always is." He smiles as he fills our glasses and passes me one. "Cheers."

"Cheers." I take a swig.

"Go on."

"Anyway, we met a few years ago when I was in Switzerland for the weekend and we had a…."

"Great time." He finishes my sentence.

"We didn't exchange details and we knew nothing about each other, but I've recently run into him."

"What happened when you saw him again?"

"We were at a charity auction and the next minute we rushed upstairs and kissed, which is a complete nightmare because we are with other people."

"Hmm, I see." He sips his champagne.

"I mean…we were with other people but we've now both become single."

"Because of each other or…."

"Well." I roll my eyes. "Maybe on my behalf but not on his. I came to Paris for the weekend to try and forget about him but he showed up today at a work meeting and was flirting with our co-worker and he's taking her on a date tonight."

He listens intently.

"And I wanted to leave, so I told a lie that I came to Paris to meet a man."

He smiles into his glass as he listens. "Nice."

"But it's not nice because he called my bluff and said we should go on a double date tonight and I panicked and said yes."

"And that's when you called me."

I take a huge gulp of champagne and slosh it around my mouth. "This story sounds worse when I hear it out loud."

"Alora." He smiles calmly. "I do this for a living. You are in safe hands."

"I don't want to have sex with you," I blurt out.

He chuckles. "Well, that's a shame, you're hot as hell."

"Thomas." I widen my eyes. "Be serious."

"It's fine, we go meet him and his date. We get on great and put on a little show. We leave and then boom."

"Boom?"

"Suddenly you have control because he knows that someone else is in the arena and maybe he should man up before you get snapped up."

My eyes hold his.

"Trust me on this, it works every time."

"I don't know." I twist my lips as I think. "This guy isn't a normal guy."

"What, is he like a vampire or something?"

"Probably." I sigh. "He's just very…dominant and bossy and…."

"I can handle him."

My eyes search his.

"We'll stay half an hour and then we're out of there."

I chew my bottom lip as I think.

"Do you want this guy or not?"

"Honestly, I don't even know anymore."

"Work that out when he wants you." He stands. "Come on, let's get to it."

"To it?"

"Tell me a little bit about you so I can at least hold a conversation."

"Oh, my name is Alora Sorenson, I own an antique shop in Nice, also American."

"How did we meet?"

"Um." I shrug. "How *did* we meet?"

"I'm a doctor and you were a patient of mine and I was besotted with you."

That sounds cool. I bite my lip to hide my smile.

"Nice to meet you, Alora Sorenson." He smiles as he clinks his drink with mine once more.

"Nice to meet you, Dr. Thomas Stone." I smile back, this guy is so unexpected, cute, and smart and not in the least what I expected. "What the hell are you doing in this job?"

He chuckles. "Having the time of my life." He drains his glass and holds his hand out to mine. "Are you ready to do this?"

"I guess." I wince. "But just so you know, we are not having sex tonight."

His eyes sparkle with mischief. "But if we do, we do. No harm done."

"We aren't." I smile as I take his hand in mine.

"Okay, only maybe." He pulls me out the door. "What's this guy's name anyway?"

"Edward."

"Okay, Edward, prepare to sweat."

We walk down the hall and get into the elevator and he steps toward me and fixes my hair, his eyes drop down to my breasts and he runs a finger over my clavicle. "You are absolutely gorgeous," he breathes as his gaze follows his finger.

Nerves dance in my stomach at his touch.

He leans in and kisses my cheek. "Let's go get him," he whispers in my ear. The elevator doors open. "It's showtime." He takes my hand and leads me through the foyer. "Where are we going?"

"Just to the bar in this hotel."

"Alright." He looks around. "This way." We walk through a corridor and into a large bar area, it's painted in a dark maroon and the furniture is all vintage. There is a huge dark wooden bar in the center with chunky big stools around it.

"Hmm, it's pretty nice in here, actually." I smile, impressed.

"It is." He looks around. "Are they here yet?"

"No, I don't see them."

"Let's go stand in the corner over there."

"Okay,"

"I'll get us a drink. Another champagne?"

"Yes please."

He disappears to the bar and I stand to the side; I still can't believe I am actually going through with this, my mind is a whirl of possibilities. "Here you are, my dear." He passes me a glass of champagne. "I got us the good stuff."

"Thanks." I smile as I take a sip. "Oh yum." From my peripheral vision I catch sight of Edward walking into the bar. "Here he comes."

"Where?"

I point with my chin as I glance over to see that he has a beautiful woman on his arm. "Who the hell is *that* girl?" I frown. "Where's Nell?"

"Which one is he?"

"The guy in the navy jacket."

"Oh fuck." Thomas spins to turn his back to them.

"What's wrong?"

"I know him."

"What?" My eyes widen in horror. "You *know* him?"

Edward and the woman go to the bar.

He drags his hand through his hair. "You didn't tell me he was a Kingsman."

"A what man?"

"That's what they call them."

"Who?"

"Society."

"What the hell are you talking about?" I whisper angrily.

"The Riviera Brat Pack, they call them the Kingsmen." He's openly rattled. "You're going to get me fucking killed."

"You actually know him?" I begin to sweat as I see Edward approaching us from my peripheral vision.

"I don't know him as such, I know who he's friends with: Sinclair Montague, and the prince, Theodore Chapelle. His name is Edward Prescott, right? He's the casino mogul."

"Yes." The blood drains from my face. "Oh my god, you *do* know him? Your ad says you were discreet," I whisper. "You don't seem very discreet so far."

"Change of plans," he whispers. "Just roll with it."

"Roll with what?"

"Good evening." Edward's swoony voice cuts the air.

"Hello." I smile.

Thomas turns toward him. "Hello."

Edward's eyes land on Thomas and he blinks as if surprised.

"Edward, this is Thomas. Thomas, this is Edward," I splutter.

Thomas holds his hand out. "Nice to meet you."

Edward nods but doesn't reply, his eyes are locked on Thomas's.

"Haha, who is this?" I laugh in a high-pitched voice.

So help me god.

"My apologies." Edward snaps out of it. "This is Colette." He puts his hand on the small of her back as he introduces her.

"Bonjour." She smiles as we shake her hand. She has long blond hair and a stunning face. She's wearing a skintight black dress that leaves nothing to the imagination.

Who the hell is this woman…and why is his hand on her back?

Does he just have beautiful women on speed dial everywhere he goes…ugh, and why are they always blond? My eyes dart around as I search for the closest exit and that's when I see his three bodyguards standing by the wall, watching us.

Perspiration dusts my skin and a fully fledged panic attack is imminent.

"So Colette, are you a local?" Thomas smiles calmly.

"Oui."

He says something to her in French and she laughs and says something back.

Edward's cold eyes hold mine; he's openly pissed.

Well, that makes two of us…get your hand off her, *asshole.*

"So what did you do today?" Edward asks me.

"Um." I try to think on my feet. "Had lunch. Went shopping, got a blowout."

Witty….

Edward's eyes roam over my hair as if deciphering whether I'm lying.

"What did you do?" I ask nervously.

"Lots of things." He sips his drink and turns his attention back to Thomas. "So, Thomas, what's your surname?"

"Oh my gosh, did you see what they have on the menu?" I cut him off.

"Yes I did." Thomas plays along. "We're going to have to get it."

Edward's jaw clenches as he glares at Thomas.

"Let's get one." I grab Thomas's hand and pull him to the bar.

"Shit. Shit. Shit," I whisper.

"What are you shitting about, I'm the one about to be murdered." He opens the menu. "Great knowing you, Alora, we should have had sex before we came down so it was at least worth it."

My eyes linger on Edward and Colette as they chat. "Do you think she's pretty?"

"Who fucking cares?" he whispers. "We need to leave. Now!"

"Oh, you think?" I widen my eyes. "And for the record, you are terrible at being discreet."

"Says the woman trying to piss off the most powerful man in Europe, have you gone completely fucking mad?"

"I'm in the middle of it right now," I whisper angrily.

"What will it be?" the bartender asks.

"Umm…." I open the menu.

"Do tell what this great thing that we have to order is?" Thomas raises an eyebrow.

"Dead in a ditch looks good." I smile through gritted teeth.

"Be careful what you wish for, Alora." He smiles sweetly. "I'm pretty sure his bodyguards kill people for less."

I look over at them. "You think?"

"I know." He widens his eyes. "You do not fuck with this man."

"Oh." I frown. "Maybe just—"

"Order some goddamn drinks." He cuts me off.

My eyes scan the choices on the menu. "If you only listened to me, I did tell you not to come."

"Oh, so this is my fault."

"Absolutely."

"For the record." He continues reading the menu. "If we do happen to survive tonight, we are one hundred percent having sex."

"Oh my god. Stop talking," I whisper angrily. "Just get me the fuck out of here."

EDWARD.

I watch Alora and Thomas at the bar, furious.

"Excuse me for a moment, I'm just going to the bathroom," I tell Colette.

"Sure."

I walk past my men and give them a subtle nod; they follow me out to the foyer.

"Yes, boss?"

"Who is that man with Alora?"

They exchange glances. "No idea."

"I want a name and address, you have ten minutes." I turn and walk back to Colette.

My phone vibrates in my pocket and I dig it out.

To use facial recognition we need a close photo.

Fucking idiots. I run my tongue over my teeth in annoyance.

This is a first.

"Let me take a photo of you, Colette." I hold up my phone. "Smile."

She smiles playfully and I take a photo. I linger with my phone out waiting for them to come back from the bar and I casually glance over.

The fuck are they doing over there?

I keep pretending to take photos and eventually they come back to stand with us. *Click*. I snap a photo of Thomas and immediately send it to Philippe.

Thomas starts yapping on to Colette again and my eyes go to Alora. "So...what's the deal here?"

"What do you mean?"

I lean in closer so they can't hear us. "Who *is* this?" I gesture to Thomas with my chin.

"He's an old friend."

A surge of jealousy runs through my system like a tidal wave.

"What kind of old friend?"

"Edward, this is really none of your business, but I would like to discuss who *your* date is."

"An old friend."

She raises her glass to me and then takes a sip, animosity bounces between us.

Touché.

"We can't stay long," Alora says. "We have a dinner reservation."

I begin to hear my heartbeat in my ears.... If she leaves with him....

"Thomas, we should get going?" she tells him.

"Sure."

"One more drink." I try to stall. "My treat."

"Umm."

"I insist." I walk to the bar and order another round.

My phone vibrates with a text in my pocket and I take it out and discreetly read it.

His name is Thomas Stone.
He's a male escort.

CHAPTER EIGHTEEN

What!

My eyes rise to Philippe and he shrugs as if he's as surprised as I am.

Why would she be on a date with a male escort? As if she needs to pay for sex, every man on earth would give his left kidney to sleep with her. This doesn't make sense.

I don't get it.

I text him back,

Are you sure?

An answer flies in.

According to our sources.

Hmm....

What the fuck is going on here?

I glance over to them standing in the corner, Thomas's hand is on the small of Alora's back. He's whispering something in her ear and she smiles up at him. Something sinister comes over me like never before, I imagine him touching her and thermonuclear rage sets in.

My body simmers as I feel adrenaline pump through my veins.

Calm down....

But I already know that's an impossible task. I collect the drinks tray and walk back to the group. "Here you are." I bite the side of my cheek to stop myself from saying something that they will regret.

Alora takes her champagne and takes a nervous sip; the rest of the room disappears as my eyes hold hers.

What are you up to?

Colette's phone rings. "I have to take this."

"Of course." I nod. "Take your time."

"Bonjour," she answers as she walks out into the foyer.

Thomas's eyes come to mine. "I didn't quite catch your surname," I repeat.

He hesitates and his eyes flick to Alora's.

"Don't look at her. Look at me, Mr. Stone," I growl.

"Edward," Alora whispers.

"Don't dare *Edward* me. What the fuck are you doing here with her?" I demand.

"We're friends," Alora splutters.

"Do *not* answer for him."

Our eyes are locked and I step forward. "So you get paid to sleep with women."

"Pissed that I don't give it away for free like you?" he fires back.

I clench my fists by my sides.

We glare at each other.

"Edward," Alora whispers. "Stop it."

"I'm going to ask you again. *What* are you doing here with Alora?"

"We are old friends."

I step forward, bringing us face-to-face. "You need to leave before you meet your maker."

"Edward, stop it," Alora whispers as she looks around. "You're making a scene."

"Why should it bother you who Alora is with?" he fires back. "Aren't you here with another woman?"

"A friend."

"Does she know that?" He smiles into his drink. "Or is she here chasing her paycheck? People in glass houses shouldn't throw stones, Mr. Prescott."

I get a vision of my hand around his throat.

"We're leaving," Alora snaps.

"Don't you dare go anywhere with him. I forbid it."

"I'll do whatever I like."

"The hell you will." I step forward again.

"Is everything alright here, Mr. Prescott?" My bodyguard Philippe interrupts as he steps in between us.

"Escort this man from the premises immediately."

"I don't know what the hell is wrong with you," Thomas spits. "We're leaving anyway."

I step forward to block his way. "You lay a finger on her and I swear to fucking god," I whisper, "you are a dead man."

"Edward," Alora snaps. "Stop it."

"Is that the best you've got?" Thomas smiles. "An idle threat."

"Let's go." Philippe pushes him on the back. "Outside."

They walk off into the distance as I become glaringly aware that everyone in the bar is watching us. I drag my hand through my hair as I try to compose myself.

"What now, boss?" Herman asks.

"Don't let them out of your sight, and if he lays one finger on her...bring him to me in a body bag."

"Yes, sir." They take off after them.

I drain my glass of scotch, heart pumping hard and so angry that I can hardly see.

"What did I miss?" Colette smiles calmly as she reappears.

"We're leaving."

ALORA.

Thomas and I rush from the hotel and out onto the road. "Holy shit," I whisper as he pulls me along the crowded footpath by the hand. "That was…."

"Hectic."

"I'm so sorry to get you mixed up in this," I stammer in a fluster. "But did you have to bait him?"

"Listen, I don't know what the hell is going on with that guy, but he is out of line."

"Oh my god, *he's on a date*?" I glance back at the hotel disappearing. "He's on a fucking date?"

We cross the road. "Are we having dinner somewhere?"

"Yeah, I guess." I sigh.

He's finally single and now he's going to sleep with her....

"What do you feel like?" he asks as he turns and looks behind us.

"Anything will do at this point." I shrug. "Arsenic?"

"We're being followed."

"What?" I spin around to see the two bodyguards walking behind us. "What the hell?"

"Don't look back." He pulls me along.

"Oh my god, why are they following us?"

"To make sure I don't touch you, I'm assuming."

"What?" I spin back to see and he turns me back to the front.

"This way." He opens the door and we walk into a restaurant.

"Bonjour, est-ce que vous auriez une table pour deux ?" (Translation: Good day, do you have a table for two available?)

"Yes, this way." We follow her inside to a small table for two at the back of the restaurant.

I give a weak smile, grateful to be away from the goons.

The front door opens and the two guards walk in.

"What the hell?" I put the menu up in front of my face. "Should we run?"

"Where are we going to run to?" Thomas sighs as he takes off his jacket and hangs it over the back of his chair. "They'll just catch us anyway and proceed to cut off my fucking balls."

I turn and watch them take a seat at a table at the front. "They're just going to sit there and watch us? I can't believe this."

"We'll just have dinner and call it a night." Thomas sighs as he opens the menu.

"We're just going to let him win?" I frown.

"I would like to live a bit longer." He widens his eyes in jest. "Thank you very much."

"Wimp." I open the menu. "What kind of escort are you, this is the perfect time to hang your dick out or something."

He chuckles. "Charming."

"Puis-je prende votre commande," (Translation: Can I take your order?) the waitress asks.

"I'll have the pasta please and a glass of red."

"I'll have the gnocchi and the same red, make it a bottle," Thomas says as he closes the menu and passes it back to her, she writes down our order and leaves us alone.

"How the hell did you get mixed up with Edward Prescott?" he asks.

"I don't even know." I shrug, my heart is still racing.

"So you're sleeping with him obviously?"

"No. That's the thing, not at all."

He frowns. "I'm confused, explain this situation to me."

"Where do I even start?" I sigh.

"The beginning."

"Okay…we met at a…club three years ago."

"What sort of club?"

My eyes hold his.

"I'm a male escort, I'm pretty sure nothing you say could ever shock me."

"I guess." I blow out a defeated sigh. "We met at a kink club."

"Oh." He smiles, surprised. "*Look* at you."

"Anyway." I roll my eyes. "At this resort you're matched with a person for the weekend and you are not told their names or any personal details."

"So it's an anonymous thing."

"Exactly."

The waitress arrives and pours us a glass of wine each.

"Merci." She leaves us alone.

"Go on." He takes a sip.

"And we were matched and we met and immediately had a huge fight."

"Doesn't surprise me." He rolls his eyes. "He is pretty infuriating."

"We ended up having the most incredible weekend together… and…." My voice trails off.

"You fell in love with him."

"No, not at all."

"Really?"

"That's impossible." I shrug. "It was just sex, and you can't fall in love with someone in only a weekend."

"Improbable yes, impossible no, I don't think so." He watches me for a moment. "What happened next?"

"Nothing. I didn't see him for over three years."

"But you thought about him?"

"Every day." I glance back to the guards, who now have soft drinks in front of them. "I live in Nice and…."

"You live in Nice?" He puts his hand on his chest. "I have a place in Antibes."

"You do?" I laugh in surprise. "That's like half an hour from me, are you there full-time?"

"I started out only being there for a month a year but most of my work now is in Europe so it's a great base for me to work out of."

"I can't believe you are an escort," I whisper as I lean onto my hand. "What's that like?"

"Actually…." He smiles. "It's great."

"Do you have a partner at home or…?"

"No, no. I couldn't do this job if I were in love with someone."

"How did you first get into it?"

"Honestly…. I don't even know. It started with helping out a lady when she needed a date for a wedding and we had a great time and it kind of snowballed."

"Do you sleep with everyone?"

"God no. Only the ones I'm attracted to and would sleep with on the outside." His eyes twinkle with mischief. "And if the chemistry isn't there then it isn't going ahead, I'm not chugging down the Viagra to get through the night or anything."

He has this charming honesty about him. "You must feel very free."

"Yeah." He smiles. "I guess I do."

I smile as I listen.

"Well, until tonight," he replies. "Wasn't planning on getting followed by bodyguards."

I laugh at the ridiculousness of this situation. "Can you believe he has them following us?"

"I guess…." He twists his lips as if contemplating saying something. "He could…."

"What is it?"

"I don't know if this guy is good for you."

"I know for certain that he's not."

"So what are you doing?"

"I don't know." Emotion overwhelms me at the mess I've made of my life lately. "From the moment I met him I have been under his spell and then we saw each other for the first time a couple of weeks ago and we kissed and…." I get a lump in my throat.

"What?"

"All the butterflies and the excitement that only he can bring returned and I remembered what it was like to feel this way."

He listens intently. "What way?"

"All consumed. Powerless, and hopelessly addicted."

His face is solemn as he listens.

"I had this beautiful boyfriend but I could think of nothing else but Edward."

"The relationship fell apart?"

I nod, feeling stupid. "What do you know about him?"

"Prescott?"

"Yeah."

"Well…." He exhales as if searching for the words. "I know his friends. There's like six or seven of them. They play in a prestigious Monte Carlo polo team called the Kingsmen and the name stuck, so now everyone calls them that."

"Who are his friends?" I ask, interested.

"Let's see, there's Alexander York and Nicholas Anastas, Sinclair Montague, um, Jacques Vermont and Prince Theodore Chapelle."

"How do you know them?"

"We have run in the same circles for years."

"You run in the same circles as the Prince of Monaco?" I frown.

He gives a playful shrug.

"Oh my god." My mouth falls open as I do the math. "You see women that they know?"

"One woman that they know."

"Do they know what you do?" I ask.

"I'm assuming they will soon now that Prescott knows."

"Oh crap, I've ruined everything, haven't I?"

"Not at all." He puts his hand over mine. "All I'm saying is to be careful. From what I hear, Edward Prescott is ruthless and will stop at nothing to get what he wants."

"I'm getting the gist of that, but the thing is he hasn't made an effort to get me. Sexual innuendo and flirting, sure, but there has been no effort to sweep me off my feet at all. It's like I'm a big game to him, just because we slept together in the past he now has the right to treat me however he wants." I sigh, I glance over to the guards and one of them points at Thomas's hand on mine and I snap my hand back like it's on fire.

"This is ridiculous." I think for a moment about what else I want to know. "Does he cheat, is Edward a cheater?" I ask. "Because I really hate cheaters."

"I don't know." He catches his bottom lip with his teeth. "I know women throw themselves at all of them and in the past they have been major players. Nicholas is gay and was married but his husband, Pierre, died in a skiing accident. His husband was a super-wealthy local and that's how he met the others." He frowns as if remembering something. "Actually, come to think of it, isn't Edward going out with Princess Hermione?"

"He was."

"They broke up?"

"Yes."

"Because of you?" His eyes widen.

"I don't know."

"How did he know you were in Paris?"

"I told him I was coming."

"So he followed you here?"

"I don't think so. I thought he came here to meet Nel, a woman he works with, but now that he's on a date with someone else I have no idea what's going on."

"Here you are." The waitress puts our meals down on the table in front of us.

"Merci."

We eat in silence for a while. "So what are you going to do?" he asks.

"I need to forget him. I know he's bad for me."

"What makes you so sure?"

"Because my heart is not safe. I have no defenses against him. If he broke me I wouldn't recover because I am totally and utterly…."

"In love?"

I shrug as I try to articulate my thoughts. "In lust, in denial, in a fatal fucking attraction movie. I know I just need to forget him once and for all."

"Somehow I don't think you're going to be able to do that."

I exhale heavily. "What would you do if you were me?"

"Run headfirst into the fire." He gives me a sad smile.

"Why?"

"Because what I wouldn't give to feel like that about someone."

"Even if you knew it was going to end badly?"

"It's better to have loved and lost than to never have loved at all."

"Why do I get the feeling that you're a hopeless romantic, Mr. Thomas Stone?"

"Maybe in another life." He smiles as he takes a bite of food off his fork. "This one's too fun as it is."

An hour and a half later we walk back to the hotel with the guards trailing behind, it's been the weirdest night, they haven't tried to hide from us and only once interacted with me when Thomas put his hand on mine. But other than that they are just loitering around. We get to the corner opposite the hotel and we stop on the spot.

"I...." He looks over to the hotel. "I would offer to come in...but."

"Of course." I smile. "Thanks for being a great listener."

"Anytime." He smiles back. "So lunch next week?"

"I'd love to. Call me."

"Okay." He kisses my cheek.

"Move along," a stern voice says from behind us.

"Yeah, yeah," Thomas scoffs. "Bye, Alora. Good luck." He turns and walks off down the street and I turn and scowl at the men. "We're just friends. Not that it's any of your business."

"Just doing our job, madam." He shrugs as he gestures to the hotel. "This way."

Great, now I'm being told to go to bed.... While Edward is off on his date.

I look left and then right, maybe I should just run for it and go and stay in another hotel for the night. But then my things are inside and I have to find another hotel at this hour, ugh it's not even worth the drama.

I trudge across the road and walk into the foyer and get into the elevator. The doors close and I stare straight ahead. Thomas is right, this isn't a healthy situation. Edward Prescott can bring nothing to me that would enhance my life; so far all he's done is decimate it.

I need to forget him.

The crack of light through the drapes has moved all the way across the bedroom. Ticking every moment of time with it along the way. The night has been long.

I haven't heard from Edward, not that I expected to I guess.

I never do.

He spent the night with Colette no doubt, while I lay here like a pathetic fool.

I'm too old for this crap, when I get out of bed tomorrow, which is actually very soon, I vow to never think of Edward Prescott again.

A day in Paris heals all wounds, it's true what they say.

The warmth of the late-afternoon sun kisses my skin as I amble through the Parisian markets. I sip my hot chocolate as I look at all the stalls. I always drink hot chocolate when I'm here, but I never seem to drink it anywhere else.

Bizarre.

"Alora." I hear a voice and turn.

"Pascal," I say, surprised. "What are you doing here?"

"I'm here for the weekend. Came to see some friends, I'm staying at the Zavier."

"You're staying at the Zavier?" I frown. "That's where I'm staying."

"Really?" He smiles. "What a coincidence."

"It is. How have you been?" I ask.

"I'm okay, you?"

"Getting there." He falls in to walk along beside me.

Shit.

EDWARD.

The Rolls-Royce comes to a stop and my driver opens the car door; cameras click as I climb out. "Mr. Prescott, you must be so proud of this event," someone calls.

"I am." I nod. My phone beeps with a text in my pocket and I quickly glance at it, a message from Philippe.

Look who's here.

An image of Alora talking to someone comes through and I frown as I stare at it.

Pascal.

The fuck is he doing in Paris?

"A photo, sir?"

"Of course." I glance up and do up my black suit jacket and straighten my bow tie and stop on the bottom stair so they can get their shot.

"Thank you, sir."

I nod and make my way into the foyer.

"Late to your own party, I see," a familiar voice says. I smile and turn to see Theo standing by the door.

"Wish I wasn't even here," I mutter as I shake his hand. "The worst host in history." He smiles. "Always so accommodating."

"Fuck off," I mutter under my breath.

Theodore Chapelle, also known as the Crown Prince of Monaco, who moonlights as one of my best friends.

"Where's Sinclair?"

"Already inside."

I straighten my cuff links as we walk through the grand foyer, my mind a clusterfuck of fury.

What the hell is Pascal doing in Paris?

Was this planned?

I've had no sleep, spent the entire night pacing while trying to stop myself from going to Alora's room and then had to return to Monaco first thing this morning to come to this stupid event, now to find out that she's in Paris with her ex... my blood is boiling.

I drag my hand through my hair to try and regain my composure.

"You hungover?" Theo asks as we take the stairs.

"No, why?"

"You look like shit."

My eyes flick over to him as we continue up the stairs to the top. "Looked in the mirror lately?"

He chuckles and then looks over and winces.

"What?" I follow his line of sight.

Fuck.

I take a drink off a passing tray and dart to the left and hopefully out of sight. Theo follows me.

"I didn't know the king was coming?"

"Neither did I." I feel my stress levels rise another ten notches. Hermione's father is here, Volter the King of Switzerland.

"You'd be pretty high on his hit list right now, I'm imagining," Theo whispers as he cranes his neck to look his way.

"There you are," Nicholas says as he comes down the corridor. "Stay out of the ballroom." He shakes my hand. "Slight problem." And here's another of my best friends, Nicholas Anastas.

"What's that?" I glance around, I'm not worried about a slight problem in the ballroom, I have a *major* fucking problem in Paris.

I just want five minutes' peace to call Philippe and see what the hell is going on.

"Oh...fuck." He spins toward me and widens his eyes. "Here it comes."

"Here he is." Sinclair appears out of the ballroom with Hermione on his arm. "I told you I'd find him."

"Oh, thank you." Hermione smiles up at me before reaching up and kissing my cheek. "I've missed you, darling."

I glare at Sinclair and he smirks and winks.

Fuck. You.

This particular best friend has no greater joy than winding us up.

The smart-ass of all fucking smart-asses.

Sinclair is the owner of a tech start-up, his family were the original owners of Formula One Racing.

The thing about living in Monaco is, the friends I keep are all as wealthy as I am. A tax-free country definitely has its advantages. We met as teenagers; our families had superyachts at the marina here in Monte Carlo. We were around the same age and started hanging out together during vacation, little did I know back then that one day we would all end up living here full-time and they would become the best friends I could ever ask for.

Eccentric assholes.

Coming from old money definitely has its advantages, but nobody quite understands the challenges it brings unless you've lived it yourself. The pressure of expectation that hangs over our heads firsthand. We live with it every day.

I guess that's why we're so tight, we get it.

"Can we talk?" Hermione asks.

"What are you doing here?" I ask her softly. "I didn't know you were coming tonight."

"I *had* to see you."

My eyes drift over her shoulder to see Sinclair and Theo smirking as they clink their champagne glasses, thinking this is hilarious.

Fuckers.

This is the setup of all setups.

"I have to work, now isn't a good time, Hermione," I say softly, screw him for bringing her to me. I'm going to kill him with my bare hands.

"Shall I go back and wait at your place for you to get home?" she asks hopefully. "We need to sort this mess out."

"No." I grab a glass of champagne off a passing tray and give it to her. "You go and have fun. I have to work for a bit. I'll come find you later."

"Okay." She smiles up at me.

I throw the boys a look and walk off before she tries to kiss me, this is a literal fucking disaster. I walk around the corner, take out my phone and call Philippe.

"Hi, boss."

"What's happening?"

"Nothing, they talked for about five minutes."

"Where is he now?"

"He walked off in the other direction."

"So.... Where is Alora now?"

"She's just crossing the road on the way back to the hotel."

"Okay." I feel myself relax a little. "Just um...." I try to collect my thoughts. "Don't let her out of your sight."

She's important.

"Yes, boss, I'll call you if there are any developments."

"Thank you." I stuff my phone back into my pocket and turn to Olivier, my guard who's trailing behind me. "Keep King Volter away from me at all costs."

He nods. "Yes, sir."

I glance over and smirk as the chance to repay the favor appears. "Margarite." I smile. "Bonjour."

"Edward." She kisses both my cheeks.

"Sinclair is looking everywhere for you." I take her hand. "Let me take you to him."

"He is?" Her eyes widen in excitement.

I lead her through the hall and Sinclair sees us approaching and turns his back to us in hope we don't see him. "Sinclair. I have a surprise for you." I tap him on the shoulder and he turns toward us acting surprised and I pass Margarite's hand to him. "Look who I found."

"Great." He fakes a smile as he gives me the side eye.

"Oh Sinclair, Edward told me how you've been looking for me all night?" She smiles all dreamily up at him. "I was looking for you too."

His eyes meet mine and I wink.

Theo and Nicholas smirk before clinking glasses. "Touché."

ALORA.

"Hello." I smile. "I have a booking."

"This way, madam," she says. "Can I get you a drink?"

"Sparkling water, please." She toddles off and I immediately take out my phone and google.

Edward Prescott
Previous Partners
Images.

The thing about snooping on a guy's past is this…it's stupid, highly unadvised and I do not recommend.

One star. Actually, scratch that…no stars.

For the last half hour I have studied in great detail every woman that Edward has ever dated, and you know what it has shown me?

Nothing.

Other than the fact that they are all famous, rich, and beyond beautiful.

"Alora." I hear a voice and look up and see Pascal walking through the tables toward me.

"Pascal." I frown. "What…."

"I was catching up with a friend down here but he's just called and cancelled. Stomach bug or something."

"Oh."

"Mind if I join you?"

"Ah…do you think that's a good idea?" I shrug. "I don't want to."

His face falls. "I thought you said we could be friends?"

"I mean, we are, I just…."

I'm such a bitch.

"Just sit with me until my meal comes out." I force a smile; it's got to be coming out any minute now.

He takes a seat and the waitress comes over. "Can I get you something, sir?"

"Yes." He smiles as he opens a drink menu. "We'll have a bottle of red to share."

Um….

I stare at him deadpan…. Seriously?

EDWARD.

Lucien and I walk through the whale gaming lounge en route to my office. "Prescott," someone calls. I turn to see King Volter sitting at a gaming table. "I'd like a word."

I subtly make eye contact with Lucien and he rolls his lips.

This isn't good.

I walk over to him with a smile. "Of course." I go to take a seat beside him.

"In private." He stands and marches out of the lounge and toward my office, his men scurry to keep up.

"Nice knowing you, man," Lucien whispers.

"Not in the fucking mood for this shit," I mutter under my breath as I follow him. He storms into my office, unimpressed, and I close the door with a sharp snap.

His eyes hold mine. "How has the event been?"

"Good. Cut to the chase." I pour two glasses of Blue Label scotch and pass him one. We glare at each other as animosity bounces between us. King Volter and I don't see eye to eye. We never have.

At first he didn't want me to date Hermione and then he tried to force me to marry her.

"I have recently heard a story." He lights a cigar and blows smoke my way.

"Such as?"

"You rejected the royal engagement ring."

I take a sip of scotch and slosh it around my mouth, it burns all the way down. "I did."

His jaw clenches. "Why?"

"Hermione and I won't be marrying."

"Since when?" he growls.

"That is *none* of your business. With all due respect, King Volter, this is a private matter between Hermione and me. I will not be discussing this with you."

"You son of a fucking bitch." He slams his drink down onto my desk, scotch sloshes over the side. "What kind of man makes a woman fall in love with him only to throw her aside when he tires of her company?"

"I have not tired of her company, stop being so fucking dramatic." I roll my eyes into my drink. "We are simply no longer compatible."

His eyes hold mine and he raises an eyebrow. "Who is she?"

"You need to leave."

"Prescott.... If I find out that you have another in the wings there will be hell to pay."

"Does this power trip work for you often?"

We glare at each other and he steps forward, bringing us face-to-face.

"If you hurt my daughter...it is not going to end well for you."

"Is that a threat?"

"That's a promise," he sneers.

"Get. Out," I whisper, my temperature rising.

"I'd hate for anything to happen to you." He winks as he bites down on his cigar, without another word he leaves and I feel my phone vibrate in my pocket.

Adrenaline is pumping through my veins. "What is it?" I answer.

"Um, boss. We've got a problem," Philippe replies.

"What now?" I snap.

"Pascal has joined Alora for dinner."

I inhale sharply as the sky turns apocalyptic red. "Put. Her. On. The. Phone."

CHAPTER NINETEEN

ALORA.

"And then I went to look at the apartment but it wasn't anywhere near what was advertised," Pascal continues as he sips his wine.

I catch my bottom lip with my teeth as I glance around, Pascal has settled right in as if we are old friends. I couldn't leave because I had already ordered and I had to stay and eat my dinner, but there is a giant elephant in the room as to why he is hanging around.

We are no longer together, and yet here he is acting exactly like he did when we were? He's talking about old stories and telling me all about what he's been doing lately and it's been nice to see him, and I mean, I don't want to be rude. He is a lovely man who I care a great deal for, but I would rather he just come out and say what he wants to say instead of acting as if we are long-lost friends.

Philippe appears through the restaurant. "Hello, Miss Sorenson."

What the hell is Edward's guard still doing here? I thought they left this morning. I glance around, wait, is he here?

Philippe passes me the phone as his eyes hold mine. "You have a phone call, Alora."

What the hell?

"I have to take this; I'll be back in a moment," I tell Pascal as I get up and walk out into the foyer. "Hello."

"What the fuck are you doing!" Edward bellows, nearly bursting my eardrum. I hold the phone away from my ear.

"Excuse me?" I glance around and head out the front door of the hotel into the street. "Where are you?"

"Monaco."

"So why is Philippe still here?" I demand.

"Keeping an eye on you. Why the fuck is Pascal there? You told me you broke up."

"Do not speak to me like that, Edward. I won't have it," I whisper angrily.

"Then do not disobey me because I *won't* have *that*."

"What the hell are you talking about?" I whisper angrily. "I bumped into him. It was a complete coincidence."

"Like hell," he yells. "There is nothing coincidental about this."

I screw up my face in disbelief, what the fuck is this guy on?

"Since when do I have to do as you say, Edward, we aren't together."

"Last night it was a male escort and tonight it's your fucking ex," he bellows as he completely loses control.

"Stop yelling like a lunatic." From my peripheral vision I see Philippe walk out behind me and I turn on him like the devil. "Go inside," I snap, annoyed.

He holds both hands up as if surrendering but doesn't move.

Fucker.

"You are purposely trying to piss me off," Edward growls through the phone.

"Keep yelling and I am hanging up on you."

"You. Will—" he screams.

I hang up on him mid-sentence. "Idiot." My phone immediately rings and I hit decline. "Don't even."

I turn and storm over to Philippe. "Listen here, you. If you are intent on following me around, do not cause me trouble. Edward is losing his living shit right now over nothing."

"Just doing my job."

"If you are following me then you do as I say," I snap. My phone rings again. "What do you want?" I answer as I move away from Philippe so he can't hear the conversation.

"Don't. You. Dare. Hang. Up. On. Me."

I roll my eyes. "Then stop yelling at me."

"I'm here trying to work while doing all I can to hide from Hermione only to find out that you are having dinner with your fucking ex."

What?

Why would he even care?

"Hermione is there?" I ask.

"Yes," he fumes.

"Did you invite her?"

"No, I did not. The casino is an open business, I have no control over who visits."

I imagine her all glammed up and looking beautiful and yet here he is being jealous over me, my mind begins to race with hope.

Maybe, just maybe...in some fucked-up psychopath kind of way, he cares.

"I was having dinner and Pascal walked in and his friend bailed on him, he asked if he could sit and have a chat, what was I supposed to say?"

"No. You were supposed to say no, Alora."

I think for a moment. "Okay," I say softly. "Why, Edward?"

Silence.

"Why don't you want me with Pascal?"

"We have unfinished business. You know we do."

"So if we have unfinished business, why did you leave with another woman last night?"

"I didn't touch her."

I screw up my face. *That's bullshit.*

"I have to go," I snap.

"To do what?"

I know this is toxic as all hell, but I want to see what he says if I play along with him. "I'm going to go inside and tell him."

"Tell him what?"

"Goodbye." I shrug. "That we are over for good and to not contact me again."

"Thank you." His voice softens.

I frown as I listen. "You do the same."

"I plan on it."

We hang on the line waiting for the other to say something.

"What's going on?" I ask. "Between us?"

"I don't know."

Wrong answer....

"If you don't know, why have you left a guard here in Paris to spy on me?"

"To keep you safe."

"From other men?"

"Just go to bed, Alora," he demands.

"You can't tell me what to do, Edward." My temper rises.

"For the love of god. You are stressing me the fuck out. Go back to your room alone and go to bed."

"Or what?"

"Or there will be hell to fucking pay!" he screams.

Click.

The phone goes dead.

Oh my fucking god, he did not just hang up on me. I dial his number. *Ring....*

"What?" he snaps.

"Do not fucking dare hang up on me." I hang up on him and turn my phone off.

I march over to Philippe like the Terminator. "Do not mess with me or I will fucking end you."

His eyes widen and he lets out a surprised chuckle.

"And you can tell your wimpy boss to go fuck himself."

He does laugh out loud this time.

"Nothing about this is funny, Philippe," I growl as I storm inside and I walk back in through to the restaurant and take a seat.

"Everything alright?" Pascal asks.

"Ahh, yes." I try to think on my feet. "Just a...family thing."

He glances over and sees Philippe sit at another table. "Who is that man?"

"Umm."

He frowns as his eyes come back to me. "Is he...."

I swallow the lump in my throat, please don't say it.

"Is he one of Prescott's guards?"

I can't lie.

"He is," I murmur.

"So you're with Prescott now?"

"Pascal," I whisper. "No."

His eyes search mine. "You left me because you kissed him."

"No. He's not the reason we broke up."

"But you *are* seeing him and it's been all of three weeks?"

"I'm not. I swear to you."

"He's with the princess, Alora." He screws up his face in disgust. "So you're going to be his side chick?"

"No," I snap.

He gives a disgusted shake of his head. "So how long were you thinking about him while you were with me?"

From the minute I saw him.

"Pascal, you're a really great man. You deserve better than what we were together."

"Did you sleep with him?" His eyes turn murderous. "Were you and he fucking while you were with me?"

"It's not like that," I stammer.

"That's exactly how it is." He slams his hand down on the table, making me jump. "That fucking asshole," he cries.

"Everything alright here?" Philippe asks.

Pascal's heartbreak is palpable and guilty tears fill my eyes, physically I've done nothing but yes, I was definitely thinking of Edward while I was with him. "Pascal was just leaving."

"I'll never forgive you for this," Pascal spits as he stands. "I hope he breaks your heart like you have mine." He marches from the restaurant.

My shoulders slump in disappointment, that couldn't have gone worse.

Philippe gives me a sympathetic smile as if only now understanding what has just happened. "Can I get you anything, Miss Sorenson?" he asks softly.

"I'm going to have another drink before I go up to my room."

"Alright." He calls for the server. "I'll just be over at my table. Edward will call me to check on you in two minutes anyway."

Why?

"How many times has he called you to check on me today?" I ask.

"At least ten."

Hmm, I need intel.... All of it.

"Will you sit down and have a drink with me?" I ask.

"I'm not...."

"I know you're not supposed to talk to me, but I did tell you that I would end you, and I'm feeling pretty gangster about it, so.… We kind of have to be friends now."

He gives me a lopsided smile and sits down opposite me. "Maybe just one drink won't hurt."

"Thanks." With a shaky hand I pour us both a glass of wine. "I didn't expect to see my ex here tonight, you know? This whole situation has me very on edge."

He takes a sip. "Miss Sorenson, if I may speak out of turn."

"Please."

"Mr. Prescott is acting very out of character at the moment."

"How so?"

"Before today he's never once called before to check on a partner. When they are with me and under my care, he never thinks twice about them."

"He hasn't?"

"No."

"How long have you worked for him?"

"Nine years."

"Oh." My eyes hold his. "But Edward and I aren't together."

"Are you sure about that?"

I stare at him as I try to connect the dots…*does he like me?*

He taps the side of his nose with a wink as if to say it's a secret. "Not a word."

Click.

The clock scrolls to 1 a.m.

I lie on my side in the darkness, sleep evades me, I thought he'd call me when he calmed down.

Perhaps he won't.

Yes, he was checking on me, but maybe right at this very moment he's probably kissing her. I get a vision of them together at the charity auction and how perfect they looked together.

The Princess of Switzerland and the English casino mogul, a match made in heaven.

With every moment that passes the more my certainty that they are going to get back together increases. She's beautiful and well connected, a fucking princess for Pete's sake.

I roll onto my back and stare up at the ceiling. My stomach is in knots, my anxiety at an all-time high, every emotion seems heightened and out of balance.

My mind goes back to where we met. Switzerland, what *was* he doing at the Establishment?

At the time I thought that he wanted to hold control over someone, but now that I know him better it's blatantly obvious that he controls everything and everyone anyway, so I'm not so sure anymore.

Maybe he's just a pervert who frequents sex clubs, looking for his next kink. Maybe that was just an average weekend for him. He's probably had another two hundred weekends just like it since.

Stop it.

I roll my eyes, disgusted by my own insecurities.

Ring, ring... ring, ring.... My phone vibrates on the side table and with a pounding heart I scramble to answer it.

Mr. Doe

He's calling me....

He wants to talk.

"Hello."

"Hi, Doe."

My heart pounds at the mere sound of his voice, husky and soft.

"Did I wake you?"

"No." I sigh, *I was hoping you'd call.*

I scrunch up my face, play it cool.

"You went straight home," he says; his voice is different than it was earlier, soft, and cajoling.

"I did."

"Thank you."

I frown, he's thanking me for doing as he asked.

"How did the event go?"

"It was good." He seems tired...or quiet.... Off.

"Are you okay?" I ask.

"Yeah." He sighs. "A bit of a rough end to the night."

"What happened?"

"I snuck out of there and went back to my yacht and…." His voice trails off.

"Go on." I bite my lip as I listen.

"Hermione turned up and was causing a scene on the marina when she wasn't permitted to board."

"Oh."

"It's a wonder you didn't hear her from Paris."

"You do crazy things when you're heartbroken." I try to make him feel better. "Did you go and talk to her?"

"I did."

I close my eyes, unsure if I want to hear what he's going to say next. "How did that go?"

"Not great."

We stay silent on the line, waiting for the other to say something.

"Eventually…I left." He sighs.

"You left her on the yacht?"

"I had no choice; she was completely losing it."

"Is she okay?"

"She had her staff with her, and mine were there too. I knew that if I was removed from the situation she would calm down and listen to them. She will be safely back at her place now."

"Where are you now?"

"I'm at a friend's apartment."

"Are you okay?"

"It's not a nice feeling to break a heart."

"I know."

"Anyway…." He tries to change the subject. "How was your day?"

"Not as dramatic as yours."

Silence….

"I didn't mean to scream at you."

I smile. "Yeah you did."

"Maybe a little," he replies. "I just saw red when…."

"When what?"

"When I think of you with someone else."

"Why?"

"You know why."

I bite my bottom lip with a smile, more than he knows…I do know why.

"I just have a lot on my mind right now," he continues.

"Okay."

"Just…." He cuts himself off.

"Just what?"

"Can you just not…."

I wait for him to elaborate but he stays silent.

"What do you want from me, Edward?"

"I don't want you to be with anyone else."

Why?

Play along.

"I'm not interested in anyone, Edward. Spending time with another man is the very last thing on my mind."

He stays silent on the other end of the phone and honestly, what is going on with him? Is this his way of telling me that we have something, or?

He's so confusing.

"Philippe said you told him that you were going to end him." I can tell that he's smiling.

"Oh, hell." I smile, embarrassed. "I don't even know what I said, I was too infuriated to think straight."

"He was impressed."

I giggle. "Where are you?"

"Lying on the couch, I called you as soon as I got in."

I picture the enigmatic Mr. Prescott lying on a couch in his black dinner suit calling me and I get that giddy excited feeling that only he can deliver.

"I should let you go…. It's late," he whispers.

I hold on the line, not wanting to get off the phone.

"Good night, Doe."

"Good night, Edward. Sweet dreams."

"With you involved, they always are."

Oh….

The line goes dead and I flop back on the bed and smile up at the ceiling.

In his own fucked-up way, I think he just asked me to wait for him.

EDWARD.

"More caviar, sir?"

"Thank you."

The waiter places another tray of caviar down onto the table.

"What I want to know is what was in those cocktails last night." Sinclair sighs, he's lying on a deck chair beside the table, wearing sunglasses and a good dose of green at the gills.

"Alcohol," I reply as I cut my bread. "You should stop drinking, you can't handle it."

"That's it!" a woman screams from a yacht a few down from the one we are on. "I'm leaving."

We all turn. "Is that coming from...."

"Good. Because if you don't, I fucking will." A male voice echoes through the marina.

"Uh-oh." Theo smirks. "Trouble in paradise."

"You're nothing without me," she screams.

"Ha," he bellows. "You're nothing without your fucking handbags."

"What a dumb comeback." Theodore screws up his face. "Seriously...handbags, is that the best he's got?"

"Fuck you!" she cries.

"I already did that," he yells back.

We all laugh at his stupid reply.

"Abysmal." Nicholas raises an eyebrow as we all listen in.

"I think I was drugged." Sinclair throws the back of his arm over his eyes. "Just the smell of that food makes me sick."

"Only you could be sick from lobster and caviar."

"Oh god, don't say it, I'm gagging."

Theo and Nicholas roll their eyes at his dramatics and I chuckle. "Drink more water."

"It's not working," he moans.

"Elsie, can you find this idiot some Tylenol or something?" Theo asks. "Put us all out of this misery."

"Yes, sir."

"Just throw him overboard, Elsie," I say as I peel a shrimp.

Elsie smiles as she disappears.

We are on the *Serene*, having lunch on Theo's yacht.

More screaming, more slamming, more dramatics echo over the marina. "That's it, I *am* leaving. For real this time."

"Promises. Promises," Alexander yells back. "Hurry up. I'm waiting to go out."

We all chuckle again.

"He's such a prick." Nicholas shakes his head as he peels a shrimp.

"Margarite looked good last night, Sinclair." Theo smirks as he crunches on some ice.

"Stop." He holds up his hand in a stop signal. "I honestly don't know how it happens."

"I think it goes something like, Sinclair, do you want to come back to my place?"

"And you say.... Yes." Theo widens his eyes. "Shocking, isn't it?"

"Christ Almighty, that was the last time. I swear," he huffs.

"Until next time." I smile as I sip my drink.

"Did you know Hermione was coming last night?" Theo asks me.

"No, and don't remind me. The night ended on a total nightmare."

"What happened?"

"I left without saying goodbye, trying to avoid a scene. Twenty minutes later she turned up at the marina screaming and crying and...."

The boys stop eating as they listen.

"What happened?"

"I brought her inside and...." I throw up my hands. "Ended it once and for all and then she was completely losing it and she wouldn't leave and the situation was spiraling. I ended up leaving her with the staff on my yacht and went and slept elsewhere."

"Fuck." Theo frowns. "What's Volter going to say?"

"He already warned me earlier in the night that if I hurt her that there would be hell to pay."

"You idiot," Sinclair says with his eyes closed. "I told you not to get mixed up with her. He'll fucking kill you."

"Not if I kill him first," I mutter, annoyed.

"I thought you two were good. Out of nowhere you just break up with her. What happened?"

I shrug. "Complicated."

"You met someone?" Theo frowns.

"Kind of. Maybe." I shrug. "I don't fucking know."

"Who is she?"

"None of your business."

"When do we meet her?"

"Probably never."

"Why not?"

"Because she has no interest in money." I shrug. "And we all know what happens if they don't want money."

"They want time." Theo sighs.

"Something that we don't have a lot of."

"You idiot." Sinclair sighs. "You break up with a princess for a no-name who hates money and wants time. How is this ever going to fucking work?"

"It won't." I shrug. "I already know that." I glance over at my green friend. "Someone hurry up and throw him overboard."

"Where is she from?"

"Not far."

"So have you gone out with her.... Or?"

"What's with the twenty questions?" I chew my food.

"This is just unlike you to be secretive."

"Because I don't want to talk about it. Next subject."

ALORA.

Ring, ring.... Ring, ring.

Mr. Doe.

"Oh my god, he's calling me." I scramble to answer my phone. "Hello."

"Good evening, Miss Sorenson," his voice purrs.

The sound of his deep, velvety voice gives me butterflies. "Hi." I swoon.

You already said that.

I screw up my face, for once in your life just act cool.

"I called to see if you got home from Paris safely."

"I did. Thank you." I glance at the clock, 8:12 p.m. "Where are you?"

"In bed."

I get a vision of him all naked and sleepy, wrapped up in blankets.

"Already?"

"I had hardly any sleep last night, I'm exhausted."

Oh…I wonder did he see Hermione again after he called me, or…?

"Can you do something for me?" he asks.

I smile as excitement runs through me, is he going to ask me out on a date? "Sure."

"Check your handbag."

"What?" I frown, not at all what I expected the favor to be. My excitement dissipates.

"I want you to check your handbag."

"For what?"

"I think Pascal has planted a tracker in your purse."

"What?" I screw up my face. "No he hasn't."

"How did he know where you were last night?"

"It was a coincidence."

"No. It wasn't. In the entire city of Paris, he ran into you yesterday and then stayed at the exact same hotel and then crashed you at dinner last night."

Hmm, come to think of it, that is a little weird.

"Humor me," he says. "Put me on FaceTime and let's go through your purse."

I have a green mask on my face and a treatment in my hair, I look like a greasy alien. "No, I will just look while I talk to you." I put my phone on speaker and get up and retrieve my purse. "I'm telling you, there is no tracker in my purse. He's not like that." I begin to look through it. "What am I even looking for?"

"An AirTag or something that isn't yours."

"Like what?"

"I don't know, something that's different. Not yours."

"Nope." I dig to the bottom. "Nothing here."

"Take the items out one by one and then feel in the lining."

I roll my eyes. "You've got to be kidding."

"Just. Do. It."

I begin to take things out one by one.

So much for calling to romance me.

"What's in there," he asks.

"A purse. Makeup bag. Lipstick. Hairbrush." I keep taking things out and I pull out a pen. It's black with the name of a restaurant on it. "A pen." I stare at it for a moment. "I've never been to this restaurant."

"What is it?"

"It's a pen, but I don't know where it came from."

"Unscrew it."

"What?"

"Unscrew the fucking pen."

"Don't swear at me." I begin to get annoyed. "It's 8 on a Sunday night and I feel like I'm in the principal's office."

He exhales as if I'm annoying him too. "Just do it."

I unscrew the pen and it pops apart. "It's popped apart."

"And?"

I go through all the bits, the usual ink cartridge and spring then there's a little black cylinder attached to the barrel of ink, I hold it up and look at it suspiciously. "That's weird."

"What?"

"Theres a black cylinder attached to the barrel of ink."

"That's it."

"What?" My eyes widen.

"Philippe will be over to collect it soon."

"Oh."

Why don't you come and get it?

"I…."

Don't ask him to come over, play it cool.

"Okay."

"He's leaving now."

"My address is—"

"I know your address." He cuts me off.

"So you're a stalker too?"

"Only in my spare time," he replies, and I can tell he's smiling.

"I'll wait for Philippe."

"Good night, Doe."

Wait, that's it?

"Umm…." I think for a moment, waiting for him to say something more.

He doesn't.

"Good night, Edward." The phone clicks as he hangs up. I sit for a moment and stare at my phone, that was the weirdest phone call of all time. He calls me to talk to me, but then he doesn't even talk to me.

How odd.

EDWARD.

The sun is just going down, my elbow is resting on the car door as I watch the building. People are leaving and the street is winding down for the day.

"Come the fuck on, you idiot." I sigh. "I don't have all day."

He appears through the rotating glass door and my phone beeps with a text from the car behind.

Go time.

I get out and cross the street, I follow him around the corner and up to his car in the parking lot, my men trail behind at a safe distance.

He turns and sees me and his eyes widen. "Prescott. What are you doing here?"

"Teaching you a lesson." I put my hand around his throat and slam him up against his car. "You go near Alora again and I will *fucking* kill you."

CHAPTER TWENTY

ALORA.

"And then what happened?" Thomas frowns.

"Wait a minute, he turned up at dinner too?" Helene asks.

"Yes, and then Edward calls me and asks me to check my bag because he thought it was sus."

"I did too, remember?" Thomas agrees, he taps his temple. "I'm telling you, that Pascal is a fucking weirdo."

We're having dinner in a café as we dissect my weird and wacky weekend in Paris.

It's crowded and the television is playing the nightly news up on the wall in a corner.

"But then, he doesn't talk to me." I shrug.

"Who?"

"Edward."

"Prescott randomly calls you but doesn't talk about anything?" Thomas frowns.

"So he only called to ask about the bug?" Helene is chewing her thumbnail as she listens.

"Yeah." I shrug.

"He's so weird." Thomas frowns. "Like really fucking weird."

"I know," I scoff. "So everybody in my life at the moment is fucking weird."

"Except me." Thomas widens his eyes.

"You're the weirdest, have you checked out your job lately."

He chuckles and pinches his fingers as if to say *little bit.*

"Oh my god." Helene's eyes widen.

"What?"

"Look." She points up at the television and we all turn to see a picture of the hospital, the subtitles read.

In breaking news,

Monaco Councilor Pascal Deschanel has been found unconscious in the parking lot of the council chambers.

He had been savagely beaten and has multiple broken ribs.

The cameras of the parking lot had been disabled and this appears to be a targeted attack.

"Oh my god," Helene whispers as her eyes come to me. "You don't think...."

"No...." I put my hand over my mouth. "He wouldn't."

"Of course he did," Thomas snaps. "Nobody fucks with Prescott and gets away with it. Everybody knows that."

"No, surely not." I glance between the two of them. "You don't think."

"But honestly." Helene smiles, all gooey-eyed. "How is he so fucking hot?"

"Beating my ex-boyfriend is not hot."

"He was tracking you," Thomas gasps. "Do *not* blame Prescott for this, I would have done the same." He sips his drink with a shrug. "Probably not as well, though, but it would have at least been a split lip."

Helene and I giggle.

"God," I murmur, wide-eyed. "It's all so dramatic."

"I know, right?" Helene whispers. "What I wouldn't give to trade places with you right now."

"But." I hold my glass of wine up to them. "Has he called me to talk about anything.... That's a big fat no."

"Because he was too busy beating people to a pulp for you," Thomas replies. "Give the man a chance."

"He wouldn't have done it himself, he would have had one of his goons do it."

"I don't know about that." Thomas twists his lips as if thinking. "He definitely has the psycho gene."

"How do you know?" I scoff.

"I can see it in his eyes. You seem to forget that he was plotting my death on Saturday night and I was scared for my fucking life."

"Wimp."

"Agree." Thomas holds his two hands up. "Wholeheartedly."

"I like you, Thomas." Helene smiles. "How much do you charge a night?"

"I don't know, five to ten thousand. Sometimes fifty."

"Fifty thousand dollars." We both gasp.

"I'm worth every pretty penny, ladies." He flicks his hair like Fabio. "But don't get any ideas, I don't work for friends. It would be weird to go to work and then rock up to lunch the next day as if nothing happened."

We giggle as we imagine the scenario.

"Can we go out on Saturday night?" Helene asks. "I need to get messy."

"Messy." I wince. "What does that even mean? It's giving me bad visuals of genitals or something."

"Eww."

"Well, I can go, but Alora might be in the Bahamas by then being wooed by her thug boyfriend."

"Who hasn't called me." Although I secretly hope I am in the Bahamas. "Do you think I should go to the hospital and check on Pascal?"

"No," they both snap. "He was tracking you, Alora, you should be going to the police."

"We don't know it was actually him or that it was even sinister."

"Yes. We do. You don't track someone and follow them to Paris."

"But he is harmless. I know him. He's got a good heart, he would never hurt me."

"No. I'm with Prescott on this." Thomas sighs. "You stay away from him."

"Are we going?" I grab my bag and my jacket. "I've come straight from work and I've got crap to do at home." We pay our bill and walk through the front doors out onto the footpath and there, standing beside the door, are Philippe and another man in a black suit.

"What are you doing here?" I frown.

"Mr. Prescott has assigned us to you."

"For what?"

"Protection."

"I don't need protection."

"That's actually a good idea," Thomas interrupts. "She does, thank you."

"He's in the hospital half dead," I stammer. "I'm pretty sure I'm safe."

A trace of a smile crosses Philippe's face.

"Who did that to Pascal?" I ask him.

"I have no idea what you're talking about," he replies, straight-faced.

"Of course you don't." I turn to look at the other guard. "And what is your name?"

"Stefan." He smiles. "Nice to meet you, Miss Sorenson."

"Well, the pleasure is all yours, because no offense, but I don't want you guys following me around."

"It is what it is." Philippe shrugs. "We follow Prescott's orders."

"Seems like everyone does." I roll my eyes, honestly this is a joke.

Helene, Thomas and I exchange glances. *Are you actually kidding me?*

"See you guys later." I kiss them both on the cheek and look up the street.

"Where are you going?" Philippe asks me.

"To get a cab."

"We can drive you."

I stare at him for a beat. "You are actually going to follow me home?"

"Yes."

"Is Edward going to be there?"

"I have no idea."

Ugh, I need to talk to him. "Okay, fine. Thank you, a lift would be appreciated."

I follow them to the car, they open the back door for me and I slink in. We pull out into the traffic and I stare out the window as the night goes by.

If he has his guards on me…. That has to mean something, right?

God, I have no idea what's going on. Everything about this man is so confusing.

Ten minutes later we pull into my street and surprise, surprise I didn't tell them where to go. They already knew my address.

I know that Pascal is the one in the hospital but damn it, at this moment Edward feels just as unsafe to me.

Two hours later, I dial his number again.

You've reached Edward Prescott.
Leave a message.

Still not answering….

"Damn it, answer the damn phone. Call me back," I demand. "I'm getting angry, Edward."

I hang up in disgust, I've called him four times and not once has he answered. What's he doing that's so important that he can't pick up a damn phone?

Is he in jail?

I want to know if he did this to Pascal, this is important.

I go to the window and peer out onto the street to see two black cars parked in front of my house. Four men are leaning up against them, red dots glow in the dark as their cigarettes light up. They look settled in for the night.

I glance at the clock, 11:14 p.m. I'm horny and exhausted and honestly don't have the energy to worry for a moment longer. I have to work in the morning and I need to go to bed. I shower and dress and with one last look out the window at the circus down below in my street, I climb into bed.

He'll call me tomorrow.

Darkness.

I read the sign on the window,

HUNTING EQUIPMENT

I make my way inside; I walk through the aisle and pick up some rope and a weighted trap. "Can I help you?" the assistant asks.

"Yes, I am after a set of knives and a pistol."

"Of course, this way."

ALORA.

Four days.

Four fucking days of being followed by security guards and I haven't heard one single word from their prick of a boss.

He's not answering his phone, he's not texted me back.

Nothing.

So he thinks that his cheap and nasty sex show can go unaddressed, he thinks he can beat my ex to a pulp and assign unwanted bodyguards to loiter around. I've come to the conclusion that if he's not dead in a ditch, he soon will be.

Because with every day that I don't hear from him, the more my anger grows.

Who the hell does this guy think he is?

Did he do this to Pascal?

I am not a possession; he doesn't get to have guards on me without even checking with me first.

And they won't go away, I've tried every day. On my lunchbreak yesterday in a rage I even told Philippe to fuck off and he laughed.

Laughed.

Another asshole who will be dead in a ditch sooner than expected.

Pascal's mother called me crying on the phone and I had to pretend I didn't know and of course I couldn't tell her what's happened.

Not that I even actually know.

I've made the decision that I'm going to call Pascal this afternoon and see if he's alright, I can't have this on my conscience. It's eating me alive.

Well.... I've got a new plan today, I grab my purse and make my way out to their car.

"Good morning, Miss Sorenson." Philippe opens the back door for me.

"Good morning." I smile as I get into the back seat.

He gets in behind the wheel and starts the car.

"I would like to go to Edward's office please," I announce.

"Edward's in London." They glance at each other as if surprised. "You don't know that?"

Oh, hell...they think that I know what's going on. They think that Edward is keeping me updated, sorry boys, that's a hard no.

Your boss is an asshole!

"Oh, I did know that," I lie. "I thought he was back already."

"No, not until the weekend. Sunday, I believe."

Red steam shoots out of my ears and I side eye out the window.

Mother. Fucker.

"Take me to my store please."

EDWARD.

The office door opens. "Edward."

I stand, walk in and sit down.

Paul smiles as he looks me over from behind his desk. "Back in London."

"Yes."

"Tell me, how has your week been?"

"Not. Great." I bite my lip.

"What happened?"

"I...."

"Go on."

"I ended my relationship."

"Good." He smiles. "This is progress."

"Is it, though?" I shrug. "It doesn't feel like progress, feels like I've just jumped over a cliff into a pit of fire."

He chuckles. "I do always love your analogies.

"How did your girlfriend take it?"

"Terribly."

"Okay." He nods. "How was it seeing her so upset?"

I shrug, a weight sits heavily upon my shoulders. "I'm ashamed of how things turned out."

"Ashamed of yourself?"

"For hurting her."

"Yes." He nods. "I understand." He thinks for a moment, "Have you seen Alora?"

"Yes."

He smiles. "How did that go?"

"Worse."

"Worse?"

"I followed her to Paris and she was on a date."

"Oh." He frowns.

"She said he was a friend."

"Is he a friend?"

"I don't know." I shrug. "Maybe."

"Why do you think maybe?"

"She's seen him since and nothing suspicious has happened."

"How do you know that?"

"I have guards on her."

"Does she know that?"

"Yes."

"What did she say when she found this out?"

"I...." I hesitate.

"You what?"

"I haven't taken her calls since I put them on her."

"Why not?"

"I don't want to fight with her."

"Edward Prescott not wanting to fight." He sits back and smiles. "I do believe we may have progress."

"Fuck off." I roll my eyes. "I just don't want to...."

"What?"

"Antagonize her."

His eyes light up. "Are you scared of Alora?"

"I'm not scared of Alora, I'm scared of losing my temper with her," I murmur.

"Why is that?"

"It's obvious, isn't it?"

"Not to me."

"Where she's concerned, everything is heightened."

He stares at me for a beat. "You're afraid your temper will be heightened too."

I roll my lips, uncomfortable with where this is going.

"Edward, you need to have more trust in yourself. You have never been violent with women."

"Not that way, I mean I don't want her to end it," I say softly.

"So something has begun?"

"No."

"But you want it to?"

"Maybe."

"Why are you afraid that she will end it?"

"Because she's the first person I've ever met that I know actually would."

"She's as strong as you?" He frowns.

"Just as stubborn."

"Which means?"

"Which means if I fuck this up she will walk away."

"And that would be a problem?"

"Oh my fucking god. Do you listen to me at all?" I snap. "I'm leaving, as usual you are wasting my fucking time."

"Hold up, sit back down." He swings on his chair as his eyes hold mine. "Why don't you take things slow with her."

"Like how?"

"Get to know her properly. Wine and dine her. No sex, show her the real you."

"Paul. Do you have a brain at all?" I roll my eyes. "I'm an angry sex maniac. If she meets the real me then she's one hundred percent leaving."

He chuckles. "I don't think so."

"So that's your answer."

He smiles over at me.

"I fly all the way to London for you to tell me to be friends with her."

"I think it's a great idea."

"I think you're talking out of your ass." I throw my hands up. "You have no idea how hot this woman is and how *not* sleeping with her is physically impossible."

"Vulnerability is a superpower, Edward."

"No." I shake my head. "You told me last week that her bonding depends on how hard she comes. *That* is my superpower."

His eyes hold mine.

"So I'm going with that option." I stand. "I should charge you for these visits, I'm the only one here with any decent ideas."

"I'll see you next week."

"No you won't." I walk to the door. "Problem solved, I'm going to fuck her into unconsciousness."

"That's not legal."

"Who fucking cares."

ALORA.

Ring, ring.... Ring, ring.

I close my eyes, hoping he won't answer and I can just leave a message.

"Alora. Hi."

"Hi Pascal," I reply. "I saw the news and spoke to your mother. Are you okay?"

"I'm getting there." His voice has a sadness in it. "Just got out of hospital today."

"Right." I chew my lip as I try to work out what to say next. "Who did this to you?"

"I don't know. I didn't see them."

"They jumped you from behind?"

"Yes."

It wasn't Edward, he would never hit someone from behind, he would want them to know it was him.

Phew....

"What are the doctors saying?" I ask.

"I have six broken ribs and a broken eye socket and nose."

"God. You must be in so much pain," I whisper. "How awful."

"I'm on the good drugs, so I'll be fine."

"Ummm." Should I just ask him? Yes, screw it, I need to know. "Pascal, I have to ask you something."

"Yeah."

"I found an…." I try to find the right words. "A tracker in my purse. Do you know anything about it? If mean, if you put it there by accident or something while we were going out then that's okay," I stammer. "I just need to know who put it there. It's really scared me."

"What kind of tracker?"

"I don't know what type it was but it was a location tracker, it was in a pen."

"Oh." He falls silent. "What kind of pen?"

He seems genuinely shocked, it wasn't him at all.

"Why don't you ask your new boyfriend about it? He would have put it there for certain."

Huh?

"Pascal, I have to ask, did you know Edward before you met him through the council in Monaco?"

"Yes."

"How?"

"We went to school together."

What?

"You went to school with Edward Prescott?" I frown, how did I not know this?

"I got a scholarship in London for my senior year and he was there."

"Were you friends or…."

"We hated each other from day one."

"Did something happen, a particular incident?"

"He's an asshole, his friends are all assholes. That's what happened. But you'll find that out for yourself in good time."

Hmm, I am beginning to pick up on that myself.

"Well…." I hesitate. "I should let you get back to healing."

"Can I see you?"

"Pascal," I sigh. "No. This doesn't change anything between us. I wish you all the best, but I just called to check on how you are."

"I'm fine."

I have to get off the phone. "Okay, well…happy healing. Look after yourself." Before I can say another word I hang up.

Shit.

EDWARD.

"Hey, boss," Philippe says.

"Hi."

"We are outside the antique store and we have a problem with Miss Sorenson."

"Is she okay?"

"She's fine, she just…." He pauses.

"She's what?" I snap.

"She's very delicate."

I screw up my face in question. "Delicate, what do you mean, delicate? Like a flower?"

"Delicate like a hand grenade."

I smirk. "Why?"

"She's becoming very hard to manage."

"How so?"

"She doesn't want us to follow her anymore and has just stormed over to our car and is threatening to call the police on us."

"Okay." I roll my eyes. "I'll handle it."

"Can you do it soon, she's very…."

I get a vision of her being angry with them and I smile. "Very what?"

"Fired up."

First woman in history who would ever dare to tell my men off.

"Okay, I'll call her. Bye."

I immediately dial her number. *Ring, ring….*

"What do you want?" she snaps.

A broad smile covers my face at the sound of her angry voice.

Even furious, she's hot.

"I believe you meant to say, Hello, Edward."

"Nope, didn't mean to say that," she fires back. "I meant to say, what do you want?"

"I'm in London."

"So I heard."

"Watch your tone, miss."

"Don't fucking dare miss me," she snaps. "You tell your guards to leave me the hell alone."

"They are there for your safety and they will be staying with you for your safety."

"No, Edward."

"This is nonnegotiable, Alora, I need you safe."

"Why? So you can ignore me all the way from London?"

"You're angry that I haven't returned your calls?"

"I'm not angry. I'm infuriated."

I smile, even fighting with this woman excites me.

"I haven't answered your calls because I wanted to see you in person, I didn't want to fight with you over the phone."

Silence.

"I will be home on the weekend," I tell her.

"No."

"We can discuss your guard situation then."

"I don't want guards at all, ever. This isn't a spy movie and you're going way too far."

"Just humor me until I'm back in the country."

"You know what I find funny?" she fumes.

Here we go. I roll my eyes.

"You tell me to not see other people and to wait for you and then you go missing for the week?"

"I did."

"And you don't answer my calls and you don't call me back and you listen to my messages and then you still don't call me back."

"That's right."

"You know this?" she shrieks.

"I do."

"You are the most infuriating man I have ever met."

"Agreed."

"I'm going because you're patronizing me and I'm about to explode."

I chuckle.

"Are you laughing?" she gasps in outrage.

"As I just told you, I'm not fighting with you over the phone."

"Well, I'm fighting with you. Good. Bye."

Click.

I chuckle and dial Philippe's number.

"Hey," he answers.

"The firecracker is fine, stay with her," I reply.

"Are you sure?"

"Big tough Philippe, has she got you running scared?" I tease.

"Not funny."

ALORA.

Is there anything better in life than a revenge night out?

Edward is still in London, but his men are here watching and damn it, I am giving them something to report back with.

Screw. Him.

I don't know who this guy thinks that he is but he is messing with the wrong girl.

Surely his idiotic society girls don't put up with his crap?

He hasn't called me, he hasn't texted me…nothing. The only reason he did call me was because I threatened to go to the police, and if I haven't heard from him by Monday I'm bombing his stupid yacht. Hopefully with him inside.

It's Saturday night and just on 11.

And tonight, Mr. Prescott, watch and weep because I am single and looking to mingle.

Thomas, Helene, and I have been drinking cocktails at the Golden Peacock and are now walking arm in arm to Lierre… The hottest club in Monaco.

We are way too tipsy and yes, I know what you're thinking. It's true, this is war and tonight is completely strategic, we've come to his stomping ground to flirt…because damn it, we decided that if you're going to push some buttons, best be sure they're the right ones.

I'm wearing a black, tight, strapless minidress and sky-high stilettos. My hair is in a high bouncy ponytail and I have my favorite red lipstick on.

"We're not going to get in," Thomas whispers as we get closer to the door. "It's a private club, I don't even know anyone who has ever been here. It's a membership-only club."

"We're getting in," Helene replies. "By hook or by crook."

"What the hell does that even mean?" He frowns. "By hook or by crook?"

"You know, in an autograph book you used to write on the last page, by hook or by crook I'll be last in this book."

"That's so dumb." Thomas curls his lip. "Don't tell anyone that story, okay?"

I giggle as we walk to the front door. "Three please." I smile confidently.

The bouncer glances over our shoulder and nods, he unhooks the red rope.

"How much?" Thomas asks.

"Free tonight."

I glance over my shoulder to see Philippe and Stefan walking up behind us.

They got us in.

"Oh my god," Thomas whispers as we head up the stairs. "We're in."

"Only because of Philippe." I roll my eyes. "Ugh, so annoying. Can't we do anything by ourselves?"

"I'm not complaining." He rubs his hands together as if he just won the lottery. We get to the top of the stairs and are stopped by a lady sitting behind a desk. "I'll need identification and for you to sign here."

"Sure." We pass our licenses over and she scans them and then hands us an iPad. "Sign here."

"What are we signing?" I ask.

"A nondisclosure agreement."

What?

We stare at her, shocked. "Are you serious?"

"Do I look like I'm joking?" she asks deadpan as she looks us up and down. "No signature, no entry. And just a warning, if you do break your NDA and share anything that you see in this club, you will be criminally charged to the full extent of the law."

Jeez.... So dramatic.

We all glance at each other and then with a shrug, sign her stupid iPad and continue up the stairs. "Who does she think we're going to tell anyway?"

At the top of the stairs we go through another checkpoint. "Identification please."

This really is over the top.

We hand it over again and he reads the license numbers out to someone over a headpiece and then passes them back. "Have a good night." He opens the large door and we walk in and stop on the spot.

"What. The. Actual. Fuck?"

"I've never seen anything like this," Thomas whispers wide-eyed.

"Holy fucking hell." Helene's eyes dart from place to place. "I don't know where to look first."

There are naked women covered in gold paint dancing on podiums.

Naked.

The barmen are all shirtless, women are dressed in black leather corsets and black lace panties and are carrying around silver trays with shots on them.

"Welcome." One smiles, she has long red hair and is absolutely gorgeous, my eyes drop down her scantily dressed body, man.... She works out, hard.

"Can I offer you a shot?" she asks.

"Umm." We glance at each other. "Sure." We all take a shot of something clear and throw it back.

"Tequila." I wince, we put the empty shot glasses back on the tray and she saunters off.

"How's her ass." Thomas smiles as his eyes linger on her.

"Tight," I whisper.

Another woman arrives with a silver tray covered in white lines of powder. "A welcome treat."

Cocaine...you can get cocaine as a welcome gift?

"What the fuck?" Helene squeaks.

"Don't mind if I do." Thomas smiles.

"That could be anything," I whisper.

"That works because I'm up for anything." He smirks.

I glance over to see a man getting a lap dance by a naked lady. "Is this a strip club?" I ask the cocaine dealer.

"This is an everything club." She winks and walks away as we all stare after her.

I look to the other side of the club to see a man in a G-string giving a woman a lap dance. Her partner is sitting beside them watching while he smokes a cigar. The dancer leans in and kisses her and then leans in and kisses her husband.

"Fucking hell, is this a brothel?"

There's a packed dance floor and a DJ box, the man dancing behind the DJ is naked and painted gold with a massive erection. It's bouncing heavily around between his legs as he dances.

"Oh my god," I whisper, the others follow my line of sight.

"Viagra, anyone?" Thomas whispers wide-eyed. "Now I have officially seen it all."

"Don't ruin our fantasies." Helene slaps him on the thigh. "He doesn't use Viagra, that's all natural."

"The women here...Fuck," Thomas whispers. "Everyone is beautiful."

"And the men, can we talk about the men?" Helene whispers back. "I've died and gone to heaven."

"I'm getting a lap dance by the gold guy with the massive shlong," I announce.

Thomas giggles. "I bet you don't."

"Oh my god," Helene gasps as she looks up, once again we follow her gaze to see a large black cage suspended from the ceiling. In it, a gold-painted man is getting a head job from another gold-painted man on his knees, he's wearing a gold-chained collar and leash.

"Fucking hell," I whisper wide-eyed. "Jeez."

Another scantily dressed woman saunters past us and Thomas's eyes drop to her chest. Thomas adjusts himself in his pants. "I am one hundred percent picking up tonight, be warned."

"Why do you need to warn us?" Helene asks as her eyes linger on the head job action. "Man or woman?"

"Woman," he scoffs. "Just so you know I am not leaving with you, that's why. I don't want it to get to 4 a.m. and it looks like I'm ditching you in the spur of the moment. Totally premeditated."

"Let's go to the bar." I smile as excitement runs through me, I grab their two hands. "Oh my god this is so exciting," I whisper as we weave through the crowd.

"Fucking hell," Helene whispers. "Here comes the blow tray again."

"Hi." Thomas waves at her. "How nice to see you again."

"This place is insane."

We get to the bar. "My treat," Thomas tells us. "What do you want?"

"I'll have a margarita."

"Me too."

"Me three."

Thomas lines up and I glance over to the entry and see Philippe and Stefan come through the doors, they immediately walk over to the corner and up to a line of men standing along the wall. They laugh and shake hands as if they're long-lost friends.

"Who are they talking to?" I whisper to Helene.

"I don't know."

My eyes linger on the men. "Oh, they're bodyguards. But who are they…." My eyes dart around and then I see it. In a roped-off section on a raised level are low slouchy leather couches around big low tables. And right in the middle of the action sits Prince Theodore.

"Oh my god," I whisper.

"What?"

"Prince Chapelle is here." I gesture to him with my chin.

"What?" Helene's eyes nearly bulge from their sockets as she sees him. "What the hell is he doing in a place like this?"

I giggle. "Snorting coke and watching gold head jobs, apparently."

Thomas reappears with a tray of margaritas. "Here you are, my loves."

"Thanks." Helene takes a sip. "The fucking prince is here."

"He is?" He smiles as he takes a sip. "How deliciously scandalous." He looks around. "Where?"

"Over there." I subtly point.

"Oh." His eyes linger on the group of men. "He's with the Kingsmen."

My eyes flick between him and the group of men. "Those are Edward's friends?"

"Yep."

"Ha." I feel the confidence drain out of my body. "If they come here, that means Edward comes here."

"Uh-huh," he replies.

"Who's who?" I ask, I met some of them before, but who are the others?

"Okay so, the dark Greek god is Nicholas Anastas."

"He's the gay one?" I ask as I watch from the shadows.

"Yeah."

"Then the guy on his left is Prince Theodore." He continues.

"Yes, I know who he is."

"Beside him is Jacques Vermont and then beside him is Alexander York." He lets out a low whistle. "Fuck me, there is some serious money in that group."

"Like what are we talking?" Helene asks.

"Billions, these men are all the rich of the rich. The most powerful men the business world has to offer."

A woman with long black hair walks up to the prince and they begin to chat, he smiles as he runs his hand up her thigh and underneath her skirt. She keeps talking as if this is the most natural thing in the world.

"That's not his fucking girlfriend," I whisper, infuriated.

"I don't think she's his girlfriend. I think she's just a placeholder."

"So they all just openly fuck around?" I stammer.

"Why wouldn't they?" Thomas replies. "I would too if I were them."

"What are you talking about?" I scoff. "Nobody fucks around more than you."

"True." He laughs as he clinks his glass with mine.

Thomas and Helene change subjects and keep chatting but my eyes keep going back to Edward's friends.

The Kingsmen.

Ugh, I'm so out of my depth with this guy. What was I thinking...that I was going to be the woman who finally tamed the tiger? He isn't giving up this life anytime soon. Ha, what a joke. You are such an idiot, Alora.

The prince looks up and sees someone and waves, I follow his line of sight to see Philippe and Stefan wave back.

Fuck.

I spin so that my back is to them but I can still see their reflection in the mirrored wall in front of me. Theodore gets up and walks down out of the roped-off area and over to them as they stand against the wall.

I watch on as they talk and then Philippe points me out and Theodore looks me up and down. Theodore has obviously just asked who they are watching over.

Shit, shit, shit.

Theodore takes his phone out and calls someone.

Edward.

He says something and then laughs.

"This place is off the hook." Helene smiles over the music. "We're coming here every week."

"Right?" Thomas agrees.

"Uh-huh." I sip my cocktail as I dance to the beat to try and look like I'm not watching the prince's every last move.

He keeps talking as his eyes linger on my ass and he says something and laughs again.

What is he saying...?

He nods and looks at his watch, says something else and then hangs up. He slaps Philippe on the back and then waltzes back to his seat in the roped-off area.

Why would he have looked at his watch? Unless....

Oh my god, does that mean...Edward is coming.

The tantric beat of the music echoes through the club as we dance for our lives.

Blurred colors, flashing disco lights and way too many cocktails.

It's late, and even though I thought he was coming, he never showed.

Edward Prescott is still in London.

Thomas is dancing with some hot woman, they're making out as they dance. His hands are roaming up and down her body and damn. "I think he's giving it away for free tonight," Helene yells over the music.

I laugh out loud and feel two hands snake around my ass from behind.

"Don't." I pull away from the hands and am snapped backward until I slam against a hard body. I spin to see Edward, towering above me and wearing black jeans and a black T-shirt that fits perfectly over his large muscular body.

Excitement screams through my every cell.

His eyes are dark and they drop to my breasts and then back up to my face.

Oh no you don't, you don't get to ignore me for a week and then turn up here like a rock star.

"We are not on speaking terms," I tell him.

He grabs my hand and puts it on his crotch, he's hard as a rock beneath. "Suits me, who needs words when you have this." He flexes beneath my hand and unable to help it I cup him as we stare at each other. If the last four hours of being in this club has taught me anything, it's that we will never work out. We come from two completely different worlds. But….

One last time….

As his eyes hold mine he puts his hand around my throat and pulls me to him and kisses me. His tongue swipes through my open mouth with a darkness that only he can deliver. His grip is near painful, my air running out.

Lord have mercy….

"We're leaving," he growls.

If I could answer, I would. But his tongue gliding across my lips has stolen my ability to form a sentence.

He takes my hand in his and turns and pulls me through the club, I glance back at my two friends who are watching wide-eyed.

Arghhhhhh!

What is happening right now?

I look over to see Theodore watching, he throws his head back and laughs hard.

Oh crap, I'm so pathetic.

One chokehold and this asshole has me in a chokehold.... Literally.

He pulls me through the club but instead of heading to the door we came in through he leads me to the other side of the room to another door. The doorman nods as he opens the door. "Mr. Prescott."

"Hi."

We walk through and are met by elevator doors. He hits the button and slams me up against the wall and lifts my leg around his waist. He kisses me hard, our teeth clash and damn it, this man is fire.

Arghhh!

The elevator doors open and he pushes me in and again pins me to the wall as we kiss. The electricity between us is like nothing I've ever felt. His hands are all over me, up and down my thighs, over my ass.

Before I have time to even think the doors open straight into a penthouse, I look around in a daze. "Where are we?" I frown.

"My place."

"What do you mean?"

"I own this club."

My eyes widen. "You own this club?" I squeak.

"Yes." He unzips his pants. "And I own you. Get on your fucking knees."

CHAPTER TWENTY-ONE

Fuck….

He lifts my dress over my head and slides my panties and bra off, his gaze drops down the length of my body, burning my skin all the way down.

"Alora." He takes himself in his hand and every fantasy I have had over the last week is coming true.

"Suck. Me," he mouths.

Yes….

Probably not a good idea, but who cares at this point. Nice girls come last.

I drop to one knee and then the other, his eyes darken as he watches on. My eyes roam over his erection, engorged with thick veins coursing down the length of it.

"All of it," he mouths.

The air crackles between us and I kiss his head, his eyes flutter closed as he flexes it in my hand. "In your mouth." He drags it across my lips and I taste the smear of pre-ejaculate.

He grabs a handful of my hair and pulls me onto him. "Open. Your. Fucking. Mouth," he growls, impatient. "Now."

I snap my teeth and he inhales sharply at the threat of pain.

Oh, I remember, it's all coming back to me now.

He likes to walk the tightrope between pleasure and pain.

He's so bad…. *But so damn good.*

I take my time. Memorizing every inch of his beautiful thick cock as my eyes roam over him, large and hanging heavily between his legs, dripping with need. His pubic hair is dark and well kept. "Take your clothes off," I whisper. "I want you naked."

With his eyes locked on mine he lifts his shirt over his head and I'm blessed with the sight of his ripped abdomen. My hands roam up and over his eight-pack of tanned muscle, broad shoulders and his wide chest with a scattering of dark hair. He kicks his jeans off and his thick quad muscles make me flutter deep inside. He's begging to be ridden.

I take him in my mouth, deep, and then bare my teeth and scrape him as I pull off.

"Ohhh," he moans, his knees give out beneath him and I smile around him. His hands tighten around my hair and I know he's hanging on to his control by a thread.

I may not have him for long, but damn it, he's going to remember this night for forever.

I take him again, deep down my throat, and his mouth hangs slack as he watches on. "So fucking good," he murmurs. "Oh…."

I pull off and lick my lips for added effect.

"Get on it," he growls as he pulls me back onto him.

I laugh around him as we fall into a rhythm, with every stroke I take him, I watch him come more undone. Deep down my throat he pumps me and damn it…. I taste his hot pre-come and I moan.

He tips his head back as he struggles to hold it. "*Fuck.*"

Watching him come undone is my favorite thing.

"I'm going to blow so fucking hard."

"Don't you dare come without me."

A flash of a frown crosses his face as he realizes that's a strong possibility. He pulls me up and walks me back to the couch and pushes me back over it and next thing I know his hands are on my thighs as he holds my legs back up over my shoulders.

His tongue swipes through my swollen wet lips and I flutter.

Oh no…hold it.

"Don't you dare fucking come," he growls, he licks me again, deeper this time and his eyes close in reverence.

Edward Prescott doesn't go down on me for my pleasure, he does it for his.

Never have I met a man who loves the taste of a woman like he does.

His tongue deepens and I see stars and then he's all in, licking me deep, his stubble burning my most intimate parts. "So fucking good," he murmurs, his dark eyes rise to meet mine and my arousal glistens all over his face.

Good lord.

He goes again, deeper, more intimate, and then he adds a finger and then another and then two more.

"Oh," I cry out as my toes curl.

"What's wrong, sweet Doe?" he whispers as he comes up over me, his lips taking mine, and I taste myself as we kiss. "You need something more."

I nod, how is he so good at this?

He fingerfucks me with his whole hand, hard and fast.

Brutal.

The sound of my body sucking him in echoes around the room and I see stars.

Oh, I remember this…nobody fucks like this man.

He's the king.

His fingers get harder and faster and my mouth hangs open as I stare at him, whimpering as pleasure steals every coherent thought.

I shudder…*no.*

"Now!" I demand as I try to pull him down. "I need you inside of me," I whisper. "Please," I beg. "Now."

With a dark smile he kisses the inside of my ankle that is being held back over my shoulder and he slowly eases himself in. Just an inch, he circles one way and then another. His thick quads are jacked as he holds himself up, my hands rise up over them as I feel his every muscle.

He goes shallow, little pumps, stretching me wider. Burning my entrance but not going any farther in, my body begins to rise off the couch by itself, searching for a deeper connection.

What is this move?

I begin to thrash beneath him. "Harder," I demand. "Deeper."

His teeth graze my neck and I feel him smile against my skin.

"What are you doing?" I cry as I lose control. "Give it to me."

He holds my legs back and slams in hard, all the way. I'm stretched open to the hilt.

He's big….

"Oh." The air is knocked from my lungs as my eyes widen, I forgot his size.

Damn….

Then he's riding me hard, fucking me with wild abandon. The couch begins to hit the wall with force, slamming loudly against the plaster.

A picture falls off the adjacent wall and comes crashing down, but it doesn't halt him.

He doesn't falter.

"So fucking good," he moans, there's no stopping him now. He's locked on to his only goal, his body chasing the ultimate goal.

Orgasm.

My body ripples around his and I scream out as I am hit with a freight train of ecstasy.

"Fuck. Fuck. Fuck." He slams into me and holds himself deep, I feel the jerk of his cock deep inside of me as his body empties into mine.

He falls over me as we both gasp for air, wet with perspiration. Our bodies still connected. "You're an animal," I pant.

He smiles as he pulls me up by the hand. "You turn me into one." Then he kisses me, his lips take mine as he holds my face in his hands. It's slow and tender, loving.

Intimacy runs through us like a river and oh…. *I've missed him.*

"Nobody makes me feel like you do," I murmur.

He smiles against my lips as his fingers drop and part the lips of my sex. "You're about to feel it again."

EDWARD.

Tangled in the blankets, she lies in my arms. Naked and vulnerable and every bit as beautiful, if not even more beautiful than before.

She was hard to leave back then, even harder to find.

Impossible to forget.

And now, like a sorceress, she holds me even deeper under her spell.

I kiss her temple and hold her close against my body, my lips rest against her forehead as she sleeps. Her breasts are up against my chest and I can't let go of her to sleep because I'm craving this new emotion she's given me a glimpse of.

A special kind of magic that only she has.

Whatever it is...I feel out of my depth, just jumped out of a plane without a parachute. With no idea of where I'm going to land or how hard I'm going to hit the ground.

There's only one thing I do know for sure: I'm spiraling out of control.

ALORA.

I wake to the sound of the shower going, and I lie in the darkness for a while to try and get my bearings.

I don't think we slept for more than an hour all night. He took me again and again until we both had nothing left to give.

And now...well, the world is just ruined, because where do you go after a night like that with a man like him? If this doesn't work...I can't imagine how I'm ever going to recover.

He owns me, body and soul.

I must look appalling and I really can't have sex again, I'm sore. My body is throbbing from being overused. Sitting up, I look around the darkened bedroom, it's luxurious and modern.

Nothing at all like my home or taste.

I see my black dress neatly folded on the chair, along with my underwear and stilettos, and I wince at the cheap feeling as it runs through me. I have to put that dress back on to get home.

The walk of shame.

Short minidresses and stilettos always feel so different in the light of day.

Edward walks into the bedroom with a white towel wrapped around his waist, fresh out of the shower. "Hi." He smiles, he leans down and kisses me, his lips linger over mine. "Good morning."

"Good morning." I drag my hand through my hair, self-conscious of how I must look.

"I have to play polo today, Doe."

"Oh." I glance around. "Of course, I'll get going."

"I'll drive you home."

"No, it's fine. I'll catch an Uber."

"Don't be ridiculous." He tucks a piece of hair behind my ear and smiles over at me, his tanned chest is broad and his biceps are bulging. "I'm driving you home."

"Okay."

He kisses me again, longer with a little suction and I feel my heart flutter in my chest. He gets up and walks into the wardrobe.

He's just so....

I scramble out of bed and grab my things and rush into the bathroom.

Naked while horny is great. Naked while feeling like a rat that's just crawled out of a trash can is horrifying. I take a quick shower and re-dress into my clothes, should I put my high heels back on?

No...too far.

I walk back into the bedroom to see him fully dressed and sitting on the bed, waiting for me. I smile awkwardly. "I really can catch an Uber."

"There's no way in hell I'm letting you catch an Uber home."

"Okay." I smile shyly. "Thank you."

We get into the elevator and ride down to the parking lot; my shoes are in one hand and I pray to god that we don't see anyone. He takes my hand and leads me to a dark green sports car, it's wildly over the top and luxurious.

We make our way around to the passenger side of the car, he opens the door and I slink down in. It's so low to the ground and has a cream leather interior. I look around it in awe, I've never even seen a car this impressive, let alone driven in one. "What kind of car is this?" I ask as he gets in behind the wheel.

"Aston Martin DB11." He starts the engine and it roars with a deep growl.

"Oh...jeez." I widen my eyes at him and he smiles. "It's so loud."

He revs the engine again. "That's the point."

He glances over at me, stops what he's doing, leans over and pulls my face to his and kisses me. "I can't stop kissing you."

My heart somersaults in my chest at the emotion behind his kiss.

Okay…stop it.

This is just stupidity, am I dreaming right now, because if I am, don't wake me up.

He pulls out of the underground parking lot as I concentrate on wiping the stupid smile from my face.

This feels so surreal.

He begins to chat casually as we weave through the traffic, he's holding my hand in his and every now and then he lifts it and kisses my fingertips as if we are long-lost lovers and this is the most natural thing in the world.

I feel stunned to silence, unable to push a word past my lips because goddamn it, Bastard Mr. Prescott was hot, but Swoony Prescott is to die for.

His dark hair is messed to perfection, and as he drives I can see the muscles in his forearm contract. The chunky designer watch he has on is probably worth more than my apartment, but it's the carefree smile he's wearing. Broad and beautiful, and for the first time it feels like he's giving it to me of his own free will.

Honestly….

It's taking all my might not to undress again right here, right now.

"Where am I going?" he asks as we pull off the highway into Nice.

"You know where I live." I smile over at him.

He smirks as his eyes flick between me and the road and he takes a right turn.

"Ha, see. You do know where I live."

"Never said I didn't." He turns again at the Mont Boron sign. "This is a nice area," he says as he looks around. "Like, really nice."

"It is." I smile calmly but my mind is racing a million miles per minute.

Is he going to ask to see me again?

Will I be waiting on tenterhooks all week for him to call me?

No. I already know that I can't put myself through that. I have to force the issue now, and if he's not prepared to lock something in then I have to cut my losses. I can't have another week like I did last week.

Stop it, *act cool.*

"It's this one up here on the left with the sandstone." The car pulls into my driveway. "Are you…." I shrug, unsure what to ask.

"I can't come in." He glances at his watch. "I have to play polo and am already cutting it fine."

"How are you going to play polo with no sleep?"

"God knows." He gives me a breathtaking smile and my heart somersaults in my chest for the tenth time this morning.

My fangirling of him is becoming embarrassing.

EDWARD.

Alora looks over at me and her eyes search mine. She wants more….

"Have a great day," I tell her.

I watch her face fall as she realizes I'm not asking to see her again, and if I were a better man, I would.

I just can't….

"You too." She forces a smile as she opens the car door. "Have fun at polo." She slams the door hard, revealing her hidden anger, and marches up to her front door.

I fight the urge to follow her inside because I know we need to be over.

Before it even began…. But maybe that's a good thing because the way she has me feeling is not okay.

I pull out onto the street and drive away deep in thought.

If only….

Dragging my hand through my hair, I feel an uneasiness run through my veins.

I'm completely rattled.

I need to sort my shit out, and fast.

I pull into the parking lot of the Monte Carlo polo club and see Theo getting out of his car and I pull in beside him.

He leans on his car as he waits for me. "Hurry up," he mouths as he glances at his watch.

"Yeah, yeah." I climb out and grab my bag from the trunk.

"How was your night?" he asks.

"Good." I slam the trunk closed and glance over to see him smirking. "What?"

"Well...." He falls in to walk beside me.

"Well, what?" I look over to see my horse trailers parked, my six horses are being led out by my stable hands.

"You've got it that bad, huh?"

"Not in the least."

"Don't give me that fucking shit." He follows me over to my trailer. "You have guards on her while you're not even here and then they tell me that the minute you found out she was out last night you immediately flew home."

"Hello." I smile to Amber.

"Hello, Mr. Prescott. Ready for your game today, sir?"

"I am, thank you." I pick up a brush and begin to brush Camelot, my horse.

"Well?" Theo puts his hands on his hips. "I'm waiting."

Ugh.... He's not going to go away until I answer his question.

"I was returning this morning anyway and..." I shrug, lost for words. "...I didn't want her out by herself. She's a...." I pause as I think of the right analogy. "Handful."

He frowns as he thinks.

"Shouldn't you be over with your horses, doing something useful?"

"Probably."

"Hey," a voice sounds from the left, we both glance up to see William, my brother, walking toward us.

"Hey." I laugh in surprise and pull him into a hug. "What are you doing here?"

"I'm moving back."

He hugs Theo. "Good to see you, man."

"What?" I frown as I do the math. "Please.... Tell me you finally left her."

"Yep." He holds his hands out. "I left her."

"Haha." I laugh out loud. "Thank the fucking lord."

"Yeah, man." Theo and him high-five. "Good for you."

My brother William is married to the coldest, most evil woman I've ever met. She had an affair and then used their son as leverage to make him stay. He's been trapped in a living hell for years.

"Where's Harrison?"

"He's with her for the time being, but she finally agreed to shared custody."

"This is great news." I smile.

"We're celebrating tonight," Theo announces as he marches toward his trailers. "My place," he calls.

"Sounds good."

My eyes meet William's and I know how hard he'd be struggling, all he ever wanted was a happy marriage. It would have taken all his strength to walk out that door and leave his son behind. "You alright?"

He shrugs and kicks the dirt.

"You did the right thing." I hug him again. "You're back now, time to start again."

"I'm just going to miss him, you know, the weeks he's with her."

"I know." I nod. "It won't be easy, but at least you know she's a good mother, he's safe."

"I know, good mother, terrible fucking wife." He sighs against my shoulder. "Never get married," he tells me.

"Don't worry, I won't be."

ALORA.

The ache of almost.

Is there a worse emotion on earth than almost?

Almost had a chance, almost hopelessly in love. Almost his.

It's been a long thirty-six hours since Edward dropped me home on Sunday.

I haven't heard a word from him since.

And I want to call him and I want to beg him to come back and make my ache of almost go away. But I can't do this alone, he needs to want it too.

He'll call…I know he will.

Be patient.

I walk into the bathroom of my store and lock the door, I stare at my reflection in the round mirror. His teeth marks on my neck have begun to fade. The physical reminder of our night together will soon be long gone, and as much I treasured our time together…I'm beginning to wish it never happened because it's opened a wound in my chest that took three years to heal. A deep, cavernous hole of fear.

I hate feeling like this, continually checking my phone and worrying about what he's doing or thinking. Wondering what's going to come next.

You see, it's one thing to be scared about never finding your soulmate. But knowing who he is and still not ending up with him….

That's a tragedy I'm not sure I can survive.

I'm keeping myself busy and acting non-bothered while playing it down to Helene, but on the inside, with every hour he doesn't call…. I die a little more.

My eyes well with tears, I'm so in love with this fucking asshole and I have no idea how to deal with it or what to do. I feel out of control and powerless; when he left on Sunday he took my heart with him.

He'll call…*he has to.*

EDWARD.

Like a caged animal, I pace. "Do something," I bark.

"Why don't you take a seat, Edward," Paul replies calmly. "You're wearing my office carpet down to a thread."

"I don't want to sit down." I drag my hands through my hair. "Delete it," I demand.

"Delete what?"

"Her. From my head." I throw my hands up in the air. "Delete it right fucking now. You're a quack, isn't this what you do?"

Paul sits back and calmly crosses his legs. "You know that isn't possible, but let's unpack what has you feeling so upset."

"I don't want to unpack anything," I fire back. "I don't have time to have a daily freakout that forces me to fly to London just to see you." I walk back and forth. "I'm very fucking busy, and this doesn't align with my schedule."

"Okay." He nods as he holds his pen and notepad in his hand. "So are you saying that you don't have time for Alora or are you saying that you don't have time for the way she makes you feel?"

"Both." I wipe the perspiration from my brow. "I need medication or something." I glance back over to him as realization sets in. "Why haven't you given me any?"

"This issue isn't going to be rectified by numbing yourself with medication, Edward, you need to work through this."

"I don't have time for this fucking bullshit."

"What exactly seems to be the problem?" Paul continues. "You spent the night together and what then...?"

"Do you fucking listen to me at all?" I cry. "I'm having a mental breakdown, that's what." I continue to pace.

"Explain to me in feelings, give me an example."

"I can think of nothing else but her. I dream of her, I stalk her on social media, I have guards on her so I know she's safe so that I can at least function." I keep walking back and forth as I think out loud. "All I want to do, all I think about doing, is going to her."

"So why don't you?"

My eyes rise to meet his. "Are you not listening, dumb, or just plain stupid?"

"I think you are struggling because for the first time in your life you have met someone who has awakened feelings in you that are completely foreign. You feel connected, satisfied and contented. Am I right?"

I listen as I keep pacing.

"Edward, have you ever considered that being the happiest version of yourself comes with goodbyes?"

"What the fuck does that even mean?" I snap.

"Goodbye to your old way of thinking, but I'm going to ask you something and I want you to think long and hard before you answer me. Why don't you want to be in love?"

"It's not that I don't want to be in love." I think for a moment.

"Go on."

"This isn't love, this is an obsession. I have an unhealthy fascination with this woman, I'm like a depraved stalker."

"You haven't felt like this about another woman before?"

"No."

"Be honest with yourself, are you in love with Alora?"

"I don't know." I shrug as sadness falls over me, I can't even do therapy right.

"Let's talk about that for a moment. What does the thought of being in love, truly all in with your soulmate, make you feel?"

I stare at him as I feel fear swirl deep in my psyche. "Terrified."

"Why?"

"None of my scars came from an enemy," I murmur.

"I know."

"And if I...." The lump in my throat blocks my vocal cords and his silhouette blurs.

"A beautiful life is not stumbled upon, Edward, it is built. You can't skip chapters, you have to live through this experience to get to the life you so badly desire. To find the deep-seated happiness that you deserve."

My eyes search his.

"Have you told Alora how you feel? Talked to her about your roadblocks?"

"Fuck no."

"Why not?"

"What, tell her I can't be in a relationship because she could fuck me up?"

"As I see it, not being in a relationship with her is the only thing that's fucking you up."

"And if I let myself love her and then something happens.... What then?"

"But if you don't let yourself love her...something *will* happen."

"What's that supposed to mean?"

"She will not wait forever, she *will* move on from you. Are you really prepared to watch her fall in love and then marry someone else? He then gets to have the life that you wanted. She has *his* children, she makes *him* happy...while you're still stuck in the same old toxic patterns with women you don't really want to be with."

My eyes hold his.

"It sounds like a very mediocre existence, if you ask me."

I begin to hear my heartbeat in my ears.

"Edward, in my experience, someone who overthinks love, is someone who over-feels it."

A lump forms in my throat and I drag my eyes away from his.

"Wouldn't it be wonderful to give that love to one woman and to have her love you with her whole heart in return?"

Emotion fills me and I drop my head to evade his gaze. "I need to go."

"Please think about what we discussed today."

"Goodbye." I walk out of his office and straight past reception.

"Do you need another appointment, sir...." she calls after me.

I push through the doors without answering, I'm not coming back here again.

What a waste of my fucking time.

ALORA.

"Hi, Dad." I smile down the phone.

"How is my favorite girl?"

Hearing his voice makes me teary. "She's good," I whisper.

Don't cry.

"What's been happening?" I push out. "How did you do at the doctor's for your yearly checkup?"

"Blood pressure is perfect." He chats away and tells me all about his week and I smile as I listen, grateful that I don't have to tell him about my week and the imminent heartbreak I'm about to go through. Like a ticking time bomb, I can feel it coming.

No missed calls.

Dear Nel,

I love your suggestions and have attached a furnishing concept. I have some beautiful pieces on hold, let me know if you want to go ahead with them.

Have a great day,

Alora.

I hit send on the email, the plans for the hotel refurb in Paris are coming along nicely. We've finally locked in a color palette and I know it's not Nel's fault, but I really can't help disliking her. Knowing that she likes Edward is like twisting a knife in my side. Who am I kidding, the entire female population likes Edward.... Ugh.

I let out a deep sigh and turn the kettle on. "You guys get going," I call to Jonty and Helene. "I'm going to take my time finalizing the cash register."

"Okay," Helene calls.

"Good luck on your date tonight," I call.

"Don't need luck," she calls back. "Just condoms."

Jonty laughs and I smile as I make my tea. I love this girl. They come out of the back room and grab their things. "What's for dinner?" Jonty asks as he grabs his backpack from his locker.

"No idea, what are you having?"

"Pasta. I think."

"Sounds good."

"Lock the door behind us," Helene says.

"Okay." I walk them to the door. "See you tomorrow."

"Bye." They walk out onto the street and I flick the brass lock on the back of the door and turn the *Open* sign around to *Closed*. I wind the blinds closed on the front windows and turn the music up.

Knock, knock, knock, sounds on the front door.

"What did you forget?" I call. I walk out the front to see Edward standing at the door. He gives me a slow, sexy smile and my heart skips a beat at the mere sight of him. I open the door in a rush. "Hi."

"Hi." His eyes hold mine, big and beautiful, just like I remembered.

How is this man so perfect?

"Can I come in?"

CHAPTER TWENTY-TWO

I smile, embarrassed that I was too starstruck to realize I hadn't asked already. "Of course." I step to the side and he walks past me into the store. I look out to see the two cars of guards parked down the street as they wait for their boss. I close the door and flick the lock and turn to see Edward walking into my office.

Nerves dance and I close my eyes to try and calm myself before I walk in after him.

"I thought you must have forgotten about me?" I joke, but it's not a joke. I'm deadly serious and even more needy.

He takes me into his arms and leans down and kisses me; his lips linger against mine as he holds me close with a warm tenderness. "How could I ever forget about you?" he murmurs. "You're all I fucking think about."

Oh….

And it's there again, the pull to him. A magnetism that I have no chance of fighting. So strong that it's a tangible force.

"I haven't seen you in four days," I whisper.

Shut. Up.

Stop being so needy, play it cool for god's sake.

"I know." He kisses me again, his hands slide down my behind. "I have a lot going on at the moment." He takes my face in his hands and stares down at me, he seems different tonight, more in touch. "But I'm here now."

"Thank god." I smile against his lips as we kiss again, deeper, more urgent. I feel his erection up against my stomach. Desperation hits and he pins me up against my desk.

"Let's go back to my place," he whispers, his hand moves up my leg and under my skirt. His fingers slide beneath my panties to find me dripping wet and his eyes darken with desire.

"But I live closer, let's just go to mine," I pant as arousal begins to pump through my bloodstream.

"I…." He slides a finger deep into my body and I whimper, he adds another and I clench around him. "Staffing issues, you need to come to mine," he says, distracted.

"Oh…okay." I clench around his fingers and he inhales sharply as he plunges them deeper. "We need to…." My eyes flutter closed, I can't speak while he's doing that.

His teeth drop to my neck and he bites me hard, goose bumps scatter up my spine.

I want a full night together.

"I'm not having sex here, Edward. Wherever we are going, we need to go now."

He withdraws and puts his fingers into his mouth and as his eyes hold mine he sucks them dry. "*Fuck*…. You taste good."

I feel faint.

"Let's go." He takes my hand and nearly pulls my arm out of the socket as he pulls me toward the door.

"Wait, I have to lock up."

"Hurry up about it." He drags his hand through his hair as if trying to calm himself down.

I grab the keys and my bag and we walk out the door and I turn, lock it and pull the security door down while he waits. I glance over at him, his dark hair is messed up and his big red lips are a wonderful shade of come-fuck-me.

"This way." He leads me to his car and now that we're out the front his demeanor feels different, he's not holding my hand like he usually does. Is that because the guards are watching or does he just not want to?

Oh my god, Alora. Stop overanalyzing every little thing.

He opens the back door of the Bentley and I slide in and over, he crawls in behind me and sits down. "My apartment, please," he says, void of emotion.

"Yes, sir," the driver in the front says, I don't know this guard, I haven't seen him before. He glances up as we pull out onto the road and we make eye contact in the rearview mirror and I drag my eyes away from his.

How many women has he driven back to Edward's apartment?

Edward sits on his side staring out the window, his elbow is on the door and his thumb runs back and forth over his lips as if he's deep in thought. With every mile we drive I feel him pull away from me a little more. Just ten minutes ago he was all over me like a rash and now we sit in a car together and he's staring out the window, ignoring me.

Is it the guards?

The half-hour trip from Nice to Monaco is made in complete silence, and I wish that I could say I didn't notice it, but his deafening silence makes me feel like we are driving to a cavern of uncertainty. One I should know better than to visit.

The car pulls into the underground parking lot and over to the elevator. The guards stay in the car while Edward comes around and opens my door for me, has he told them to do that or….

"Here we are." He forces a smile as he takes my hand in his and helps me out.

"Thank you."

He drops my hand again and we walk to the elevator and get in and turn to face the doors, still not a word said.

What the hell is going on here?

He drags his hand through his hair and seems weird and distracted…off. Something is not right with him.

This man is so confusing, he tells me that I'm all he can think about and then pulls away. Why would he….

Is he still in love with his ex? Is that what this is…guilt?

The double doors open straight into his apartment and he strides out. "Would you like a drink?" He disappears into the kitchen.

"Yes please." I put my bag down on the side table and look around the swanky apartment. "It seems surreal that this apartment is above a nightclub and yet so silent," I call.

"Yes."

I peek around the corner and see him down a glass of scotch in one gulp and then with a shaky hand fill his glass again.

I don't know what's going on with him, but I do know I need to calm him down.

Ha, the irony, Miss Freaking Out Herself has to calm *him* down.

He reappears with two glasses of wine and passes me one. "Here you are."

"Thank you." I smile, I hold my glass up and touch it with his before taking a sip. "Are you alright?" I ask.

"Yes," he snaps way too quickly. "Why do you ask?"

I shrug as I try to think of the right wording. "You seem unsettled."

"Nope." He rolls his lips as his eyes hold mine.

"Is this about Hermione?" I ask softly.

"What?" He screws up his face. "Why would it be about Hermione?"

"Do you still have feelings for her, is that why you're acting weird? Do you feel guilty for being here with me?"

His eyebrows shoot up in surprise. "Trust me, I do not have feelings for Hermione. We are well and truly over."

"Oh." I force a smile. "I just…." My voice trails off, embarrassed that I brought her up. "Never mind."

"What were you going to say?" he asks.

"You just seemed to change once we left the store."

"I…my apologies." He gives a subtle shrug. "I have a lot on my mind lately."

Hmm…. About what?

It's obvious he isn't going to elaborate, so I try to change the subject. I sip my wine again as I look around. "Do you know how many times I've watched the video of you jerking off in my store?"

His eyes darken as he sips his wine again. "Do you know how many times I've jerked off thinking about you in your store?"

"How many?"

"Too many."

"Why would you jerk off thinking about me when you can have the real thing?"

He opens his mouth to say something but no words come out.

"I like you," I whisper.

"I like you," he replies without hesitation.

"But you make me feel needy," I murmur. "I'm not used to this feeling, and if I'm being honest, I'm not sure that I like it."

Satisfaction flashes across his face before he quickly covers it. "You just like my cock."

"Probably." I smile as we stare at each other and like smoke in the wind I feel the tension leave his body.

Whatever I just said made him feel better. *You make me feel needy*, is it possible that he's feeling needy too?

"So now that you have me here, what are you going to do with me?"

"Hmm." He rubs the backs of his fingers through his stubble as his eyes drop down my body and back up to my face. "I'm going to get you naked. Tie you up and put my cock so far down your throat that you choke."

I snort my wine up my nose. "What?" I splutter before launching into a full-blown coughing attack.

"Just like that." He smiles as he rubs my back.

I cough and cough and cough and he gets me a glass of water and passes it to me. "Drink this, wimp."

I take a sip of the water. "You did say you wanted me to choke."

"On my dick, not air."

I bite my bottom lip to hide my smile. "Is that why you were nervous in the car, you were frightened that you were going to choke me to death."

"Not nervous." He smiles. "Excited."

"About?"

"Finally getting you alone." He tucks a piece of hair behind my ear and cups my face in his hands. "You're all I've thought about all week."

The air swirls between us, a magical aura that only he can activate.

He's just so....

"Same," I whisper.

His lips take mine as he kisses me softly, his eyes flutter closed and I know he's as lost in the moment as I am. We kiss again, more urgent, and him confirming that he and Hermione are well and truly over has taken down my guardrail.

I am irrevocably his.... Even if only for tonight.

I don't want to think about tomorrow, I want to be lost in the here and now.

"Can we shower?" I murmur against his lips.

"Hmm." He bites my bottom lip as his two hands grab my behind and drag me across his erection.

I've been at work all day, if I'm getting tied up I at least want to be clean and fresh.

He takes my glass of wine from me and puts it down on the counter and leads me to the master bedroom. He turns the shower on and comes back to stand in front of me, his dark eyes drop down my body and my breath catches in anticipation.

This is where the dynamics change between us; from the moment he gets me naked we both know I hand over my control.

He leads, he dominates and conquers my every fantasy.

And I, well, I just ride the waves of pleasure as he dishes them out.

Watching and feeling him come undone as he uses my body for his pleasure is my most favorite thing in the world. And it's hard and messy and rough and a level of arousal that nobody else has ever brought out in me before.

He begins to undo the buttons on my blouse one by one.

"You incite a darkness in me that I didn't know I needed," I whisper.

His eyes rise to meet mine. "You incite a lot more than that for me."

"Like what?" I hold my breath as I wait for his answer.

"You're very talkative tonight, Alora." He peels my shirt off and throws it to the side, he turns me away from him and glides down the zipper on my skirt.

"Hmm." He runs his fingers over my black lace G-string. "I like this." He bends and kisses my behind.

Ha! My plan worked, I've been wearing sexy underwear to work all week on the off chance he would show up.

Diabolical.

He slides my skirt down my legs. "Step out."

I step out and he turns me back to face him. "In." He leads me into the shower.

"But my…."

"You will shower in that."

"Oh." Deviant wants to have sex while I'm in my lace underwear, my plan wasn't diabolical, it was a complete home run. I adjust the water temperature as I watch the strip show.

His eyes hold mine as he undoes his shirt buttons and as his broad tanned chest comes into view my insides begin to ripple with excitement.

So fucking hot.

He kicks off his shoes and socks and next the fly on his suit pants comes down with a sharp snap. I stand back under the shower and let the hot water fall down over my head, my eyes locked on his every move. Every time I watch him undress feels like the first time. I will never tire of this.

He slides his pants down and his large erection springs free, and I swallow the lump in my throat as I stare at it. Thick and long with veins pulsing down the length.

A weapon to behold.

With his dark eyes fixed on mine, he steps under the water and jumps. "Argh, why is the water so fucking hot? Are you preparing for hell?"

"Well, I'm here with the devil, so I guess I am," I tease.

He cuts me off with a kiss as he pins me to the wall; his hands run up and down my body as if memorizing every inch of my skin. His hand reaches down the front of my panties and I smile against his lips, *yes*.

His fingers slide through my dripping flesh as he parts me wide open and he's completely right, underwear left on somehow feels naughtier, more forbidden.

His teeth bite my neck as his fingers begin to ride me, one, then two, then three fingers. Deep and plunging. His teeth graze my jawline as I see stars, my eyes roll back in my head as my mouth hangs slack.

Oh god….

How is he so good at this?

The water echoes as my body sucks him in, and never have I craved being fucked by a hand so much before. It's like he knows what I need more than I do.

He brings me to the edge, and just before I cry out: "Hold it," he demands as his fingers slow.

"I…."

"Hold it," he breathes into my ear, his fingers slide in and out of me slowly and even just hearing his deep English voice tell me to hold it is orgasm-inducing in itself.

"I can't…" I whimper. "I need…."

"Alora," he commands. "Look at me."

I drag my eyes to meet his.

"Focus." His fingers are slow and deep inside me. "Focus on me."

"I…." I try to detach my emotions, I want to be able to do as he asks.

"Lift your leg, baby," he breathes in my ear.

"What?" I pant. "I can't, I'll come."

"Hold it and I'll give you what you need." His teeth graze my skin. "Lift your leg and clench for me." He bites my ear harder. "I want to feel you contract."

I wrap my leg around him, his fingers are deep inside me as we stare at each other in the steam-filled room.

"One," he breathes.

I clench and he smiles darkly. "Good girl."

"Oh…." My eyes close, I can't do this and not orgasm, it's impossible.

"Two."

I clench again and he inhales sharply as he feels my body ripple around his fingers.

"So fucking hot," he moans as his fingers ride me harder. "One more and you can have me."

"Three." I nearly pass out with the pleasure as I contract around his fingers.

"Yesssss." He smiles. "Just like that." He lifts me and wraps my legs around his waist and he pulls my panties to the side and slides in to the hilt.

My body ripples around him and just from the sheer size I cry out as an orgasm steals the air from my lungs.

"Fuck. Fuck. Fuck," he moans as he lifts me and slams me back down onto his body.

He rides me with wild abandon, hard and up against the tiles. The sound of the water slapping echoes off the walls. My lace panties are burning me and I'm sure him, but I think that's the point, he wants his pleasure wrapped in pain.

I grip his muscular shoulders and I watch his beautiful face as he comes undone. Water beads over his skin and his big blue eyes are hooded. "Yeah," he begins to chant. "Fuck yeah." He slams me hard, almost painful, and holds himself deep. I feel the telling jerk of his cock as he ejaculates inside my body.

And then he kisses me, tenderly, loving.... And everything wonderful in between.

We stay like this for a long time, kissing up against the wall. Taking our time and drinking every last drop of each other in.

"Do you feel better now?" I whisper up at him.

"Still needy." He smiles, and it's a beautiful broad smile that melts my heart into a puddle.

"Lucky I'm here for the night, then, isn't it?"

He chuckles. "It is."

The scent of aftershave lingers in the air and I stretch while sitting up.

I've woken up alone.

The bedroom is in semidarkness and I can hear muffled talking in the distance.

I go to the bathroom and wrap myself in the bathrobe that is hanging on the back of the door and go in search of my Mr. Doe.

His voice is coming from the last room down the hall and I tentatively walk down and stand at the door.

He's fully dressed in his suit and sitting behind a desk on a Zoom call. He's speaking in another language.... Is it German?

What time is it?

He glances up at me and flicks the camera off and mic off and pats his lap, I go and sit across him. "Good morning, Miss Sorenson." He kisses me softly, his aftershave dances around me, inciting memories of the heaven he took me to last night.

"Hi." I swoon.

I can hear the voice on the other end of the Zoom still going through his headphones.

"I have back-to-back meetings this morning," he tells me.

"That's okay." I think for a moment. "I have to get back to Nice, I have to open the shop."

"Philippe can drive you now or I can drive you around eleven."

"I'll go with Philippe soon if that's okay."

"Of course." He kisses me again, our lips linger over each other's. The voice continues to talk through the headphones.

"Can I cook you dinner tonight?"

"Um." His eyes hold mine and I can almost see his mind ticking a million miles per minute.

"It's just dinner." I pull a whiny face.

"Edward," the voice calls, realizing he isn't answering.

"Okay." He nods, with another quick kiss he pushes me off his lap. "I'll see you tonight," he mouths. "I'll pick you up from work."

"Okay." I act cool but what I really want to do is jump in the air.

Dinner…like a real date.

I make my way back into the bedroom and quickly dress and make the bed. I take one last look around, have I got everything?

I go back down to Edward's office and wave from the door, he frowns and points to his cheek.

He wants a kiss.

Ahh, things are going very well indeed. I walk in and kiss him and he slides his hand up my thigh as he keeps talking and honestly, seeing him in work mode is a major fucking turn-on.

Who am I kidding, everything this man does is a major turn-on.

"Phillippe is waiting downstairs for you," he mouths.

"See you tonight." With one last kiss I make my way to the elevator and once the doors close I break into a goofy smile.

I think the night was a success.

5 P.M.

"He's here," Helene squeaks as she peers out the window.

"Okay, then." I try to play it cool as I finish up with the cash register and eventually we all make our way out the front to lock up.

"Seriously?" Helene whispers as she looks up the street. "I fucking hate your guts right now."

I giggle and look up to see such a beautiful sight that I nearly gasp out loud. His dark green sports car is parked and Edward is leaning up against it. He must have finished work a little early because he's wearing blue jeans and a white T-shirt. His skin is tanned and he's wearing aviator sunglasses.

Dear lord, he looks so gorgeous that I can hardly stand it.

Eeeeek!

A broad smile covers my face and I want to run to him and jump into his arms like some lovesick fool. But I won't, I'll pretend that cool stuff like this happens to me every day.

Philippe and Stefan are already in their car waiting and honestly, how is this real?

I make my way over to the car and he smiles warmly. "Hello, Miss Sorenson."

"Hi."

Don't get carried away, I remind myself to bring me back to earth. This is just one night and maybe it means nothing. He opens the car door and I slink in.

He pulls out and we drive in silence and suddenly I'm nervous.

What if tonight doesn't go well?

"Everything alright?" Edward glances over.

"Yes." I fidget with my fingers, nervous for what's about to happen. He reaches over and takes my hand into his and holds it on his thick quad muscle.

"How was your day?" He glances over at me.

Long without you.

"Good. What about you?"

"Much of the same." We pull into my street and suddenly the nerves really hit home. This is weird having him here, he comes from such money. I have no idea what he's going to think of my humble abode. "You can park in my garage if you want? It's usually filled with furniture, but thankfully it got emptied out last week."

"Good timing."

I rattle through my purse, take out the remote and hold it tightly in my hand. He looks around. "You have a water view?"

"I do."

"I didn't notice it when I dropped you home." He glances around the tree-lined street. "This is actually *really* nice."

"You were expecting a dump?" I tease.

"I never said that."

"It's the place with the sandstone on the right."

"Yes, I know."

I push the remote and the garage door slowly goes up, we pull into the driveway and it's then I see the car of guards pull in behind us. Damn it, I thought I had him to myself for a while.

"Are they coming?" I frown.

His eyes flick over to me as if surprised. "No. They just…." He gives an embarrassed shrug. "Have to check the place and then I'll tell them to go."

"Check for what?"

"Just the safety of things."

It's all I can do not to roll my eyes. "Do they think I have someone in here waiting to take you out?"

"Do you?"

"Do I count?" I clench a fist. "I reckon I could beat you in a fight."

"I have no doubt." He smiles as he drives into my garage, suddenly the sound of the engine echoes loudly off the walls. It's like a low and rumbling jet plane.

"Are you serious?" I laugh. "What even is this car?"

"Don't you love it?" He puts his foot on the pedal and it roars loudly.

"Stop." I laugh. "The neighbors will call the police." He turns the engine off and the garage falls silent. Philippe and Stefan and one other man are in the car, I have seen him before but I don't know his name. He must be Edward's personal guard, he's so huge he looks like the Terminator. They walk up the driveway and into the garage. "Hello," I say awkwardly.

Edward must sense my agitation at them being here. "Just come in and look around and then I'll be fine, you can go."

"I—" They exchange glances.

"I'll be fine." Edward cuts him off. "Nobody knows I'm here and we weren't followed."

They still don't seem mollified.

"We won't leave the house," I tell them as I hold the remote up to close the garage door. "This way." I open the internal door and secretly want to die.

"This is Aleki." He introduces me to the other man, he's Polynesian or maybe Hawaiian, very handsome, and very scary.

"Hello." I smile.

He nods but doesn't say anything, how many women has he met in the past?

Insecurity screams through my bloodstream, they are used to rich women in palaces and here I am…my house is anything but rich.

We walk in and my eyes flick to Edward in a silent plea. *Get them out of my house.*

"You have two minutes," he tells them.

They walk past us and begin to look around, they open the cupboard doors and peel the curtains back to check the window locks before disappearing upstairs. I stand on the spot, feeling violated.

"They'll be gone in a minute," Edward says softly.

I nod, I know this isn't his fault but damn it, I hate this invasion of privacy. While he's out and about is one thing, but damn it.

This is my home.

What do they actually think is going to happen here? Annoyed, I go to the kitchen and turn the kettle on and I hear them come back downstairs. "So we…."

"Baisse d'un ton." Edward murmurs. (Translation: Keep your voice down.)

My ears prick up, Edward is speaking to them in French, he doesn't want me to know what they're saying.

"Ton sac est en haut. L'arme est dons la poche latérale." I hear a muffled voice. (Translation: Your bag is upstairs, the gun is in the side pocket.)

"Merci."

L'arme?

Gun…did I just hear something about a gun? I don't speak French, but there are some words I recognize. I walk back out into the living area, "Au revoir, Mademoiselle Sorenson." They nod.

"Goodbye." I fake a smile; my mind is reeling.

Good riddance.

"Ne quittez pas la maison, Monsieur Prescott." (Translation: Do not leave the house, Mr. Prescott.)

"Je n'en ferai rien." (Translation: I won't.)

"Verrouille la porte derrière nous." (Translation: Lock the door behind us.)

Lock, another familiar word.

They walk out the door and I close it behind them and lock it, get out of my house, fuckers.

Edward's eyes find mine and he gives me a soft smile. "You don't like my men in your house?"

"No."

"They're gone now." He takes me into his arms. "Forget about them."

"Why did they say gun?"

"What?" He plays dumb.

"I heard the word gun."

"They left a gun upstairs for me."

"Why?"

"In case I need it."

"Why would you need a gun to stay at my house?"

"Alora." He holds me at arm's length. "It's a precaution and we won't need it, but just in case something goes bump in the night, we have protection."

"Has something happened before?"

"It has." He walks to my back French doors and looks out to my little terrace garden. "This is lovely."

"Don't change the subject, Edward."

"I'm not, your garden is lovely, but I told you before. I am a target and precautions need to be taken. I don't sleep at premises other than my own, but seeing…."

His voice trails off.

"But seeing what?"

"Seeing as we are new and you wanted to cook me dinner here in private."

In private?

I stare at him as I try to read between the lines. "Is Hermione going to be calling on your houses and you don't want her to see me, is that what you're saying?"

"No."

"So what are we hiding from?"

"The paparazzi, as soon as I am photographed with you there will be a media frenzy and Hermione doesn't need that added pressure right now." He takes me into his arms. "And neither do you." He kisses me softly. "Besides, I would like some time for us to be alone for a while without distractions." He kisses me again, his tongue sliding through my lips. "Wouldn't you?" I feel myself melt into his arms, he puts his finger under my chin, bringing my face up to his. "Okay?"

"Okay." I smile, honestly, this man could sell honey to a bee.

He steps back from me. "So…show me around."

"Well." I snap out of my annoyance. "This is the living room." I hold my hand out and point to the furnishings. "Armchair. Armchair. Couch. Coffee table."

"You have beautiful taste." He smiles as he looks around. "Something tells me that you like antiques?"

"Maybe a little." I smile proudly as I look around the room as I try to see it through his eyes for the first time. I'm not going to lie, I love my home more than anything in the world. The walls are a warm cream with crown molding, the drapes are a deep coffee-colored velvet and hang from the twelve-foot ceilings. There is a huge, gilded mirror above the cream marble fireplace and Gobelin tapestries are hung in assorted gold frames. Chandeliers and pleated gold lamps add ambience. The details are in the deep red cushions and vases of flowers. The most beautiful thing about living here has been the joy of being over the top with my extravagant French furnishings. My place is small but it's decorated as if it's a palace.

"This is the kitchen." I show him proudly. "I had this remodeled just last year." I point to the oven. "My pièce de résistance."

He eyes it over. "You like your oven?"

"I *love* my oven."

"You are in love with your oven?" Amusement flashes across his face.

"I love to cook."

"Hmm." He walks around with his hands clasped behind his back as he takes it all in. "And what is…that?"

I glance up to where he gestured. "What do you mean?"

"That plant thing growing up the wall."

"Oh, right." I laugh. "That's a devil's ivy, she was my first family member I bought when I moved to France, she's lovely isn't she?"

"Hmm." A trace of a frown flashes across his face. "A family member?"

"Plants are living things too, you know."

"If you say so." Amusement crosses his face. "I would assume you'd have bought a better-looking family member."

"You don't like devil's ivy?"

"I just never saw one growing up a wall on the inside of a house."

"How sad for you."

He gives me a slow, sexy smile and I feel it all the way to my bones.

"Oh." I remember something. "Come out here." I open the French doors to my garden; it has stone walls on either side blocking out the neighbors but the most beautiful view of the ocean. There's a small table for two on the patio and two deck chairs on the small, round grassed area. "Let me show you my pride and joy." We walk down a little stone path and I hold out my hands, "Ta-da."

He frowns as if confused. "What's that?"

"It's my vegetable garden."

"You grow vegetables?"

"I do." I smile proudly and then I rush to the other side. "Ah, and over here is my flower garden. I'm growing peonies, they've always been my favorite." I pull out a weed.

He gives a subtle shake of his head. "I've never met anyone quite like you, Alora."

I pull out another weed. "What do you mean?"

"You have a body built for sin and fuck like an…." He shrugs as if searching for the right word. "Animal demon. And yet…you cook and garden like a farmer."

"An animal demon?" I smile as I slide my hands around his waist. "How does an animal demon fuck?"

His dark eyes hold mine. "Really fucking good."

I giggle as I take him by the hand and begin leading him back inside the house. "Here's how tonight's going to go, Mr. Prescott."

"I'm listening."

"I'm going to cook you dinner and then I'm going to take you upstairs and you can meet a *possessed* animal demon." He stops and pulls me back to him and we kiss. Really hard. Our lips linger over each other's and I feel that throb of arousal that swirls between us.

"This night is sounding very promising indeed." He takes my face in his hands and kisses me again, this time with suction, and I feel his erection grow between us.

I know if I don't stop this there will be no cooking, and I want his first night here with me to be more than sex. I pull out of the kiss and step back. "Your job is to light the candles and set the table."

He frowns. "What do you mean?"

"I'm cooking."

"And."

I pass him the matches. "Go around and light the candles and turn the lamps on to set the mood."

"Oh." He looks around as if having jobs is totally foreign to him. "Okay. I could do that." His phone beeps with a text and he digs it out of his pocket and reads it.

"Why don't you switch it off?"

He glances up. "What?"

"Switch it off." I take his phone from him and I put it on the fireplace mantle. "When you're here with me, then you're here with me." I slide my hand down and cup his crotch. "Time to relax."

EDWARD.

I stand at the window looking out into the back garden, garden lights are shining into the garden and lit solar lanterns hang from the trees. I have a glass of wine in my hand, music is playing through the sound system and not your usual music, something called "Sunny Mornings." It's all piano and zen

with birds and shit. Alora is happily chatting away from the kitchen and whatever the hell she's cooking smells divine.

I turn and look around the house, home. *This* is a home. Candles flicker, and lamps throw a warm glow through the small and intimate space, and the weirdest feeling runs through my veins, though I can't quite put my finger on exactly what it is.

"Babe," Alora calls.

Babe....

"Yeah?"

"Do you want béarnaise or Diane sauce?"

What is this alternate universe? I take a gulp of my wine, almost shocked to silence.

"Whatever," I call back. "Both sound good."

"Dinner in ten."

"Okay, I'll just freshen up." I tentatively walk up the stairs, unsure what new surprises lie in store. There are two bedrooms on the next level and a small bathroom. Is one of these hers? I duck my head in to see that one bedroom has been converted to a wardrobe, it's full to the brim of clothes all hanging neatly. Boxes of shoes are lined up but they aren't your usual boxes, they seem very old.

Ah yes, I remember that she has a love of all things vintage. This must be where she keeps her collection. I keep going up the stairs and find the main at the top, my eyes roam around as if I'm a child in a candy shop. "Fuck. Me."

This isn't a grand room by any means, it's small and intimate.

Romantic.

The walls are a shade of blush apricot, the drapes are an antique lace. A beautiful chandelier hangs in the center of the room and there's a giant picture of a vase of roses. There's a cream marble dresser with a gilded gold mirror above it. Over the bed is a sheer canopy and the bedside tables are a matching cream marble. This is probably the most feminine and luxe bedroom I have ever been in...and I've seen a lot of bedrooms in my life. "Wow," I whisper as I drop to sit on the bed and look around.

I can feel Alora in every inch of it; her presence is so strong in here. My eyes roam around the space and I see a book on her side of the bed and I pick it up.

I skim over the blurb and place it back down, not at all the type of book that I imagine she would read. My eyes go to the shelves and I go to them, my finger runs across the spines. They're worn as if read time and time again, like an old companion that's constantly brought out, a friend she revisits. I pick up an oval photo frame of a woman, she has long dark hair and a pretty smile, she looks like Alora and my heart sinks. This must be her late mother. I carefully put the frame back where it was. My eyes land on an old metal tin, it's obviously an antique and very well loved. Red and gold and very worn, I wonder what's inside. My guilty eyes rise to the door to check the coast is clear and I pick it up, slide the lid off and frown as I stare down at the contents. Needles and thread, with a selection of black or white satin fabric labels in different sizes, huh, what are these for? I pick one up and turn it over to see that it has been embroidered with the initials.

AS

I don't understand why she would have this, *AS* what does that stand for...oh, Alora Sorenson. What the hell? She embroiders her initials onto labels for her clothing? I've never met anyone who would take the time to do such a thing. I close the tin, unsure how to unpack that piece of information.

The bathroom is small and cream marble, quaint and understated. I hate to admit this, but Alora is the first normal person I've ever been with.

The women I date have all come from money and a lot of that has to do with the circles we run in, but a lot of it also has to do with the fact that I have no interest in meeting a gold digger.

Alora doesn't fit into either category, or any that I've ever known for that matter. She isn't even normal, she's eccentric with weird grandma hobbies.

Completely happy as she is.

I sit for a moment with my thoughts, blazingly aware that she wouldn't give up anything here for the life that I live. My world is fast, hard, and competitive. Nocturnal.

A million miles away from a vegetable garden, embroidered initials and playlists called "Sunny Mornings."

This will never work.

"Dinner." I hear her voice echo up the stairs.

"Coming."

Before I know it my hands are under the faucet and as the hot water runs over them, I'm wondering if this thing between us is even worth pursuing.

Let's face it, I already know how this ends.

I make my way downstairs to see that she has set the table outside in the garden in amongst the lights. Two long, thin, white candles are in the center of the table, crystal glasses of water are beside the delicious-looking meal and everything looks perfect.

I smile as I sit down. "You are quite the entertainer, Miss Sorenson." I pick up my napkin and place it on my lap.

"Don't get too excited." She smiles as she picks up her knife and fork. "You haven't tasted it yet."

I take a bite of the melt-in-the-mouth steak and my eyebrows flick up in surprise. "I knew this smelt good, but that was nothing in comparison to how it tastes."

She smiles proudly and we eat in silence for a while as my mind scampers through this new information.

"Tell me." I finish my mouthful as I try to get the wording right in my head. "Where do you see this going?" I wipe my mouth with the napkin.

"What?"

I gesture to the air between us. "This."

"Well." She cuts her steak with a subtle shrug. "I'm happy today." She smiles with another shrug as she bites the steak from her fork.

I stare at her with a frown. "What does that mean?"

"I live for the day, I'm happy in the moment."

"What the fuck does that mean? Speak English."

"Well...." She thinks for a moment. "So many people live

in the future and are always thinking ahead as to what will make them happy, but in the meantime are walking around miserable."

"True." I sip my wine as I listen.

"And up until recently I had always been very happy on a day-to-day basis."

"Why until recently?"

"Well." She smiles softly over at me. "You were this beautiful book that I started to read in Switzerland but I got interrupted and felt like I didn't get to finish the story." She takes a sip of wine. "But I always had your page turned down in hope that one day I could pick it back up to see how it ended."

My heart swells as I stare at her.

"And then I saw you at that auction and instantly I was back in the unfinished book. And no matter how hard I tried to live in the moment and enjoy my day, I couldn't do it."

"Why not?"

"Because I was back in there with you."

We stare at each other as the air crackles between us.

"So my days became sad and lonely and I felt like I wasn't where I was supposed to be."

"And now you're here and back in our book."

"Yes." She holds her glass over and I tap it with mine.

"Where does this book go, Alora?"

"I don't know." She shrugs. "But I do know that I'm happy being back in the moment and I want to just take it one day at a time with us. As long as we're both happy today is all that matters."

I stare at her for a moment, uneasiness falls over me at her answer.

If your plan is to make me fall in love with you...only to leave me as soon as things get hard.

"You like to live a simple life?" I ask.

"I do. Stillness changes me in a way that busy can't."

"I have never been still."

"I know." She chews her food as if thinking. "But how do you know what's in your heart if you are never still enough to listen to it?"

"Maybe my heart doesn't speak." I shrug.

"Or maybe you just never listened to it."

I eat in silence, unsure how she wants me to respond.

"Love isn't always loud, Edward."

My eyes rise to meet hers. "What does that mean?"

"Lust is loud, love is quiet. It grows in between spoken words and offers a sense of belonging between two people."

"That's *if* you're looking for love."

"That's true."

"You know...." I hesitate. "If you're looking for a grand love, I'm not the man for you. That's not what I'm looking for."

"I get that." She nods. "But do you ever ask yourself why you wouldn't want a grand love in your life?"

"No."

"Well, then." She shrugs casually. "Maybe this will be our last night together."

Don't say that.

"Why?" I put my cutlery down.

"Because I'm not going to dim my light to feed your shadows."

My eyes hold hers.

"In my eyes...if you give up on true love then you are making a conscious decision to live a life with an average love. But no matter how you look at it, they both hurt."

Her words hang in the air between us.

"Is that what you're looking for?" I ask. "True love."

"I'm looking for a best friend. Someone who knows what's in my heart even when I don't speak. A teacher, a protector, a beautiful father for my children." She shrugs and sips her wine. "At my age this isn't about orgasms, this is about finding my soulmate."

I snap my eyes away from hers, typical fucking bullshit.

"I mean...." She stops herself mid-sentence.

"What?" I snap, annoyed.

"What can you offer me, Edward?"

"What does that mean?" I huff, she's getting annoying now.

"Let's be real, apart from orgasms and money...what can you offer me?"

"Apart from orgasms and money?" I frown. "Is that all I am to you?"

"Not at all, but I believe that's all *you* think you are."

I throw my napkin down onto the table. "I didn't come here to get lectured on my shortcomings."

"What *did* you come here for?"

"I came here to see *you*."

"And yet you shy away from a hard conversation."

"I'm not shying away from anything. I just don't need this bullshit."

"Okay." She shrugs and picks up her cutlery and begins to casually eat again.

"What does okay mean?" I snap.

"It was fun while it lasted, but the reality is that this probably *will* be our last night together, and I hope you have a nice life with your white-hot money and your lukewarm love."

I blink, surprised.

White-hot money and your lukewarm love.... She hit the nail on the head.

If she stabbed me through the heart it would hurt less.

She's ending it.

I drop my head, rattled.

"I believe that at some point in your life you have to take a big swing and truly go all in, or else what's the point?" She shrugs.

"It's not that simple, we come from different worlds." I drag my hand through my hair, completely flustered. "I've told you already, I'm not good at relationships and as soon as we put pressure on it everything is going south."

"Why do you think that you are not good at relationships?"

"I don't think it, I know it. I'm not...." I pause. "Wired the same as most people."

She reaches over the table and takes my hand in hers as her eyes search mine. "My love will not heal you, Edward, but I can hold your hand while you heal yourself."

Emotion unexpectedly fills me and her silhouette blurs.

What the fuck is going on with me lately?

"Hey...." She gets up and comes around and sits across my lap, her lips dust mine. "We can work it out together."

"I'm not capable of giving you what you want, Alora," I murmur as my arm tightens around her. "You need to move on."

"No." She kisses me again. "I'm not leaving you where you are."

"You need to because..." I shake my head, "...I can't...."

"Yes. You can."

I lean my forehead against her shoulder, words escape me. There is nothing I can say that will make either of us feel any better.

"If you can't do it for you...then do it for me."

CHAPTER TWENTY-THREE

ALORA.

"Alora." He pushes me off his lap and stands in a rush. "I have to go…."

Shit…*too much, too soon.*

"No. You didn't eat your dinner yet," I stammer in a panic. "If this is our last night together, let's just enjoy it."

He twists his lips as he looks around.

"Enough of the deep talk." I hold my hands up. "I promise."

He begrudgingly sits back down.

Stop making demands, you idiot.

"All you have to think about is how many orgasms I'll have tonight."

He gives me a lopsided smile. "*That*, I can do."

Darkness.

Glasses on, headphones secure, I aim the pistol at the target and fire.

Bull's-eye.

I load the gun and take aim again and shoot.

Bull's-eye.

Everything is falling into place, I'm nearly there.

Locked, ready, and loaded.

ALORA.

The steam envelops us as the hot water falls from above.

My head is on Edward's chest and his big safe arms are around me as we stand under the shower. My legs still shaky, it's late, and like every time we sleep together, more of the façade came down. We always start off rough, fucking hard. Feeding our bodies with an animalistic attraction, but then it turns into something else, something more.

The bad girl in me loves Mr. Doe in all his dark glory, but the soft girl in me is falling harder for Edward.

Mr. Prescott the powerful mogul seems a million miles away from us, which in itself is ridiculous because I know he's the same man. But how do you reconcile craving a powerful sex maniac, while yearning for the softer, more loving man who is buried deep within him?

His lips are at my temple as he holds me in his arms and every now and then he kisses me softly as if he, too, is trying to make sense of this.

What started as a carnal attraction is developing into so much more.

"You need to sleep, Doe," he says softly. "You're exhausted. Let's get you into bed."

I smile sleepily, my favorite thing in the world is hearing him call me Doe. "Okay." But I don't move, because being here under the hot water with him is like being in our own little love cocoon.

Eventually we get out and he wraps me in a towel and dries me as if I am a child.

I'm not sure why he does this, but perhaps it's to make amends for how hard he uses my body during sex. I smile sleepily up at him as he dries my hair.

"What?" He concentrates on his task.

"You know.... You're a really, really great fuck."

He chuckles as if surprised. "Just really, really great?"

"Like otherworldly." I widen my eyes.

"Otherworldly?" He hangs the towel up and leads me into the bedroom. "How many other world creatures have you slept with?"

"Just you." I smile as I lie down. "The others didn't let me sleep."

He chuckles and lifts the covers up as he tucks me in and turns and walks around my bedroom naked as I watch on. His large body is ripped, every muscle is proudly on display. He has that distinct *V* that leads down to his groin. His thick cock hangs heavily between his legs and damn….

I'm not even joking. Edward Prescott is a beast to behold. My body throbs for hours after. His size, his domination, his sheer will over my body, an addiction that I have no idea how I'm going to break.

This can't be our last night together…. It can't be. We are too good together; he will see it. I know he will.

He bends and gets a black velvet bag or something out of his bag and puts it in the drawer beside the bed and it's then I remember what I heard earlier.

"Why do you need a gun?"

"For protection." He turns down his side of the blankets. "There are no guards here, so just in case."

"Hmm."

He slides in behind me and pulls me close to his body, we lie spooned together and I feel myself relax again. "Good night, Doe."

"Good night, my sweet Edward." I put my hand up to cup his face over my shoulder.

I feel him smile into the darkness.

"What?" I smile too.

"I've never been called sweet before."

"That's not true. I'm sure your mother thought you were the sweetest little boy she ever knew."

He falls silent and I inwardly kick myself, why did I say that? *Too far.*

I love talking about my late mother, I love being reminded that she loved me, but it doesn't bring everyone happiness, I need to remember that. He kisses my cheek as I hold his face to mine, his lips linger on my skin, and a beautiful intimacy holds us together.

Unspoken words hang between us; I can feel them in the air. Building, growing…. Manifesting into a tangible force.

This feels a lot like love….

Brrrrr, brrrrr, brrrrr.

I wake with a start and reach over for my phone to hit the alarm and lie back and smile sleepily.

What a night.

Hours and hours of time with him.

Wait….

I open my eyes to see his side of the bed is empty, and I sit up. "Edward," I call.

Silence….

I can't feel his presence, surely he wouldn't have left without saying goodbye…. Would he?

"Edward," I call again as I climb out of bed and grab my robe. I rush down the stairs. "Edward." But I can already tell he isn't here, perhaps he's out in the garden.

As I get to the bottom of the stairs my fears are realized, he's not here. Did he not want to wake me or….

Then I see it, a note on the kitchen counter.

Good Morning Alora.

As usual in your company I had a wonderful time last night, you are so very beautiful.

My heart sinks as I read on.

On greater reflection over our conversation last night I've come to the realization that we cannot continue on this journey.

Unfortunately I am not in a position to offer what you are looking for, if only I could, I promise you, I would.

I cherished our time together, and please know that I will never forget you.

I sincerely hope you find the grand love you are looking for and I wish you all the happiness in the world.

All my love
Edward.
XX

"Wow." I puff air into my cheeks. "Here I was falling in love and there he was drafting a breakup letter." I slump onto the stool at the kitchen counter.

I read it again and again. Disappointed but not surprised, and even though I thought I made a valid case last night I guess on some level I knew the writing was on the wall. The end was always near.

I'm not a princess or an heiress and obviously once he saw my humble abode, my love of simplicity and my beloved vegetable patch, he knew I wasn't the girl for him. His words from last night come back to me: *we come from different worlds.*

The reality is, I know he's right and this is probably for the best. Better to cut ties now rather than later when I'm hopelessly in love with him. Who am I kidding, I already am.

Fuck.

I make myself a cup of coffee and walk to the kitchen window, two blackbirds are sitting side by side on the fence. Chatting away and bouncing along together.

Happily oblivious to the complications of being human and the heartache it brings.

I watch them for a long time, my mind runs over the last two months.

Are you happy, Alora? You broke up your relationship for a man who didn't even care about you.

Betrayal washes over me and my eyes well with tears.

I'm such a fool.

I walk into work with a spring in my step, I'm not going to cry over a man who doesn't want me.

Screw him.

"So…." Helene's eyes widen with excitement. "How did it go?"

"How did what go?" I take my scarf off and hang it up on the hook.

"Your night with Edward."

"Oh." I sit down and turn my computer on. "It was okay." I shrug. "I don't think we'll be seeing each other again, though."

Her face falls. "Why not?"

"I woke up to an it's-not-you-it's-me letter."

"You did." She drops into the seat opposite me. "But I thought—"

"Doesn't matter." I cut her off. "I don't want to talk about it and I don't want to talk about him ever again."

"Right." Her eyes hold mine. "You okay?"

"Yep." I force a smile.

Not really, I'm hanging on to my sanity by a thread, but damn it, I'm going to fake it till I make it. Like that motivational book says, I can do hard things.

"But there are two guards still out the front." She frowns.

"I have to put a stop to that as well." I open my emails.

"Do you want to film this morning?"

"Not today." I can't bring myself to act happy. "Tomorrow?"

"Sure." She disappears out the front and I stare at my cold, hard and lonely computer screen as my heart sobs in silence.

He broke me….

Hard.

PHILIPPE.

"Get out of my office," Edward yells at the top of his voice. "Now."

The door opens and a man practically runs down the hallway to get out of the line of fire.

Bang.

Something hits the back of the door.

"What the hell is wrong with him this week?" Stefan leans in and whispers.

"No idea," I whisper back.

"Melissa," he yells as the door comes flying open. "Where the fuck is my phone charger?"

Melissa comes running with a charger. "I have it here, Mr. Prescott."

"What good is it out there?" he growls as he snatches it from her. "Don't take it again."

"Yes, sir." She follows him into the office.

"What are you doing in here?" he bellows. "Leave."

She closes the door as she walks out and widens her eyes at us. "Heaven help us."

I bite my lip to hide my smile.

Ten minutes pass. "What do you mean?" he yells. "Why are you so fucking incompetent?"

"Who's he talking to on the phone now?" Stefan mouths.

"Fuck knows, some poor bastard."

Bang.

Something hits the back of the door again.

"What is he throwing in there?" Stefan frowns. "He's going to break a window in a minute."

More time passes, more screaming and more things thrown.

"I'll go talk to him," I murmur.

"Are you crazy?"

I knock quietly on the door.

"What?" he yells.

I tentatively open the door. "Mr. Prescott?"

"What do you want?"

"Shall I get the plane ready for a trip to London, sir?"

"What the fuck are you talking about?" he bellows. "Mind your business. I'm fine."

"I know, sir." I force a smile. "But I think a trip to London would be very beneficial."

His eyes rise to meet mine and the look he gives me is sheer evil. "Get out before I fucking strangle you with this charger cord."

"Yes, sir." I close the door behind me.

"How did it go?" Stefan smirks.

"How do you think it went?"

ALORA.

The wind and the rain lash against the glass. Sitting on the window bench seat, I sip my tea as I stare out into the storm.

My mind has been a clusterfuck of confusion and hurt, and I honestly don't know if I could have made more of a mess of my life lately.

I knew Edward Prescott was a walking red flag, but I was right with my underestimate, he was a red carpet.

A giant, loveable, addictive and toxic red carpet.

One that I'm hopelessly in love with and no matter how hard I try to forget him, I can't escape the feelings I have. The sheer desperation to be with him and share a life.

The worst part is my heart tells me he feels the same but just can't allow himself to go there with me…but maybe that's just wishful thinking.

They always say that men aren't hard to read, that their actions speak louder than words. It's what they don't do or say that you need to listen to….

And he does nothing, he gives me nothing other than orgasms and I was dead on the money the other night giving him the third degree. The next morning I was kicking myself for pushing so hard, but as the days have gone past I'm proud of myself for being honest. I wanted more and I told him…. And he ran. I can't say I'm surprised, just sad.

I get a vision of the life we could have had together, laughing and rolling around in the sheets, a family full of love and children, growing old together…and damn, I need to stop this before I have a full mental breakdown over him.

No man is worth this heartache.

Ring, ring…ring, ring…. I glance at the screen: *Sis.*

I smile, my beautiful sister. The built-in best friend who I can always depend on, she never lets me down. "Hi."

"Hey, babe," she says. "How are you?"

"I'm okay," I lie.

"Did you hear from him?"

"No." I shrug. "I think it's officially over."

"Well, screw him, you can do better anyway."

My heart twists because I know there isn't better, he's the cream of the crop.

"Yeah." I force a smile. "Screw him."

"Why don't you come home for a few days?"

"I can't, I've got to work. Can you come here?"

"I wish, I have to work too." She falls silent for a moment and we hang on the phone. "Put me on FaceTime, I'm going to wash the dishes while I talk to you."

"Okay, I'm going to make another cup of tea." I make my

way downstairs, and flick FaceTime on. "It is raining cats and dogs here."

"Really?" The camera comes on and I see her and laugh. "Why is your face mask bright orange?"

"I don't know, I bought this shit on TikTok. It's the latest trend." She turns her head to look at her reflection in the camera. "Do you think it will stain my skin?"

"I would get that shit off immediately if I were you."

She carries the phone into the bathroom and sets it down, I watch on as she washes her face and I smile at the normalcy of us.

I'm going to be okay.

EDWARD.

"I just don't get it," Nicholas says as he reads out loud from his phone. "It says here...." The voices trail off.

I walk to the staircase and then back to the door, I look out over the sea and glance at my watch, it's 6 p.m.

She'd be finishing work soon.

"You know how it works...." Theodore's voice blurs into the distance.

I walk to the bottom of the staircase and back to the door.

Why hasn't Philippe called me yet?

I walk to the staircase and then back to the door, I glance at my watch again.

Time passes and it's now 7:30 p.m... hmm.

Maybe I should call him?

I walk to the staircase and then back to the door.

"Will you sit down?" Theodore snaps. "What the fuck is wrong with you?"

I continue to pace, I glance at my watch again.

Is she working late tonight?

"Prescott," Theo snaps.

I glance up. "What?"

"What the hell is wrong with you? You're like a cat on a hot tin roof."

"Nothing. Why?"

"You're wearing the carpet down with all the pacing."

"I'm not pacing." I screw up my face in annoyance. "Can you all fuck off back to your yachts and leave me alone."

"What *is* wrong with you lately?" William frowns.

"Nothing," I snap. "I've just got a lot on my mind."

The need to know she's okay is slowly sending me insane.

I walk to the staircase and then back to the door.

Fuck this, why hasn't he called? I storm out to the deck and dial his number.

Ring, ring....

"Boss," he answers.

"What's happening?" I snap.

"She hasn't left yet, she's still in her store."

I glance at my watch. "What's she doing in there?"

"I don't know, the other staff left half an hour ago."

"Go in and see if she's alright."

"She's alright, I can see her cleaning through the front window."

"Why is she cleaning after hours?" I bark.

"I don't know, why don't you ring *her* and ask."

"You are beginning to piss me off, Philippe."

"Yeah, yeah. I'll call you when she's home safe."

I hang up and walk to the staircase and then back to the door.

Is she alright?

ALORA.

ONE WEEK LATER.

I click through and type into Google.

Best beach holiday destinations.

I've made an executive decision, I'm going on a vacation all by myself. Where I can lie in the sun, drink margaritas, and have daily massages. Somewhere that I can lick my wounds and get myself together in private, away from his guards.

For a while there having his guards still loitering around gave me hope, I mean if he cared enough to have me watched over then maybe he was coming back.

But as the days go by I realize this isn't about coming back, this is about control.

Him knowing where I am at all times, and I'm sorry, Mr. Prescott, but I've had enough.

Screw. You.

The crying, heartbroken and wimpy version of Alora has morphed into the angry and mean version of Alora. And I like her a lot better.

Even if Edward came back now begging on his knees for forgiveness, I wouldn't take him back. No way in hell, that chapter has closed for good. He had his chance and he blew it.

Asshole.

EDWARD.

"Good morning, I'm Alora from Sorenson Antiques," she says, my heart constricts at the sight of her smile, I feel it all the way to the pit of my stomach. Her hair is down and she's wearing a fitted cream dress.

Always so effortlessly beautiful.

I don't know why I keep putting myself through this by watching her morning videos, all it does is screw up my entire day. She's clearly composed, happy, and carefree. While I'm over here dying a slow and painful death.

"Today we have a beautiful chest that I want to show you." She runs her hand over the chest. "It's early seventeen hundreds and would have been used as a blanket or storage box." The camera angle circles the chest. "Perfect for hiding useless things." She opens the lid. "Perhaps even spineless cowards and their pathetic letters." She slams the door shut. "Just joking, those things belong in the trash with all the other nasty things."

Adrenaline surges, even when not addressing me directly she still has a way of pissing me off.

"And these marble lamps are beautiful." She picks one up and pretends to swing it. "Excellent for knocking people out."

I click out of my phone in disgust.

I won't be watching these stupid videos again...who am I kidding, until tomorrow when her next one comes out.

The club is loud, the drinks are strong. My mind...distracted.

It's been two weeks since I last saw Alora, although she's haunted my every thought. Starred in my every dream.

Beautiful women are sauntering past, circling like vultures.... And yet all I can think about is her.

I've got it bad...really bad.

My friends are laughing and chatting, having a great night. And me, I think I'm having a midlife crisis. Perhaps even an existential crisis.

A big one.

I drag my hand through my hair, annoyed with myself.

Get the fuck over it.

She's just another woman and this feeling will pass. From the depths of my dark soul a little voice whispers:

What if doesn't?

I slam another shot back and slosh it around in my mouth, I feel it burn all the way down. I lick my lips and take another off the tray.

I'll do anything to numb this feeling.

Mikaela saunters over, she's wearing a silver minidress and has legs up to her ears. She straddles my leg and bends down to whisper in my ear, "I need to be fucked." Her teeth graze my ear and my cock twitches with approval. "And only your cock will do."

Hmmm....

Perhaps a good hard fuck with someone else is all it would take.

It would be so easy to lose myself in someone for a while.

But then.... The thought of having another woman doesn't interest me in the slightest.

I only want her.

What the fuck is wrong with me?

I pull my ear away from her mouth. "Not tonight." I wave her away and glance at my watch. It's only 1 a.m.

Screw this.

I need to go home.

PHILIPPE.

"Good morning, Philippe." Alora smiles as she walks out of her house.

"Good morning, Miss Sorenson." I open the car door for her, she slides into the back seat and I walk around and get in behind the wheel.

"If you could please give me a lift to work and then I won't be needing your services any longer."

"Ah...." My eyes meet hers in the rearview mirror. "I'm here for your safety, Miss Sorenson." I pull out from the curb and onto the road.

"I'm not in any danger, Philippe."

"But you had a tracker in your handbag, remember?"

"Did I, though?" She narrows her eyes. "Or did Edward plant that in my bag so that he would have an excuse to have you follow me around?"

Stefan and I exchange glances.

"Edward and I are no longer together and he has you following me so that *he* can keep track of me." She looks out the window as she talks, seemingly detached.

That's why he's been a lunatic lately.

"You broke it off with him?" I frown.

"No. He broke it off with me, so you can understand how infuriating it is that he still has you trailing me everywhere I go. I am not his possession and I won't be treated as such."

"Ahh." I'm unsure how to answer.

"Today will be your last day with me."

"I'll have to check with Mr. Prescott."

"There is nothing to check, Philippe," she fires back. "If you follow me tomorrow I *am* calling the police and having you charged with stalking. What he is doing is illegal and I will no longer stand for it."

"Yes, Miss Sorenson." I nod. "I'll let him know."

"Thank you."

"Just call him and get it over with." Stefan lights a cigarette as we lean up against the car.

I give a subtle shake of my head, why do I get all the good jobs? I dial his number.

"Yes," Edward answers.

"Miss Sorenson has let us know that this will be our last day with her."

"No."

"She said she's calling the police if we turn up tomorrow."

"So let her call the fucking police," he snaps. "Somebody is tracking her."

"She thinks that you put the tracker in her bag."

"Why the fuck would *I* put a tracker in her bag?"

"To control her."

"Stop insulting my intelligence. Stay. With. Her."

"I don't want to get arrested."

"The police are on my fucking payroll," he fires back. "Who the hell is going to arrest you?"

"She said you broke up with her."

"That is none of your business and your high horse is a fucking donkey. Do your job and do not let her out of your sight."

Click.... The phone goes dead.

Stefan raises an eyebrow. "Well?"

"We stay."

ALORA.

With my garage door down and hidden from the world I put my suitcase into the trunk of my car. Today's the day, and I'm not telling anyone but Helene where I'm headed. I'm going to pick her up and she's going to bring an empty suitcase with her and then she's going to drop me at the airport under the guise I am taking her there. Just as I suspected, the guards have turned up this morning, and our only goal is to outrun them.

I do a last check of my place, water my plants and grab my purse.

It's vacation time.

I start my car and the garage door slowly goes up, they're both leaning up against the car chatting away and I floor it and drive right past them. I glance into the rearview mirror to see them scrambling and I put my foot on the gas.

I giggle, proud of myself.

Catch me if you can.

CHAPTER TWENTY-FOUR

EDWARD.

"And then moving forward I want to build...."

Bzz, bzz, bzz, my phone vibrates on my desk and I glance at the screen.

Philippe

Why is he calling me?

"I have to take this," I tell the four people at the board table. I stand and walk to the window and look out over the view. "Yes."

"We've got a problem."

"Such as?"

"Alora drove off this morning and we've followed her but we got caught in traffic and have lost sight of her car."

"Where are you?"

"At the international airport."

What?

Fury fills me.

"Alone?"

"No, Helene is with her."

"Find. Her." I hang up as adrenaline screams through my bloodstream and I turn back to the eight eyes watching me. "Get out."

They exchange glances and stand.

"Now," I growl.

They scamper from the room like rats.

I call Philippe back. "Yes, boss."

"Did you find her?"

"No."

"What the hell are you idiots doing?" I scream. "You have one fucking job."

"She's purposely tried to lose us."

"And she succeeded," I fume. "Do not let her get on a fucking plane. Do you hear me?"

"If she's already through customs then it's too late, we can't get through."

"Buy a fucking plane ticket to get through."

"Yes, sir."

I pace back and forth. If she gets on a plane to god knows where...without protection...if something happens to her... if....

I dial her number as my blood boils. *Ring, ring.*

"Hello," she answers.

"Where the fuck are you?" I yell.

"That's *none* of your business."

"Alora, I'm warning you. Do not dare get on a fucking plane."

"I'll do whatever I like."

"Stop being so childish, have you forgotten someone is stalking you? It is not safe to travel alone at the moment."

"Give me a break."

"Why are you purposely trying to piss me off?" I scream.

"What?" she scoffs. "Are you for real?"

"Get your ass back to Nice. Right. Fucking. Now."

"Swear at me again and I'm blocking your number."

Veins are pulsing in my temples; the sky is a red shade of fury. "Stop being irresponsible, I want you safe."

"And I want to forget I ever met you. So leave me alone. You've made it abundantly clear that I'm too much for you. So go find less."

"Don't you fucking dare threaten me. You *will* take a guard with you."

"Stop trying to control me with your money, Edward, my love isn't for sale. Stay the hell away from me. I never want to see you again."

Click.

"Are you fucking kidding me?" My anger explodes and I dial her number again.

Ring, ring.... Ring, ring...ring, ring.

"I swear to god." I'm so angry that I can hardly see straight. "Answer the fucking phone," I growl as I pace. I hang up and dial her number again.

Ring, ring.... Ring, ring...ring, ring.

"Fuck," I scream. I call her immediately.

Ring, ring.... Ring, ring...ring, ring.

ALORA.

Heart hammering in my chest, I turn my phone off and shuffle forward in line.

"Tickets please." The stewardess smiles.

I pass my ticket over and walk through and onto the plane. I take a seat and peer up the aisle of the plane. "Come on, come on, just close the door already," I whisper.

He's going to march onto this plane any moment and cause a scene, I just know it.

I wipe the perspiration from my brow, how the heck did my life get so complicated?

He doesn't want me but still wants to control me

Talk about a toxic situationship.

For fifteen minutes I hold my breath, praying to get in the air. The doors finally close and I let out a sigh of relief. Thank god, two weeks of sun, sand and relaxation.

Thailand, here I come.

PHILIPPE.

I stand on the dock and stare up at the yacht to see the dark silhouette pacing back and forth like a caged animal. It's near midnight and the marina is in silence.

"What the hell is going on with Prescott?" Stefan murmurs as he stands beside me watching him. "I've never seen him like this before."

"Me neither." I light my cigarette. "He's got it bad for this woman."

"Yeah, well, he just fucking lost her, so get over it."

I watch him for another half hour and I can't let this go on, I go through my phone and walk up the marina so that nobody else can hear me. Ring, ring....

"Philippe," William answers.

"Hi."

"Is everything okay?" he asks.

"Ahh...." My eyes flick up to the yacht. "Are you around tonight?"

"I'm in London, why, what's wrong?"

I twist my lips as my eyes flick back to the yacht. "Edward is just—"

"What?" He cuts me off.

"Agitated."

"What's happened?"

"I'm not sure, I was just thinking that you may be able to come over, but if you're in London—"

"I'll call him now," he replies.

"Okay."

"Thanks, man."

I walk to the end of the marina as I do another check and ten minutes later my phone vibrates in my pocket, the name William lights up the screen.

"How did it go?"

"He didn't answer."

I twist my lips as my eyes go back to the yacht. "Thought as much."

"Can you go in and check on him please?"

"He doesn't want to see me."

"He doesn't want to see anyone, just go in and make him go to bed to sleep it off. He'll be fine by morning."

"Yeah, okay."

"Call me if anything else is going on."

"Alright."

I make my way onto the yacht and stand at the door. "Edward."

He turns toward me, his eyes are wild and he's totally disheveled.

"Let's get you to bed, hey?"

"I'm fine," he replies, his voice is weak, broken.

But he's not fine, his soft and sad reply is so unlike him that it only worries me more.

"I've got some of your sleeping pills."

"Go away please," he murmurs.

"Sir, I need you to go to bed and get some sleep or else as a duty of care I'm going to have to call your brother."

He exhales heavily. "Leave me be."

"A good night's sleep will fix everything; in the morning you will feel so much better and we can make a new plan."

He stares at me for a while and eventually nods, resigned.

I follow him up to his bedroom and get his sleeping pills and pass them to him; he takes them with a glass of water.

"What would I do without you, Philippe?" he says softly.

"Probably murder a lot of people." I smile as I gesture to the bathroom. "Shower."

I wait as he showers and then eventually he comes back into the bedroom with a towel around his waist and drops it as he dresses into boxer shorts.

"Have you eaten?" I ask.

"Yep." He pulls the blankets back and climbs into bed, and I know he's lying. He hasn't eaten all day.

"I'm going to stay on the yacht tonight, okay?" I tell him.

"Whatever."

"I'll be in the room next door; you call me if you need me."

"I won't need you." He sighs.

"What if you have a bad dream?" I tease.

"Fuck off," he replies with his eyes closed.

"Well, can I call you if I have a bad dream?" I smile.

"Get out before I kill you," he mutters dryly.

I flick the light off and leave his bedroom door ajar. "Tomorrow will be a better day."

"Stick to your day job, you're a terrible therapist."

"Sweet dreams." I smirk.

"Shut the fuck up."

EDWARD.

I roll my lips as I park the car, can't believe I'm about to do this.

I push through the doors of the antique store and walk in. "Hello, Helene."

Helene turns and her face falls when she sees me. "What are you doing here?"

"I...." What am I doing here? "I need to know Alora is okay."

"She's fine." She picks up the feather duster and walks to the shelving as if to dismiss me. Not one to be deterred, I follow her.

"Is she alone?" I ask.

"Well." She dusts a shelf. "I talked to her a half hour ago and she was at the beach bar and she had just met a lovely man." She keeps dusting. "Funnily enough...he just broke up with his girlfriend as well."

I glare at her, my tongue slides over my teeth as I get a vision of Alora talking to another man, my fists clench at my sides.

"Where is she?"

"That is *none* of your business."

"It's all of my business, I want her to be safe."

"Oh, she's safe." She smiles sarcastically. "But let's be real for a moment, you don't want her, you just don't want anyone else to have her. But my prediction is that tonight she's going to fuck you out of her system with a long, hard night grinding in the sheets." She smiles. "And by morning she won't even remember who you are. You snooze, you lose, Prescott. Letting her go was the biggest mistake of your life."

My jaw clenches in fury. "I don't like you."

She shrugs with a smile. "But Alora does, and we both know that her opinion is the only one that matters."

"Where is she?"

"Get out."

I hate this woman, although her loyalty is admirable.

"When will she be back?"

"In a while."

"How long?"

"Goodbye, Edward." She turns to dust the shelf. "Tell Philippe to ask me out on a date."

"Dream on." I march toward the door. "That will absolutely not be happening."

"Toodle-oo." She waves with her fingertips. "Have a nice life," she says in a singsong voice. I march out of the store and onto the street, I can feel my blood as it pumps angrily through my veins.

What a fucking witch.

ALORA.

"Where are you from?" I ask.

"New York," he replies with a playful smile. His sandy hair has a curl to it, and even while sitting down on a bar stool I can tell that his tanned body is built for sin. I thought men like this only existed in brochures, I've never met a man like him while on vacation before. "It's beautiful. Like you."

"Really?" I smile as I feel myself blush, there is definitely something about this guy. "My sister lives in New York."

"Yeah? What part?"

"Manhattan."

"Next time you're there visiting we will have to catch up." His eyes dance with mischief. "I could show you around the city that never sleeps."

"I'm sure if I went I would be sleeping." I smile into my drink.

"I wouldn't be so sure about that." He smiles as he sips his cocktail.

Oh...

I'm at a beach bar in Koh Samui and have unexpectedly just met another solo traveler, funnily enough he's here recovering from a breakup as well.

"We have a lot in common, Alora." He smiles as he sips his cocktail.

"Apparently so." I tap my cocktail glass with his and frown. "What was your name again?"

"Brennan."

"Well," I smile, this guy seems just so wonderfully … normal. No bodyguards, no baggage and there is absolutely no heart left for him to break. "It's nice to meet you, Brennan."

"After we finish our drinks would you like to go and get some dinner?"

"Um." I glance around in search for a reason not to.

Oh, that's right…. There are none. I'm a free agent who can do whatever the fuck I want to. I'm single, painstakingly heartbrokenly single, and maybe Helene is right.

Maybe the best way to get over Edward Prescott is to get under someone else.

"That sounds lovely."

EDWARD.

I stare at the graph on my computer screen and add a comment in the drop box.

Knock, knock, sounds at the door.

"Yes," I call.

The door opens. "Hello, Edward."

I know that voice, I glance up to see Paul walking into my office.

"What are you doing here?" I snap.

"Your brother has called me, apparently something is currently transpiring with you."

"Nope." I keep typing. "Go back to London, I'm fine."

"Okay." He sits down, ignoring my request.

"Leave please. I'm very busy."

I can feel his eyes on me as he looks me over. "Does this have to do with Alora?"

"No." I keep typing to evade his glare.

"So are you still seeing her?"

"No."

"Why not?"

"I am not interested in a relationship and she wants more." I shrug. "Wanted."

"Wanted as in past tense?"

"I guess."

"So she doesn't want that anymore?"

"No." I exhale and keep typing.

"How does that make you feel?"

Crazy.

"I don't care."

"You don't care?"

"No."

"You know, Edward, real love is messy, and not everyone is brave enough to let themselves feel it."

My heart sinks.

"Just get out," I whisper.

"You have come so far and you are so close."

I close my eyes to block him out.

"What's the worst that could happen.... You get your heart broken?"

I clench my jaw.

"From where I stand, your heart is already breaking by not being with her."

My eyes hold his.

"Are you really going to let her go?"

"She's better off without me."

"But are you better off without her?"

I swallow a lump in my throat. "I just don't need to deal with this shit today." I turn back to my computer and begin typing. "If I wanted to see you I would have come to London. You've wasted your time coming here."

"Everyone is worried about you."

"No need to be." I hit the computer key with force. "I'm fine."

"Okay, that's fine. You keep hiding from your emotions." He stands. "Throw away five years of our work together because you are too stubborn to let your heart out in the open. Too afraid to love someone."

The computer screen blurs. "Get out."

The door clicks as he closes it behind him and his words hang in the air like an echo. *Your heart is already breaking by not being with her.*

Make it stop.

An Aloraless life is a sad existence.

I sit in my car and stare through the windscreen as I watch her cross the road.

She's talking to Helene and laughing as they walk along together, she has a takeaway coffee in her hand.

She's back, and while she looks refreshed and happy, I've had two weeks of feeling like the world is coming to an end.

Complete insanity.

Her long dark hair is swept up into a ponytail and just the sight of her beautiful face flutters my stomach. She's wearing a cream cashmere turtleneck and a chocolate skirt with long, dark brown suede boots.

So classically Alora.

How does she always look so effortlessly perfect?

I'm ashamed to say it, but as soon as I saw her morning video this morning saying she was back, I came straight here...I literally couldn't help myself.

I had to see her.

She walks into her store and my heart drops in disappointment.

I close my eyes; I need to get a handle on this obsession.

This isn't healthy.

ALORA.

We walk into the store.

"Oh my god," Helene whispers. "What is he doing here?"

"Who?" I frown.

"Didn't you see? Edward was sitting in the car up the street, watching you."

"He was not."

"He is." She drags me to the front window. "See?" We peer out the front window and sure enough I see him sitting in his Bentley, elbow on the window, looking forlorn.

My heart begins to beat hard.

"What the hell is he doing?" I whisper. "Is he going to come in or...?"

"Go and find out." She pushes me toward the door.

Before I can stop myself, I storm out and up the street to the car. I get in the passenger seat and slam the door. His big blue eyes find mine and instantly I'm reminded of what he means to me.

Of how much is at stake here.

"What are you doing?" I ask, I can feel stupid tears are simmering dangerously close to the surface.

"I just um…." He stops himself with a shake of his head.

"Edward." My eyes search his. "I don't know what's going on with you, but I'm going to tell you what's going on with me."

His teeth catch his bottom lip as he listens.

"We're not right for each other," I whisper.

"I know that."

"No, stay quiet. *You* will listen to *me* this time. I have had two weeks alone to think about this and I need to get it off my chest," I snap. "We come from different worlds. I love peace and quiet and you love to party. I want to garden and you own a coke club. I'm looking for my forever man and you're looking for an escape route. But for some stupid crazy reason that I can't explain—" my eyes well with tears, "—I love you." I swipe them away. "And maybe that makes me a fool, and the fact that you're watching me from your car weeks after we were last together… makes me think that maybe you love me too."

His eyes search mine and he opens his mouth to say something but no words come out.

"Well?" I wait.

Silence.

My heart begins to hurt as it cracks wide open.

"I tell you that I love you and you can't even say one word?" I whisper through tears.

"Doe…." He gives a subtle shake of his head. "I'm…I just… it's not…."

I wait but he falls silent once more and it's obvious that he has nothing to say.

My tears break the dam and I angrily swipe them away. "Don't apologize for not loving me. It's not your fault." I get out of the car and lean back in. "Can you just do me one last favor?"

He nods.

"Please stay the hell away from me." The tears roll down my face. "I never want to see you again because it only reminds me of what we nearly had. And what you couldn't give me. I'm done," I spit as my heart breaks in two pieces. "I'm so fucking done." I slam the door and angrily wipe my tears as I storm back to my store. All his guards are watching, judging me for being so pathetic.

I'm such a fool.

I lie in the darkness; my eyes are swollen and my throat is sore. Seeing him today has torn me to shreds, I can't stop crying. That whole trip I tried to convince myself that I was stronger than this but the truth is, I'm heartbroken.

And not for the time we've had together, because I know it's been limited.

For what we could have been, for the future we could have had. And I can't imagine feeling the way I do about him with anyone else.

He well and truly broke me.

My phone beeps with a text and I know it's Helene checking on me for the fifteenth time tonight. I roll over and read it: Mr. Doe.

I'm at your front door.

I sit up, huh? I concentrate and read it again, am I seeing things? I get up and turn the light on, walk downstairs and open the front door.

"Hi, Doe," Edward says softly as his eyes search mine. "Can I come in?" He walks past me into the house and I close the door behind him.

"What are you doing here?" I cross my arms as I try to shield myself from his hurt.

"I love you." His eyes search mine. "More than anything…I love you."

CHAPTER TWENTY-FIVE

I stare at him, shocked to my core, unsure and confused.

"You said you loved me?" He frowns. "Today in the car…."

"I do."

He takes me into his arms and kisses me softly, his lips linger over mine.

A thousand emotions run through me all at the same time, disbelief, betrayal….

Fear.

"Why…." I frown as I step back from him. "What made you realize this now?"

"There's no point to anything. To having everything." He holds my face in his hands as he stares down at me. "If I don't have you it…all means nothing. I have to try."

My eyes search his, that doesn't sound very convincing. "Try?"

"I can't do this without you, nor would I want to."

"Since when?"

"Since Switzerland," he whispers against my lips. "And I can't fight myself over loving you any longer."

Oh….

Intimacy runs between us as we kiss, and holding him in my arms makes everything instantly better.

"You've had me since the day we met, you took my heart with you and never let me go," he murmurs against my lips.

"It was you who kept mine." I smile though tears as he holds me close, and I feel the tectonic plates slowly shift into place.

After the worst month in history, we can finally kiss and make up.

I take his hand and lead him up the stairs, he's somber and quiet and I don't know what he's been through but he doesn't seem to be himself.

As if finally opening up to me has broken him on some level.

We walk into my bedroom and I turn to face him. "It's okay now."

His eyes hold mine.

"It's okay now, babe, talk to me." I run my hand through his hair. "What's wrong?"

"Last time I was here, you asked me other than orgasms and money what could I offer you?"

I nod. "I did."

"The truth is, I don't know." He shrugs sadly. "When you walk into a room, you emit a light so bright, this beautiful calm aura, and I…." He swallows the lump in his throat as his eyes hold mine. "I have nothing to give you in return."

"Edward." My eyes well with tears, is this really how he feels? "You have everything to give me."

"Like what?"

"Love and honesty, respect and laughter." I smile up at him. "A family of my own and a future with the man that I love."

He puts his head into the crook of my neck and holds me tight in his arms and it becomes apparent that the last month has been hard on him too. "It's okay, babe," I whisper. "We'll work it out together." I pull his T-shirt up over his head, it's true that Edward and I are bad at a lot of things.

But physically, we're perfect. Our bodies fit together like a glove as if made only for each other.

I unzip his jeans and he kicks them off and I push him back to sit on the bed and as he watches my every move, I lift my nightdress over my head and straddle him.

"Kiss me," I breathe.

His lips take mine with reverence, and the feeling behind his kiss is heartfelt.

Deep.

"I love you," I whisper against his lips.

He screws up his face against mine and I push him back onto the bed. I get up onto my knees and guide his body into mine, his hands grab my hip bones and he pulls me down onto him.

We both moan as his large body takes possession of mine, he pulls me down to kiss him as we lose control.

Like a tsunami of love, slowly…and tenderly…we ride the wave of pleasure and for the first time in our history, we make soft and slow love.

Three hours later I'm curled against Edward's chest, his arms are around me and even though I'm exhausted, I don't want to go to sleep. Because then this wonderful night in our love bubble will be over. It's not often Edward lets his guard down, so I'm savoring every single second while it lasts. I know I'm going to wake up with a different man tomorrow.

Edward's finger circles aimlessly on the skin of my bare shoulder. "Were you with anyone while we were apart?"

"No." I look up at him. "Why, were you?"

"No." He kisses my temple. "Helene told me you were with a man at a beach bar. She told me you were going to fuck me out of your system."

"Of course she did." I smile, god I love that girl. "I did meet a man at a beach bar, but it wasn't like that. At least not from my side."

"Did he hit on you?"

"Yes, but I told him that I was still with another."

He stays still as he listens.

"Even though I wasn't with you, the thought of being with someone else made me physically sick."

He kisses my temple again, deep in thought. "I kept having this reoccurring dream every night," he murmurs. "More like a nightmare, actually."

"About what?"

"You told me that you were in love with another man and then when I saw him he was bald and had no teeth."

"*This* is what you dreamed about?" I smile. "Toothless men stealing me."

"His name was Cecil."

I giggle in surprise.

"If I ever see that guy…." He clenches his fist and holds it up.

"Nobody is going to steal me, Edward." I kiss his chest.

"Don't leave me again," he murmurs.

"I won't."

He holds me tighter, and unable to fight it, my eyes close. Finally safe in his arms, I fall asleep.

EDWARD.

I pull my suit coat over my shoulders and tie my tie. The boys brought me my clothes early this morning so I could leave for work from here.

Alora walks into the bathroom; she's wearing a tight black pencil skirt and a cream silk blouse. My eyes drop down her body. "You look…" I grab her roughly and push her against the bathroom counter, "…fuckable."

I'm feeling more myself today.

"Stop, I have to go to work." She puts in her pearl earrings as she looks in the mirror.

I turn her toward me and do the top two buttons up on her blouse.

"You don't like my buttons undone." She undoes the top one and I do it back up.

"No, I don't." I brush my hands down over her hips as my eyes linger on her breasts.

Maybe ten minutes late won't hurt…. I turn her to face away from me and I cuddle her from behind. I feel myself harden.

"Cecil lets me keep my buttons undone." She smiles up at me in the mirror.

"Well, he's not expected to live long, is he?"

I feel her smile against my cheek and damn it, I want to undress and get back into bed with her, if I didn't have back-to-back meetings I would be doing just that.

"I'll pick you up from work," I tell her.

"We can go to your house if you want?"

"No." I pump her with my hips. "The last two weeks at my place have traumatized me. We'll stay here for a while."

My phone beeps with a text.

"I have to go." I pull out of her arms and head downstairs; I lock the door and head out to the car. Philippe is standing beside the second car and I walk over to him. "Good morning, Philippe." I smile.

"Morning, boss." He rocks onto his toes with a big smile.

"Stay with her all day please."

"Of course, sir."

I look back up to the window in her bedroom and I imagine her finishing getting ready.

"Beautiful day." Philippe smiles as if reading my mind.

"It sure is." I get into the back of the waiting car and smile out the window as we drive down the street. It's been a very long time since I felt this happy.

It's a perfect day.

10 A.M.

"You have a meeting at ten with Mr. Kennedy."

"Uh-huh." I go through my emails as Antoinette, my assistant, reads my day out for me from my calendar.

"And tonight you have the Biffa Gala event."

I glance up from my computer. "Tonight?"

"Yes, sir."

Hmm, I think for a moment. I want to see Alora alone tonight. "I'm unable to attend, please cancel on my behalf and send my apologies."

She glances up. "I don't know if—"

"Do it." I cut her off.

"It's very late notice, sir."

"I'm taking a break from all engagements for the foreseeable future."

She looks up again. "What do you mean?"

"I'm burnt out. I won't be attending anything after hours at night or weekends until further notice."

"This weekend you have the Formula One."

"Cancel."

"But you always go.... You host an event?"

"Antoinette." I cut her off. "What don't you understand with this conversation?"

"Yes, sir." She writes something down in her calendar. "Is there...." She hesitates as if choosing her words wisely. "Is there anything the matter, sir?"

"No." I open a new email. "I have a personal project that I'm currently working on and it requires my full attention."

"Yes, sir." She scribbles something down. "When will your schedule be reopening?"

"I'll let you know."

ALORA.

If walking on sunshine were a feeling, I am the golden girl.

My feet haven't touched the ground all day.

"Just help me put this couch by the window?" I ask.

Jonty holds one end and I lift the other as we struggle to carry the couch. "Why have you decided to move the entire shop around today?" He grimaces as we lift.

"You'll see." We put the couch down and I glance around the store. "Okay, now we move that coffee table in front of this couch and a lamp on the table in the corner."

"Okay." We lift the coffee table over and Jonty goes and finds a lamp. "How's this one?"

"Great, turn it on and see how it looks."

He arranges it and turns it on, a beautiful glow warms up the space. "That's perfect." I keep looking around. "Now we need some books and magazines and things to put on the coffee table."

"Okay." He takes off in search of them. The best thing about owning an antique store is that we have at least ten of every item you could ever think of. He returns with stacks of books and arranges them in piles and puts a bunch of flowers down beside them. "How's this?"

"Looks great. Thanks for helping me." I go out the front doors onto the street and look around, I see Philippe standing to the side against a wall.

"Philippe," I call. "Stefan."

They push off the wall. "Yes, Miss Sorenson."

"Come." I wave them over. "I made you something."

"Excuse me?"

I usher them into the store and hold my arm out to the corner. "Ta-da."

Philippe looks around confused. "I don't understand."

"This is your new couch area."

"What?"

"If you're going to hang out with me, which Edward is insisting on, I'm not having you stand in the street. I won't hear of it."

Their faces fall as they looks around.

"You can stay in the shop with us, you can sit here on the couch and read a book or you can go out the back to the office and hang there. Hell, you can even work and learn to serve customers if you want."

"I don't know what to say."

I smile. "Jonty, meet Stefan and Philippe. They are going to hang out in the store with us from now on, and this is Helene."

"Hello." Jonty shakes their hands. "I guess, welcome aboard."

"Merci." Philippe smiles, he seems embarrassed and unsure what to do.

"I'm making coffee," Jonty calls as he heads out the back.

"I can do it," Philippe calls.

"Or I could," Stefan offers.

"Yeah, okay, come and I'll show you where everything is."

They head out the back with Jonty. "What's going on?" Helene mouths.

"Edward and I got back together last night. He professed undying love."

"He did?" Her eyes widen in shock. "He actually said he loved you?"

"Uh-huh." I beam. "I'm quietly optimistic."

"You know I was a real bitch to him when you were away."

I giggle. "I heard."

"Great, so now he's going to hate me."

"He'll warm up." I smile as I look around the store.

"So what's with the guards in the shop?"

"I don't know, but I can't have them stand out the front any longer."

I swipe through to the next invoice and glance at the clock on the wall of my office: 3 p.m.

Three hours until I see him.

I hear the bell over the front door. "I have a delivery for a Miss Alora Sorenson," I hear a voice say.

Huh?

I glance up from what I'm doing, who's that?

"Oh my god," Jonty gasps. "I'll go get her."

His head pokes around the corner. "You have a delivery." He laughs as he twists his hands together in excitement.

"She's going to freak." Helene laughs out loud.

"What is it?"

"Wait until you see." He hunches his shoulders and I poke my head around the corner to see a delivery man with the biggest bunch of red roses I have ever seen.

"Alora Sorenson?"

"Yes."

"These are for you."

"Oh my." My mouth falls open in surprise. "What the hell?"

"Sign here, please." He gives me an iPad and I digitally sign for them. He passes me the giant crystal vase and I struggle to hold it up. "Have a nice day." He disappears out the front door.

"Holy fucking shit. It's a Lalique vase," Helene cries. "The vase alone is worth a fortune."

I put them down on the front counter and open the envelope to read the card.

From the day we met.
Edward
x

"Ahhh," I cry as I hold the card to my chest.

"Fucking hell," Jonty murmurs as he looks them over. "He doesn't mess about, does he?"

I hold the card back to my chest. "My sweet Edward." I glance over and see Philippe and Stefan smiling broadly as they watch on, oh crap, I forgot they were here. "You don't tell him anything you hear around here, will you?" I warn. "You're on my side now and anything that comes out of my mouth is top-secret information."

"I won't." Philippe holds his two hands up with a chuckle. "Sweet Edward? You must have another Edward somewhere, though, because our boss is anything but sweet."

I laugh as I look over the roses, huge, big heads with the most perfect perfume.

"How many are there?" Jonty asks as he counts. "Twenty-four." He lets out a low whistle. "These would have cost a pretty penny."

Gah.... *I'm giddy.*

I grab my phone. "I'll be back in a moment." I head out the front door as I dial his number.

"Hello," his deep English voice answers.

"I just got a really beautiful bunch of red roses delivered." I beam.

"Who were they from?"

"From this really hot guy I know." I unapologetically swoon through the phone. "Thank you."

"You're most welcome." I can tell that he's smiling too.

"It means a lot." And suddenly I feel overemotional, teary even. For so long I dreamed about us and now it's....

"I'll be home to pick you up around six," he tells me.

Home.

"Okay, I'll see you then."

I practically float back into the store and read my card again and again.

From the day we met.
Edward
X

I feel like I'm in a fairy tale.

The day has been hectic and we're here late, still moving furniture around to try and fit the large shipment of the furniture that arrived today.

The bell above the door rings and I glance up to see Edward, he's wearing a charcoal suit and the look he gives me could set the place on fire.

"Good evening, Mr. Prescott." I smile.

"Hello." He kisses me on the cheek as he takes my hand in his.

Helene walks around the corner. "Oh." She rolls her eyes in a dramatic way. "Hello, Mr. Prescott," she says sarcastically. "Still don't like me?"

"No." He looks at her deadpan. "I don't, actually."

She smiles at his reply. "And how long are you not going to like me for?"

"Five to ten business days," he mutters dryly. "At least."

She giggles and gets back to cleaning.

Edward looks around. "Where's Johnathon?"

"My name is Jonty," Jonty calls from the back room.

"Whatever it is," Edward calls back. "Hello."

"Maybe I don't like you either," Jonty teases.

"Feeling is mutual, so not offended."

I smile up at my gorgeous man, I love that he's trying to be friendly with them.

He's not great at it, but at least it's a start.

"Let's get going, guys, we can finish this in the morning."

"Okay." They begin collecting their things as Edward stands to the side with his hands in his suit pockets. His dark hair has a curl to it and the power emanating out of him makes the space feel so small and insignificant.

Even when out of his kingdom, he feels like a king.

"See you," the others call as they leave.

"Goodbye." He nods politely and I smile. I think watching him trying to be nice to people is my favorite new sport. I can almost hear his sarcastic inner dialogue from here.

"I haven't even thought about dinner, babe." I grab my purse. "I've had the busiest day."

He puts his arm around me and kisses my forehead. "Let's go out."

"Like a real date?" My eyes widen.

He chuckles. "Sure, like a real date."

"Where do you want to go?"

"I don't know." He shrugs. "This is your neighborhood, you tell me."

Hmm, I know his snobby food choices, where the hell *will* we go?

"French or Italian." I screw my lips as I think. "Japanese?"

"Japanese sounds good."

"Okay." I smile up at him. "It's just around the corner, we can walk. Hopefully they have a spare table." We walk out the front and I lock the doors as Edward goes and talks to Philippe; he must be telling him we are going out to dinner.

It's so weird having to report every move to others, I need to talk to him about this. I really don't think they need to come to work with me every day, it's overkill.

He comes back and throws his arm around my shoulder as we walk. "How was your day?" he asks.

"Better now you're here. How was yours?"

"About the same."

"You know, I've been thinking, and I really don't need guards with me." I turn back to see them trailing us.

"Yes, you do."

"I get it for you or when we are out or something, but every day?"

"You had someone put a tracker in your purse, Alora, we still don't know who's responsible."

"You said it was Pascal."

"We don't have confirmation on that, though, he denied it."

"When did you see him?" I frown.

"I saw him." He rolls his lips as we walk along. "Let's just leave it at that."

"Wait..." I think for a moment. "Did you beat him up in the parking lot?"

He shrugs. "I don't know, did I?"

"Edward."

"He needs to find a safer hobby than following you around."

"So it *was* you?"

"You're with me now." He tightens his grip around my shoulders. "And nobody touches my things and gets away with it."

Uneasiness fills me at his tone, he's saying it as a joke but I know that he's deadly serious.

We get to the restaurant and walk in. "A table for two, please."

"Sure, this way." We follow the waitress to a table for two by the window, candles are on the table and it has an eclectic and beautiful feel. We take a seat and Edward orders a bottle of wine and she comes back and fills our glasses before leaving us alone.

"So…." I smile over at him.

He slides his hand up my thigh. "So."

I hunch my shoulders in excitement, this is really happening between us.

He reaches into the inside pocket of his suit coat and brings out a little red box and sets it on the table in front of me. "I bought you a present today."

"What?" I stare down at it. *That's a Cartier box.* "Why did you buy me a present?"

"Because I can." He gives me a come-fuck-me look and butterflies swirl in my stomach.

"You don't need to buy me things."

"But I will." He picks up my hand and kisses my fingertips. "Open it."

Ahhh!

I carefully undo the ribbon and take the lid off the box and my mouth falls open.

"Edward," I whisper, it's a gold diamond bangle. "This is too much."

"Nothing is too much for you, my love." He smiles.

I look at it in my hand and I see cursive writing on the inside. "It's engraved?" I gasp.

I love you,
Edward.
X

"Oh." I put my hand over my heart as emotion overwhelms me. "You bought me an I-love-you bracelet?"

"I did." He smiles.

"Why?"

"Because I *do* love you." His eyes hold mine and my heart melts, he's getting more open with me day by day. "Let me put it on you." I hold my arm out and he opens it and puts it on me. "Never take it off."

"I won't." I stare at the shimmering diamonds on my wrist. "It's so beautiful. Thank you." I reach over and take his face in my hands and kiss his lips. "For the record, I love you more."

"Impossible." We get lost in the moment and kiss a little too much.

"Ahem." The waitress interrupts us and we pull back from each other. "Can I take your order?"

Edward opens the menu with a sharp snap and I look through the box to see a small tag of authenticity, I take it out and read it.

Agrafe Bracelet, rose gold, set with 459 brilliant-cut diamonds totaling 10.69 carats.

"Holy crap," I say louder than expected.

The server and Edward glance over at me and I smile, embarrassed. "Never mind."

"Are you ready to order?" the waitress asks.

From my peripheral vision I see Edward smile into his wineglass as if reading my scrambled mind.

"Umm." I open the menu, too flustered to even think. "I'll have whatever he's having."

EDWARD.

The car pulls up to the curb and I climb out. Picking Alora up from work has become my favorite part of each day.

This last week with her has been a dream, a simple happiness that has meant so much. I'm a little late today and she's already locking the shop up as I walk up to her.

"Miss Sorenson." I slide my arms around her from behind.

"There you are." She turns in my arms and kisses me.

"You ready?"

"Yes, but we have to stop by the grocery store before we go home."

"Huh?" I stare at her, confused.

"I need some ingredients for dinner."

"Well, write a list and I'll send someone out."

"Are you above grocery shopping for yourself?"

"No," I scoff. *I've just never done it before.*

She turns back to lock the roller door and I go back to Philippe. "We're going grocery shopping, apparently."

"For real?" He chuckles. "This I've got to see."

"Shut the fuck up."

I go back to Alora and take her hand in mine and she leads me up the road and into a grocery store. I look around, there's a million things on the shelves and people are everywhere. There's beeping sounds and children crying in the distance. People are lined up everywhere, the place is pure chaos.

What fresh hell is this?

"Here." She takes a basket and passes it to me. "Carry this."

"Oh." I take it from her. "Okay." I glance back to see the boys snicker under their breath.

"Fuck. Off," I mouth.

She walks up and down the aisles as I trail behind her like a puppy, she's looking at every little detail, occasionally putting things into the basket, and this thing is getting heavy.

Does she think I'm a fucking packhorse now?

She grabs a three-liter milk and puts it in. "That's enough shopping for today," I snap. "This basket weighs a ton."

"Few more things." She keeps going up and down the aisles and as we walk past the fridges I see my reflection, I'm trailing behind her while carrying her shopping and the sight brings a smile to my face.

Who even am I?

ALORA.
6:30 P.M.

Dinner is in the oven, I've showered, have a glass of wine in my hand and I am lying on a deck chair in my back garden in my cream silk dressing gown. The afternoon light has a beautiful glow lighting up the sky. I've watered my plants and stared at my roses and honestly, this is the happiest I have felt in what seems like forever.

I feel him before I see him, an undeniable energy shift. I turn to see Edward leaning with one shoulder against the French door, watching me. Wearing a navy suit; his dark hair has a bit of a curl to it. His jaw is square and his big, kissable lips are a beautiful shade of come-fuck-me.

"Hi." I smile.

"Hi." He keeps standing there and tonight there seems to be a different look in his eye. An edginess that I haven't seen for a long time.

"Come sit with me." I tap the chair beside me.

"Come sit *on* me." He grabs his crotch.

Yes....

I get up and go inside and he closes the door behind me, it's obvious that he has one thing on his mind and it's going to be noisy.

He takes my face into his hands and kisses me as he walks me backward toward the kitchen. "I've been thinking about you all fucking day," he murmurs against my lips; I can feel his erection push into me through his suit.

He lifts me onto the kitchen counter and lays me back, his dark eyes hold mine as he spreads my legs. "Open." His eyes drop to my sex and he licks his lips.

Ahhhh....

He pulls the lips of my sex apart with his fingers and bends to lick me, softly at first.

Barely a whisper, but enough to drive me wild.

My breath quivers as I try to control it.

Jeez.

When he's intense like this is when he's at his best, the beast of a man who's come to feed and take from my body what he needs.

He licks me deeper and his eyes close in pleasure as he tastes me. "So good."

I feel faint, the blood drains out of my face. Dear lord, how is this man so hot?

He really begins to lose control as he licks me deeper, his stubble burning my most intimate parts, his big hands hold my legs back as my body begins to take a rhythm all of its own. My hips circle and pump as they try to ride his face.

His dark eyes rise to meet mine and he slides two of his thick fingers deep into my sex and I moan as my body contracts around him. "Edward." I reach for him.

He pumps me and adds another finger as his mouth drops to my swollen, wet lips again. My back arches off the counter.

Fuck…what must we look like? He's been home for all of two minutes and here he is going down on me on the kitchen counter, fully dressed in a suit.

His teeth graze my clitoris as his eyes flutter closed. "Hurry," I whimper.

He flicks his tongue again.

"Edward," I demand. "I want to come on your dick." I clench around his fingers. "I want you to blow inside me."

His jaw clenches and he lets out a guttural moan.

"Now," I demand.

He unzips his suit trousers and pulls his hard cock out and then lifts my legs up high in the air.

In this position I am completely at his mercy. "Careful," I whisper.

"Why would I be careful when I know you like it rough?" He slams in deep, knocking the air from my lungs, and I cry out somewhere between pleasure and pain.

He puts both of my legs over one of his shoulders to bring me tighter and lets out a low whistle as he slowly pulls out and pushes back in. "So fucking good," he murmurs as perspiration dusts his brow. The sound of my wet body sucking him in echoes through the room and he smiles darkly. "So wet and creamy for me."

Pump.

I nod as I see stars.

Pump.

I can feel it building, an orgasm so strong that it might steal my sanity.

"You be a good girl and clench for me."

Pump.

"So perfect." He tightens his grip on my ankles and my eyes roll back in my head, as soon as he starts dirty talking it's all over.

"I've been thinking about fucking you all day."

Pump.

"I jerked off twice and blew so *fucking* hard."

I get a vision of him jerking off in his office bathroom thinking of me and it nearly sends me wild.

He picks up the pace as he begins to moan, and damn it, I can't hold it. Seeing him so unhinged does things to me that I can't control.

I cry out as he rips an orgasm from my body…but he doesn't stop there, he keeps pumping, harder and harder. His moans so loud the paint could peel from the walls and a thought races through my head.

I hope Philippe is gone and can't hear us.

"Oh fuck yeah," he cries out, he grabs a handful of my hair and pulls out. "Open your mouth."

Ahhh.

He slides his cock down my throat and as his eyes hold mine he blows hard; I gag and choke but he doesn't falter.

He stays deep down my throat, giving me every last drop of what he has. Overtaking every single one of my senses.

He knows what he wanted…and he took it.

Owning me on his terms.

Love conquers all.

I look around the store with a renewed sense of accomplishment, everything feels like it's finally falling into place, new routines have been set and the store has never been busier or looked better.

Like clockwork, over the last week Edward has arrived at my place every day after work at 6 p.m. We talk and laugh, make love, and have the dreamiest of nights and then he leaves for work from my place in the morning. There are no games or wondering if I will see him, he sets it in concrete before he leaves every day as if he needs to know as much as I do. This new reality between us feels too good to be true.

My phone lights up on my desk and I glance at the name,

Thomas Stone

I glance up to see where Philippe is and I get up and close the office door before answering. "Hello." I smirk.

"Hey you," his happy voice replies.

Just the sound of his cheeky voice makes me smile. "I was just thinking of you, how are you? What happened to our coffee date on Wednesday?"

"Well, I'm in America, family emergency."

"What happened?"

"My mom fell and broke her leg, so I'm here for a few months to help her."

"Oh no, is she okay?"

"Honestly. I don't know how these fucking nurses do this job full-time. It's exhausting."

"I know, right. So can you work over there or...."

"Yeah I can, probably won't but I could if I wanted to. How's things going for you?"

"Great." I beam, I glance up guiltily through the glass window in the door at Philippe sitting on the couch in the store with his book. "Oh my god, things are going so well with you know who?" I say with a lowered voice.

"Really?" He says. "How so?"

"Well, he's stayed at my place every night now and he sent me a huge bunch of red roses and honestly...I feel like we're falling in love."

"Wooow, woo, woo, slow down, old girl."

"I know it's very early." I roll my eyes, feeling foolish. "But it just feels different, you know?"

"I hope it is love, but be prepared for finding out that it might not be."

"I know." I shrug. "Thank you for checking in, it feels like you're the only one who pulls me back to reality about him."

"Have you formally met any of his friends yet?"

"Not yet. We haven't even been to his place yet." I frown as I come to that realization. "Which is weird, now I think about it."

"He's probably just wanting to come to yours while you get into a rhythm."

"Maybe."

"I have a date tonight," he tells me.

"You do?" I smile. "A job or a date?"

"Like a *date* date. A real date."

"Does she know what you do?"

"No, and to be honest, I'm a bit nervous about it."

"Why?"

"I haven't been on a real date for years, what the hell do you even do?"

I giggle. "Have sex for free, I'm assuming."

"Fuck, my life…."

I glance up to see that the store is crowded with people. "I've got to go, the shop is swamped."

"Okay."

"Good luck tonight."

"Thanks."

"Call me tomorrow and let me know how it goes." I smile.

He chuckles. "Yeah, okay."

"Bye." I hang up and smile, Thomas has a real date…. For free.

The regulated sound of Edward breathing is a peaceful sound.

I lie on my side propped up on my elbow as I watch him sleep in the semi-dark room.

Naked, his beautiful olive skin is a stark contrast to the white bed linen that's pooled around his waist. His hands are up behind his head, his large biceps demand my attention as my eyes linger over every inch of him.

I've never known a man like this, so masculine that his body calls to mine on a primal level. It's like the testosterone pumping through his veins has become my very own brand of heroin. An addiction to flesh is not something I've ever battled before.

The more I crave him, the more I physically have him, the more I need him.

Whenever he's near, I'm in this semi-aroused state at all times as if our bodies are talking to each other. Speaking a language that only they understand.

Its early, 6 a.m., and I could watch him sleep all day but I won't, I'll pretend I'm not totally smitten and play it cool. I get up to go to the bathroom and his phone lights up on the bedside table and I pick it up, a text:

Hermione

CHAPTER TWENTY-SIX

What?

Why is she still texting him?

Jealousy runs through me and I quietly put his phone back down, grab my robe and make my way downstairs.

The coffee machine percolates as a million scenarios run through my mind, have they spoken? Do they still see each other? I know she meant a lot to him because he's hell-bent on not letting her find out about us…maybe I'm a secret because he's still with her?

Stop it.

I make my coffee and head out into my back garden; I need to stop being insecure.

This isn't who I am.

I'm not even going to ask him about it, I already know they're still friends and I want to respect that.

I turn on the hose and call my favorite person in the world. "Hello, my darling," he answers.

"Hi, Dad." I smile, and suddenly the world is right again.

Two weeks of loving Edward Prescott….

He's the sky, the moon, and all the stars in the night sky, I worship the air that he breathes.

We walk through the markets in town, the morning sun is shining and my arm is linked through his. He's wearing jeans and a T-shirt with a baseball cap and sunglasses, his usual disguise. We haven't been to his place yet because he seems to have unofficially moved into mine. On the weekend we pottered around my neighborhood. Dinners in small intimate restaurants, walks at sunrise and drinks at sunset in my garden.

We were normal, more normal than I could have ever dreamed.

I never imagined that it could be like this. So in tune with each other that it's like he's an extension of me.

We're inseparable, so in love and haven't spent a single night apart. My second bedroom has somehow turned into his wardrobe, it's filled with designer suits, shirts, and shoes. I have a stupidly expensive Aston Martin in my garage and Rolex watches just lying around in my bathroom.

It feels so natural and right, we laugh and talk about everything and yet at the same time nothing at all.

EDWARD.

Bang.

My eyes flutter as my sleep is disturbed by an echo in the distance.

Bang.

I roll onto my side in the darkness.

Bang.

My eyes spring open, what the hell *was* that?

I reach over and grab my phone off the nightstand to see the time.

3:08 a.m.

Bang.... It's coming from downstairs.

The hell?

Someone's in the house.

I sit up and reach over to wake Alora; her side of the bed is empty. Where is she?

Bang....

My eyes dart around in a panic and I get up, tiptoe to the bathroom, and flick the light on. She's not in here, and then I see it. A large droplet of blood on the bathroom floor.

Fuck.

My heart begins to pump and I pull on a pair of boxer shorts and slowly slide open the bedside drawer and grab the gun from the black bag.

Adrenaline screams through my veins as I pull back the slide and cock the gun. I go to the door and peer around the corner. Lights are on downstairs.

Bang.

I hold the gun up and walk down the stairs, if they've touched a hair on her head I swear to god....

I make my way to the second level and check the bedrooms, in one of the bedrooms the window is open and the curtains are blowing in the wind. I creep down the next flight of stairs, the lights are on and my eyes fly around.

"Alora," I call.

Silence....

"Alora."

I can hear water running in the bathroom and my heart hammers in my chest.

Am I going to find her body in there? Is she dead in the bathtub...? Is this some fucked-up scene from a horror movie?

Holding the gun to my chest, I walk toward the bathroom.

Bang.

I look up at the ceiling, that sound came from above, it must be from the open window on the second level.

"Alora," I call.

I close my eyes, deep down I always knew this day was coming. I knew that one day someone would make me pay. With my heart in my throat, I slowly push the door open to see Alora is standing under the shower with her back to me, she's naked.

"What?" My eyes fly around to see nobody in the room with her. "What are you doing?"

It's then that I notice that the water running down the drain is red. Oh my god.

"What's wrong?"

She turns and, catching sight of me, jumps in fright. "Argh, what are you doing?" she screams. "You scared the hell out of me." She takes AirPods out of her ears.

"What the fuck are you doing?" I point to the floor of the shower. "Are you hurt?"

"Why do you have a gun?" she stammers.

"Because I thought you were down here getting fucking murdered," I snap.

"No." She screws up her face as if I'm an idiot. "I have my period really heavy and I needed a hot shower to stop the ache."

"Are you fucking kidding me right now?" I fume. "I saw the blood and you were gone and I was calling out to you," I whisper angrily.

"Oh...I didn't hear you; I didn't want to wake you up, so I came down here and thought I'd listen to my audiobook while I stood under the hot water." She shrugs as she holds her AirPods up. "I didn't realize I dropped blood upstairs. Sorry."

"My god." I drag my hand through my hair. "I just lost ten fucking years of my life."

"Who would be down here killing me?" She screws up her face. "What's wrong with you?"

My shoulders slump and I look down to see the water in the bottom of the shower is fully red. "What is happening here?" I gesture to the floor.

"My period."

"Surely it's not that much blood, you'll need a fucking transfusion."

"This is normal, what are you talking about?"

"I don't know about that; I think we need to go to the hospital."

"You can't be this clueless about periods."

I stare at her as I reconcile what I know about women's monthlies.

Nothing.

In fact, I have never even had a partner bleed in front of me.

"Edward?" She frowns.

I shake my head in confusion.

Why haven't I had a partner bleed in front of me...now that I think about it, it's fucking weird.

"See you upstairs." I rush back upstairs, put the gun away and climb into bed.

Adrenaline is still pumping, and I pull the blankets up around my ears as an unknown emotion fills me.

Twenty minutes later Alora comes into the room, she flicks the bathroom light on as she dresses and cleans up the blood. I lie with my back to her pretending to be asleep. She eventually climbs in behind me and cuddles my back. "Sorry for worrying you."

I lie still as I try to make sense of my emotions.

"What's wrong?" she asks.

"Nothing. Go to sleep."

"Edward." She pulls my shoulder, rolling me onto my back. "What's wrong?"

"Why wouldn't I ever have seen a woman have her monthlies?" I murmur.

"Never?" She frowns.

I shake my head. "Not once."

"Hmm." She thinks for a moment. "I guess it's a very personal thing for women."

I stare at her and an overwhelming sense of sadness fills me.

"They didn't trust me enough to...."

"Hey." She leans over and kisses me. "Not necessarily. They probably had IUDs and didn't even have a period."

"That doesn't make me feel any better," I murmur.

"Why not?"

"Because I never even noticed. Not once has the thought ever crossed my mind." My eyes search hers. "Am I so self-absorbed that I don't even know a woman's body other than for my pleasure?"

She nods as if finally understanding my point. "Maybe...in the past."

We lie in silence, surrounded by darkness, and while I reflect on one of my countless flaws.... She holds me in her arms and loves me.

ALORA.

I sit in the back of the car as we drive through the streets of Monaco, I'm consulting on a house here today and Philippe and Stefan are taking me there.

I glance at my watch. "We're early, can we grab a coffee and kill some time before we go to the house?" I ask.

"Sure thing." They make a turn. "We'll go to the main street."

"Okay."

Ten minutes later they park the car and we get out and walk along, I see a café. "I'll go in here." I walk in. "Bonjour, can I have a café Americano please?"

"Of course." She turns to make the coffee and I glance out to the street to see a beautiful blond woman go to walk into the café toward me, Philippe intercepts her at the door and begins to walk her backward as he says something in French. What's going on? She seems to try and catch my attention before Philippe turns her away from me.

What?

Stefan steps in and grabs her too and then they pull her around the corner and out of view, what the hell is going on? I walk out the front to see both boys missing.

"Café Americano," the lady calls.

I look left and I look right, no sign of them, what the fuck is going on? It's not like them to leave me here alone.

I walk back in and collect my coffee and then back out into the street, a good five to ten minutes later Philippe comes around the corner; he seems flustered. "Let's go," he says as if hurried.

"Who was that woman?" I ask.

"She was …." He pauses as if searching for the right answer. "She looked dangerous, I didn't want her near you."

I stare at him as I reconcile his words, they bounce around in my head like an echo.

Bullshit.

"Where is Stefan?"

"He…is getting some lunch. We will meet up with him later."

Why are you lying to me?

Who was that fucking woman and why wasn't she allowed to talk to me?

EDWARD.

"And this point here." I point to the screen.

My phone vibrates and the name *Philippe* lights up the screen.

"I have to take this, excuse me." I stand and walk out of the boardroom. "Yes," I answer.

"Isadora just tried to approach Alora," he snaps.

I clench my jaw. "Where was she?"

"In the street, Alora was in a café and she saw her and tried to enter."

"What did you do?"

"We stopped her."

"Where is she now?"

"Stefan has her."

Fury fills me. "I'm on my way."

CHAPTER TWENTY-SEVEN

"And through here I was wanting it to feel really luxe," Mrs. Dupont tells me.

"Yes." I smile as I continue taking notes. "The color of the drapes, are you keeping that aesthetic?"

"No. We are changing it, but I guess it depends on the pieces you find as to where we go with it."

"Right." I continue to scribble in my pad, I walk over to the window of the upstairs bedroom and look down out onto the street, Philippe and the car are gone.

What the actual fuck is going on?

They would never leave me unaccompanied at a random house.

"And this over here," Mrs. Dupont continues as she walks through to a dressing room.

Ugh.... I just want this over with so I can call Edward for answers. I don't know much about anything, but I do know that woman was no stranger and the boys didn't want her talking to me.

But why?

"Thank you, Mrs. Dupont, I shall have some ideas back to you by Thursday at the latest. It was lovely meeting you."

"You too, dear." She smiles as she walks me out, I glance up to see the car is back and the two boys are out and leaning up against it.

"Have a good day." I smile as I walk down the front steps and the door closes behind me.

After the longest hour of my life, I've finished the appointment, but I'm not waiting another minute to call him. "I just have to make a call," I mouth to the boys.

Philippe nods and Stefan says something to him and Philippe smirks.

What the hell are they saying to each other.... Am I the village idiot here?

Anger begins to heat my blood, it's one thing to have men follow me around but for them to know shit that I don't is just damn infuriating. I dial Edward's number.

Ring, ring.... Ring, ring.... Ring, ring.... The answering machine picks up.

You've reached Edward Prescott.
Leave a message.

"How convenient," I mutter, infuriated, as I hang up. I call him again.

Ring, ring...ring, ring...ring, ring.

You've reached Edward Prescott.
Leave a message.

I begin to fume. "Call me immediately." I march to the car.

"You ready to go?" Philippe smiles as he opens the back door for me.

"Yep," I snap as I climb in.

Don't talk to me, asshole, I'm annoyed with you too. When I ask you a question, you fucking answer it. My phone beeps with a text, it's from Edward.

Hi babe,
Can't talk, I'm in a meeting, and back-to-back all afternoon.
I'll pick you up from work.
x

He doesn't want to talk to me?

Why?

I stare out the window as Monaco flies by; a million scenarios are running through my mind and none of them good.

This should be interesting.

"So what's going on?" Jonty asks as he peers out the shop front window to the men standing out on the curb. "Why are there four of them now?"

I try to act casual. "Oh, I don't know, they must be rotating soon I guess." I keep dusting. The shop has never looked better, I've been rage cleaning all afternoon.

I'm always so much more productive when I'm pissed.

"Oh, fuck." Jonty runs away from the window and I know that he must have arrived.

There's only one person who can frighten the living daylights out of everyone just on sight.

I walk out the back and sit down at my computer to pretend to work.

Just stay calm.

I take a few deep breaths to try and calm myself down, I've been imagining the worst scenarios in my head all day and I don't even know what's going on.

She's probably a reporter or something completely innocent.

My gut tells me she isn't, I know she isn't.

The bell sounds over the door. "Good afternoon, Jonty." I hear the deep English accent.

"Ah.... Hello, Mr. Edward," Jonty replies nervously.

"I trust you are well?"

"I am, and you?"

"I'm great. Where is Miss Sorenson?"

"She's in her office."

I puff air into my cheeks as I prepare for battle.

"Good afternoon, Miss Sorenson," his sexy deep voice purrs.

I look up to see him leaning on the doorjamb with his shoulder, he's wearing a perfectly fitted navy suit and crisp white shirt. His hair is messed to just-fucked perfection and he looks like a walking orgasm.

Infuriating.

"Hello." I fake a smile. "I'll just be a moment." I go back and open my email to try and look busy and important.

"How was my girl's day?" he asks as he walks in and closes the door.

"Interesting." I hit the computer key with force.

He walks around behind me and leans down and kisses my neck, his teeth graze my skin.

Don't dare try and hypnotize me with your magical dick tonight, Edward, I am *not* in the mood.

"Let's go and have some dinner." He bites me again and goose bumps scatter up my arms.

I wiggle away from him. "We're at work. Stop it."

He smiles against my skin. "That just makes me want you more." He bites me again.

Ughh....

How am I supposed to be angry with him when my traitorous body just wants him all the time?

This attraction is becoming very inconvenient.

I close my computer down. "Let's go." I stand.

His hands are in his suit pant pockets and his eyes hold mine. "Where's my kiss?"

"Later." I brush past him and collect my things. "Jonty," I call. "Let's go, honey."

"Honey?" He raises an eyebrow, unimpressed.

"Yeah." I widen my eyes. "What about it?" Fight me, asshole, I dare you.... I am *in* the mood to end you tonight.

Amusement flashes across his face. "You need to eat."

"I'm not angry because I'm hungry, Edward, not even you could be that stupid."

"Careful," he warns.

"Who was she?"

He runs his tongue over his teeth, angered by my tone.

"And before you say anything, I want you to think long and hard about how you answer. Because believe me, Edward, when I say this, I can forgive anything as long as I am told the truth. But if you lie to me there is no coming back from that."

He rolls his eyes.

"Do not dare roll your fucking eyes at me," I whisper angrily. "*Who* was she?"

"We will have this conversation *later*."

"When?"

"Alora," he snaps. "Do not give me your *fucking* attitude. I said we will talk about it later, and we will." He turns and walks out of my office and out the front door of the store.

I stare after him as my blood boils.

Of course he's going to be angry with me, well, if that's the best defense he's got then I've already won.

I loiter in my office for a while as I try to calm down, that didn't go to plan. If there's one thing I've learned about Edward Prescott, it's that if I want my way it's all in the delivery of what I say. If I demand it, it's a straight-up hard no. If I'm sweet and vulnerable, he'll give me whatever I want.

I swear to god he's got oppositional defiance…hmm, maybe I should get him tested for that? It would sure make my life easier if this could be fixed with a pill.

I pack up my things and Jonty and I walk out together. "Thanks for today," I tell him.

"Have a great night," he says as I lock the door.

"You too." I force a smile and turn to see Edward talking to the guards by the car, his hands are in his pockets and he's listening to Stefan as he talks intently, are they filling him in on today's activities?

Oh, to be a fly on the fucking wall….

He sees me and smiles. "There she is." He walks over and kisses my cheek. "Let's go and have some dinner."

"Okay." I clench my lips together to stop myself from saying something snarky. He takes my hand in his and we walk down the street toward the restaurant strip. "Italian?" he asks.

"Whatever."

He raises his eyebrow again, unimpressed with my tone.

"I swear to god. Don't push your luck tonight, Edward, you are on thin ice."

He rolls his eyes and drags me into a restaurant. "Bonjour, est-ce que vous auriez une table pour deux ?" he says. (Translation: Hello, do you have a table for two, please?)

"Oui, par ici s'il vous plaît." (Translation: Yes, this way please.)

We are seated at a small table toward the back. "Puis-je vous apporter quelque chose à boire ?" she asks. (Translation: Can I get you something to drink?)

"Une bouteille de votre meilleur rouge, s'il vous plaît." he replies. (Translation: A bottle of your best red, please.)

She leaves us alone and he takes my hand over the table and lifts it and kisses my fingertips while I stare at him deadpan.

"Explain to me why you're angry," he says softly.

"You know damn well why I'm angry."

"Tell me it from your side. How you see it."

"Okay, so…." I try to collect my thoughts. "Today we were in Monaco and I was in a café and a beautiful woman tried to talk to me but was intercepted by your men."

"I see." His eyes hold mine.

"And they tried to tell me that they stopped her because they thought she was dangerous, which is just a straight-out lie, and I want to know who she is."

"Okay." He nods.

The server returns with a bottle of wine and as she goes through the whole opening-the-cork thing, he starts talking to her in French again and whatever the hell they are talking about seems to be taking forever.

I just want to slam my hand on the table and scream *not now, fucker.*

Eventually she leaves us alone and his eyes come back to me. "Where were we?"

I roll my eyes; I can feel an inferno building and I'm about to blow. "Who. Is. She?"

"So…." He rubs the backs of his fingers through his stubble as if doing an internal risk assessment. "Her name is Isadora."

"Why did they stop her talking to me?"

"Because she is unhinged." He sips his wine and sloshes it around his mouth as he waits for my reply. "She obviously saw my men were with you and then put two and two together to work out that you are important to me."

"How do you know her?"

"She is a woman from my past."

"A woman you have slept with?"

He takes another big gulp and I do believe this is the first time I have ever seen him this uncomfortable. "Yes."

I stare at him as I try to think on my feet. "When was the last time you slept with her?"

He swallows and then takes another gulp of wine. "It is in the past, Alora. It is best left there. It doesn't matter."

"It matters to me, Edward." My eyes search his. "You're right, it is in the past, it doesn't matter. Whatever you tell me is not going to affect us and our relationship. But if this woman ever approaches me at an event, and going by her actions today, she probably will, I want to be prepared and I need to know what the hell she's going to say to me."

He rolls his lips as his eyes hold mine. "This isn't going to affect us?"

"You have my word."

He nods and takes another gulp of wine.

"How long ago did you sleep with her?"

"Three months."

What?

I begin to hear my heartbeat in my ears as I stare at him. "You cheated on Hermione?"

Oh my god, *he's a fucking cheater.*

"No."

"I don't understand. Explain this to me."

"Umm...." He looks out over the restaurant. "I've gone over this conversation in my head all day and still it...." He shrugs. "It sounds bad every way I put it."

"Just spit it out."

"She used to join Hermione and me in bed."

I blink, in surprise...in shock...in sheer fucking horror.

"What?" I whisper.

Wherever I thought this conversation was going...this is not it.

He clears his throat and refills his glass of wine.

"You and Hermione used to have orgies?"

"Not orgies, just the three of us."

What?

"You would fuck her in front of Hermione?" I whisper.

He sips his wine and raises his eyebrows.

That's a yes.

"How.... Did...." I frown as I try to collect a thought. "So you and Hermione had an open relationship?"

"No, well." He shrugs. "It's complicated."

I put my fingers to my temple. "You need to explain this to me because my mind is completely blown right now." Actually I need some wine too, hell, I might start drinking from the bottle. I pick up my glass and take a giant gulp. "How did this start?"

"She was Hermione's friend."

What?

"You fucked her friend in front of her?" I whisper, horrified.

"I told you it sounds bad." He rolls his lips.

"Wait, go back to the beginning. So is this how you all started, like the three of you hooking up and then you sided with Hermione or...."

"I was with Hermione and we were." He cracks his neck, seriously uncomfortable with this conversation. "Struggling."

"Struggling how?"

"Sexually."

I stare at him, my mind a clusterfuck of confusion. How the hell could you struggle with this man sexually? He's the GOAT.

"So there was an attraction issue or...." I frown.

"I tried to end it because...." He stops himself.

"It's okay, just tell me."

"I feel bad giving out this information."

"It's just me and you know it won't go anywhere."

"Hermione isn't a sexual being, she isn't like you or me."

I stare at him as I listen.

"We were perfect on paper and I adored her, but sexually it wasn't there for me."

"But you were attracted to her friend."

He swallows the lump in his throat as his eyes hold mine. "Hermione was the one who suggested it."

"How did this come up?"

"We were partying one night on my yacht and after everyone went home, Hermione asked me if she could join us in bed. She thought that it would reignite a spark between us."

I listen intently as I get a vison of how it went down.

"The problem was...." He stops himself again.

"You liked it." I finish his sentence.

He nods.

"So it happened a lot?"

"Yes."

"How did Hermione...."

"Watch me with her?"

"Yeah."

"Looking back, it isn't my proudest achievement. Isadora and I both loved to fuck."

I get a vision of them going hard at it as Hermione sat to the side and waited her turn.

Poor Hermione.

"So Hermione thought she was saving her relationship and all she really did was put herself through the heartbreak of watching you fuck her friend?"

He twists his lips and I know that I'm right.

"You cold bastard," I whisper. "How the hell could you do that to her?"

"She was all for it. Trust me, I wouldn't have done it if I knew it upset her at the time. Hindsight is a wonderful but sometimes upsetting thing to have because things are a lot clearer than they are at the time."

"I don't even know her and I know she wasn't all for it."

"You said that this wouldn't affect us?" He grabs my hand over the table. "It isn't like that with us. We are different, I'm in love with you and I would never even dream of doing that to you."

I stare at him; the rose-colored glasses are well and truly off.

"What then?" I ask.

He sits back, unwilling to share more.

"I shouldn't have judged you. I was just shocked," I apologize. "Go on. From then to now, what happened?"

"There was one night when we were all fried that things got a little out of hand."

"Like how?"

"Hermione asked us to stop. We couldn't."

I get another visual, I know how Edward gets when he's fucking hard and in the moment. He's like an animal.

"God," I whisper.

"Anyway, the next day I was horrified by Hermione being upset and I called Isadora and I told her it was never happening again and that's when things turned ugly."

"Ugly how?"

"She told both me and Hermione that she was in love with me."

Of course she did.

"When I told her that it was just a purely sexual thing for me she went postal and demanded I end it with Hermione for her."

I stare at him, shocked to my core, what the ever-loving fuck is this story?

"Around this time I had already made my decision that Hermione and I needed to end. This was toxic for both of us, we were both trying to be something we couldn't. But then Isadora threatened to go to the press and so I stayed to support Hermione through it."

I blink, just when I think this story can't escalate.... Up it goes.

"You must understand, Alora, Hermione is the Crown Princess of Switzerland, can you imagine the absolute fucking nightmare if this gets out?"

"My god," I whisper.

"Hermione's father, the king, has already threatened to kill me for hurting his daughter when I broke up with her. Can you imagine the carnage if he finds out what has actually gone on?"

"Fucking hell, Edward," I whisper.

"So basically the story in a nutshell is, at the time I thought we were having harmless fun and that Hermione was enjoying it too. Looking back, though, that wasn't the case, and I was absolutely in the wrong and that is why I have tried to protect Hermione from the press. That is why I have kept you hidden. She has been through enough."

"Does anyone else know about this?" I ask.

"No. My closest friends. That's it."

"And your staff?"

"They don't know the details, none of them was ever around and we were always very discreet.

"But they do know that Hermione and Isadora had a falling-out because she professed her love for me. The day Isadora went postal she was screaming the yacht down and everyone was there."

I take a huge gulp of wine, unsure what to even make of this situation.

Just what the actual fuck?

"Here you are." The server puts a big bowl of pasta down in front of me and I look down at it, I just lost my appetite.

He begins to eat while I sit and watch him.

"I feel so out of my depth here."

"Do you not remember where we met?" He takes a mouthful of food. "You're not exactly an angel, Alora. Like I said, if I had an inkling that this was ever going to hurt Hermione, I would never have done it. She's a beautiful person, she doesn't deserve to be blackmailed by a former friend."

"I know, but…."

"But what?"

"Who is this Isadora anyway?"

"She's the daughter of an oil tycoon and a very well-connected socialite around Monaco."

"So I will run into her?"

"Yes."

My shoulders slump. "Well, I'm on Hermione's side…. For the record. Not yours."

"Of course you are." He shovels another mouthful of food in. "I feel better now that you know."

"Well, that makes one of us." I gulp my wine. "Fuck this shit, I need tequila."

He smiles and keeps eating and I watch him in a detached state, halfway between hell and denial. The man that I'm in love with seems a million miles away from the story I just heard, and an uneasiness begins to crawl across my skin.

An eerie snapshot into my future rears its ugly head.

He glances up and smiles over at me. "I love you."

Is that so….

Who even are you?

CHAPTER TWENTY-EIGHT

It is possible to know too much about someone?

I would have thought no, but as I lie here in the dark as he sleeps beside me and I contemplate my life choices, I would have to say it's a hard yes.

I want to erase my newfound information from my mind; nothing good can come of knowing how cold Edward can be.

For the first time since we've been together, Hermione is weighing heavily on my mind. Which is ridiculous in itself because I didn't care that he left her for me…it was a fair game. But now that I know that she never stood a chance, I really feel sorry for her.

The thing is, I know what it's like to be in love with Edward Prescott. I know what it's like to want to move heaven and earth to please him sexually. The fact that she couldn't, breaks my heart for her. I can't imagine loving him and everything being perfect on the surface and yet underneath in the shadows…. Him needing more than you are.

Is this a peep into my future?

We made love tonight, and while he was completely lost in the moment and whispering words of adoration and love, I was hovering up above, absent and detached. Wondering what he was really thinking. Gauging his every moan…. Trying harder to bring him undone.

I close my eyes, disgusted where my thoughts are taking me.

I roll onto my side and watch him in the darkness, he's sleeping and relaxed. He's relieved that I know, his dirty little secret not his to bear alone any longer.

The irony is I know that's just the tip of his secrets.

My mind goes back to the charity ball and his three friends that he was with. Handsome, powerful, royal, and wealthy.

They all had beautiful women on their arms…but what goes on behind closed doors? They would never tell, I'm positive the secrets run deep.

I want to know how and when the attraction started?

Was he checking out Isadora while she was with his girlfriend, did his friends all know that he was lusting after his partner's friend? Was he having thoughts about her when he was alone…. Was she his fail-safe? Was he just waiting for Hermione to suggest that he sleep with her?

I get a vision of Hermione sitting to the side as he went down on Isadora, and I know he would have because he loves it more than anything.

Hermione lying there…watching him enjoy her friend's body, my heart constricts.

I can't imagine that pain….

He stirs and opens his eyes, he blinks while he tries to focus his eyes. "What's wrong, baby?" he whispers sleepily.

Everything.

My eyes fill with tears and his silhouette blurs.

"Doe," he says softly as he pulls me into his embrace. "I told you that you didn't want to know."

I nod through the lump in my throat.

"Our relationship is different," he whispers into the darkness. "Stop thinking about it."

I nod, knowing he's right. I do need to stop thinking about it, this is not good for my mental health.

"Promise me you'll tell me," I murmur against his chest.

"Tell you what?"

"If you…if you want someone else, promise me you'll tell me first."

"I won't."

"But if you do."

"I'll tell you." He kisses me softly. "I promise. But only if you promise me the same."

I nod.

We lie in silence, the hot tears run down my face and damn it this is the most unstable I've felt in a very long time.

He has my entire heart in the palm of his hands.

"When I tell you I love you, I fucking mean it." He rolls me onto my back and comes over the top of me. "We. This…. What we have. It's different to anything I've ever felt before."

I stare up at him. "I so badly want to believe you."

"You can believe it. And you *can* trust me." He leans down and kisses me tenderly. "I looked for you for three long years. Don't let something from my past hurt what we have."

He's right…. I can't let this poison us; I'd be a fool.

"I love you," I whisper through tears.

He nudges my legs open with his knee and rolls on top of me, his thick cock slides through the lips of my sex as his lips take mine. "Show me how much."

He said it was time, so here I am.

Edward wants me to join him in his world and announce our relationship.

Last time I was here seems like a lifetime ago, so much has happened since then.

The car pulls into the Monte Carlo marina and I nervously glance down at myself. I hope I'm dressed okay. I thought I'd go all feminine and wear a pretty floral dress, but now as we pull up and I peer out to the sleek five-story black superyacht…I'm not so sure this dress was the right choice.

I should have gone sexy….

My breath quivers as I inhale and I have no idea why I'm so nervous but I am, and I feel sick to the stomach.

This is the first time since Edward and I have been together that I've been in his world, the Monaco one. The life so far removed from who am that it isn't even funny.

The car door opens and Philippe smiles down at me. "Miss Sorenson."

"Thank you." I climb out to see Edward walk out onto the main deck to greet me.

He's wearing blue jeans and a white T-shirt; his hair is messed up. He looks up and sees me and gives me a breathtaking smile, and my heart stops.

My god…. How is he so perfect?

"This way, Miss Sorenson." Philippe and another guard walk

me toward the yacht, Philippe is carrying my overnight bag and another two guards in black suits are standing by the gangplank. "Hello, Miss Sorenson." They nod.

How do they know my name?

"Hello." I force a smile. Seeing him here in his natural habitat reminds me of who he actually is; up until now I've been living in a fantasy world with him in Nice, and it was easy to forget his past and his name and all that comes with that.

They usher me across the gangplank and Edward smiles and takes my hand. "Here she is." He leans in and kisses me, his lips lingering over mine, and I discreetly pull back. Everyone is watching.

His eyes dance with mischief as if knowing exactly what I am thinking. "Place Miss Sorenson's things in my bedroom. We can pull out now and will redock in the morning," he tells them.

"Of course, sir."

I swallow the nervous lump in my throat, we're staying out to sea all night? What if there's like an earthquake or a tidal wave or a damn tsunami for that matter.

I glance around, does this thing have a lifeboat? I make a mental note for later to find out how to work it just in case.

"Come." He takes my hand in his and leads me inside and my stomach flips at the grandeur. Suddenly I'm taken back to the day when I came to visit him here and he told me I was his surefire and god, I'm so overwhelmed that I can hardly breathe.

"Hey." Edward takes me into his arms and looks down at me. "What's wrong?"

"Nothing."

The engine on the yacht starts and I see people out on the deck undoing ropes. People seem to be everywhere doing everything at once.

He tucks a piece of hair behind my ear. "You seem nervous."

"Maybe a little."

"Why?"

"Just…." I give a subtle shrug. "This is just all new, I guess." I glance around at the luxurious furnishings and this doesn't seem real. That I'm here with him…. Doing this…that we're officially together.

"Would you like a drink?" he asks.

"Yes," I reply way too fast. "It's a margarita kind of night."

"It is." He smiles, his eyes have a certain warm glow in them tonight. "It's so good to have you here."

I twist my fingers in front of me, I wish I could say it felt good to be here.

"Go put your purse down, sweetheart, slip into something more comfortable," he says as he walks behind the bar.

Slip into something more comfortable.

Something about that sentence triggers me and I stare at him as I have an out-of-body experience, he's said that before.

Many times.

Right here…on this yacht.

To how many women I can't even imagine.

I begin to hear my heartbeat fast and hard in my ears and damn it, I don't want to feel like this. Tonight is about celebrating us making it, the start of our journey together.

"I'll just take my purse up to your room," I murmur.

"Our room," he corrects me as he pours the tequila into the glass.

I nod and take the stairs, he needn't worry about putting tequila into a glass, I'll drink it straight from the fucking bottle tonight, right before I jump overboard. I climb one staircase, then another, then another and I hear music sound through the speakers down below. A low chill-session vibe…*is this his fuck playlist?*

Stop it.

"What the hell are you doing, Alora?" I whisper as I get to the top level, and I know that if I keep feeling like this that I'm going to ruin the entire night. "Snap the hell out of this shitty mood." I walk into his bedroom to see black lingerie laid out on the bed.

Suddenly what he wanted me to slip into becomes very apparent. My heart sinks, because normal Alora would put this on and vow to blow his mind, make him beg for mercy and then some.

But for some reason I'm not her tonight, I'm some weak insecure version that not even I want to be around.

I go to the window and watch on as we pull out of the port, people stand in crowds on the marina watching the grand yacht leave and I close my eyes.

Disappointed with where my thoughts are taking me.

Ever since I found out about Hermione and his past with her I've felt unsettled, like there's a huge part of him that I don't know.

I knew who he was, I knew this was his life. So why am I letting his past upset me?

It doesn't change a thing between us in the here and now.

I know that tonight more than ever.... I need to fake it till I make it. I want to have a good night, I want us to enjoy each other and celebrate in style, maybe after a few drinks I'll be able to relax and be more present. Let go of all this bullshit.

Yes.... Good plan.

I pick up the lingerie and look it over, I'll come back up later and put this on.

"Okay." I talk out loud to myself. "Let's do this."

EDWARD.

"Serve dinner now and then I would like privacy for the rest of the night. You may all retire and I want nobody above deck," I tell the server.

"Yes, sir." She disappears downstairs and I continue making Alora's margarita.

She's upstairs right now putting on the lingerie that I bought her and I smile at the thought.

Nobody blows my mind like Alora Sorenson, *nobody....*

The spa is hot and bubbling and damn it, I can't wait to replay the last time we had one together.

"Hi," she says softly. I turn to see her still in her dress.

"Ah...." She shrugs, sensing my disappointment. "I'll put it on later."

I nod and pass her the margarita and she tastes it. "Perfect." She walks out on deck and looks out over the port as it twinkles in the distance. I go and stand beside her as she watches the land in silence.

She seems different tonight, distant.

"A penny for your thoughts?" I ask.

She sips her drink. "I'm thinking this is a great margarita."

My eyes hold hers and I know there's something bothering her. I sip my drink as I contemplate my word choice, in the end it just blurts out. "What's wrong?"

"Nothing." She forces a smile.

"Alora." I rub my thumb over her bottom lip. "I don't like being lied to."

"God," she whispers, as if exasperated. "I'm just feeling really weird."

"Why?"

"Because...." She looks around the yacht and throws her hand up. "This place is just...." She shrugs. "And then I can't stop...." She cuts herself off. "But then I know."

"Land the plane," I snap, impatient.

"Your history on this yacht is whispering through the walls and taunting me with visions of you with other women."

My eyes hold hers.

"And I logically know. *I know* that it doesn't matter and that it makes no difference to us or our relationship."

I concentrate on trying not to cut her off.

"I guess." She sips her drink. "It's hard to put into words."

"Try harder."

"I just feel insecure tonight, and I don't want to, and I don't like feeling like this but I have been wondering. Why *do* you love me, Edward?"

"Can you hear yourself right now?" I frown. "You feel insecure because I love you?"

"The irony is not lost on me." She rolls her eyes. "Believe me."

"Alora." I exhale. "You are a very different species of woman to who I usually spend time with."

"I know that, and that's what has me confused."

She listens as her hair whips around in the wind.

"Don't be confused, because this—" I gesture to the yacht, "—is an illusion of happiness. And from the moment I met you, I was also back in our book and I realized I didn't want the fake life I was living anymore and maybe that's why I fought against it so hard. On some level I was giving up everything I knew to be with you. I've always been rich, but it's only now that I have you that I am truly wealthy." I take her into my arms and kiss her. "Forget my past. *You* are my future."

Her eyes well with tears and she nods as if understanding.

"Why didn't you put your lingerie on for me?" I kiss her again.

"I don't know."

She's still struggling and I know I need to pull her out of her head.

"Here's what's going to happen." I put my mouth to her ear. "Tonight we're going back to the first weekend we met."

I hold her close as she listens.

"You don't know me, and I don't know you." She smirks as I hold her ear to my mouth. "And you have arrived on my yacht to pleasure me on request."

She bites her lip to hide her smile.

"Get upstairs. Get that fucking lingerie on and get back down here and suck my cock." I grab a handful of her hair and pull her head back; I lick her open lips.

Her eyes darken with desire and I feel myself harden with a deep throb.

"You have two minutes," I growl.

"Yes, sir." She turns and I slap her hard on the ass.

"Let's fucking go."

ALORA.

I stare at my reflection, I'm in the bathroom of the main bedroom with wall-to-wall mirrors. The black lace lingerie fits like a glove. It cuts away at the breast, barely covering my nipples and it laces up the front like a corset. It has lace and velvet panels with black satin ribboning and a snap crotch. It looks like something from a hardcore bondage porn film, not something your wife would wear…but maybe that's the point. I smile as I turn and look at my behind, barely covered with lace.

Deviant.

Where did he even buy this?

I feel him before I see him and turn to see Edward leaning with his shoulder against the doorjamb. His hair is messed and his olive skin looks stark against the crisp white T-shirt and light blue jeans. Big, deep blue eyes hold mine and he has something in his mouth.

"Hi."

He pulls it out and licks his lips. "Sucking on your butt plug." He gives me a slow, sexy smile.

"Why would you be sucking on a butt plug?" I breathe.

"To warm it up for you." His hungry eyes drop down my body. "To warm you up for me."

Jeez….

I swallow the lump in my throat.

"Come here," he whispers as he unzips his jeans. "Suck me." He picks up a towel and drops it to the floor and points to it. "Kneel."

His words snap me out of my mood and I want to please him, more than anything I want to please him. I drop to my knees and his hands go to my hair as I struggle to pull his jeans down over his hips.

His cock is hard, making pulling his jeans down over it difficult. Damn this thing has its own zip code.

"Hurry. The. *Fuck*. Up," he growls.

The jeans finally give way and his thick hard cock springs free; my eyes linger on his manhood. God, his dick is beautiful, the joy it brings my body is like nothing else.

Thick veins course down its length and pre-ejaculate drips from the end.

It looks angry…. *Hungry.*

Holding himself at his base, he rubs the tip over my mouth, smearing the pre-come across my lips. "Open." He fists my hair in his hand and I part my lips, purposely not enough so that he has to pry them open.

This is what I love doing…teasing him, just enough so he loses control.

He lets out a low growl as he pushes forward. I keep my mouth parted only slightly, I want him to fight to get it in.

Cupping his balls, I slowly lick his end and his breath catches. "Yes...."

I smile as I lick him again, his grip on my hair tightens as he guides my head where he wants it to go.

Watching Edward Prescott come apart is my favorite extreme sport. And extreme it is, because once he loses control there's no going back. There's a very fine line between pleasure and pain. He fucks hard and unapologetic.

Primal as the human race, this man was built for sin.

His dark eyes hold mine as I open my mouth and he slides it deep down my throat until my gag reflex kicks in. "Take it." He fists my hair harder. "All of it."

I close my eyes as I try to calm myself, this is nothing new. I fight to take him every time, but I know the payoff is more than worth it. I open my throat and he slides right in.

"Yesssss," he hisses. "Good girl. Just like that." He pulls me by the hair out and then back onto him. My sex ripples in excitement at the sound of his moan.

Satisfying this man is a need in me that I can't describe, a deep ache that I need to fulfill.

"Oh yeah," he breathes. "Like that." He pulls me back and then slides back in deep. "Swallow," he whispers darkly, and I smile around him.

Fucking deviant.

I swallow around his cock and his lips go to a perfect *O* as his eyes flicker closed. "Fuck yeah."

I fist him as I suck, hard and just the way he likes it.

On a normal man, this would be painful.... But not Edward. He likes to ride the pain, the harder and more brutal, the stronger his orgasm.

So fucking hot I can't stand it.

I fist him harder and harder and his breath catches as his hands twist in my hair and he tips his head back and....

He snaps out of his trance, realizing that he's about to blow without me. He pulls me off and up to my feet. "Up." He pulls a velvet stool over to us. "Kneel on it."

"What?"

"Do it," he demands.

I kneel onto the stool.

"Lean over it."

I swallow the lump in my throat, he scares me sometimes… how far is too far?

"It's okay, I've got you." He runs his hand down my spine in an act of tenderness. "It's okay."

I lean over and my behind is up in the air and I hear the cupboard open and I close my eyes as I wait for his next move.

He slowly unsnaps the crotch buttons and pulls the lingerie up and I stare at the tiles as I try to calm my breathing. I feel his tongue on my back entrance. He licks me, softly at first and then deeper, hungrier.

Oh…

I close my eyes as I try to deal with him…. With this.

Whenever he touches me here…it's always so intimate, and knowing he's the only man who's ever done this only amps up our connection.

My breath quivers in anticipation and I hear a cap click open.

What's he doing?

I feel something pour over my skin, dripping down my thighs, and his finger rubs it in.

Oil….

He pours more on and his fingers slowly rub it into my ass, around and around, and my eyes flutter closed.

And then in….

Fuck.

Softly at first and then deeper…. More urgent. He pours more oil onto me and my body begins to slurp as his fingers dive deep. He rides my ass and then I feel the bristles of his whiskers as his tongue slides through my sex.

This man….

I'm dripping wet, swollen and so ready to come.

"Sharp sting," he murmurs. "Relax."

I feel the hardness of the butt plug nudge my back entrance and I close my eyes as he slides it in deep.

I see stars…as my eyes roll back in my head.

"Oh, yes," he breathes. "My dirty girl loves it here." He pulls it out and slides it back in. "Doesn't she?" He bends and kisses my behind and I quiver, the orgasm so close I can nearly taste it.

"Don't even think about it." He rearranges me on the stool, I'm bent over, completely at his mercy, and he nudges his tip through my weeping lips.

He slowly slides his thick cock deep into my sex and the air leaves my lungs. In this position with a large butt plug firmly in place…. Taking all of him feels impossible.

My senses are so heightened that every move has me quivering, shaking at the knees as I try to hold myself up.

He pulls out and pushes back in and a deep moan leaves my body like an earthquake and he picks up the pace and I feel the sharp sting of a slap to my cheek.

Dear god…I'm in heaven.

The ceiling spins as we pant, staring up at it.

Both covered in oil, gasping for air, and completely spent. He's had me every which way, in every position known to man, and damn, it feels like we've run a marathon.

We've been fucking for hours.

He looks over at me, his chest rises and falls as he tries to catch his breath. "You should hydrate."

I bubble up a surprised giggle. "No shit."

Darkness.

Meanwhile…. Alora's house.

2 a.m.….

I slowly open the gate and quietly close it behind me. I creep down the side of the house and once at the back door, put the mini flashlight into my mouth and shine it onto the lock. My hands clad in black leather gloves, I grab the tension wrench and begin to pick it. The lock doesn't budge, and I take out my glass cutters but then think better of it. No. Then someone will notice.

I go back to picking the lock and with ten more minutes of maneuvering, the door clicks open. I slink inside and close it behind me, relocking it on my way.

I'm in….

Carefully taking off my backpack, I slowly unzip it and grab the plans of the house. I shine my torch to see them, looking between the wall in question and the plans, I finally locate what I'm looking for. The wall-to-wall bookcase.

My hands run over the moldings on the front of the bookcase but I don't feel what I'm looking for. I shine my torch on the plans again, it should be just.... I feel behind the books to more molding.

Nothing.

Restudying the plans, I notice I'm on the wrong side.

Ahh....

I change sides and feel around the molding and it clicks, that's it.

I push it hard and it gives way, it still works. Slowly I pull the entire wall of shelving toward me to reveal a hidden staircase.

A satisfied smile creeps across my face, I walk in, close the hidden door behind me before hitting the lock button.

I shine my torch up the staircase, it's musty and the air is heavy and dense. This secret part of the house, uninhabited for decades.

I walk up the three flights of stairs until I get to the floor above the main bedroom. I sit down and begin to unload my backpack, I bring out a camping light, set it up and turn it on. The large room lights up and I smile at my newfound haven.

Perfect.

I take out the air mattress and hand pump it up and throw the sleeping bag on top, then I take the drill and tool kit.

Reading the plans once again, I retrieve the tape measure and carefully mark where I need to drill. In the light fitting over the bed, and in the bathroom ceiling and the back of the shelves in the staircase.

It takes me hours, and just on daylight my work is done.

I lean down and look through the hole in the floor, Alora's bed is right beneath and I get an overhead view of the room and bathroom. I sit up and smile.

Now.... I wait.

CHAPTER TWENTY-NINE

ALORA.

The sound of an engine in the distance wakes me from my sleep and I stretch out like a cat. My body aches where it shouldn't and I sleepily smile as oily memories of last night reappear. My eyes float around the luxurious bedroom but my man isn't beside me. God, what time is it? I have to work today. I grab my phone from the side table, 7 a.m. Hmm.... Time to get up.

Pulling on the black silk dressing gown that I found hanging in the bathroom, I head off in search of him. I peer around the bedroom door, wait...what's the day etiquette around here?

Are people just like walking around or....

Maybe I should get dressed first. I walk to the top of the stairs and duck down to see if I can see anybody on the floor below.

Edward did say just be normal.... Okay, so here goes. I drag my fingers through my hair to find knots the size of a bird's nest. Mental note, oil and carnal activities with my head being rammed into a bed doesn't do well for the blowout. Maybe I should wear a swimming cap next time?

Walking down the stairs, I see Edward sitting at a table out on the deck in the sun. He's sipping a cup of coffee and I make my way out to him. "Hello."

"Good morning." He smiles darkly into his coffee cup and I smirk at his naughty look.

Deviant.

He taps his lap and I walk around and sit on him; his big arms slide around me. "Hmm." He nuzzles my face. "How did you sleep?"

"Well, considering I was fucked into unconsciousness, I don't remember."

He chuckles and kisses my lips. "Just the way I like it. Coffee?"

"Yes please." I get up and take a seat opposite him, my eyes go out to the water that surrounds us. "Where are we?" I ask.

"Barbados?"

"What?" I stammer. "I have to work today."

"Relax." He throws me a sexy wink. "That's Monte Carlo just over there."

"Oh." I smile, feeling stupid, and pick up a morning paper, wait a minute.... How does a newspaper get here, is there like a water postman delivery driver or.... I open the paper as Edward fills my coffee cup.

"Are we going back in soon? Because I have to work today."

"Yes, have some breakfast first and we'll head in." He sips his coffee. "I've been giving your situation some thought."

"My situation?"

"Yes. I think it's time you put a manager into your store."

"Huh?" I frown. "Why would I do that?"

"So that you can—"

"Be at your beck and call?" I cut him off.

He smiles at my comeback. "Travel with me when needed."

"Oh."

"Don't be mistaken, being at my beck and call is high on your to-do list." His eyes dance with mischief.

"Edward." I sigh, unimpressed.

"I'm just saying...you want to launch more into the decorating space and working with interior decorators but you are tied down so hard to that store that you can't even take a day off."

"I like working." I sip my coffee.

"I know that, and you can every day if you wish, but wouldn't it be nice to have someone to share the load with you and cover if we need to go away?"

"I'll think about it, but no rush. We aren't going away anywhere soon."

"Yes we are."

"Like where?"

"I have to be in Vegas soon and I want to take you home and meet your father while we're in the States."

"You do?" I smile.

He picks up his phone and calls someone. "Hello, we are ready for breakfast. Two egg-white omelets, fresh fruit, and a side of pancakes with bacon. And an almond croissant for Alora. Thank you." He hangs up without saying goodbye.

So bossy….

"We have a full weekend of social engagements, so I've organized for my personal shopper to call on you."

"What?" I snap, annoyed.

He looks up over his paper. "Tone." He raises an eyebrow.

"Why would you think I would want a shopper?"

"Well, we have a ball on Friday night. I'm playing polo on Saturday, which you will be coming to with drinks after, and then we have a private party at Theodore's house on Saturday night."

Oh, hell no….

"Four things in the one weekend?" I slump into the chair, "That's a bit of overkill, isn't it?"

"No." He keeps reading.

"Well, they say that being out too much and being too available isn't a good look."

"Who says that?"

"You know, the styling shows."

"What styling shows?"

"I don't know." I shrug. "Life of the rich and famous and stuff."

His eyes rise above the paper as amusement flashes across his face.

"That sounded ridiculous, even to me." I smile, embarrassed.

He raises an eyebrow in agreement.

"You know what I mean."

"No. I don't."

"Do I *have* to come?"

"Yes." He goes back to reading. "Don't even start that shit."

"Polo…you're such a blue blood snob."

He sips his coffee. "I've been called worse."

"Why do you think I need a shopper? Don't you like the way I dress?"

"I do, I just thought.... She's a stylist, she's very good."

"Has she styled any of your ex-girlfriends?"

"No. Why would you even ask that?"

"Well, I don't want anyone young and hot and in love with you." I imagine them all fawning over him and my blood boils. "I don't want anyone who even knows you, actually? And I'm only interested in vintage fashion."

His eyes flick up to me. "Would you prefer a male stylist?"

"Do you have one?"

"No, but Theo's stylist, Laurent, is apparently very good."

"Can I have him?"

"I suppose so." He keeps reading his paper and turns the page. "If he looks at you the wrong way I will end his life, but hey, that's on you."

"Your breakfast, sir," the server says, he has a man behind him and they are both carrying huge trays; they carefully place it all down in front of us.

"Thanks." I smile, embarrassed, did they just hear what we were talking about?

"You're welcome." They disappear.

"Jeez," I whisper as I look over the table. "There's enough food for ten people here?"

"Yeah, well, I worked up the appetite of ten men last night." His eyes meet mine and we smirk at each other, the air crackles between us.

"More like fifteen."

"Eat your food." He smiles as he unwraps the napkin.

I begin to cut my toast. "Can we stay at my place tonight? I need to get some more things and I want to water my plants."

"I guess." He exhales. "But I want you to move in with me full-time."

My eyes rise to meet his. "You do?"

"Yes, our principal residence will be here. Bring all of your clothes."

I roll my eyes, unimpressed that he just assumes we can live here.

"What?" he asks.

"Why can't we live together at my house?"

"Because it won't work."

"Why not?"

"Because we need more room and your house isn't suitable for my men. I need a gym and to be close to work in case of an emergency."

"Ugh."

"What?" He snaps.

"Are we really going to live on the boat?" I mutter dryly.

"Yacht," he corrects me. "And a four-hundred-million-euro yacht isn't good enough for you?" He bites his food off his fork as if annoyed.

"There's just...." I shrug.

"There's just what?"

"There's no dirt here, Edward. How can I have a vegetable garden if there's no dirt? You know gardening is my first love."

"I thought I was your first love," he mutters dryly.

"Yes, but you know what I mean?"

"Hmm." He keeps chewing with an eye roll.

"What does hmm mean?" I snap, annoyed.

"Alora." He exhales. "You're killing me."

"What, I'm just being honest. This yacht is nice and all, but as a forever home I'm not so sure. I want a kitchen I can cook for us in and I want a garden I can garden in. I want to touch the earth with bare feet whenever I feel like it."

"Fine." He bites the food off his fork as if annoyed. "I'll buy us a new fucking house in Monaco."

"Good. You do that." I bite my food off my fork too as I fake annoyance as well. "Make sure it has good soil."

The car door opens and Philippe smiles down at me. "Good night, Miss Sorenson."

"Thank you, Philippe." I climb out of the car. "Good night." Edward gets out the other side, it's just after 9 p.m. Edward picked me up from work and then we went and had dinner and are just arriving back to my place. Edward takes my hand in his and we walk up my driveway and I unlock the front door. Edward turns and waves the boys off and they leave us for the night. I flick the lights on and throw my keys down. "You want a cup of tea, babe?" I ask.

"No. I'm dead tired, I'm going to have a shower." He kisses me before disappearing up the stairs and I turn on the kettle on and flick the television on and notice that a book has fallen out of my bookshelves.

Weird.... How did that fall down?

I pick it up and slide it back into its place, make my tea and flop onto the couch to watch the late news. Ugh.... I'm tired.

EDWARD.

Alora climbs into bed and I go to the window and look out over the street below. Shrouded in darkness, silent and calm.

There's an uneasiness surrounding me.

I can't put my finger on it but something feels off here in her place tonight, there's a different energy to how it normally feels. I check the windows are locked and close the heavy drapes, then do the same in every room.

I'll just recheck downstairs to put my mind at ease. I check the second-level windows and pull the drapes and then walk to the ground floor and flick the lights on.

A book is on the floor in front of the bookcase, Alora must have got a book out and knocked it loose. I pick it up and place it back in the shelving and walk around and tighten all the locks and close the drapes.

My eyes roam over the place as I walk around, why do I feel so off....

I'm being paranoid.

I dim the lights, make my way back upstairs and slide into bed, I pull Alora close and wrap my arms around her. "Good night, my darling," I whisper.

She doesn't answer, she's already asleep.

ALORA.

"I'm off, Doe." Edward leans down and kisses me softly. The bedroom is semi-dark, only early, it's not fully light. "See you tonight."

"Okay," I whisper sleepily. "I love you."

"I love you too. Have a good day." Another kiss and I hear him walk down the stairs and then the front door open and close, moments later the car drives up the street and around the corner.

I snuggle back into bed, close my eyes and doze for what feels like a long time.

Creak….

I frown with my eyes closed, what was that?

Creak….

There it is again; I drag my eyes open and look up to the ceiling as I listen.

Hmm, great, just what I need. A damn mouse in the roof.

I lie for a few more minutes, it's raining and really coming down outside. There's thunder rumbling in the distance and the sky is dark. Eventually I drag myself out of bed and walk into the bathroom and catch sight of myself in the mirror and wince as I pull my hair up into a high bun.

I turn on the shower and get in under the hot water. The room fills with steam and I smile into the heat, my favorite way to start the day.

Ring, ring…. Ring, ring…. My phone vibrates across the counter.

I walk out of the shower dripping wet to see that it's Philippe. "Hello," I answer.

"Hi, Alora, we're at the front door. Edward said you had some extra things that needed carrying out to the car this morning."

Oh crap, they're at the front door in the pouring rain and I'm not even ready.

"I'm just in the shower, Philippe, you have a key, don't you?"

"Yes."

"Let yourself in and have a cup of coffee, I'll be about fifteen minutes."

"Alright then."

I hang up and rush back through my shower, damn it I haven't even packed.

"Thanks for today." I smile to Jonty as I lock the store door. It's been a productive day and we got so much done. We moved the store around, got in four deliveries and sold two large armoires, three big mirrors and nearly every lamp we had in stock. I am thoroughly exhausted and for once am happy that I don't have to cook dinner tonight.

The blacked-out car is across the road, the waiting guards sit inside as they patiently wait. The rain has thrown everything out today, the guards haven't been able to walk around the street as usual and I'm sure they have gone a little stir-crazy being cooped up in a car or in the front of my store. As per Edward's instructions I have packed a few bags of my things and the boys put them in the trunk this morning and I will be staying with him in Monaco most nights from here on in.

I'm a little sad to be leaving my place here in Nice, but I'll be going back there every day or two to water my garden before or after work and we will stay there a night or two each week. Not sure yet what we're going to do with my place long term moving forward, but I guess we'll work it out when we need to.

I walk across to the car where Philippe is standing waiting for me with the back door open. "Good afternoon, Miss Sorenson." He smiles.

"Hello, Philippe, thank you." I slink into the back seat. "What a day."

"Yes, it's really coming down out there."

As the car drives through the rain in Nice, I open my phone and begin to scroll through Instagram. I need to get used to this drive.

EDWARD.

I read the email.

"Mr. Prescott, Laurent is here for his appointment with Miss Sorenson."

"Just show him up to the upper-level living room and ask him to set up there." I keep typing. "Can everyone help bring in anything he needs carried."

"Yes, sir."

"Close my door on the way out, please."

As they leave me alone, I keep working for another hour and my office door slowly opens and I glance up, Alora peeks around the doorjamb. "Hi."

Just the sight of her brings a smile to my face and I slide my chair out and tap my lap. "Hello, Miss Sorenson."

She walks in, sits down and I wrap my arms around her. She kisses me softly and puts her head down onto my shoulder. "How long until you finish?"

"At least another hour."

"Hmm," she grumbles. "I'm going to go upstairs and soak in the bath, I'm so tired."

"Have you forgotten something?" I kiss her temple.

"What?" She looks up at me.

"Someone is coming to see you tonight?"

"Who?"

"Laurent, the stylist."

"Oh god." She screws up her face. "I'm way too tired to try on clothes tonight. Can we reschedule, please?"

I put my mouth to her ear and whisper to try and soften the blow, "He's upstairs already."

"What?"

"They've been carrying clothes inside in the rain for over an hour."

"Oh god." She throws her hands over her eyes. "I don't even want to go to these stupid things on the weekend."

"You're going." I tap her behind. "Upstairs now and get it over with."

"Edward." She sighs.

"What would you like for dinner, I'll order and have it ready for when you're finished."

"I guess if I had to pick..." she rolls her eyes, "...chocolate cake."

I smile and kiss her big, beautiful lips. "Go do this and I'll have a chocolate cake waiting."

"I'm not trying anything on. I'm just picking any old thing." She stands.

"Okay." I turn back to my computer. "Luckily, dressing in old things seems to be your jam. But don't complain to me on the weekend when you have nothing to wear to two black tie functions."

"Ugh.... This is a literal hell," she whines. "Going out with you is becoming very high maintenance." She stomps to the door. "And this is a real hassle that I don't have time for," she moans as she leaves.

I chuckle, only Alora Sorenson would complain about designer clothes waiting for her with a stylist.

She's one of a kind, I'll give her that.

ALORA.

Edward smiles as he looks me over, his eyes dropping to my toes and back up to my face. "You look beautiful." He takes my face in his hands and kisses me, his lips lingering over mine.

"I feel like a peacock."

"A beautiful peacock."

It's Friday night and we're about to leave for the ball, a hairdresser has been in and styled my hair in big Hollywood curls and a makeup artist came and did my makeup. I'm wearing a strapless ice-pink gown and I know I should feel beautiful, but in reality, I feel like a fish out of water. My hair is too bouffant and my makeup looks like a drag queen. I feel overdone and awkward.

"I'm doing my own hair and makeup from now on."

"Okay." He smiles down at me. "Why did you even get them to do it in the first place?"

"Laurent told me to."

"Well, Laurent is used to dealing with nightmares who need glamming up." He kisses me again. "You can't enhance perfection."

"You're so biased." I smile up at him and slide my hands under his black suit jacket. "Luckily for me."

"Let's have a glass of wine and then get going."

"Okay, I need some Dutch courage."

"Are you nervous?" He frowns.

"I guess."

"Why?"

"Well." I shrug. "It's my first time out with you as a...."

"Girlfriend?" He picks up my hand and kisses my fingertips.

"At all," I reply. "We haven't done anything in public and now I'm coming out of the closet as a girlfriend."

"Out of the closet?" He chuckles. "You sure do have a way with words, my love." His eyes glow with tenderness. "You don't need to worry about tonight. Nobody that I know personally will be there. It's a work function only, one of my board members asked me to go and in good faith I wanted to be there for him."

"So no…" I widen my eyes, "…women from the past?"

"No."

I smile, feeling a little bit better. "What about the party tomorrow night at the prince's house?"

"Prepare yourself for that one, straight into the fire." He fills our champagne glasses and passes me one. "Your initiation into Monaco." He clinks his glass with mine and winks. "It will be fun."

I fake a smile as dread fills me.

Great….

Chatter, laughter, and a grand soiree.

Edward's having a great time and me…. Well, I'm standing beside him as he does.

I smile on cue as he chats and laughs, I'm physically by his side but not mentally here.

Not one person has spoken to me all night.

Not one.

I'm the handbag, here for show.

And it's not his fault, he's holding my hand and introducing me to everyone and trying his best to include me. But after the introduction, the conversation goes straight to him and work subjects that I know nothing about.

As the hours tick over I have this sinking feeling about the party tomorrow.

How the hell am I going to get through a night with all his exes in the same room, at the same party? Him knowing everyone and me knowing not a soul.

And I don't want to be that girlfriend that demands he stand beside me all night; I want him to have fun and see his friends and talk and socialize.

But what do I do while he does that?

Do I just stand there awkwardly like I am tonight…. Hoping and praying that we can go home soon?

Fuck….

The people he is talking to finally leave us alone.

"You alright?" he asks softly.

"Yep." I force a smile, an abysmal lie but whatever.

"Are you having fun?"

"Uh-huh." More than anything I know that it's not Edward's job to make me feel comfortable in his world. I need to work this out for myself, and I'm not going to beg him to take me home early every time we go out.

I love him, I want this to work and I need to suck it up and learn to love this life.

"Do you want to go home?" he asks softly.

"Whenever you're ready." I smile.

"That smile didn't touch your eyes," he murmurs. "Why are you lying?"

Unexpected emotion fills me and I get a lump in my throat as my eyes hold his.

Because if I tell you the truth, that I hate this world…where does that leave us?

My eyes well with tears and I drop my head to hide them.

"Doe," he says softly. "It will be okay, sweetheart. You'll get used to it."

I nod. "I know."

He puts his mouth to my ear. "I love you."

"I know." I blink away the tears and kiss his cheek. "I love you too."

That's the only reason I'm here…believe me.

He squeezes my hand in his. "Another hour and we can go."

The car trip home is made in silence. I stare out the window into the darkness.

As if sensing my inner mental breakdown, Edward is watching his words. Or maybe he's just second-guessing his life choices too.

I had the worst night tonight…. Like really bad.

I felt like an outsider, a spectator to a glamorous life that I don't belong in…and Edward knows it, and there's not a damn thing he can say to make me feel any better because this isn't a him problem, this is a me problem that only I can fix.

The car pulls up at the marina and we climb out, he takes my hand in his and we walk up the dock with the guards trailing behind us.

I mean, what the actual hell is wrong with me?

I'm with my dream man, who lives the dream life, who is the absolute love of my life and here I am upset because I felt left out at a glamorous event.

Wake the fuck up, Alora. You spoiled little witch.

"Miss Sorenson." Philippe smiles as we walk across the gangplank.

"Good night, Philippe, thank you." I smile as I walk onto the yacht.

"Thank you," Edward says. "We can depart when ready."

"Yes, sir."

We go out to sea overnight, every night. Apparently it's safer out there. From what, I don't know. It's not like there's a boogieman waiting to get us or anything. In honesty, I think all this money has made Edward paranoid. He's imagining danger that doesn't even exist.

We walk inside and I put my purse down. "Would you like a nightcap, Doe?"

"No." I just need to go to bed and sleep off this depressing entitled little bitch mood I'm in. "I'm tired, babe." I go to walk upstairs and Edward pulls me back by the hand to him.

"You okay?"

"Yeah." I nod, tears threaten. "I don't want you worrying about it."

"Talk to me."

"I just…" I shrug, not even sure how to answer, "…I feel like a duck out of water and…."

"And what?"

"Honestly." I throw my hands up. "I guess I'm dreading tomorrow night and I think maybe you should go by yourself and I'll just wait here at home for you."

His eyes hold mine.

"I want you to have a good time, I don't want you worrying about me, Edward."

"I want you in my world, Doe."

"I know." Tears do break the dam this time and I swipe them away, embarrassed. "I'm sorry.... I don't know why I'm being so dramatic about this. I knew it was going to be hard in the beginning."

"Look." He pulls me into his arms. "Why don't you bring a friend to the party tomorrow night?"

"I don't want to be a burden."

"No burden at all. They could come here for a drink first and we can go together and then at the party you will have someone to talk besides me, someone who has your back."

"Really?" I smile hopefully. "Would that be okay?"

"Yes, of course. Invite a friend who's fun and friendly and who can help you relax and meet new people."

"That would be amazing." I smile. "Thank you."

"Now, I'm going to ask you again. Would you like a nightcap?"

"No. But I'll take your dick in the shower."

"Excellent plan." He grabs my hand and leads me upstairs. "The ultimate nightcap."

EDWARD.

"Miss Sorenson has a friend joining us tonight," I tell the guard on the marina.

"Yes, sir."

"Just show them in when they get here."

I walk inside as Alora walks down the stairs and *holy fuck*.

I let out a low whistle of appreciation.

She's in a black strapless tight minidress with her long legs on display. Sky-high strappy black stilettos, her long dark hair is loose and bouncy and she's wearing my favorite red lipstick. "You look fucking hot." I grab her roughly. "Maybe we should both stay home."

"You like?"

I turn her around so that her back is to me and I bend her over. "I fucking love." I bounce her off my hips and feel myself harden. "I'm not even joking, let's go upstairs and fuck."

"Edward." She laughs and swats me away. "Behave yourself."

"Yes. This way." We hear a voice. "They're expecting you."

I turn to see Thomas Stone walk through the door. "What the fuck are you doing here?" I demand.

"I invited him," Alora replies.

"Wait." Thomas's eyes flick between the two of us. "You didn't tell him?"

"What do you mean?" I growl.

"He's the friend I'm bringing tonight. You said I could invite someone fun and friendly to help me meet new people. This is who I chose."

"Over my dead body."

CHAPTER THIRTY

ALORA.

"Leave. Right now," he tells Thomas.

"Edward." I put my hands on my hips. "Where are your manners?"

"If you think for one minute that we are taking your male escort to a fucking party, you have another thing coming," he growls.

"Shh," I whisper as I close the door. "Keep your voice down."

"I will not keep my fucking voice down," he fumes.

"Hey, I can just leave." Thomas points to the door with his thumb. "It's fine." He widens his eyes in an *are you trying to get me killed* gesture.

"Don't you dare leave." I turn to Edward and poke him hard in the chest. "Listen here, you." I poke him again. "If you want me to live in and accept this ridiculous over-the-top world of yours. I'm allowed to choose my own friends. You told me to bring my friendliest friend."

"Him." Edward's eyes nearly bulge from the sockets. "Out of all the people in the world.... *He* is who you choose?"

"Yeah." I throw up my hands. "Helene is away and Thomas is friendly, he gets on well with both men and women. He knows this type of women like the back of his hand, but most of all, he has my back."

"Oh, I'm sure he does, your back isn't all he wants."

"With all due respect." Thomas interrupts. "Alora and I *are* just friends. There is no way in hell I would risk getting killed for her."

Edward narrows his eyes at Thomas. "Wise."

"But seriously, you're a little over the top, am I right?" Thomas replies.

"Over the fucking top," Edward fires back. "I'll tell you what's over the fucking top. You thinking that a male escort is coming to a party with me and my girl as I introduce her to the world."

"He can be my cousin." I try to think on my feet.

"Your cousin?" Edward fumes.

"Yeah, good idea," Thomas replies. "This way I can innocently come and blend in but then disappear when you two are spending time together. But if you need me to step up and talk to either men or women, I can do that too."

"No." Edward straightens his cuff links.

Time to bring out the big guns.

"Edward, I'm not coming unless you let me bring him." I put my hands on my hips.

"Why are you intent on ruining our night?" Edward barks.

"Because I need backup and I know I only have one friend who can hold his own at a party like this."

Edward's eyes meet Thomas's and I can see his brain ticking.

"Completely innocent, I swear." Thomas holds his hands up. "If you want me to leave at any time you just have to say the word."

Edward runs the backs of his fingers through his stubble as he thinks and I can feel his fury, simmering dangerously close to the surface.

"What about if he just came for an hour." I try to sweeten the deal. "Until I'm comfortable and then he can go."

"I don't like this," Edward replies.

I slide my arms around him and go up on my toes to kiss him. "I know, but you'll do it for me."

"Alora," he sighs with an eye roll, and I know that I've won.

He turns to Thomas. "You even look at her the wrong way and I will kill you with a smile on my face."

"Well.... That's great." Thomas widens his eyes at me and I bubble up a giggle.

Poor Thomas.

"Are we going to have a drink before we leave?" I try to lighten the mood.

"I don't know, am I allowed to drink?" Thomas teases.

"No," Edward snaps. "You are not."

Have you ever had a moment in your life that is so surreal that it just doesn't seem real?

I'm in one, right now.

Walking toward the front gates of the Prince of Monaco's private residence. Holding the love of my life's hand, who I anonymously met at a kink club three years ago and also happens to be a billionaire. I'm dripping head to toe in vintage Chanel, and my stilettos cost more than my car. The man walking beside us: a gorgeous male escort who somehow has become a trusted friend.

Shit like this just doesn't happen, but whoever's recently taken over as my guardian angel is doing a mighty fine job up there.

We walk along the pathway that leads around to a private road and a huge set of gates. There's a giant twenty-foot stone fence covered in vines, and lanterns strategically light up the space. Guards are standing around, laughing and shaking hands when they see each other as if seeing long-lost friends.

My god....

It never even occurred to me that the guards of the rich and famous have their own social clique; they meet at these events regularly. I wonder if they ever exchange information about each other's bosses.... Of course they would.

People stop talking and turn their attention to us as we approach. "Good evening, Mr. Prescott."

"Good evening." He nods.

Their eyes linger on me as they watch us walk by.

Edward squeezes my hand in his, as if reading my thoughts.

"Wiggle that ass, girlfriend," Thomas mutters under his breath. "Give them something to talk about."

A trace of a smile crosses Edward's face as we walk, and I smile too, hopeful that in time Edward will come to like Thomas. They have a lot in common, sarcastic wit. One grumpy and one sunshine...opposite sides of a similar coin.

Though not the same.

We get to the front gates and the three guards standing in

front of it, there's three women in front of us, scantily dressed and hot as hell. "Identification and phones, ladies," one of the men asks them.

"Of course." The girls show them their licenses and their names are ticked off a list, they fill out a piece of paper and pass their phones over to a woman, she gives them a ticket and they walk inside. I watch the woman put them into a giant numbered shelving unit. They then walk through a metal detector.

Jeez....

Thomas and I exchange looks, a silent *what the fuck?*

The guards glance up and see us and move to the side. "Good evening, Mr. Prescott."

"Good evening." He walks straight through the metal detector, leading me by the hand.

"Ahh," Thomas says from behind us. "I'm going to leave my phone too." I glance back as he hands it over.

I pull Edward's hand to make him wait for Thomas. "Wait," I whisper. Edward subtly rolls his eyes. Thomas fills out the paperwork, hands his phone over, shows his license and then catches up with us.

"Why did you do that?" I ask.

"Because I'm not being the only fucker in a party with a phone."

"Why not?"

"Because if something gets leaked I don't want to be blamed."

"Ah, smart."

"Come." Edward pulls me forward. "Are you my date or his?"

"So hostile," Thomas mouths behind his back and I get the giggles.

As we walk through the private courtyard and around the large circular water feature, people stop mid-conversation to watch us.

All eyes on me.

The mystery woman with Edward Prescott.

I have never been so grateful to have a friend by my side, if I had to do this alone I would already be hiding in the bathroom.

Fairy lights twinkle in the trees above us, and waiters are carrying silver trays of cocktails up on their shoulders.

Jeez....

"Are there fish in there?" Thomas squints into the water feature. "Yes, there are. Giant fucking fish."

"You might be swimming with them by the end of the night," Edward mutters matter-of-factly.

I giggle and we walk up the split stone staircase that leads into the house, even the handrail is carved from stone. Once inside, my eyes widen.

"Fucking hell," Thomas whispers as he looks through wide eyes too. "This is...."

Wall-to-wall marble, giant archways and painted ornate ceilings that would give the Sistine Chapel a run for its money.

Glamorous beautiful people, with waiters and staff everywhere catering to their every need.

Edward looks over the crowd, not even noticing the splendor. "This way." He leads us through the people and as the crowd dissipates I see Prince Theodore standing in the corner with another man.

My stomach flutters with nerves.

"Hello." Edward smiles as we approach and they shake hands, happy to see each other, before he turns to me. "You remember my Alora."

My Alora.

"Alora, you met Theodore Chapelle and Sinclair Montague at your store that night, two of my best friends in the world."

"Hello." I smile nervously.

"Hello, Alora, good to see you again." They both smile warmly and kiss my cheek. Their eyes linger on my face as if memorizing every freckle.

"This is Thomas," Edward says as if an afterthought. "He's Alora's cousin."

"Hello." They smile as they shake his hand.

"Nice to meet you." Thomas smiles, I can tell that he's a little nervous too.

Theodore lifts his hand and a waitress immediately appears from nowhere. "What would you like to drink, Alora?" he asks me.

Tequila.... All of it.

"I'll have…." I glance around at what other people are drinking.

"She'd like a top-shelf margarita." Edward slides his hand around my waist and pulls me close.

"That would be amazing, thank you." I smile, embarrassed. I turn to ask Thomas what he would like but he's gone. "Where did he go?" I whisper to Edward.

"Who fucking cares," he whispers back.

"Prescott," a man says from the side, and Edward turns and laughs as he shakes his hand.

"So." Theodore comes to stand beside me. "You are responsible for our friend missing of late."

"Haha." I smile shyly. "That's on him, don't blame me."

Theodore smiles warmly. "I've never seen him so happy."

"I'm very happy too." I beam, jeez this man is hot as hell. Sandy brown hair and big brown eyes, tall and well built, he has the whole Theo James vibe going on, which is ironic because his name is Theo too.

Say something…. And quick.

"Thank you for having us, your house is incredible." I smile, that was lame but anyway, at least I said something.

His eyes float around the room as if trying to see it through my eyes. "It is. A little big if I'm being honest. That's the problem when you inherit things, you don't get to choose." He widens his eyes with a cheeky smile.

Oh…he's nice. Not at all what I imagined.

A group of girls are talking to Sinclair and then they include Theodore, my eyes wander over to them, all gorgeous and talking and laughing. Not a visible nerve in sight. My mind wonders if these are the kind of women Edward usually dates.

Beautiful and confident.

"Your margarita." The waiter passes me a cocktail.

"Keep them coming, please," Edward asks him.

"Yes, sir."

I casually look around in hope to spot Thomas.

"He's over by the bar," Edward tells me.

"Oh." I stand still, not wanting to move.

"Go on, then." Edward sighs. "You have ten minutes."

I smile and kiss his cheek. "See you soon." I turn and head toward the bar, I need to dissect this party with someone stat.

EDWARD.

Jerome, Theo's bodyguard, appears through the crowd and whispers something to him, Theo's eyes rise to meet mine.

I lean closer. "What?"

"There's a disturbance at the front gate, sir," Jerome replies.

"What kind of disturbance?"

"Miss Auclair was refused entry and is demanding to see you, Mr. Prescott."

Isadora.

My eyes meet Theo's.

"She's being very vocal and says she's not leaving until she speaks to you, sir."

Theo crunches on a piece of ice, unimpressed. "Go deal with your problem."

"Yeah, yeah." I drain my glass, this is the last fucking thing I feel like.

I follow Jerome through the party and out to the front gates. Isadora is standing to the side with her arms folded.

"What the hell are you doing?" she spits when she sees me come around the corner.

I pull her to the side and out of earshot. "What the fuck are you doing is the question," I whisper angrily.

"I'm trying to get into a party that I would have always been invited to.... And now for some unknown reason...I am not."

"Don't play games with me, Isadora," I sneer. "You made your bed, now fucking lie in it."

"No," she fires back. "You made the bed, Edward. Remember?" She raises her voice in the hope someone hears us. "There were three of us in it."

I grab her elbow and bring her to me as I drag her farther into the garden. "Shut. The. Fuck. Up."

"Why am I not invited tonight?"

"Because you are threatening Hermione and I won't stand for it."

"So you're just going to erase me from society?" she gasps.

"You asked for this, not me. I have no problem with you. However, I *do* have a problem with you threatening Hermione."

"If I tell everyone about you and her." She smiles sarcastically.

"Then you are *dead*." I look her fair and square in the eye and step forward so that we are only millimeters away. "What do you think King Volter is going to do to you if he finds out what you've done?"

"He's going to kill you," she fires back.

"*After* he kills you."

"He wouldn't touch me," she spits.

"Are you sure about that?" I fire back. "It's one thing to betray a girlfriend, but I did not betray her. I engaged in some extracurricular activities with her and her friend. But you.... You've threatened to sell sex scandal stories about the Crown Princess of Switzerland to the media...."

Her face falls as she stares at me. "Did you tell him?"

"Be very careful, Isadora," I whisper. "Or he will find out."

"Let me in."

"Go. To. Hell."

"Is Hermione inside?" she replies. "Is that why I can't come in?"

Yes.

"I don't know, I haven't seen her," I lie. Hermione was the first person I saw when I walked through the door with Alora.

"So let me get this straight," she fires back. "You get to break Hermione's heart and use me for all your deviant kinks and then you get to walk away scot-free with a new shiny girlfriend that we all know you are going to dump as soon as this blows over."

My eyes flicker red.

"Hey, this has nothing to do with me and my life. I'm doing my job and protecting my ex-girlfriend, Hermione, *from you*. If you hadn't been threatening her, trying to blackmail her and ruin her life, you could have come to any party you wanted to."

"Fuck you."

"Get. Out," I sneer.

"You're going to pay for this." She steps onto her back foot. "I'm going to make sure of it."

"Don't play with matches, Isadora, and then cry when I arrive with the fucking kerosene."

"Is that a threat?"

"That's a promise."

"Everything alright here?" Theodore approaches us in the darkened corner of the garden.

"Edward isn't letting me into your party," Isadora replies.

"I think it's for the best, Isadora," Theo replies. "Not tonight."

"You're siding with him?"

"Always."

"You make me fucking sick too. The Kingsmen. You think you're so untouchable." She looks him up and down in disgust. "You let me into this party or I'm going to bring you down too, you and the pathetic Sinclair Montague."

"Please." Theo rolls his eyes. "You've got nothing on us."

"Oh really?" She crosses her arms for effect. "What happened in St. Barth last year, *Prince* Theodore?" She smiles. "I have video footage to prove it...I'm sure Daddy the King is going to be so proud of his gangbanging son."

His eyes hold hers. "Liar."

She smiles darkly.

He steps forward. "I'd be careful who you threaten, Isadora."

This fucking woman....

"I'd hate for you to have an accident."

"If I go missing, my instructions are that all of my evidence goes straight to the press. Do you think I'm that stupid?" She lifts her chin as if happy with herself. "So am I coming into the party?"

"No. You're not," Theodore replies. "And you've just made damn well sure that you never come to one again." He holds two fingers up as his eyes hold hers. "Nobody threatens me and gets away with it."

Three guards walk over. "Escort Miss Auclair from the

premises and see that she never enters a social engagement of mine again."

"Yes, sir."

"You son of a fucking bitch," she whispers as they grab her elbows.

Theo and I turn and begin to walk into the house.

"I'm going to bring you all down," she calls from behind us. "Just you wait...."

Theo's murderous eyes meet mine. "You have the worst taste in women."

"In this instance—" I drag my hand through my hair, "—I have to agree."

ALORA.

The music is playing, the dance floor is packed and I have to say, this is actually a fun night. Thomas has been a godsend, he's swooned every female he has met off her feet. Laughed with Sinclair and Theodore and I may have even caught Edward half listening as he talks.

"Do you want to get some fresh air?" Edward asks me.

"Is that code for do I want to come outside while you and your friends smoke cigars kind of fresh air?"

Edward's eyes dance with mischief. "Perhaps."

"No, thank you." I smile and he kisses me softly.

"Back soon." His hand runs down over my behind as he nips my neck.

I watch him walk through the crowd and smile, see…this is why I brought Thomas, Edward would never have left me here alone. He would have been chained to my side to the detriment of us both and we would have both gone home frustrated.

I walk over to the bar and wait in line and I feel someone standing to the side of me, not in the line but close enough that I can feel them watching me.

Hermione.

We don't know each other and have never been introduced, but I know who she is from all my stalking…. Which is actually pretty pathetic now, given the circumstances.

It's obvious she has something she wants to say…here goes nothing.

"Hello." I smile.

"Hello." She nods shyly.

I don't know why, but I just get the feeling that she's a good person, from everything Edward has told me and the vibe she has surrounding her. I move closer. "Hermione, is it?" I ask.

"Yes." She nods. "You're Alora?"

"Yes." I hold my hand out to shake hers. "It's nice to meet you."

She forces a smile. "Can I ask you something?"

"Yes."

"Were you and Edward together behind my back?"

"No." I shake my head.

"But he bid for you at the auction when we were still together. Is that where you met?"

My heart sinks and I don't know why but I have to fess up my sins to this woman, she deserves to know the truth.

"Edward and I knew each other a long time ago. The auction was the first time we had any contact in years."

"Did you date him back then?" Her eyes search mine.

I nod.

She presses her lips together as if processing the information.

"When we saw each other at the auction we both…." I shrug.

"Knew?"

I nod again. "I was in a relationship also."

"You broke that off?"

"Yes."

"Did he know you left someone for him?"

"No. I didn't want him to know, I didn't want it to affect your relationship."

"Did you sleep with him while he was with me?"

"No. We kissed hello at the auction but I swear to you, nothing else happened while the two of you were together." I shrug, ashamed that I even let us kiss. "I'm not like that. I would never…"

She nods and I know that she believes me.

"I'm sorry for what happened with your friend, you deserved better."

"He told you?" She frowns.

I nod. "And I want you to know that I'm on your side. There is no excuse for what transpired. I'm absolutely appalled on your behalf, and if you ever need anything or any help with that so-called friend of yours, please let us know."

She gives me a lopsided smile.

"Edward isn't innocent in this; his behavior was inexcusable and it's not okay," I add.

"It wasn't his fault, I suggested it."

"To try and help a situation, not because you wanted to. This isn't on you, don't ever let anyone tell you that."

"Thank you." Her eyes well with tears and I know that hearing this from me means a lot to her. "Can you do me a favor?"

"Anything."

"Look after him."

Oh….

"I will." I take her hands in mine. "This is just a roadblock, Hermione. Your happiness is coming."

"You think?"

"I know."

She looks at the ground for a bit as if wondering what to say next. "I should let you go."

"It was lovely meeting you."

She smiles. "You too." She turns and I watch as she disappears into the crowd.

The crack in her heart is iridescent under the lights.

Fuck.

It's just past 1 a.m. and I have no idea what time these kinds of parties finish.

I sip my margarita, about my tenth tonight, and Thomas smiles into his.

"What?"

"Everyone just stares at you as they walk past."

"They do not." I smile.

"Yes they do, and whenever Edward touches you, nearly the entire party turns and watches."

"They do not." I laugh, embarrassed.

"Hey, it's a good thing." He smiles as he looks around.

"How is that a good thing, everyone probably can't believe that I snagged the bachelor of the universe."

"They can't believe that he snagged you." He taps his glass with mine.

"Alora," a voice from the side says.

"Pascal." I smile in surprise. "How are you?"

"I'm good, how are you?" His eyes hold mine and he's all doe in the headlights as he stares at me.

What is he doing here?

"I've been thinking about you, nonstop."

"Pascal."

"I'm sorry," Thomas interrupts us. "Who are you?"

"Please excuse my rudeness. This is Pascal."

"Her ex-boyfriend." He cuts me off.

"Oh." Thomas nods as he sips his drink. "Hi."

"I really miss you," he says as his eyes search mine. "I can't sleep. I can't eat...."

Thomas rolls his lips as he listens in.

"Pascal," I say softly. "It's not like that between us anymore."

"I can't accept it," he says angrily as he grabs my hand in his. "I won't."

Thomas steps forward. "I think you should move along," he tells him.

"And who the fuck are you?" he demands as I weave my fingers out of his. "Stay out of our way, we'll get through this."

"Ah, no you won't, and I'm the guy who's about to beat you to a pulp, that's who." He steps forward again. "Leave her alone."

Edward walks back through the crowd. Edward sees Pascal and narrows his eyes and then without another word Pascal turns and practically runs away.

"That's what I thought," Thomas calls after him.

I watch Pascal cross the room with a deep sense of regret, it's a terrible thing to break a heart, especially when I'm so happy.

THOMAS.

I stand against the side wall as I watch him watch her.

Pascal, hiding in the shadows, hasn't taken his eyes off Alora all night.

Something is off with this guy.

I turn in Alora's direction to see what he's watching. Edward has his hand around her waist and they are smiling as they talk. Edward leans down and kisses Alora and I turn back to Pascal, his face is stone cold and I get an off feeling.

This guy is a weirdo.

I walk over to Edward and Alora.

"Hey."

"Hi." Alora smiles.

Sinclair leans in to talk to her and I walk beside Edward and subtly lean in. "You need to watch Pascal."

Edward frowns. "What do you mean?"

"He's here."

Edward's eyes shoot up and scan the crowd. "Where?"

"He's a fucking weirdo and he hasn't taken his eyes off Alora in the last two hours."

"How did he get in?" Edward's eyes come back to meet mine.

"How would I know?"

"He must have come as a plus-one."

"Don't trust him."

"I don't."

"She's too nice, she thinks he's harmless."

"You don't?"

"*No.*"

"Me neither."

Alora grabs Edward's hands. "Let's dance."

"Okay." He walks her backward and winks at me as they disappear.

I'm going to go for a walk and see if I can see him, I don't trust this fucker for a second. I walk around the bar and through the dance floor. Edward and Alora are dancing and laughing; they look so in love. I smile as I keep walking around.

I go out onto the veranda and out into the garden and there, sitting on the side of the fountain, is a sight so beautiful that it stops me in my tracks.

A blond woman, with peachy cream skin and dimples. The biggest, most perfect blue eyes I have ever seen.

The air leaves my lungs as I stare at her, riveted to the spot.

She looks up at me and I swear, the earth moves beneath me. Our eyes are locked as the air crackles between us.

What is this?

She stands and walks to me. "Hello."

"Hello." My stomach flutters in excitement, I don't ever remember having such a physical reaction to someone before.

Visceral.

"Have we met?" she asks. Her voice is soft, and angelic.... Ethereal.

"I...." I stare at her, lost for words. "Unfortunately not."

She puts her hand out to shake mine. "My name is Amaya."

"Hello, Amaya." Before I can stop myself I have her hand lifted to my mouth and I kiss the back of it. "My name is Thomas."

She smiles and puts her hand up in a stop symbol, I glance around in a daze, what's she doing?

"Let's go and talk somewhere." She takes my hand in hers and pulls me through the garden.

"What are you doing?" I ask as we walk.

"Giving us privacy. Just around here." She pulls me into another courtyard, it has a smaller water fountain and a stone bench, which she sits on. "Sit with me." She taps the bench beside her.

I sit down, my heart in my throat, confused by the effect she has on me.

We stare at each other and it's like I know her...but I don't. Her eyes linger on my face. "You're beautiful," she whispers.

"My god," I whisper, embarrassed. "It's you who is beautiful."

Her eyes drift to my lips as if she wants me to kiss her.

The air leaves my lungs and for the first time in my life I think I'm too nervous to actually pull this off. There are no words in my head, none.

The air between us is electric and I don't remember anyone having this effect on me before.

Unable to help it, I lean in and takes her face in my hands and kiss her softly, her lips a gentle whisper across mine. Her eyes close and oh....

Thump.

Thump.

Thump, blood rushes from everywhere to the erection she's incited.

Fuck....

We kiss again, this time with a little tongue, and I feel it all the way to my toes.

"Dear lord," she murmurs against my lips.

My hand snatches around her waist and I pull her to me with hunger as our kiss deepens and she pulls out, flushed and panting. "I have to go." She stands in a fluster. "I have to go now."

"What?" I stand. "What do you mean?"

She leaves the courtyard in a rush and I follow her out, trying to think of a way to make her stay. We get back out to the main party and she walks straight up to two bodyguards, who appear that they were looking for her.

As I blend into the crowd I watch her, mesmerized by her beauty. After chatting briefly, she walks inside with the two men and out of view.

Who is she?

ALORA.

4:30 A.M.

Edward, Thomas and I totter up the private road toward the waiting cars.

"Oww." I bend down and slip one high heel off. "Wait a minute."

They turn back as they wait for me.

I slip the other one off and pass them both to Edward. "Carry these."

He holds them by the straps in one hand and takes my hand with the other.

"My biggest takeaway from tonight was," I slur, "that stupidly expensive shoes are even more stupidly uncomfortable than cheap ones." I tiptoe over the cobblestones.

"That is your biggest takeaway from that whole night?" Edward slurs back.

Boy…we are all very tipsy, those cocktails were lethal.

"Uh-huh." I nod. "What's your biggest takeaway from tonight, Mr. Prescott?"

"It's confirmed that I have the hottest woman on earth." He grabs my behind and bites my neck as I giggle.

"Ugh, make it stop." Thomas groans. "You two are fucking pathetic."

"What's your biggest takeaway from tonight, Stone?" Edward asks.

"That love at first sight does actually exist." He smiles proudly.

"You fell in love tonight?" I smile as I stumble over my feet. "Oww."

"I do believe so." He rolls his hands out and does an overexaggerated bow.

"With who?" I screw my face up. "I didn't see you with anyone."

"The most beautiful woman on earth."

"Couldn't be," Edward slurs. "She's taken." He grabs me roughly again and we laugh like idiots. I swat him away. "Behave, Prescott."

"Who was she, Stone?"

"She has blond hair and blue eyes. So fucking perfect."

"What was her name?" I ask.

"Amaya," he says. "Didn't quite catch the surname yet, it's a work in progress."

Edward's eyes meet his. "Blond hair, blue eyes, white dress, Amaya?"

"That's her."

"Ha." Edward tips his head back and laughs, a deep belly laugh. "Fucking yes. Hilarious."

"What?" Thomas and I frown.

"Did you talk to her?" Edward thinks this is the funniest thing he's ever heard.

"Yes I did, actually." Thomas puts his hands on his hips, indignant. "We even made out."

"You made out?" He laughs hard again. "Oh, this is the fucking best."

"What the hell is so funny?" I frown.

"Do you know who he made out with?" he slurs as he points to Thomas.

"Who?"

"Princess Amaya of Switzerland."

"Huh?"

"Hermione's little sister." He widens his eyes.

"Why is that funny?" I frown.

"Because the king will fucking kill him."

CHAPTER THIRTY-ONE

EDWARD.

Sunday morning and I pull the SUV into Alora's driveway in Nice.

We're here to collect more of Alora's things and water her damn garden, I glance over to her in the passenger seat. "These vegetables get more attention than I do."

"Probably." She bounces out of the car and up to the front door and I hang back to talk to the car that's just pulled up behind us. "Morning, boys."

"Morning," they reply as they climb out of the car.

"I wanted to talk to you," I say. "It's come to my attention that Pascal Deschanel is still hanging around."

They listen intently.

"I don't want him anywhere near Alora at any time at all, and when she arrives here at her house I want you to go inside and check it before she enters, please."

"Yes, sir." Philippe glances into the house. "Has something happened that we are unaware of?"

"No. But last time I was here I got the feeling that something was off.... I can't quite put my finger on it but for some reason my senses are heightened around Alora's safety right now."

"Okay." Philippe listens. "I'm sure it's just that there's a lot going on with her moving house and whatnot. I can assure you she's completely safe, we won't take our eyes off her."

"Thank you."

"I take it she's still wearing her bracelet?" he asks.

"Yes, but...." I put my finger to my lips. "If she knows

there's a tracking device in it she won't wear it. I don't want to frighten her."

"Of course, sir."

I think for a moment. "You know what?" I look in at the house. "Fuck it, I'm not taking any risks, put a trace on Pascal Deschanel. I want two men on him."

"Yes." He takes out his phone. "How do I spell his name?" I spell it out and he sends it off to his sources. "As soon as we have an address I'll send a crew over."

"Just watch him," I reply. "Stay at a distance and unnoticed if possible, but we need to know his whereabouts at all times."

"Agree, better to be safe than sorry."

"We're just packing up a few more of Alora's personal things and then we'll be returning to Monaco later this afternoon," I tell them.

"Okay."

I head inside and walk through to the back of the house; the French doors are open and Alora is out in the sunshine, watering her beloved garden. She's hosing and walking around pulling out weeds, and I smile as I watch her in her happy place.

I flick the coffee machine on and turn to notice a book on the floor. I walk over and pick it up. "Why the fuck is this book constantly falling off the shelves?" I set it on the kitchen counter. "Keep falling on the floor and I'm throwing you in the trash, fucker." I make us both a cup of coffee and walk out and pass her one.

"Thank you." She takes it from me.

"Did your carrots grow in the rain?" I blow into my coffee cup as I look over the garden.

"They did."

"And what about your chili?"

She smirks, knowing I'm making fun of her. "Still hot." She flicks the hose up at me. "Go and lie on the deck chair before I hose you down."

"You'll be the only one getting hosed down around here, Miss Sorenson." I grab my crotch and she smiles and flicks the water up at me again.

I take her advice and lie down on the deck chair. Alora potters and waters and weeds, she snips and rakes the leaves.

I lie in the warm glow; the afternoon sun moves across the sky as the hours tick by. It's funny how life throws curveballs, if someone told me a year ago that watching my love enjoy being in nature would become my favorite pastime, I would never have believed it. Yet here I am, doing something that brings me a great deal of happiness. Who knew such a perfect simplicity existed?

When we're here doing this, nobody else exists, the world is calm and centered.

Peaceful.

I take out my phone and scroll through my Realtor contacts. I need to find us a new house...one with good soil.

MONDAY MORNING.

I stride through the casino on a mission, I have way too much work to get through this morning. My first Zoom starts in fifteen minutes and I haven't even gone through my notes yet. I take the elevator and step out on my office floor to see an angry face.

Fuck.

I am not in the mood for this fucking bullshit today.

"King Volter," I say. "To what do I owe this pleasure?"

He glares at me, his face solemn. "I'd like a word."

"Of course you would." I brush past him. "This way." We walk up the large corridor and into my office and I close the door. "I am on a very tight schedule." I gesture to my desk. "Take a seat, but we will have to be quick."

We both sit down.

"How can I help you?" I ask.

His cold eyes hold mine and he links his fingers together on the desk. "I've heard a story."

"Story?" I ask.

"Don't act oblivious. You know exactly what the story is."

"No." I shrug. "I don't."

"Let me enlighten you."

I roll my lips as I concentrate on not rolling my eyes. "Please do."

"It has come to my attention that you were on a night out with my daughter when you bid on Alora Sorenson at a charity auction."

"For charity."

His eyes hold mine. "I know what you did."

"And what was that?" I snap. "Land the plane."

"You were having an affair with her behind Hermione's back and now there is a sordid story about to come out in the press."

"You're wrong." I stand and on autopilot go to the bar, fuck...it's too early for scotch. "Water?"

"No," he barks. "I don't want fucking water."

"I knew Miss Sorenson." I sip my water as I choose my words carefully. "We dated years ago and I bid on her internship at the auction to help her professionally."

He narrows his eyes as he listens.

"Hermione and I had not been working for a long time and our relationship had run its course. It organically ended and if I hadn't done it, she would have."

His calculating eyes hold mine.

"Hermione is fine, I have kept in contact with her. This was the best decision for both of us."

He slams his hand onto my desk. "Hermione is anything but fine," he yells. "I want to know what this scandal is."

"What are you talking about?"

"I've heard rumblings from our guards that there's a scandal brewing and it involves you and Hermione."

I shrug. "News to me."

"If you think for one moment that you can treat my daughter like this and get away with it, you have another thing coming."

"I have treated your daughter with nothing but respect," I bite back. "I care for her a great deal. Hermione does not need you defending her to me, I will defend her against anything or anyone."

"If something goes to the press, if you bring her name into disrepute...you're a dead man."

I exhale in an overexaggerated way. "I'm very busy and do not have the time or the energy for your dramatics today." I turn to my computer.

"When did you date Alora *Sorenson*?" he sneers.

My eyes rise to his, something about the way he said her name triggers me. "That is *none* of your business." I stand and open the door. "I have a meeting I have to attend."

He stands, his eyes fixed on mine. "Be very careful, Prescott."

"Get. Out."

He storms out of the office and down the corridor and I slam the door behind him.

Fuck off.

ALORA.

Jazz music sounds loudly through the store and I smile as I look through the window out onto the street. The sun is shining and it's a beautiful day, Philippe and his two partners in crime are playing cards out the front of the café next door.

My phone vibrates on the counter and I turn and pick it up,

MR. DOE

"Hello, Mr. Doe," I answer.

"Hello, Miss Sorenson," he replies, and I can tell that he's smiling. "Tell me you love me."

"I love you."

"Ask me if I found you the perfect house."

I smile. "Did you find me the perfect house?"

"Maybe."

"Really?"

"Finish work early and we will go and look at it."

"Alright, meet you at the yacht around three?"

"Okay, love you."

"I love you too." I hang up and smile broadly, how is this my life?

Edward smiles as he pulls into the driveway of the mansion perched high on the hill, he insisted on driving here in his favorite green Aston Martin. Maybe he thinks it's lucky or something. "This looks—"

"Over the top." I cut him off.

"Nice." He reaches over and squeezes my thigh. "Can you just look at it with an open mind, please?"

"Okay." I circle my finger over my head to symbolize a halo. "Open-minded is my middle name."

"Thank you." We climb out of the car and he takes my hand in his, the front doors open and an elderly man in a gray suit is standing there with a folder in his hands. "Good afternoon, Edward." He smiles.

"Hello, Marcel." They shake hands. "This is my partner, Alora Sorenson."

Gah, that will never get old.

"Hello, nice to meet you." I smile as I shake his hand.

"So here we are." Marcel gestures to the house as he leads us inside. "Welcome to one of the most prestigious and breathtaking properties in Monte Carlo."

Jeez.

My eyes rise to the three-story-high ceilings....

"There isn't a doubt that this mansion is the ultimate expression of elegance, sophistication, and exclusivity," he continues as we walk through the living area, the back wall is giant arched windows with the most beautiful view. I stare at it, mesmerized, as Marcel carries on talking. "Architectural masterpiece offering breathtaking panoramic views of the Mediterranean Sea, world-class amenities, this spectacular estate seamlessly blends classic European elegance with modern luxury."

Edward squeezes my hand in his, *he likes it.*

It's classically French but with a romantic grandeur. Large archways and windows, molded cornices, and super-high ceilings with low-hanging giant chandeliers.

I look around with my heart in my throat, I've never been in such a beautiful house.

Marcel continues his sales spiel. "Featuring high ceilings, grand arched windows, intricate detailing, and the finest materials, every corner of this mansion radiates opulence. The spacious open-plan living areas, designer chandeliers and premium finishes make this home an unparalleled work of art."

As we walk through the home, each room gets better than the last. Up the grand staircase to a beautiful master bedroom with its own terrace. The lights of Monaco are just beginning to twinkle. It has a view of the city that meets the sea, the ocean a deep blue, the sky is a beautiful shade of pink and I wonder if Mother Nature has joined the sales team.

I stand on the terrace and stare out over beauty.

"She sure is putting on a show tonight." Edward smiles as he kisses my temple.

"She is." I smile.

We walk back downstairs and through the large arched door that leads to outside and I don't know where to look first.

"Unrivalled outdoor spaces set against the backdrop of Monaco's stunning coastline, the mansion boasts expansive terraces, lush gardens, and an infinity pool that appears to merge with the sea. A large vegetable garden. The perfectly designed outdoor entertainment areas, with comfortable lounge spaces and al fresco dining setups, make this the ideal retreat for relaxation or lavish gatherings."

Oh....

My eyes meet Edward's and he smiles as if reading my mind.

"This is luxury at its finest." Marcel holds his hands out to the surroundings. "World-class amenities. This Monte Carlo estate comes equipped with everything you need for an elite lifestyle, including an infinity pool overlooking the Mediterranean. Private cinema room for the ultimate movie experience, a state-of-the-art wellness and spa center. A high-end gourmet kitchen with premium appliances. Sophisticated wine cellar, a grand master suite with a private terrace. Multiple luxury guest suites for friends and family. High-tech security system and smart home automation."

"How much?" Edward cuts him off.

"The price is €100,000,000 and is a complete steal, featuring six bedrooms, an infinity pool, a private spa, cinema room, wine cellar, breathtaking terraces, staff quarters and a security watch house."

"One hundred million?" I gasp, wide-eyed. "That's...."

"I'll give you some privacy, I'll be inside."

Edward turns me toward him and takes my hands in his.

"Do you like it?" Edward asks.

"That's too much money," I whisper.

"*Do.* You like it?"

My eyes roam over the infinity pool, the gardens and grassed area. I thought inside was magical, but the outside has blown my mind. "This is the vegetable garden of my dreams."

"Can you see yourself being happy here?"

"I'll be happy wherever we are together."

"Liar," he teases. "You don't like my yacht."

"That's just because I can't garden."

He leans in and kisses me. "Would you like this house?"

"It's too much."

"You can't put a price on happiness."

"Will you be serious?"

"I am." He kisses me again. "Am I going to make an offer on this house, or not?"

I bite my lip to hide my smile as my eyes float around. "Let's go back inside and look again."

"Okay." He leads me back through the house and into the perfect kitchen. "Can you see yourself cooking in here?"

I nod.

We go back through to the living room and down into the cellar and through to the wellness center and oh my god, this is really something else.

We end up back in the main bedroom and walk out onto the terrace, the sun is setting in a beautiful glow of pinks.

"So?" He kisses me. "Can I give you this?"

"But that's not fair because I have nothing to give to you."

His eyes twinkle with a certain something. "Your heart is the ultimate gift." He takes me into his arms. "The only thing I would ever wish for."

Oh….

My eyes well with tears. "I love you," I whisper. "So, so much."

"Is that a yes?" He smiles against my lips.

I giggle through tears. "That's a hell yes."

Darkness.

With my eye pressed firmly to the wall I watch.

Naked, she's straddled over him, his body deep inside hers. Moving together as they ride the wave of pleasure. The room is dim, lit only by a bedside lamp.

But I can see everything.... Feel everything.

They pant harder as I struggle for control.

No.

My breath is ragged, tugging at my lungs as it begs for an exhale.

I press my face harder to the wall.

He tips his head back and moans as she rides him. "Fuck yeah." His hands are on her hip bones and the bed begins to hit the wall with force. "Just there. Just like that."

"Fuck me," she whimpers.

He rolls them and his full naked body comes into view, he lifts her legs up over his shoulders and begins to ride her hard.

I push myself closer to the wall, my eyes wide as I watch from the shadows.

"Yes, yes," he chants as he gets closer.

Deep punishing hits as their skin slaps together.

Thump.

Thump.

Thump....

Adrenaline surges as my grip tightens around the handle of the knife.

CHAPTER THIRTY-TWO

EDWARD.

PARIS.

"And this here." Alora points to the plans. "That needs to be a monumental piece because it's the first thing you see, so I want that to have a real wow factor."

"I agree." Nel studies the plans. "So over on this wall here."

Their voices drone out. I'm sitting in the meeting about our hotel refurb, but I'm not in the meeting.

Too mesmerized by Alora's beauty to be able to concentrate on a single word they're saying.

Her long dark hair is swept up into a casual knot, she has her signature makeup-free face, glowing skin and red lipstick. She's wearing a black turtleneck woolen dress and boots. So effortlessly chic, she has no idea how beautiful and stylish she is. Honestly, how the hell did I ever get this woman to fall in love with me?

Photographers have started following her and commenting on her fashion sense, they're calling her a modern-day Audrey Hepburn.

But to me.... She's mine, the woman who has turned my entire existence up on its head. I can't go a day without seeing her, I won't travel unless she can come and I don't do any after-hour events now unless she can attend alongside me.

Being in Paris this week is the very last thing I have time for, but she needed to come and that means so did I.

After this meeting we're going saucepan shopping.... Yes you heard me right.

Not a sentence I would have ever imagined coming out of my mouth in a million years. Alora is so excited about our new house and being able to have privacy that the yacht can't offer us. She's mapping out furniture room by room and it will be just the two of us in our new home, no cook, no cleaner, no guards inside. Normal is how she wants it, and I have to admit, after spending time alone in her house, I now find myself craving privacy too.

Having her run our house returns me to a simplicity that brings me a great deal of peace. I get it now....

While I read at night, she spends her time scrolling through recipes of things she wants to cook for us and apparently there's some big kitchen catering place here in Paris that she wants to look at.

With anyone else I would just say buy whatever you want online, but not Alora.

No...it's all about the tangible experience, touching things with your hands and being lost in the tactile moment. Buying with your heart and not your wallet.

I wish she got to meet my mother.

They are so much alike, glamorous and beautiful with the purest souls.

A heart full of love, the healer of all healers.

Sometimes I look at her and choke up with emotion, she truly is the biggest gift in my life. A love that I never knew I needed.

"Edward."

I glance up as she pulls me from my daydream. "Yes."

"Nel's going."

"Oh." I nod, embarrassed. "Lovely to see you, Nel. Today was very productive." I lean in and kiss her cheek.

"Goodbye." She toddles off across the restaurant but I don't dare look after her.

Alora's temper is spicy as fuck and she has no problem ripping me a new asshole.

"Alone at last." She smiles over at me as she takes my hand in hers; she lifts it to her lips and kisses the back of it. "Did you hear anything we were talking about?"

"Every single word."

"You're such a liar."

I throw her a wink.

"Are you ready to go and buy saucepans, Mr. Prescott?" She widens her eyes in excitement.

"Yes." I smile, her joy is infectious.

"Are you as excited as me?"

"No."

She giggles. "Can you at least act excited?"

"No."

"And then we can get some dinner on the way home."

"I've booked a table at my favorite restaurant."

"Okay." She bounces out of her chair. "Do you think we should get new cutlery too?" She pushes her chair in.

"If you like."

"Well, what would you like?"

"I would like to be naked."

"Of course you would." She rolls her eyes as she takes my hand in hers. "Find me the right saucepans and you might have half a chance."

ALORA.

"Doe," Edward calls from the balcony.

"Coming." I pull the fluffy white robe around my shoulders. The bathroom is steamy, we've just soaked in the sunken tub for over an hour. We talked and laughed, made sweet gentle love and after the dreamy three days we have just had, Paris may be my new favorite city.

We aren't staying in the hotel, this time we're at his penthouse.

My hair is in a messy topknot and I walk out onto the balcony to see Edward in his white robe standing at the rail looking out over the twinkling Eiffel Tower. His dark hair is messed to perfection and his broad shoulders make that robe hang in all the right places.

This man....

There's a silver bucket with champagne sitting on ice and two crystal flutes and music is playing in the background.

"What are we celebrating?"

He turns and takes me into his arms, his big blue eyes hold mine. "Us."

My heart swells.

"Oh, Edward," I whisper. "I'm so in love with you."

A new song comes on. Elvis Presley, "Can't Help Falling in Love."

"Dance with me." He takes me into his arms and we sway to the music as he sings the words. Barefoot in our bathrobes, all alone on the balcony with the Eiffel Tower twinkling in the background, I fall in love with him all over again.

"Okay, so what happens here?" I say as I read the pamphlet. "Tell me the rules."

Thomas, Helene and I are at the polo watching the Kingsmen. We are lined up in fold-up chairs and wearing big hats. Beautiful people are everywhere watching, and apparently this is our new normal weekend thing. Edward has finally succumbed to having my friends come to the things that he wants me to go to. I can't do this alone, I need backup with these glamorous women everywhere.

"So...." Thomas points to the field. "As far as I can see, they all ride around on stupidly expensive horses and hit a ball with a hockey stick."

"Right."

"And let's not forget look hot," Helene adds.

"True." The team are all wearing tight white pants and fitted red shirts.

"Fuck me dead." Helene looks around. "There is some seriously hot man meat here today."

"Right?" I giggle. "Okay. So they ride a horse and then what?"

"No, they ride like a lot of horses," he replies.

"What do you mean?" I frown.

"What for?" Helene asks.

"They keep changing them out." He shrugs. "I don't know."

"It's like an hour?" I frown. "How tired can a horse be in an hour?"

"I don't frigging know." He opens the program. "Maybe they all just wank over their expensive horses or some shit."

"That sounds about right." I nod.

I look over to the other side of the field and see Edward walk out of the dressing room, he's wearing his tight white pants and his red shirt, he has his polo mallet in his hand and is wearing a helmet. I can see every muscle underneath his outfit. He looks over, our eyes meet and he gives me the best come-fuck-me look of all time.

We stare at each other and I feel myself heat under his dark gaze.

His strapper holds his foot and lifts him onto his horse and he looks back at me again as he rides off in the other direction.

"God." Helene fans herself. "The way he looks at you."

"Right?" Thomas agrees. "You two must have some seriously good sex."

I smile as I look back down at the program. You have no idea....

He is so getting laid tonight....

Hard.

"Pass me the sunscreen." I hold out my hand and Helene passes the bottle over.

The sun is beating down on us as we lie on sun loungers on the deck of the yacht overlooking the Mediterranean Sea.

"Can I offer you a drink?" Harmony asks us. "Any lunch?"

"Umm." I glance over to Helene and Thomas. "You guys hungry?"

They shrug. "A little."

"Sashimi?"

"I guess."

"Can we please have some sashimi and a garden salad and rice paper rolls please?"

"Shrimp rice paper rolls or lobster?"

"Guys?"

Thomas and Helene exchange glances. "Whatever is fine."

"What would you like to drink?" she asks.

"I'll just have a sparkling water." I glance over to my gobsmacked friends. "What do you guys want?"

"Whatever is fine," they reply, too shy to make an order.

"Can we have some Aperol Spritzes too, please."

"Of course." She smiles before disappearing.

"How the fuck is this your life?" Thomas shakes his head.

"Honestly." I shrug. "I don't even know."

"Fuck. Please set me up with one of his friends." Helene lies back down and puts her face up to the sun. "I need this life for myself."

I giggle and I hear voices down below, I get up and walk to the edge to see Edward fully dressed in his suit, he's walking out a man, they shake hands as the man leaves. Another Sunday business meeting.

"Edward works very hard for this life." I watch him walk back inside to prepare for his next meeting, he's got them back-to-back all day. "He never stops working."

Thomas closes his eyes to the sun. "At least it pays well.

I hold the phone up so that Edward and I can see my family's faces. I've made a habit of FaceTiming them when he's here every few days so that they feel like they are getting to know each other too. I know it's not the same as meeting in person but at this stage it's all we have to work with. He's chatted to my sister, my brother and dad a few times and they seem to be getting on like a house on fire. "Alright, Dad, I have to go. I have to get this packing done."

"Have a great time in the UK, kids," my dad replies.

Edward smiles and waves. "Bye."

"Love you."

"Love you too." I hang up and stare into my wardrobe as I look over my choices. "So what will we be doing all week?"

We're going to the UK to meet the rest of Edward's family.

"Not much, just hanging out with my family," he replies.

"Yeah, but what does your family wear while they—" I air quote the word, "—hang out."

He smiles as his eyes stay fixed on the screen; he's lying on my bed with his hands behind his head as he watches television. "I don't know, whatever." He keeps looking straight ahead.

"Will you concentrate and listen to me for one minute," I snap, annoyed. "I'm meeting your family; I want to look nice. What the hell do I pack to wear?"

"Anything will do. Relax, who cares."

"Edward." I let out a deep sigh. "You're not helping one little bit."

"Why are you so stressed out about this?"

"Because I don't know what they wear at your farm. I don't know what's acceptable. I want your dad and your sister to like me and I'm probably going to look like a troll who crawled out from under a fucking bridge."

He turns the television off and pats the bed. "Come here." I flop to sit on the bed beside him. "It doesn't matter what you wear, it matters who you are."

I roll my lips as I look over my choices. "It does help if you look the part, though."

He tucks a piece of my hair behind my shoulder. "Would you like to go shopping tomorrow to get a few things?"

"No," I huff. "I don't have time, I have so much to do before we take the week off and besides, I have enough clothes. I just need to find the perfect outfits to take."

I shrug. "Tell me about your father."

"Well." He smiles wistfully, "My father is...." He looks up to the ceiling in an overdramatic way. "Is an earl who comes from a long lineage of old money, and possessions do not impress him at all."

"An earl?" I act surprised.

"And he's kind and generous and loves shortbread and he will not give a flying fuck as to what you're wearing."

"He loves shortbread?"

"Yes. With English tea."

I smile. "I love English tea too."

"Yes. I know." He taps me on the nose. "Something in common already."

"What about your sister?"

"Charlotte."

"Yes."

"Charlotte is the most beautiful human on the face of the earth."

I smile as I listen. "I love that you two are close."

"We weren't for a while, for a long time I wasn't keen on the man she wanted to marry."

"What was his name?"

"Spencer Jones."

"Why didn't you like him?"

He shrugs. "Lots of reasons, he was older than her and a renowned playboy, and Lady Charlotte was a very wealthy, complete innocent who I knew was way too good for him."

"She's a lady?" I smile goofily, *this I didn't know.*

"In every sense of the word."

"Whatever happened to him?"

"She married him."

"She did?"

"She did, and no matter what any of us said, she never listened."

"Do you like him now?"

"I like how happy she is. As long as he loves her then I'm happy too."

"That's a nice way to think about it." I stand and look back into the wardrobe. "What was your mom like?"

"Honestly?"

"Yeah."

"She was a lot like you."

My eyes meet his. "How so?"

"She was calm and centered, kind and good."

I smile softly. "You think I'm good?"

"At fucking. Yes."

I giggle as I stand on my tippy toes and pull a sweater down. "You had to ruin it, didn't you?"

"You know, so many times when we are talking you remind me so much of her."

"Like how?"

"Your belief systems."

"What belief systems?"

"Like how you think *I'm* a good person."

I turn back to him, surprised by his admission. "You *are* a good person."

"Not always."

"Always, Edward." I lean over and kiss him. "I wouldn't be here if I didn't truly believe that you are a good person. You're kind and sweet and loving and all things that are good."

It's his turn to smile softly.

"With a *really* good dick."

He rolls his eyes. "You had to ruin it, didn't you?"

I giggle as I turn back to my wardrobe. "You know, I keep hoping I will miraculously find something perfect to wear in here."

"Who cares, just go naked."

"Oh, that would go great, wouldn't it? Hi, Earl of Nottingham, here are my tits."

Amusement flashes across his face as he holds the remote up and turns the television back on. "That would win me over."

EDWARD.

I glance up to the golfing green and back down to the ball as I line up my shot.

"What happened to you on the weekend, Prescott?" Sinclair asks as he practice swings his golf club in the air.

"Nothing." I take the putt. "Go. In." I try to will the ball into the hole but it rolls straight past. "Fucker." I roll my eyes. "This has to be the most infuriating sport of all fucking time."

"What's going on with you lately?"

"What do you mean?"

"Since when has a girl held you prisoner for two months?" he huffs. "How boring can you get. What the hell is happening to you?"

"No holding necessary." We begin to walk to the next hole. "I'm there by my own free will and trust me, she's anything but boring."

"Since when do you hang out with the same woman all the time?"

"Since her. I bought us a house to live in together this week."

Theo lets out a low whistle as he smiles down the fairway. "Careful, old boy."

"That's what I was thinking," Sinclair chips in.

"It's crossed my mind...that's for sure." I shrug and line up my shot.

Theo's face falls. "Surely not?"

"Maybe."

"You think she's the one?" He frowns.

I know she is.

"Who knows," I lie.

"Well...fuck me dead." Sinclair sighs. "It's all over from here, my advice is to run while you can." He hits the ball. "And get working on that iron-clad prenup. I don't envy her," he adds.

"What do you mean?"

"The wolves are going to eat her alive."

"Just worry about you," I snap. "Still fucking your married PA?"

He winces. "Little bit."

"I can't wait for the day when her husband cuts off your balls in a public hanging." I smirk as I put my putter back into my bag.

"In my defense, she's putting it on me all the time because he has no interest in sex. So if he were doing his job correctly I wouldn't have to do it for him."

"So it's a public service then?"

"Exactly," he agrees. "He should be thanking me for taking one for the team."

"Hey, bring Alora over on Saturday night, I'll host dinner," Theo says as he lines up his ball.

"I can't, we'll be away."

"Where you going?"

"I'm taking her home to the UK to meet the family."

Their eyes all come to me. "Are you serious?"

"Uh-huh."

"Alright, this is going too far. Who the fuck are you, and what have you done with Prescott?"

ALORA.

"Good morning, Mr. Prescott."

"Good morning," he replies as he climbs out of the car and onto the tarmac.

He holds his hand out for me. "Come, my love."

My love.

Edward is in his customary perfectly fitted suit; his back is ramrod straight and power oozes out of his every cell. Just the sight of him makes me weak at the knees.

Seriously…this man.

People run and rush around to move the luggage from the car to the plane. "Watch your step." Edward calmly holds my hand to lead me up the stairs.

It's funny, I don't see much of Edward with or around his guards. They are either alone with me or leaving us alone. Though this week since the whole Isadora saga they've been around more and it's quite comical how different they are around him. Everybody is on high alert as if he's about to blow at any moment.

Is he really that much of a tyrant?

Somehow seeing him in all his bossy, dominant glory just makes him even more delicious.

The captain and flight attendants stand at the top of the stairs. "Good morning, Mr. Prescott." The captain smiles.

"Good morning." Edward shakes his hand, he smiles to the flight attendants. "Hello."

"You remember Alora."

"Yes, hello." Everyone politely smiles.

Hmm, it's the same crew as last time. Do they work full-time for him? What happens when he's not flying anywhere…. Do they just sit around waiting for the call-up?

God, this man has more money than sense.

He leads me by the hand up the aisle and I take a seat; he puts my purse in the overhead and fusses around.

"Can I get you anything to drink, sir?"

"I'll have a fresh juice, please." He looks over to me. "Would you like anything?"

"I'll have champagne, please."

Amusement flashes across his face. "It's 8 a.m."

"Yes, I know, but I decided whenever I get on this plane that it's time for celebration." I click in my seat belt.

The flight attendant tries to hide her smile and fails miserably.

"Am I right?" I say to her.

"I would have to agree." She smiles.

Edward gets his laptop, sits down beside me, and opens it up. "I have to work for a while, sweetheart." He slides his hand up my thigh as his eyes stay on the computer.

"Okay." I look up to catch the flight attendants exchange glances at him calling me sweetheart. It's obvious the both of them are crushing hard on my man.

Grrr….

Yeah, you heard it straight from the horse's mouth…wench.

I'm his sweetheart, so eyes off.

And get me my damn champagne.

I twist my lips, annoyed, and look out the window to see that they are still loading suitcases.

"Jeez," I whisper. "How many suitcases did you bring?"

"A few." He types.

"Your champagne." Wench number one smiles.

"Thank you." I take it from her, now feeling a little embarrassed about my alcoholic ways. I wait until she's out of earshot and I lean in and whisper, "Couldn't you have at least ordered a drink to make me appear less loserish?"

"Perhaps being less loserish would help your situation," he mutters as he types.

I think for a moment and then lean in to whisper to him again, "I'm going to get rolling drunk and do a striptease while I stand on the seat."

"I look forward to it." He smiles as he reads something.

I sip my champagne and look around. "What do you think we will do today when we get there?" I take a big gulp.

"Fuck," he says loudly.

I snort my champagne up my nose and cough. "Shh," I whisper as I look around. "They're going to think you're a complete sex maniac."

"Says the stripper."

The plane begins to move. "Did you pack me stripper clothes?" I whisper.

"Absolutely," he whispers back as he plays along.

"What else did you pack for me?"

"Handcuffs."

I smile goofily as the plane hurtles down the runway and I grip his hand in mine. "This pilot knows what he's doing, right?"

"I sincerely hope so."

BONUS CONTENT

EXCLUSIVE TO THIS PAPERBACK EDITION

The car pulls into the driveway and we come to a stop. Giant black metal gates slowly open and a white mansion comes into view. My eyes widen in surprise. "*This* is your house?"

Edwards picks up my hand and kisses the back of it as the car drives up the driveway. "It is."

My eyes drink in the splendor, the house is painted white and three stories tall with charcoal slate roofing. There are black shutters on all the windows and big black double doors with brass door knockers. Lanterns line the driveway, perfectly trimmed hedged gardens line the perimeter, and with so many beautiful things, I'm not sure where to look first and they land on the purple flowers that surround the veranda. "Wysteria." I gasp. "Oh my god, that's the vine of my dreams," I whisper in awe.

I glance up to the rearview mirror to catch Philippe's smile, and embarrassed at my over-the-top reaction, I try to regain my composure. "You said it was just a house." I act casual.

"It *is* just a house." Amusement flashes across his face.

"This isn't just a house, Edward, this is a frigging mansion." I scoff, annoyed that once again he has the ability to shock me. Just when I think this man can't get any snootier, up he goes and raises the bar. Where does his wealth stop, honestly?

A huge mansion on a giant piece of land like this smack bang in the middle of London, what the hell is this place worth?

The driveway is made up of crushed limestone and the lawn is a brilliant shade of green. "The upkeep of this garden would be insane," I announce as I act unimpressed.

"We have permanent gardeners," he replies as the car pulls into the circular parking bay.

Gardeners as in plural?

Ugh.

Of course he does.

Philippe pops the trunk and gets out of the car, and the second car of guards pulls in behind us.

"And you used to live here?" I peer out through the window. "Full-time?"

"I still live here, half the time." He takes my hand in his and kisses it again. "*We* will live between here and Monaco."

"Edward." I twist my lips as I look around. "Have you forgotten that I own an antique store in France?"

"London would be a great second-store location." He arches his hand in the shape of a rainbow. "Sorenson Antiques, London." He widens his eyes. "It has a ring to it, don't you think?" His door opens and he climbs out. As soon as he's out of sight I smile goofily.

Yes. Yes, it does.

My door opens and he holds his hand out for me. "Come." I smirk up at him and he pulls me from the car and takes me into his arms. "Welcome to London, my love." He kisses me.

"You're crazy." I smile against his lips.

"For you."

The front door opens and we turn to see an elderly woman standing at the door. "Hello, my darling Edward." She smiles down at us.

"Hello, Wilhemina." He beams. "I brought someone special to meet you." He presents me as if I'm a prize.

She laughs and rushes down the front steps and Edward kisses her cheek as she hugs him and then she turns to me. "Hello, my dear."

"Wilhemina, this is Alora. Alora, this is my beloved Wilhemina," Edward says proudly.

"Hello." I smile.

She holds my two arms and looks me over. "So beautiful, Edward," she says in her snooty accent.

"She is." He smiles softly over at me.

"I've been waiting for you to arrive, sweetheart." She links her arm through mine and leads me inside. "I've made us morning tea."

I glance over my shoulder to Edward and give him an awkward smile. I don't know who this woman is, but it's obvious she's very close to Edward. She leads me in through the house.

"This is a beautiful home," I tell her, unsure what to say.

"It is." She leads me into the kitchen. "We will have tea and then I will disappear and get out of your way."

"You're never in the way," Edward says from the door.

I glance between them, unsure of their relationship.

Edward must be able to read my mind. "Wilhemina has been with me for many years."

"She has?"

"She was my nanny while I was growing up."

"Oh." I smile as my eyes flick to her. "You were?"

"I was." She nods. "Gave me hell, he did. If ever there was a naughty child, this one was the king. Sent my hair grey overnight."

We all laugh.

"Wilhemina lives here full-time; she has her own apartment on the property," Edward tells me.

"I'm so blessed." She gets up and hugs Edward. He slides his arm around her shoulders. "I could never thank you enough, my dear." She looks up at him. "You look after me so well."

"Hush now," he replies.

I smile as I watch their interaction. I love seeing him with her. There's an obvious deep affection between them. I imagine Edward as a small child, having lost his mother, just how much impact she would have had on his life growing up. I keep getting little snippets, puzzle pieces of the man that I love. Just when I think I know everything there is to know, another puzzle piece clicks into place and shows me a deeper layer of who he is, more depth and sweetness to add to his repertoire.

We sit down at the table in a giant glass orangery that looks over the back garden; it's set with a fine, beautiful, pink bone China teapot and cups and saucers. "Oh," I whisper as I trace my finger along the top of the teapot, "this tea set is divine." I turn the cup over to see if it's been stamped. "This is just absolutely beautiful," I whisper, "I've never seen such a beautiful tea set in all of my life."

She and Edward exchange glances as if they have a secret.

"What?" I smile as I look between them.

"Nothing," Edward replies.

Wilhemina chuckles, and I'm not mistaking it, there's a definite silent message passing between them

"What is it?" I frown.

"I'm telling her." She smiles.

"If you must." Edward rolls his eyes.

"Edward had me return home and retrieve a few things from Nottingham for your visit; this tea set was one of them."

"You did?"

"It was his mother Angelique's favorite."

Oh.

Emotion overwhelms me and I unexpectedly tear up. I know how much my own mother's possessions mean to me. The fact that he wanted her favorite tea set here when I arrived melts my heart.

"Just because I know you like old things and my mother liked old things too," Edward replies as if to try and justify his actions.

I lean over and kiss his cheek. "Thank you, that means so much to me."

Wilhemina smiles as she looks between us. "Tell me all about Alora."

"Well, where do I start?" Edward begins.

The love hearts in my eyes nearly block my vision as I stare over at him, the conversation fades to black as I reconcile him wanting his mother's favorite tea set to be here for me, so sentimentally beautiful.

So very Edward.

All I really want now is for Wilhemina to leave us alone, someone's about to get seriously lucky.

Edward closes the door, leans on the back of it, and turns to me. "I thought she'd never leave," he mouths.

"I *was* beginning to have my suspicions," I whisper.

Clearly lonely, Wilhemina was so excited to see Edward that she forgot all about time; she sat at that table and talked for over two hours. She's been traveling and they haven't seen each other in person for months. She told us every little detail about every single day, complete with going through the photos on her phone and explaining each and every one of them to us. Edward sat there with a patience I haven't seen from him before; it's obvious how much he adores her.

He takes me into his arms. "Now, where were we?" He kisses me softly.

"I think you were going to show me your house and … your bedroom."

His eyebrow flicks up. "Was I?"

"Aha." I kiss his big, beautiful lips.

"Was there something specific that you wanted to see in my bedroom, Alora?" He bumps his hips against mine as he gives me the look.

"The pillows."

"The pillows?" He smirks. "You want to look at the pillows on my bed?"

"Aha."

"Perhaps at close range?"

"Is there any other way to look at them?" I smile as I undo the top button on his shirt and kiss his neck. "And while I'm looking at the pillows on your bed maybe you could be…." I kiss him again.

"Behind you?" He grabs a handful of my hair and drags my face up to his and kisses me. His tongue plows through my open lips with intensity.

"That could work." I smile against his lips.

"It always works." He bites my neck and goose bumps scatter up my arms as he takes my hand in his. "The bedroom is this way."

"Wait, show me the rest of the house first."

He rolls his eyes and holds his hand up in annoyance. "The kitchen."

"Right."

"Oh, look, there's your favorite thing, an oven," he mutters dryly.

I smile as I look around. "You're my favorite thing."

"Behind your vegetable patch and your oven, you mean."

I giggle, he knows me better than he thinks. "Exactly."

"Living room." He gestures to the large television and super slouchy tan couch. There's a marble fireplace with a large gilded mirror above it and beautiful art on the walls.

"I love this style." I look around in wonder. "It's kind of a meld of new meets old."

"Yes." He pulls me by the hand. "Down here is the office." He takes me down a corridor that has a few doors off it before opening the last one in a rush. "Nothing much to see in here."

I brush past him and walk in. The walls are a deep green and the wall of bookcases are custom painted the same shade. Leather-bound old books are lined up on the shelves, adding to the ambience. The grand desk is mahogany with a glass overlay on the top of it, and the office chair is dark brown leather. The heavy curtains that run from the ceiling to floor are a fawn color with a matching green velvet ribboning sewn on about five inches up from the floor. "This is…." I smile in awe, "Magazine worthy. I love it."

He takes me into his arms. "This will be your office."

I frown up at him.

"I'm hoping that one day…." He shrugs as his voice trails off.

"One day what?"

"I would like to live here full-time at some stage."

"You want to live in London full-time?" I frown. "This is the first I've heard of this plan."

"I want my children to go to school in London."

"Your children?"

"*Our* children. That's if we are fortunate enough to be blessed with them, of course."

Oh….

We smile at each other as if hearing the words out loud have put a magic spell into the air.

"I hope we *are* blessed," he murmurs.

"We will be," I whisper.

He bends and kisses me softly. "I love you."

"I love you more."

My heart swells. This is the first time he's talked about a long-term future. I mean, I know he bought the house in Monaco for us to live in, but he owns houses everywhere and he bought the house alone, I'm not on the title deeds.

This feels different. This feels like a real plan. A family plan.

I turn back to look around at my surroundings. "Well..."

"Well, what?"

"Well, I think I will be very happy living here and having this as my office." I run my hand along the desk. "Although with ten children, I'm not sure how much work we'll be getting done."

"Ten," he repeats. "That's about five too many."

"Just checking that you're listening." I smile as I walk back out into the hallway.

"Laundry room." He opens the next door, it's huge and the floors are a black and white check marble and the cupboards are all custom cream with matching marble countertops. There are two commercial washing machines and dryers. "Oh, the big ones. I could wash the king-sized quilts when I need to. Now, *this* room excites me."

His eyebrows flick up in surprise. "Each to their own, I guess." He opens the next door. "Gymnasium." I peer in to see a full gym, equipped with a sauna and filled spa bath sunken into the floor.

"That spa bath has to be removed," I tell him.

"It's a cold plunge."

"Well, it's dangerous. Children could drown in there."

"Or we could just keep the door shut."

"You can't just keep the door shut, children run the house. We won't even be able to keep the bedroom door shut."

"Well, we will be." He widens his eyes. "Or else they will just be watching porn every night." He ushers me out and closes the door behind us.

"Do you actually think mothers of young children do porn every night?"

"Absolutely." He takes my hand in his. "Where do you think the term *yummy mummy* comes from?"

"From cake-making, of course," I tease.

"Hmm." He shrugs as he leads me up the stairs. "I beg to differ."

My eyes float around and I don't know what to look at first. The staircase is curved and made of white marble to match the black and white checkered marble tiles from below. The carpeted runner is black and held in place with brass rods. "This is.... So beautiful, Edward."

"Up here we have seven bedrooms, I'll show you them later." He leads me to the end of the hall. "This one is ours."

The bedroom is calm and welcoming. The walls are a soft grey and the afternoon sun peeking through the large windows bounces a gentle lighting throughout the room. Plush carpet is on the floor, and a large bed sits in the center. My eyes roam around the space, so different to his yacht. This place feels homely and lived in, which seems weird because he doesn't live here full-time. "This is just stunning." It's then I glance over and see eight suitcases. "Why on earth do you need so many suitcases?"

"I bought you a few things."

"Such as?"

"Open them and see."

"Edward," I sigh. "You need to stop buying me stuff, there is nothing I need."

"Open them." He unzips the first case and lays it out flat and my mouth falls open.

"What the..."

The suitcase is full of clothing wrapped in blue tissue paper.

"I know that tissue paper." I begin to unwrap at double speed to see the most beautiful vintage clothing, perfectly folded and some with price tags still attached. "Oh my god." I pull out a cream cashmere Chanel cardigan and hold it up over my body as I look down at myself. "What the.... Edward," I whisper.

"I wanted to fill your wardrobes here with things you love."

My eyes float over the other suitcases and I can't even imagine what's inside of those.

He knows me.

I see my red tin and pick it up. "You even bought my labels?"

"Well, I know you like to label your things before you wear them."

He really knows me.

I get a lump in my throat as I stare at the old red tin.

A trace of a smile crosses his face. "How did I do?"

"You did…. Really good."

All my life I wished for a love like this, and now it's found me.

He stands before me, his eyes dark and intent. He traces the line of my jaw before taking my face in his hands as he stares down at me, and I know exactly what's on his mind.

"Do you know how much I love you?" I whisper.

He kisses me softly, his lips lingering over mine. "Show me, my love. Show me."

My eyes roam over the huge stone wall that is covered in ivy as my stomach flutters with nerves.

We're here, at Edward's family home and I'm about to meet his father for the first time and I can't help but feel that I'm here to get his seal of approval, what happens if I fuck this up? The black Bentley pulls into the drive and stops at the giant metal gates, a guard smiles from the watchhouse and pushes a button, the gates slowly open.

My breath catches at what I see….

A light gravel driveway lined with giant trees, rolling green hills and white fences. This place is straight out of a movie. "What are those beautiful trees?" I whisper in awe.

"Oak trees." Edward smiles as he holds my hand in his. The car slowly drives in and the gates close behind us. We drive up and over the hill and past giant white stables with horses, and not the usual kind of horses you see, like sporty horses. There are people wandering around, one person is leading a horse by its lead, another is sweeping out a stall. There's a tractor driving along with a load of hay on its tipper.

"What kind of horses are they?"

"Racehorses."

"Racehorses?" I squeak.

"My mother instilled the love in us."

"Oh. Well, that's just." I search for something nice to say. "Really great." I look back out the window as another level of inadequacy hits, I don't know anything about fucking horses. Only that they scare the living crap out of me.

Seriously…what in the hell does this guy see in me?

I feel myself begin to sweat.

We keep driving up the perfectly maintained road and pass more paddocks, this time filled with huge black cows. "These cows look like they are on steroids."

He chuckles as he looks out at them too. "Black Angus."

"Right."

Of course they are…. Ugh, is anyone inferior around here apart from me?

We drive around a winding road and up over a hill and my heart stops as I see the sight over the next hill.

A castle, a fucking bona fide sandstone castle. Complete with giant circular driveway and perfectly manicured gardens. A man in a hat is watering flowers and a woman is raking some leaves under an oak tree.

"How long has your family lived here?" I ask.

"We are the sixth generation," he replies calmly as his eyes remain out the window. "My children will be the seventh."

I feel the blood begin to drain from my face…. Honestly, what am I playing at?

Edward at my house in Nice is just the hot guy that I met in Switzerland, he's just a normal man who I have fallen in love with. He could be Joe Blow from the street and I would love him just as much.

On a deeper level in the background, I know that he has money, but when I'm confronted with just how much…. It freaks me out. It doesn't reconcile, I can't compete with this, I can't… he dates princesses, for fuck's sake.

What am I even doing here?

Fuck.

I feel perspiration dust my skin and I want to jump out of the car and run as fast as I can to a cheap and nasty hotel where I would at least fit in.

The car doesn't pull into the castle, it keeps driving along the white gravel road. "Where are we going now?" I ask.

"To my place."

"Oh...how great." I fake another smile, of course he has his own place here...because one family castle isn't enough.

From the corner of my eye I see the driver smirk.

Not funny, asshole.

We go over another hill and drive a few miles and another sandstone house comes into view. It's still huge but nowhere near the castle's size; it has a lake with ducks swimming around and a separate garage, dark green vines are growing over it. The same beautiful oak trees surround it and this could literally be heaven on earth. "This is my place," he says as we pull into the drive.

"Oh." I bite my bottom lip to hide my smile as the car comes to a stop. "It's beautiful."

"Like you." He leans over and kisses me. "Come." He gets out of the car and walks around and opens the door for me, he takes my hand in his and leads me up the path. I've noticed that when he's with me nobody is allowed to open my car door but him. Has he told them that he wants to do it or is this some kind of rich-person etiquette that I don't know about?

We walk up the giant sandstone steps and onto a veranda with heavy double doors and he opens them and pulls me inside. "Welcome to my home, Doe." He kisses me softly. "I hope you love it here as much as I do."

My eyes widen as my heart stops.

"Edward," I whisper as my eyes float over the heaven. "My god, it's beautiful." The walls are a warm cream, the furnishings are a perfect blend of modern and antique, there are dark timber floors with giant rugs and the back wall is glass looking over the green rolling hills. "It's kind of like—"

"Your place." He cuts me off.

My eyes search his. "Yes."

"We have the same taste." He cups my face in his hands and kisses me again. "I had the same thought when I went to your place the first time."

My heart swells, just when I think this man can't get any better, he ups the ante.

"Where would you like the bags, sir?" the guard asks.

"Upstairs in our bedroom, please."

Our bedroom.

They disappear up the huge staircase and I smile as I look around.

"A penny for your thoughts?" he asks.

"I think it was stupid of you to bring me here."

"Why is that?"

"Because I'm never going to want to leave."

He cups my face in his hand before kissing me softly. "That was my plan."

"What else is in your plan for today?"

"First.... We go meet my father in the main house."

Oh crap...anything but that.

"Great."

Stop saying great.... You sound like a frigging idiot.

EDWARD.

"Shall we go?"

"What...now?" Her eyes widen.

"Why not?"

"I'm just...going to freshen up." She glances up the stairs.

"Okay. Last bedroom at the end of the hall is ours."

She nods before taking off up the stairs at double speed. I walk over to the window and stare out over the view as I feel the tension leave my body.

It's always so good to be home.

I head into the kitchen and check the fridge to make sure it's been stocked. I do a walk-around just to make sure everything is in order; it's been a few months since I've been home. Fifteen minutes later Alora still hasn't returned, what is she doing up there?

I find her in the master bedroom, standing in front of the mirror close to tears.

"What's wrong?" I frown.

"Does this look okay?" She looks down at herself.

"It looks perfect." She's wearing a flowing pink dress, her thick dark hair is pulled back into a loose ponytail and she has a fresh face, without makeup.

She spins and then turns to the bathroom and then goes back to her open suitcase and then spins again. "What are you doing?" I frown.

"Freaking the fuck out, Edward," she stammers. "I feel stupid, I've brought stupid clothes and I packed stupid things and I made a present for your dad and now that I'm here, it's just *so* ridiculously stupid."

"What do you mean, you made a present for my father?" I drop to sit on the bed.

She picks up a large square red tin, the kind you see in antique stores. "I won't give it to him." She shrugs as if embarrassed. "I don't even know what I was thinking."

"What is it?"

"I baked him some shortbread."

"When did you have time to bake shortbread?" I frown, confused.

"I got up at 3 this morning and did it while you were sleeping, I wanted it to be fresh for him."

Oh....

My heart swells, and if I didn't love this woman before, I sure as hell do now.

"How are you so perfect?" I take her into my arms and kiss her.

"Should I change?" Her eyes search mine.

"Don't you dare. I love you exactly the way you are."

"I mean my clothes, Edward. Focus...."

"Alora." I take her hands in mine. "Just be you. My father is no idiot, he will love you if you just be yourself."

"But this house is just so fancy and...I'm out of my depth here."

"Listen to me." I place my finger under her chin and bring her face up to meet mine. "I fell in love with you because of who you are, not what you have."

Her eyes well with tears.

"Show yourself to my family, the real you. Not who you think they want you to be." I wipe her tears with my thumbs. "Alright?"

She nods. "Okay."

I pick up her old red tin and I put it under my arm and we make our way downstairs and out through the front door as we hold hands, and I want to run to my father's. Because for the first time in my life I have someone worthy to introduce to him.

Someone I'm proud to call mine...and what she sees in me, I'll never know.

We arrive at the front door and I hand her the red tin. "You ready?" I ask.

She nods again, perhaps too nervous to speak.

I push the door open. "I'm home," I call.

My father comes around the corner and his face lights up when he sees us. "Ah, my son." He laughs, he pulls me into an embrace. "It's been too long."

"Dad." I smile. "This is Alora Sorenson."

"Hello, my dear." He smiles.

"Hello," she says timidly, with shaky hands she holds out her red tin. "I...." She swallows the lump in her throat. "I made you a present." She passes it over.

"You did?" He frowns as he looks down at it.

"Open it." I smile.

He opens the tin and unfolds the white tissue paper and his mouth falls open. "You made this?"

"It's probably not very good," she whispers. "Umm...." She points into the tin. "This is macadamia and this side is lemon, and this row is traditional English shortbread."

"Alora got up at 3 this morning while I was sleeping because she wanted it to be fresh for you," I tell him.

His eyes meet mine and an unexpected emotion fills me.

"Well.... Alora." He smiles. "This is the most thoughtful present I have received in a very long time."

She smiles softly and honestly...*how is she mine?*

"Shall we go and make some tea to have with it?" my father asks as he holds his hand out toward the kitchen.

"Okay." She walks in front of us.

"Alora loves English tea too, Dad, don't you?"

"I do," she replies.

My father's eyes meet mine. "Finally."

ALORA.

If heaven were a place on earth, this is it.

Our week in London has been a dream come true. We've spent our days in the sunshine with his father and sister, Charlotte. We had dinner with the extended family at Charlotte's place one night and I got to meet all of the aunts and uncles; her husband, Spencer, is hilarious.

But by night, when we've been alone, is where the magic has happened.

We've fallen even deeper in love.

I don't know what happened last week when Edward saw me in the shower, but it did something to him, changed him somehow. It's like an invisible wall he was keeping me out with came down and everything I knew that he could be, was waiting for me on the other side.

To have what we do now has been worth every single second of heartache, I couldn't possibly love him more than I do in this moment.

I kiss his chest as we lie in the darkness, the red glow of the open fire flickers across the bedroom and his regulated breathing tells me that he's fast asleep. This house, this family…this man.

I've found my happily ever after.

I lean over on my hands and knees and pull out the weed. I have gardening gloves on and a giant hat. I'm in Harold's vegetable patch; we've been working in it together for hours over the last week, turns out that we really do have a lot in common.

"How did you get into gardening?" he asks as he snips bean vines.

"My mother loved gardening and when she died I wanted to keep it alive for her." I lean over and pull out some more weeds. "And then I don't know." I lean back onto my knees and wipe the perspiration from my brow as I look over at him. "It made me feel closer to her, so I did it more and more." I shrug. "It kind of became my happy place, I guess."

He smiles as he listens.

"Why do you like gardening?" I ask.

"My dear Angelique loved gardening."

"She did?" I frown. "Edward's mother liked gardening?"

"She did."

"He never told me that."

He smiles wistfully. "Charlotte is like you, it brings her closer to the memory of her late mother and connects the two of them, but for me, I guess it grounds me." He thinks for a moment. "You can have everything in the world, but if you don't feel grounded and calm, then you have nothing."

"True." I lean back over and keep weeding. "I wish I could get Edward to garden, I think it would be good for him. He needs to chill out."

"Trust me, I've tried everything over the years." He keeps snipping. "Ever since his mother was murdered he has never been the same."

I glance up. "She was murdered?"

He twists his lips as if contemplating his next words. "She was run off the road by another car. That car has never been found."

I stare at him, shocked to my core.

"I blame myself."

"Why?"

"It was the one day she went out alone and I knew she shouldn't be driving around without her guards with her but she was sick of having no privacy so I...." His voice trails off.

"Oh." I go back to weeding. "You can't blame yourself for that." I think as I keep working. "Did they ever find who did it?"

"No. But it was premeditated."

"How do you know?"

"A fake road detour had been put up, she was ambushed and didn't stand a chance. She died because of me...because of who I am."

I stare over at his sad face as he keeps snipping and I can feel the deep-seated heartbreak that he's lived with.

"Is that why Edward is so hung up on security?" I ask.

"Yes." He nods. "He's so hung up on protecting everybody. Charlotte wore it the worst, he was unbearable with her before she married." He glances over to me. "I'm assuming he put you through a lot before you started formally dating?"

"Why do you say that?" I keep weeding so that he keeps talking.

"He's always been terrified that his love will be a target too. I imagine he would have pushed you away to try and protect you."

Oh....

A piece of the Edward Prescott puzzle falls into place...*this is why he's like this.*

"In his mind, control means safety." He keeps snipping. "The more he controls people, the safer they will be. The more distance he has from people, the safer they will be."

I look over at him as he snips away and my heart breaks for my beautiful man.

"I'm not sure if you know this or not, but Edward has been in therapy for years to try and heal his demons."

"I did know that." I go back to weeding. "How...." I try to articulate my thoughts. "How do I help him through this?"

"You love him through his flaws." He smiles sadly over at me. "But watching you two together, I know that you already accept his scars and love him unconditionally."

His silhouette blurs and I get a lump in my throat. *He's been through so much.*

"I love his scars." I smile. "Every last one of them."

"Yah." A loud voice echoes from the distance and I look up to see Edward and Charlotte are on horseback, sprinting as they race across the paddock and up into the hills.

"You need to learn how to ride." He smiles as he watches them disappear.

"Probably not." I go back to weeding. "If you want me to stay alive, you keep me away from horses. I'm so uncoordinated that I fall over my own feet."

He chuckles and keeps snipping. "Give it time."

Golden rays shine from above as we walk across the meadow. I have a bunch of handpicked daisies and huge old trees are lined up along the boundary fence. I smile up at the sun. "You know, Edward, I think this is my new favorite place on earth."

He throws his arm around my shoulder. "You're my favorite place on earth."

"Actually." I smile. "Yours sounds better, and you're right. You're my favorite place on earth and this place is just a by-product of that."

He pulls me closer and kisses my temple as we walk. "You know, I've been thinking."

"Hmm." I scan the ground for more daisies.

"When we get home and we move in together I want something to change between us."

I glance up at him and stop on the spot. "You do?"

"Yeah." He turns me toward him and takes my hands in his. "I want you to move in as my fiancée."

My eyes search his. "What are you saying?"

"Marry me."

CHAPTER THIRTY-THREE

What?

My heart stops.

He drops to his knee as he holds my hands in his. "Marry me, Alora."

"Edward," I gasp as I drop to my knees too. "We don't have to rush.... I mean...of course...but so soon.... I mean—"

"It's a yes or no question." He cuts me off.

My eyes search his. "Are you seriously asking me to be your wife?" I whisper.

"I am." He smiles softly. "When you know, you know." He takes my face in his hands and kisses me. "And I know."

His silhouette blurs. "I know too."

"So answer the question. *Will* you marry me?"

"Yes." I smile through tears. "Oh my god. *Yes.*" His lips take mine and we kiss and it's the perfect moment in time.

Kneeling in a field of wildflowers at his beloved home, so simple and yet so out-of-this-world romantic.

"You have two choices for your engagement ring." He smiles over at me, his eyes full of love.

"Is this real?" I laugh out loud.

"You can have my family heirloom ring. Or you can have a new one, the choice is yours."

"Oh...." I think for a moment. "Was the family ring your mother's?"

"Yes." His eyes hold mine.

I think for a moment. "I would like that one, please," I whisper.

His nostrils flare and I know that it means a lot to him. "Good choice." He digs a red ring box from his pocket and opens it to reveal the most beautiful ring I have ever seen. It's an Edwardian antique style, a large European-cut center diamond with diamonds around it, all encased in filigree rose gold.

"Oh my god." My hands fly over my mouth.

He takes my hand and slides it onto my finger and once again my vision blurs. "Oh…Edward. It's so perfect," I whisper as I hold my hand out to look at it. "It looks like a diamond flower."

"It does."

I laugh out loud. "What the hell just happened?" and he laughs too.

"We got…." He shrugs as if unable to believe it himself. "Engaged."

"Are you sure?" I ask as I continue to stare at my hand, I can't take my eyes off it for even a second. "This is very soon, we can wait if you want."

"It took me thirty-six years to find you, Alora, and I'm not wasting another minute."

My eyes search his. "We're really going to do this?"

"Yes…. To forever." He takes my face in his hands and kisses me. "Mrs. Prescott."

"Ha." I laugh against his lips. "It sounds so grown up."

He chuckles and pulls me to my feet and we kiss again, our lips lingering over each other's in a perfect moment of tenderness. "I love you so much," I whisper.

"And I love you."

"When are we telling everyone?"

"Right now."

I turn and run across the field, unable to control my excitement. "I'll race you back to the house."

He takes off after me and we laugh as we run and as we get to the top of the hill I see Harold, Charlotte and Spencer waiting for us with a small table set up on the grass. There's a silver ice bucket, a bottle of champagne and five flutes.

"They knew?" I laugh as I gasp for air.

"They knew." He smiles as he catches up to me. "From the minute they met you, they knew."

"What happened if I had said no?" I pant.

"Then I would have killed you and buried you in the field so that nobody ever found out." He takes my hand in his and holds it up in the air as if he just won a title fight and they all cheer and jump around in excitement.

"FaceTime your father and brother and sister," he says. "I want them to celebrate with us."

"I hope my dad answers." I take out my phone.

"They're expecting your call."

"You called already?" I get a lump in my throat.

"Of course I called them."

Oh….

"I love you," I whisper through tears, he grabs me and takes me into his arms and to the sound of cheering in the distance, he kisses me with everything that he is.

A moment so perfect that it will forever be burned in time.

Forever his.

EDWARD.

The fire glows, flickering warmth filters through the room and I know there's something I have to do before the day ends... an elephant in the room, I have no idea how to bring this up without ruining the perfect day. But then if I don't, tomorrow it will be worse...it's already eating me alive.

Alora is lying with her head on my lap as I sit with my feet up on an ottoman and a glass of red in my hand. My fingers aimlessly run through her hair and every now and then she lifts her hand to look at her ring as if still in disbelief.

"Doe." I twist my lips, trying to find the right words. "There's something we need to run over."

"Yeah?" She looks up at me with those big, beautiful innocent eyes.

"Umm...." My stomach sinks.... ***Fuck.***

"What is it?" She sits up.

"I...." My eyes hold hers.

"Edward, spit it out."

"I have something that I need you to take to your lawyers when we get home." I stand and open the drawer and pull out a large white envelope.

"What's in that?" She frowns.

I sit back down, put it on the coffee table and puff air into my cheeks, wishing I was anywhere but here having this conversation. "It's a prenup."

"Okay." She shrugs and looks around the room. "Where's a pen?"

I frown as I stare at her. "No, no." I shake my head; she obviously doesn't understand what this is. "It's not something that you sign willy-nilly. You take it to your legal team and they negotiate with my legal team."

"Willy-nilly?" She smiles as she gets up and walks to the desk. "Who says willy-nilly?"

"I do." I smirk. "Will you be serious for a moment, please?"

"I am being serious." She pulls out a drawer and grabs a pen and clicks it. "Let's go."

"No, Alora." I take the pen from her. "This is a ninety-eight-page document. You are not just signing it without legal representation."

"I don't care about money, Edward, you know that." She snatches the pen back from me. "If we break up I don't want a penny of yours. I already have everything I need." She begins to flick through the pages. "Wait a minute." She looks up at me. "Is there anything in here about children?"

"What do you mean?"

"The only thing I would want is equal shared custody of my children."

"Oh...." I frown. "No. God no, there is nothing about children at all. This is a monetary-only prenup."

"Okay." She flicks through to the last page.

"What are you doing? Read it, take your time. This isn't something you just sign."

"I don't need to."

"Alora, don't be ridiculous."

"I trust you, Edward." She smiles over at me. "I know you would never...." She shrugs. "You know."

"You shouldn't trust someone this much, Alora."

"I trust you with my heart and that's the only thing of value that I have." She signs her name on the last page and dates it. "And your heart is the only thing I would ever want. If we break up and I lose that, no amount of money would ever compensate for losing you." She leans over and kisses me. "I'm going to take a shower babe, see you upstairs?"

I nod, the sound of my heartbeat echoes through my ears.

I listen to her go upstairs and I stare at her signature on the last page. She didn't even read it.

She trusts me.

Alora Sorenson is the only person apart from my family who has ever trusted me.

Ever really loved me.

I pick up the thick wad of paper and its envelope and walk over, open the safety grill, and put it into the fire.

I watch the red flames blaze high as they burn the paper. Weeks of work from my legal team goes up in flames.

I sip my wine as the red glow lights my face, her heart really is the only thing worth value and if I lose that, I have nothing.

"I choose to trust you too." I watch it burn. "For better or worse."

ALORA.

I stare at the headstone.

ANGELIQUE PRESCOTT

LOVING WIFE, BELOVED MOTHER.

FOREVER IN OUR HEARTS.

Edward carefully places the bunch of pink roses into the vase and wipes the headstone. He makes a cross symbol across his chest with his finger as if having done this a thousand times before.

We are in the meadow across the hill and over the stream, there, beneath more oak trees is a family cemetery. Surrounded by an ornate iron fence, climbing roses grow over statues, there's a large circular water feature made from white marble with lilies floating on top of the water, surrounded by perfectly kept lawns. Old tombstones are in lines, Prescott after Prescott, and I try to imagine the people who are buried here.

Edward's ancestors, every single one of them.

And it's one thing to visit your mother's grave, but for her to be buried in the grounds of her own house is something else. In one way, it's comforting that she's close. In another way, it's a constant reminder that she isn't above the ground anymore.

That she lies here…. Her life in the past.

A distant memory of love that echoes in the wind.

Edward stares at the tombstone with his hands in his pockets, his face void of emotion. He doesn't introduce me. He doesn't seem happy; in fact, we only came here to say goodbye to her before we leave for home.

I wonder does he do this every visit. Come to see her only before he leaves. I get the feeling that he does, but then I may be misreading the situation.

I do know that this week after our engagement I have missed my mother more than I have in a long time. She should be here celebrating with us, helping plan a wedding. Sharing in my joy, and I wonder if he feels the same.

He holds his hand out for me. "Come." I take his hand and we turn and begin to head back to the house. His mood is somber and I glance back at the tombstone of his mother.

Goodbye, Mrs. Prescott, I promise to take care of him.

"Goodbye." I hug Harold, and then Charlotte.

"Goodbye." They smile and wave as I get into the car. I watch through the car window as Edward says goodbye to them; his father holds him close for an extended time and tears up. He wipes his eyes as he pulls out of the hug. Edward then turns to Charlotte and she does the same.

Goodbyes are never easy, but for some reason when the matriarch of the family has passed…. It seems harder. Leaving a parent alone isn't something that anyone does by choice. With Edward being so busy at work, I don't imagine that he checks in enough; that's just an assumption of course, but going off their reaction to him leaving I think it's a fair guess.

Edward climbs into the car and forces a smile and wave as the car pulls away, he takes my hand in his and then looks out of the window as if also saddened.

It hurts to say goodbye to parents, to see their face as they try to act brave, especially when you know that leaving is your choice.

He doesn't say a word all the way to the airport and I don't try to chat or change the subject because I know that sometimes you just need to sit in your guilt for a while.

Feel the distance between the people you care for grow greater with every mile that you drive away.

His stance is sad as he stares out the window, my hand is on his thick quad, held tightly in his. "It was a wonderful week, thank you for bringing me to meet them." I smile.

"It was." He nods. "Thank you for coming."

The car pulls up on the tarmac beside the plane, it's raining now and our driver produces a black umbrella and holds it over us as we climb out of the car. "Thank you." Edward takes it from him and holds it above as he leads me up the stairs. I watch my step closely, always so scared that I'm going to trip and fall over while everyone watches.

"Hello." The captain smiles and shakes his hand, he turns to me. "Hello, Miss Sorenson."

"Hello." I smile. I'm just busting for someone to see my ring; I desperately want to scream it from the rooftops. I have news, big news. The best news that I could have to tell you.

We're getting married.

Somebody notice, for god's sake.

Edward leads me to my seat and I sit down, he takes off his suit coat and walks to the cupboard and hangs it up on a coat hanger.

"I'll have a scotch, please," he tells the flight attendant, his eyes come to me. "What would you like, Alora?"

"I'll have a champagne, please."

"Of course, sir." She smiles as she disappears up the aisle.

Edward falls into the seat beside me and takes my hand in his again, his gaze goes out the window, no chitchat, and no banter.

No lovey-dovey man that I've had the pleasure of spending the last week with.

"You okay?" I whisper as I kiss his shoulder.

"Yes." He kisses my temple. "I hate goodbyes."

"We'll come back soon."

He nods and turns his gaze back out the window and I lean my head back against the headrest.

My man is human.

Two long hours later the plane doors are opened on the tarmac in Nice. It's late, nearly 9 p.m.

"Goodbye and thank you." Edward shakes the captain's and flight attendants' hands and we make our way downstairs.

Philippe is waiting by the black Bentley and our things are loaded into the car behind it.

Edward opens the back door and I climb in; Philippe gets in behind the wheel. "Where to, sir?" he asks.

"I...." He shrugs. "I wanted to spend the night on the yacht but it's late and we are tired. Take us to Miss Sorenson's, please."

"Yes, sir." He pulls away and the car drives through the night and I smile out the window, happy to be going back to my place.

Edward doesn't tell Philippe about us and it doesn't feel like the right time.

Everything seems surreal, in my wildest dreams I would never have imagined the wonderful week we have just had. I just want to scream it from the rooftops.

We're engaged.

"Doe, I'm going," a husky whispered voice wakes me.

"Huh?" I drag my eyes open to see Mr. Orgasmic sitting on the bed beside me, it's still quite dark and he's dressed in his power suit and ready for work.

"Okay." I smile sleepily.

"Don't wear your ring today, sweetheart."

"What?" My eyes snap open. "Why not?"

"I want to make an official announcement and I don't want anybody hounding you at work."

"Oh." I stretch. "Who would hound me?"

"Reporters." He kisses me. "Just keep it in your purse today."

I pull a sad face.

"I'll do it this morning and then I'll call you." He kisses me again. "And tonight we will stay on the yacht and celebrate. The boys will bring you after work."

"Okay." I hold my ring as it sits on my finger. "I'm not taking it off. I'll wear gloves."

"Okay."

I smile goofily up at him. "Can you believe it?"

"I can." He kisses me again.

"You're giving me your last name." I hold my hand up and smile down at my ring.

"So you can moan my first." He bites my neck and I giggle as I twist beneath him, with one last kiss he disappears down the stairs. I hear the front door and then the car start out the front.

I doze back into slumberland. I'm not taking it off.

You can't make me.

I slide the lip tint brush over and roll my lips, carefully brush the mascara on, add blush and put in my gold earrings, and have even straightened my hair. So much effort just to go into work but today isn't just any old day.

Today I'm engaged.

To the swooniest, most utterly gorgeous man of my dreams, and I want to look the part. I'm wearing a black pencil skirt and a black cashmere turtleneck. My long dark hair is loose and straight and my makeup is attempting to be chic, complete with red lipstick.

I'm not taking my ring off; I contemplated it, but in the end I decided that it was a hard no. Nobody is going to see me at work anyway, and even if they do, they have no idea who I'm dating. Besides, if Edward is making an announcement today, the cat is going to be out of the bag. With one last look in the mirror I grab my purse and head downstairs. I lock up the back door and head out the front to see Philippe and Stefan leaning on the side of the Bentley as they wait for me. "Good morning." I bounce down the driveway.

"Good morning, Miss Sorenson." Philippe smiles as he opens the back door. "I hear congratulations are in order."

He told them.

"Yes." I beam. "Can you believe it?"

"I actually can't." He laughs as I climb into the back seat. "But it is fantastic news. Congratulations."

"Thank you."

"Congratulations, Miss Sorenson." Stefan smiles as he gets into the car.

"Thank you."

We pull out onto the road and I smile goofily out the window. "You must be excited to get organizing," Philippe says as his eyes meet mine in the rearview mirror.

"Organizing…." I frown, a little lost as to what he's talking about.

"What with the wedding being in four weeks."

"Four weeks?" I squeak. "Umm…. That's not happening, Philippe."

"Oh." Philippe's face falls, worried that he has spoken out of turn. "My mistake, I must have misunderstood Mr. Prescott."

"No, you probably didn't." I shrug as I stare out the window. "You know how he is; Edward wants everything yesterday."

"He does," he agrees.

Poor fool has no idea…. Nobody can organize a wedding in four weeks.

Not even him.

Ten minutes later we pull in beside my store and park the car. "I'm just going to race and get a coffee next door; do you want one?" I ask them.

"No, thanks."

"See you inside."

"Okay."

I climb out of the car and with my purse over my shoulder I walk around the corner and run smack-dab into someone. "Oh my gosh, I'm so sorry." I glance up to see a familiar face.

"Pascal."

"Hi." His eyes drop to my hand as it holds my bag strap that's over my body.

Fuck.

“What are you doing here?” I try to discreetly put my hand behind my back. “Have you got the day off?”

“What’s on your finger?” he asks, seemingly annoyed as he shoves his hands into his suit pockets.

“Oh, just a costume ring,” I stammer. “I have to get going.”

His eyes search mine and guilt runs through me.

Fuck.

“Actually, Pascal…. This is probably a good thing that I ran into you because I want you to hear it from me anyway. Edward and I got engaged last week.”

A frown flashes across his face as he processes my words.

“I know it seems sudden, but—”

“It does.” He cuts me off. “You know he’s using you.”

“Pascal.”

“You think it’s a coincidence that suddenly in a few weeks he wants to be a respectable husband when he’s been nothing but a player for years? You can’t be this stupid, Alora.”

“Pascal….” I sigh. “Don’t be like that.”

“Like what? A realist?”

I roll my eyes, annoyed. “Can’t you just be happy for me?”

“No.” His eyes hold mine. “So… knowing Prescott the way that I do, my guess is that he’s involved in some sort of scandal that’s about to break and he needs a cover to hide behind. What better disguise than being happily married.”

CHAPTER THIRTY-FOUR

I step onto my back foot, surprised by his prediction. "That's ridiculous," I fire back.

Wait….

There *is* a scandal brewing…could his story have some merit?

"He doesn't love you, Alora." He twists his lips. "Not like I did."

"Pascal, we haven't been together for months."

"Eight short weeks and you've already promised to marry someone else? You don't even know someone in eight weeks."

My eyes hold his.

"Did our relationship mean so little to you that you would marry someone like him just to get back at me?"

"This has nothing to do with you," I whisper.

"Wake up, Alora. He's going to throw you aside as soon as he gets bored, because that's what Prescott does. Speak to his long list of broken-hearted ex-girlfriends; they were all promised the same things as you and look where they are now."

"Pascal."

"Edward Prescott looks after Edward Prescott…. But I guess you'll find that out the hard way."

I feel Philippe walk up behind me. "Everything alright here?"

"Yes," I lie. "I'm coming now." I look Pascal dead in the eye. "Goodbye, Pascal."

"Is it?" he replies sarcastically. "It doesn't feel so good to me."

I brush past him and walk into my store, rattled by his accusations. I put my purse out the back and sit at my desk. My heart is racing and my face is flushed.

Damn it.

Why did I have to see him…. This is supposed to be a happy celebratory day.

Why did he have to put that into my head?

I know his accusations are utterly ridiculous because we are in love and I know that Edward wouldn't do that to me.

Adrenaline pumps through my bloodstream as alarm bells scream in the distance.

Would he…?

3 P.M.

"Oh my god." Jonty waves his arms around in excitement as he holds his phone. "Here it is, here it is."

"Shh," I mouth, and I gesture to Philippe, who's reading his book at the front of the store. "Come in the office," I mouth.

Don't ask me why…. But since I saw Pascal this morning, I don't want to be openly gushing about the engagement.

On one hand, I know that Pascal's a jilted ex and I'm not going to let it come between Edward and me, but the truth is that it has taken the shine off my excitement.

In fact, it's kind of filled me with dread.

What if he was right? What if this is all some elaborate plan to hide from the story about Hermione that's going to blow up?

It's not….

"It says…" Jonty reads the story from the newsroom. "The casino king Edward Prescott has announced his engagement to a mystery woman, Alora Sorenson." He hunches his shoulders up in excitement. "It says here, Edward Prescott, who has been noticeably absent from social gatherings for an extended period of time, has re-emerged a taken man. He made a statement this morning. 'Alora and I dated years ago and she was always the one that got away. We reconnected and are very much in love. We are very excited to be planning a life together and would appreciate privacy at this special time.' Oh my god." Jonty reads on. "There's a picture of the two of you."

"What?" I frown.

"Oh, you look good too."

I snatch the phone from him to see a photo of the two of us just after we got engaged, I think Charlotte took this photo. We are in the garden, drinking champagne, and his arm is around me, we are both laughing and my ring is front and center. "I didn't know he was using this photo?" I frown.

"You don't like it?" Jonty takes his phone back and studies it again.

"No, I do. I just assumed he would have gotten approval that I wanted to use it."

Jonty smiles as he stares at the photo. "As if he would ask for permission for anything."

Hmm….

Even Jonty has an opinion of Edward.

My phone lights up on my desk as a call comes in. Thomas Stone.

Actually…I could use a Thomas pep talk right now. "Hello."

"Hey." I can tell he's smiling. "I just read a very interesting story about a future Mrs. Prescott."

"Ha." I hold my finger up to Jonty. "Back in a minute." I walk past Philippe. "Just going to sit and have a coffee in the café. You can watch me from here, I'll sit by the window."

He glances around. "Yeah, okay."

I rush out into the street. "Oh my god, thank god you called," I whisper.

"Are you on cloud nine?"

"I was until I saw my ex this morning." I try to keep my voice down.

"You think you're marrying the wrong guy?"

"No," I scoff. "Nothing like that. Hang on." I put the phone down and ask the server, "Hello, can I just grab a table by the door please?"

"Sure thing." She leads me to a table and I sit down. "A café Americano, please."

"Of course."

"What's going on?"

"So…I need you to tell me I'm being an idiot."

"Why?"

"Well, Edward and I, we are so in love and it feels right, you know?"

"Okay," he replies.

"And he took me home to meet his family in London and he spontaneously asked me to marry him and gave me his mother's engagement ring."

"What?" He gasps. "Are you serious?"

"Yes."

"My god, congratulations."

"I have a problem now."

"What?" He listens. "So…."

"On the way to work this morning I ran into my ex, Pascal."

"Is this the guy you ran into in Paris?"

"Yes."

"Why is this guy running into you everywhere?"

"I don't know. But he said that he thinks that Edward only asked me to marry him to cover up a scandal."

"Oh, fuck off," he scoffs, "Jilted lover much."

"You think?"

"He's such a fuckwit. Do not listen to this asshole."

"It's really upset me."

"Why would he say that to you? Even if you thought it, you would never say it unless you were purposely trying to hurt someone's feelings."

"You think?"

"I know. Alora, let's break down what he actually said…he thinks that the only reason someone would ask you to marry them is because of a scandal."

"I guess."

"And that someone like Edward Prescott couldn't possibly love someone like you."

"Basically."

"Fuck. Him."

I smile, feeling better. "You think?"

"Babe, if Edward Prescott didn't want to get married, not even the devil himself could make him do it."

"You're right." I feel a weight lift off my shoulders. "God, I've had the worst day."

"Honestly…. This ex of yours is a narcissist. You dodged a bullet with that one."

"Yeah, perhaps you're right." I smile. "Thank you, I feel like I can't talk to anyone. You have such a great perspective on things."

"Lucky you've got me as a friend, then, isn't it?"

"It is. When do you get back?"

"I fly in on Friday. I've got the weekend off; do you want to grab a coffee or something?"

"Sure."

"Hey, congratulations, babe. I'm so happy for you. Enjoy this special time and don't let anyone steal it from you."

He's right.

"Thank you." I smile down the phone, feeling happy for the first time today. "I'll see you on the weekend."

"Okay, bye." I hang up and my coffee arrives, and I hold my hand out and look down at it, finally I can sit here and stare at my beautiful ring in peace.

5 P.M.

Jonty and Helene stand at the window and peer out onto the street. "Another carful just pulled up."

"Surely not," I stammer as I nervously reapply my lipstick. "What the hell are they all doing here?" I pull my fingers through my hair and straighten my skirt. "Damn it, I should have worn something nicer."

A swarm of activity has begun outside, paparazzi are gathering out the front of my store. "Get back," Philippe instructs them as he holds his hands out to direct them the distance he wants them to stay away.

"How do they even know who I am?" I frown as I dial Edward's number.

"It wouldn't be hard to find you, they just have to google your name," Helene calls.

"Hello, Miss Sorenson," he purrs through the phone.

Butterflies swirl at the sound of his voice, it's so damn delicious that I can't stand it. "Hello." I swoon.

"How was your day, sweetheart?"

"Wonderful," I whisper. "How was yours?"

"Even better than that." I can tell that he's smiling too. "What's up?"

"Photographers have started congregating outside my store."

"Yes, so I heard."

"Well...."

"Well, what?"

"Well, what do I do?"

"Ignore them."

"What?" I frown. "How do I ignore them?"

"You walk out to the car with your guards and you get into it and then they will drive you into our secured garage and then they'll leave."

"Oh." I frown as I think. "So I don't have to do anything?"

"No. Not unless you want to."

"Want to what?"

"If you want to answer their questions you can, although I would advise against it because if they know you are going to entertain them then they will hound you even more."

"Oh." I begin to pace as I think.

"Is that all?" He cuts me off.

"I mean.... Are you in a rush or something?"

"No, but the ten men sitting around the conference table who are all watching and waiting might be."

I hear a collective chuckle of men.

"Oh, crap. Sorry. Okay, bye." I hang up in a rush and screw up my face in horror. How do I always forget that he's busy in meetings all the time? I'm not sure I'll ever get used to dating someone important.

"What did he say?" Helene calls as she stands at the front window. "It's becoming a real circus now, and can we talk about how hot Philippe is when he's being bossy?" She puts her arm out all dramatic like. "Get back," she says in a deep voice as she mimics him.

Jonty and I roll our eyes at each other.

"He said ignore them and just get into the car without saying anything to them."

"That makes sense," Jonty replies. "Don't want to encourage the fuckers."

"That's what he said." I pack up my things. "Okay, are we ready?"

"Yep." The others grab their things and we turn off the lights and make our way over and open the front doors. "Miss Sorenson," someone calls. "Can I have an exclusive please?"

"Miss Sorenson, congratulations on your engagement."

"Miss Sorenson, how did you meet Mr. Prescott?"

"This way." Philippe leads me to the car as cameras flash and I am quickly ushered into the back seat and the door is slammed behind me.

Cameras flash through the windows and I glance up to see Helene and Jonty walking down the street alone and my heart sinks. I didn't even say goodbye to them.

Ugh, I need to get better at this.

CHAPTER THIRTY-FIVE

Breakfast on the deck of the yacht is always so perfect.

"And we have a honeymoon to go on next month," he says matter-of-factly.

"Edward." I roll my eyes. "What makes you think that we're getting married in a month?"

"Because we are."

"No we're not." I widen my eyes. "I want to take my time and pick my dream dress and organize every little detail and have fun doing it."

He rolls his eyes this time. "Fine. You have six weeks."

"Edward."

"It's not up for discussion. I want to be married."

"Well, if you want to be married in six weeks we have to elope."

"Suits me."

"What?" I stare at him. "You want to elope?"

"No. I want a small wedding. My family, your family. A handful of friends each. That's it."

"Oh." I think for a moment, that does sound nice actually. "Where do you want to get married?" I ask him.

He presses his lips together. "Wherever *you* want."

"Really?" I smile. "Elvis wedding in Vegas?"

"Absolutely not."

"Underwater while we scuba dive?"

"Hard no."

"Skydiving above Mount Kosciuszko?"

"Will you be serious?" he snaps.

"Okay then." I narrow my eyes as I pretend to think. I already know where I want to get married. "I guess if I had to choose I would like to get married on your family property."

Tenderness glows in his eyes and I know this was his dream. "Really?"

"Really."

He gets up and comes around to my side of the table and leans down and kisses my cheek from behind. "Thank you. This means a lot to me."

"Six months," I tell him.

"No."

"Four months."

He squeezes my shoulders. "No."

"Edward."

"You have six weeks and that's it." He sits back down at his side of the table and picks up the newspaper, no longer interested in the topic. "What would you like for breakfast?"

"Whatever." I stare out over the sunshine dancing across the water, my mind already buzzing.

What kind of wedding dress do I want?

"Hello, is Miss Sorenson here?" the pretty young girl asks me at the front counter. She's around twenty-two with beautiful red hair, olive skin and big brown eyes.

"Yes. I am her," I reply, *who is this?*

"Hello, my name is Freya Barber. I am one of Mr. Prescott's PAs." Her eyes dart around as if she's nervous.

"Right…." Where the hell is this going? "How can I help you?"

"Umm…." She shrugs awkwardly. "Mr. Prescott had me driven here to offer my services to you for the next few months to work as your personal assistant."

"What?"

"He said that, umm…." She swallows the lump in her throat. "He said that I could perhaps help you organize the wedding."

"Oh." The penny drops as to why she's here and I smirk. "He did, did he."

Such a control freak.

"This is a really big honor for me." She smiles hopefully. "He said that you might decline, but I want you to know that I am very organized and I can do all the running around for you and

I'm great with spreadsheets and am multilingual. If you show me what you want I can find options and bring them back for you to look over. I can work all hours and am happy to do site inspections or anything that you may need," she blurts out in a rush.

Hmm, that does sound pretty good, actually....

"But where do you live, is Nice too far for you to come every day? I'm based here, so I would need someone in my store with me."

"Mr. Prescott said that a driver would pick me up and drop me off each day if you accept," she fires back without hesitation. "And I can be your PA for other things too, not just the wedding. I could work in the store here with you when you need me, and I can help you in the office. I can do payroll and ordering."

I can tell she really wants to do this.

"Okay, Freya." I smile. "That sounds wonderful. Thank you."

"Really?" She seems surprised.

"Yes. I could use the help, but you must know that maybe I will steal you away from Mr. Prescott permanently." I throw her a playful wink.

Jonty walks around the corner and stops dead on the spot as he sees Freya, her eyes light up when she sees him and they stare at each other in awe.

Aww, cute.

Her eyes flick back to me, embarrassed that she just ogled my worker. "That could work out well."

"Great." I smile, my eyes flick to Jonty, who looks like he just saw a ghost. "Jonty, this is Freya, she's going to be working with us from now on."

"She is?" He smiles goofily.

Oh god.

"Can you start tomorrow, Freya?" I ask her.

"Of course." She gives an awkward wave to me and Jonty. "See you tomorrow. Thank you for the opportunity."

She disappears out the door and Jonty smiles after her. "Well, isn't she just the most perfect thing to have ever stepped foot in here."

"Behave, Jonty." I air quote the word. "Work friend."

EDWARD.

"Throw the rope," he yells.

I whip the heavy rope as it lies along the deck.

"Harder," he yells. "Move it."

My two arms scissoring, I whip the rope as hard as I can. It's heavy, cumbersome, and fucking hard work. I started fully dressed, shorts, shirt, and sweater, but as the training heated up, so did I.

I'm now in shorts only, wet with perspiration, and gasping for air; my personal trainer, Marko, is kicking my ass.

Fuck this guy.

"Edward," Marcel calls as he leans over the balcony from the floor above. "You have a visitor."

I pant in search of air and unable to reply. I walk around in circles with my hands on my hips, trying to catch my breath. "Who?"

"Miss Anant."

"Who?" I yell.

"Miss Anant." His voice is muffled.

"Who?" I screw up my face. "I can't fucking hear you."

Isadora walks around the corner and I roll my eyes. *Fucking great.*

"Give me five," I tell Marko.

He leaves us alone and disappears upstairs.

"What do *you* want?" I snap, annoyed.

"Hermione just tried to kill me."

CHAPTER THIRTY-SIX

"What?" I pant, still trying to catch my breath. It wouldn't surprise me if I'm about to have a heart attack here....

"I thought it was a random accident yesterday but then it happened again this morning." She screws up her face in tears. "I didn't know what to do or where to go," she stammers as she looks around, her eyes darting along the marina.

"Slow down," I snap. "What happened?"

"Last night when I was crossing the street a car nearly hit me and I thought it was just a crazy driver, you know."

"How did a car nearly hit you?"

"I was standing on the corner waiting to cross the road and a car veered off the road and went up onto the curb. Missed me by inches and it rattled me, but I thought nothing of it."

"Okay." I listen with my hands on my hips. "It probably *was* an accident."

"It just happened again, except this time they targeted me and chased me until I ran into a store."

I stare at her as I imagine the scenario. "Did you see who was driving?"

"They were wearing a black ski mask." She begins to pace back and forth. "It's Hermione, she's going to kill me."

"It's not fucking Hermione." I roll my eyes. "She's not capable of running someone over, she won't even swat a fly."

"She's hired a hit on me, then."

Car tires screech from the street and she ducks for cover, her face screwed up. "Argh," she cries.

"Jesus." I grab her arm. "Calm down, you're a nervous wreck."

She falls against my chest in tears.

"You're safe." I pull away from her and grab a towel and wrap it around my shoulders. "Come inside." I pick up my T-shirt and she follows me inside and I glance around.

Hmm.... I don't want her in my personal space.

"Up to my office." I take the stairs as she follows. "Take a seat." I throw on my T-shirt and catch sight of my blood-red face in the mirror, fucking hell.

"So what happened?" I pour two glasses of water. "Have you spoken to anyone or done anything since I saw you on Saturday night?"

Her face falls as she stares at me. "Oh my god, of course. It was Theodore, wasn't it?"

"What?"

"He hired the hit."

"Nobody has hired a hit, you nutcase." I take a sip of water. "Although.... You are fucking asking for trouble with the bullshit threats to everyone. It's only a matter of time."

"Oh my god." She puts her head into her hands. "What am I going to do?"

"It will be fine."

"You have to protect me," she stammers. "This is all because of you, you have to give me some guards."

"Firstly, this isn't because of me. Let's get that absolutely straight from the get-go. I have done nothing but respect you and treat you well. You started this blackmailing bullshit with Hermione, and let me tell you, I saw her father recently and he is not fucking happy."

Her eyes widen. "You think it was him?"

"He doesn't know anything, but if he did, it would definitely be him."

"How do you know he doesn't know?"

"Because he was asking me what the scandal about Hermione is and threatening that if I'm involved he's going to kill *me.* If he knew, he wouldn't be asking questions, would he?"

"Oh, god."

"So stop threatening people," I snap, annoyed. "You have no one to blame but yourself."

"You have to protect me. I beg of you."

"You need to go to the police."

"I can't go to the police."

"Why not?"

"I'm going through a lot right now, okay?" she fires back.

"What does you going through a lot have anything to do with the police?"

"I know it's Hermione."

"I'll bet my life on it that it's not Hermione."

Her eyes widen as she stares up at me. "It was you?"

"Trust me, if I wanted you dead, you *would* be dead. There would be no missed attempts."

"You need to help me, I want protection," she stammers.

"No." I get up and open the door. "Call your father, get some of his men."

"He's cut me off."

"Why?"

"Long story."

I frown as I contemplate the question, what the hell could she have done for her own father to cut her off?

"What about me and you?" she whispers. "We have something, Edward, I know you love me."

My eyes hold hers but I remain silent, there's nothing I can say that won't cut her to the bone.

Her pleading gaze turns to one of anger. "So I meant nothing to you?" she spits.

"We were friends." I gesture to the door, knowing this is about to turn ugly.

"So you used me and now you're done?"

"Isadora." I roll my lips as my temper rises, how many times do I have to repeat myself to her? "Never once have I contacted you privately, never once have I called or texted you, or had any kind of sexual relations with you where we were alone. We never once had a conversation about emotional attachment or anything of such nature. I knew you through Hermione. I liked you as Hermione's friend, and it was great at the time, I'm not going to lie. I enjoyed your company immensely. We had a lot of fun together, but the fact is you turned on her when she trusted you. For you to then go on and threaten to expose our private matters to the public knowing her role in Switzerland and the carnage it would cause is unforgiveable."

"I could end your reputation," she spits.

"Ha," I huff. "That's laughable, my reputation is built on exactly this. This is on brand for me, and I don't give a flying fuck who knows it. I'll gangbang whoever I fucking want, whenever I want. But what I won't tolerate is Hermione or Theodore being blackmailed. Now get out."

"This is your last chance, Edward."

"Get out."

"You'll be sorry."

"Yeah, you told me that and oh look...here you are asking for my protection."

She stomps out the door.

"Don't steal anything on your way out," I call after her.

"Fuck you," she fires back as she walks down the stairs. "I could sink this fucking yacht if I wanted to." She must run into someone on the lower level. "What are you looking at?" she screams. "Get away from me."

I listen to her yell at everyone on her way out and a commotion as people scurry to get out of her way and I roll my eyes.

Crazy fucking bitch.

ALORA.

"What are they all doing?" Jonty asks.

"There's so many of them," Freya says as she cranes her neck to watch them.

We're cleaning the front window of my store as six guards circle around outside. Dressed in their customary suits, they're talking as they walk up and down the block, while two of them stand either side of the front door.

"It's like they're taking over the street, I wonder what the other shop staff think about it," Jonty replies.

"Right?" Freya says.

"And now that they've deadlocked the back door closed, we can't even go out there."

"You're right, this is going way too far. It's getting ridiculous." I throw down my cleaning cloth in disgust. "Enough is enough." I march out the back and dig through my bag for my phone.

I call Edward. *Ring, ring…ring, ring….* It rings out. I hang up and immediately dial his office. "Prescott Holdings, how may I help you?"

"Hi, Babette."

"Hello, Alora."

"Is Edward in his office?"

"He's just stepped out for a minute but he has his phone on him."

Well, he's not fucking answering it….

"Okay, thank you. Can you ask him to call me, please?"

"Of course, dear."

"Have a nice day. Goodbye."

"Au revoir."

I dial his number again.

You've reached Edward Prescott.
Leave a message.

I narrow my eyes and contemplate giving him what for, but hang up before I do; if there's one thing I've learned it's not to leave him an angry message. Nothing fires him up more, and he calls me back looking for a fight. I slump into my chair and sit behind my desk as I feel anger seep into my bones. Is this really what my life is going to be like forever?

No privacy.

Unable to go anywhere alone.

I know why he's like this, but honestly it's getting out of hand, I don't know if he's just nervous about the wedding or what it is, but security seems to be ramping up more every day.

I'm over it.

What the hell does he think is going to happen? History is not going to repeat itself. It's Nice, I live in a boring little terrace house and go nowhere and do nothing. Nobody is going to do anything sinister; this is beginning to affect my staff and it's not okay.

I dial his number again and it rings out…ugh. Where is he and why isn't he answering his damn phone?

Infuriating!

EDWARD.

"She's here," I hear Marcel tell the others.

It's after 6 p.m. and Alora is arriving home from work. I watch out the window of the second floor as she walks along the boardwalk with Philippe close behind her. She's wearing a cream trench coat, patent high-heeled pumps and her dark hair is swept up into an effortless loose knot, even straight from work she looks a picture of perfection. I pour two glasses of red wine.

Finally, time to relax.

"Hello, Marcel, hello, Josephine."

"Good evening, Miss Sorenson."

"Did you have a nice day?" I hear her say as she walks in through the doors.

"I did, and you?"

"It was okay." I hear her reach the bottom of the stairs. "Just another day."

"Are you ready for dinner?" Josephine asks.

"That would be lovely, thank you."

"I'll let the kitchen know. It will be about twenty minutes. I'm finishing for the day soon, can I get you anything before I log off?"

"No, sweetie, I'm fine. You get going."

I sip my wine and smile as I listen on, no wonder all of the staff adore her. She's always so thoughtful and present with each and every one of them.

"Okay."

"Thank you for today, have a lovely night." I hear her walking up the stairs.

"You too, Miss Sorenson."

She appears at the top of the stairs and I smile and tap my lap. "Here she is."

"Hi." She walks over and sits sidesaddle on my lap and I kiss her softly and she takes her glass of wine from the coffee table. "Where were you today?" she asks.

"What do you mean?"

"I was calling you but you didn't answer."

"Oh, yes." I remember now. "I went to lunch with some associates and forgot to take my phone."

Her eyes hold mine. "You didn't think to call me when you got back to the office."

"Well, it was late, and I knew I would see you soon anyway."

"Hmm." She sips her wine and gets off my lap as if annoyed, she kicks off her high heels, sits down on the couch opposite and curls her legs up underneath her.

"How was your day?" I ask.

"Annoying." Her eyes hold mine.

"How so?"

"I don't want so much security anymore."

"What?" I frown. "It's nonnegotiable, you know that."

"I had six men out the front of my store today." She widens her eyes. "Six."

"And your point is?"

"It's overkill. Enough is enough."

"You will be having security. End of story."

"Don't end of story me," she snaps. "I have a say in my life too, you know."

I sip my wine and slosh it around in my mouth, annoyed by her tone.

"I am well aware of that, but you have guards for a very good reason."

"Such as?"

"Such as." How do I say that my gut is telling me something is off? I try to word it right so as not to scare her. "Dangerous people are everywhere, Alora."

"You're being overdramatic." She rolls her eyes.

"What's with the fucking attitude," I snap. "Cut it out. I don't like it."

"You know what I don't like?" she fires back. "I'm under guard and can't even fucking sneeze without your men watching what I do, and yet you can go missing all afternoon and that's okay."

"I was at a work lunch," I spit.

"Really?"

"Where else would I fucking be?"

"Who knows." She widens her eyes at me in a silent dare.

She's looking for a fight.

"I don't know what fucking mood you're in tonight but snap out of it." I get up and walk to the stairs. "I'm going to have a quick sauna before dinner. Are you coming?"

"Nope." She sips her wine. "I'm very comfortable."

"Really?" I snap. "You're looking kind of pissy to me."

Her eyes flicker red.

"Maybe you should come and take some of that anger out on my dick?"

"With a pair of scissors?" she mutters dryly.

I chuckle as I make my way to the gym, strip off to my briefs and walk into the sauna.

I lean my head back against the back wall as the infrared lights glow red, it's steamy and hot and I feel myself begin to relax.

ALORA.

I sit on the couch scrolling through my phone. I *am* in a pissy mood tonight. Hormonal as fuck but damn it, he's annoying.

A text bounces in, the name Thomas Stone lights up the screen.

You okay?

Huh? I reply.

Yeah, why wouldn't I be?

I see dots as he types back and then they stop. I wait again as they start to bounce and then they stop again. What is he writing, a fucking novel? Too impatient to wait, I dial his number.

"Hi." He answers first ring.

"Why are you asking if I'm okay?" I snap.

"Umm." He hesitates.

"What?"

"I know this is probably all bullshit or old footage or whatever, but I just wanted to check on you, that's all."

"What is?" I snap.

"You haven't seen it?"

"Seen what?"

"I'm going to send you a link."

"Fine." I roll my eyes and sip my wine, honestly, all men are annoying tonight. He sends me a link to a story on TMZ, the celebrity gossip page. The heading reads:

Busted.
A leopard never changes its spots.

"Huh?" I read on.

Edward Prescott was caught red-handed last week entertaining one of his past love interests, Isadora Auclair, on his yacht.

"The fuck?" I murmur.

I look through the images, it's daytime and Edward is shirtless and cuddling Isadora on the below deck near the gym.

Marcel his guard is standing to the side as if watching on.

This is the woman who was trying to approach me in Monaco that day. I narrow my eyes as I zoom in on the photo. She's wearing a tight dress and her hair and makeup are done. Her hand is resting on Edward's bare chest and she has super-long red nails. There's no denying that she's hot as fuck.

Jealousy runs through me as I scroll through the pictures.

"It would be old footage for sure," Thomas replies. "Where even are they?"

"On this yacht," I fume. "He told me he never saw her through the day, that it was a nighttime-only thing."

"So you know who this person is?" he asks.

"Yeah, it's one of his old fuck buddies. Her name is Isadora."

"It could be doctored, probably is actually."

"Hmm." I keep scrolling through the photos, there are ones of her getting onto the yacht as security stands around and then ones of her leaving. I scroll back to the top and then I see it. Angelo is one of the guards on the gangplank as she boards.

"Fuck," I whisper.

"What?"

"The guard in the photo."

"What about him?"

"He only started two weeks ago."

"What?"

Fury begins to pump through me. "I've got to go."

"It's probably doctored, don't believe it—" I hang up on him mid-sentence and storm to the sauna and tear open the door. Edward is lying on his back with his eyes closed.

"What the fuck is this?" I hold my phone out.

"What?" He lifts his head, half asleep.

"Why does this say that Isadora was on this yacht last week?"

"What?" He sits up suddenly. "Show me." He snatches the phone off me and looks at the photos. "Calm down." He stands and something about the way he says *calm down* confirms my worst fear.

"Was Isadora on this yacht last week?"

"It's not how it—"

"Was she on this fucking yacht last week or not?" I scream as I lose all control.

"She came to me for help," he stammers as he wraps a towel around his waist.

"Obviously." I growl as I look at the photo of him shirtless and holding her in his arms. "I know what she needed help with." I storm from the sauna.

"Get back here." He scrambles to pick up his clothes.

"Go fuck yourself." I grab my handbag and he runs after me and grabs me from behind, he throws my bag on the floor and holds me, my arms down by my sides.

"She thinks someone is trying to kill her and she came to me for help," he stammers. "I swear to you that's all it was."

"When was this?"

"Last week."

I fight out of his grip. "So she was here last week, in my home. In your fucking arms while you are undressed and you didn't mention it once?" I shriek. "Not. Once."

"Because I knew this is how you'd react." He tries to throw it back on me. "That's why I didn't tell you."

"Ha." I pick up my bag from the floor. "You gaslighting prick."

"Where are you going?"

"Home."

"*This* is your home," he growls.

The waiters appear with a tray of our dinner.

"No. My home doesn't have booty calls come to it," I scream. "You fucking sleazebag."

Their eyes widen and they freeze on the spot, they glance at each other, scared for their lives.

I march down the stairs.

"Alora," he yells. "Get back here."

"Go fuck yourself." Adrenaline is surging through my veins and I can hardly see through the rage. I stumble out the front door and across the gangplank.

"Stop her," Edward yells from the balcony above.

"Miss Sorenson." Marcel runs along beside me as I march up the boardwalk. "Come back inside." He grabs my arm.

I rip it out of his grip. "Touch me again and I'm calling the fucking police."

"I must insist." He grabs my arm again and I completely lose control and turn and rip it from his grip.

"Leave me alone," I cry.

Edward comes running up the boardwalk. "Alora," he says sternly. "Calm down."

I trusted you.

His silhouette blurs.

"Come inside so we can talk about it."

"I want to go home."

"This is your home."

I angrily wipe the tears from my eyes. "Marcel, can you take me to my place please?"

His eyes flick between Edward and me.

"I'll drive you home myself," Edward replies.

"I don't want you to drive me anywhere." My nostrils flare as I try to hold it together.

I can feel my world collapsing around me.

I trusted you.

"Come inside and talk for ten minutes and if you still want to go home then I'll let you go."

"You'll *let* me go?" I screw up my face as my anger resurfaces. "Can you hear how fucked up that is?"

His eyes hold mine.

"You don't get to tell me what I do." I turn my back and start walking.

"Alora," he growls.

I turn like the devil himself and am now well aware that we have an audience, every yacht's staff is now out on deck listening. "What?" I fume as I fight to keep my voice down.

"I want you to come inside," he says softly. "Leave us, Marcel."

"Yes, sir."

Marcel disappears up the boardwalk and he comes to me. "You said you wouldn't leave when the chips are down. You promised," he says softly.

"Yeah, well." My eyes well with tears. "You promised to be faithful."

"I was, I swear to you. Come inside and we can talk about it."

"I just want to go home," I whisper.

His face falls. "Doe, don't cry," he whispers as he takes me into his arms. "I swear on my life I didn't touch her." I pull out of his grip and step back from him. "I love you, there's no way I would risk that," he whispers as he reaches for me again. "Come inside."

I look back to the yacht to see all of the staff there waiting and watching. I'm officially the town fucking idiot. What do they see when I'm not here?

"I just want to go home tonight," I say.

"We need to talk about this."

"Tomorrow."

His eyes search mine. "I want to come with you."

"No."

"Why not?"

"Because I don't want you to," I snap, annoyed.

"Nothing can be sorted when we're apart."

"I need some distance, Edward."

"Don't say that."

I know he's not going to let me go unless I'm civil.

"It's fine. I just want to go home and calm down and have the night to myself and we can go out for lunch tomorrow."

"I don't want to be apart from you."

"It's one night."

His eyes search mine. "Is it one night?"

I cross my arms, unsure how to reply.

"Alora, I promise you. I didn't touch her. She came to me for help. I was working out downstairs and that's why my shirt was off. She turned up crying and scared because someone had just tried to run her over and I hugged her."

My eyes hold his. *Is he lying?*

"She was here for fifteen minutes tops. That's why I bumped up your security, because I was scared they would come for you too."

Oh…. Kind of makes sense, I guess.

I feel a little better, but still unsure. I glance back to the yacht and the staff are all still watching.

I hate that we have no privacy.

"Okay."

"Okay?" he whispers.

"I still want to spend the night alone at my house, I'll see you tomorrow."

"I don't want you there alone."

"Stop this control bullshit, Edward. I can't stand it, let me go home and I'll see you tomorrow."

"Do you promise?" He takes me into his arms and kisses my temple as he holds me close.

"Yes."

"What time?"

"I have the day off, so come over around lunchtime."

"Why do we have to be apart tonight, you can ignore me all you like from the same bed."

"Oh my god. Seriously, Edward," I snap as I lose the last of my patience. "We have no future if you can't respect my boundaries. I am not a prisoner here. I am allowed to think for myself."

"Fine," he snaps. "The boys will drive you home and stay out the front. You call them if you need them."

I don't want them there but I know that if I don't agree there's no way in hell he'll let me go. He raises his arm for the boys.

"Fine." I pull out of his arms. "See you tomorrow."

"I love you."

My eyes hold his.

Do you?

"Do you love me?" he asks.

"Not tonight." I sigh.

"Will you love me tomorrow?"

"I'll think about it."

He gives me a lopsided smile.

"Take Alora back to her place, please, and stay with her overnight."

"Yes, sir."

"Goodbye," I murmur.

He kisses my face. "Good night, I love you," he says in front of everyone.

I roll my eyes and trudge to the car; he opens the door and I climb into the back seat.

"See you tomorrow." He forces a smile.

"Yep." The car pulls away and I sit and stare out the window into the darkness.

FORTY MINUTES LATER.

"Thank you," I tell the boys as I get out of the car.

"We'll be here if you need anything."

"I don't need anything, you can go." I sigh as I trudge up to the front and go inside. I close the door and flick the deadlock on.

What a nightmare of a day.

I walk into the kitchen and flick the kettle on.

I'm dead tired, confused and a little heartbroken. I mean, I know I perhaps should have at least talked about it, but I'm honestly too mad to be around Edward right now. Rummaging through my purse, I dig out my phone and see the missed calls, I'm not calling him back tonight.

I wasn't lying, I really do need some time alone tonight. I want to sit with this information for a while without him influencing the way I feel.

Something hard and cold comes to my temple as I am grabbed around the neck from behind.

"Move a muscle and I'll blow your fucking head off."

CHAPTER THIRTY-SEVEN

"What?" The arm strangles me hard from behind. I see our reflection in the oven door. They're dressed fully in black and wearing a balaclava and goggles. A weird tape recording of a man's voice plays; it's been doctored and isn't familiar. It repeats the same line from before. "Move a muscle and I'll blow your fucking head off."

What the fuck?

I fight.

I fight hard as I'm held from behind and we struggle for control. We hit the cupboard and then stumble forward and hit the fridge, it rocks to the side. "What do you want?" I cry. "Just take it, take everything."

What the hell is happening?

"Help," I cry as I struggle. I can feel myself being overpowered.

They're too strong.

"Philippe." I fight back harder and lash out; the person stumbles back and I run for the knife drawer.

Crack.

I'm hit on the side of my head from behind with the butt of the gun, the blunt force knocking me to the floor.

"Philippe," I cry as my vision blurs; the room begins to spin. "Help me," I whimper.

Try harder.

"Philippe," I call again, but my voice is weak, an echo into the silence.

A sharp stab goes into my neck and I try to kick out and pull away as something is injected into me.... I raise my hand and try and pull the needle out but my hand is held away. The same recording plays again. "Move a muscle and I'll blow your fucking head off."

No….

"Help me," I whimper as the room begins to spin. "Edward…."

Unable to move, my head flops to the side and time seems to stand still, sound is muffled and the blurred room begins to spin.

On the diagonal, I see someone in black go to the shelving unit and somehow open it. A staircase appears….

My eyes flutter as I fight for consciousness.

What the hell is going on…what is that staircase….am I dreaming?

Is this a nightmare?

The person walks back over to me and kicks me hard in the stomach, intense pain radiates through me but I'm paralyzed, unable to react.

No…. No…. I can't open my eyes and sound begins to fade.

Pain…darkness….

Nothing.

EDWARD.

Pacing back and forth, I throw down another glass of scotch. I keep going over and over tonight in my head.

I see the pain in Alora's hurt face and I close my eyes in regret. She didn't deserve that.

Fuck.

I drag my hand through my hair, why didn't I just tell Alora that she came here?

To be honest it wasn't even a conscious decision, after she left I didn't think about it again. We had such a hectic week without a moment to spare. Alora and I met with an architect and were excited and talking about our new house and then Alora was obsessed with wedding crap and she was talking about that every night. I was preoccupied with work stuff too.

Isadora never entered my mind.

Not once.

I link my fingers on top of my head as I continue to pace. I can't stand not being with her.

I feel like I'm about to lose my fucking mind here.

With a shaky hand I pour another glass of scotch and take a large gulp. I slosh it around in my mouth and feel it burn all the way down.

Calm down.

I continue to pace back and forth like a caged animal.

Alora's alone.

It's not safe...I'm going over there.... Her parting words come back to haunt me. *"We have no future if you can't respect my boundaries. I am not a prisoner here. I am allowed to think for myself."*

Fuck....

If I go over there and force entry into her house...I'm going to fuck this whole relationship if I'm not careful.

I've already fucked it.

Just call her and say good night. With my heart in my throat I dial her number.

Hello, you've reached Alora Sorenson. I'm sorry, I can't take your call right now.
Leave a message and I'll call you back as soon as I can.
Have a nice day.

"Doe," I say softly. "I just wanted to see that you got home safe and to say good night." I hold on the line as I try to articulate my thoughts. "I promise you on my life.... It isn't how it looked. I love you, I would never jeopardize what we have." I keep pacing. "Even now I can't hang up the phone. I can't stand the thought of even one night apart," I murmur.

Fuck.... I'm pathetic.

"Can you call me back, please?" I ask. "I need to know you're okay." I hold on the line again, willing her to pick up. "Speak soon, I love you." I hang up and let out a deep exhale.

What if she ends it over this?

She wouldn't...would she? My anxiety picks up again and I call Philippe.

"Hey."

"Did you get home safe?" I ask him.

"Yes."

"Where is she?"

"She went inside about half an hour ago."

"Is she in bed?"

"Her upstairs bedroom light is on now, so I'm assuming she's in the shower or getting ready for bed."

That's why she didn't answer my call.

"Okay."

Hopefully she'll call me back when she gets out of the shower.

"Keep your eyes and ears peeled."

"Of course, boss, there's nothing going on here, it's dead quiet."

"Okay." I think for a moment. "Did she say anything on the way home?"

"No, she kept to herself. Cried a little."

My stomach twists.

"Boss...." He cuts himself off mid-sentence.

"What is it?"

"May I speak out of turn?"

"Of course."

"Do you not think it's odd that Isadora turns up with a TMZ crew trailing her?"

Hmm....

I was so distracted by Alora being angry I didn't put the pieces together.

Of course.

My eyes flicker red and my grip tightens around my phone.

"Isadora set me up."

"That would be my guess, sir."

I feel adrenaline surge through my bloodstream. "Thank you, Philippe." I hang up and throw the phone hard at the wall.

"That fucking woman," I growl.

She told me I would pay.... And here I am paying.

I down my glass of scotch as fury heats my blood. "You're messing with the wrong man, Isadora. Your time will come."

AN HOUR LATER.

I can't stand this, I can't relax until I know she's okay. She's probably crying right at this minute over me. I call her again.

Hello, you've reached Alora Sorenson. I'm sorry, I can't take your call right now.
Leave a message and I'll call you back as soon as I can.
Have a nice day.

Ugh…her phone is still switched off. She really doesn't want to talk to me at all.

I hang up and call Philippe.

"Hey, boss."

"What's happening?" I ask.

"All lights are off, she's asleep."

"Can you walk around the house and do a perimeter check please?"

"Now?"

"Now. I'll wait on the phone while you do."

"Okay."

I wait on and listen to him walk around the house. "Check every window is locked."

"Of course." I hear the side gate open and then his footsteps on the pebbles. "I'm in the backyard now."

"Anything off?"

"No. The blinds are open downstairs."

"Why would the blinds be open? She never leaves them open."

"She's otherwise occupied, I guess."

"True." I think for a moment. "Is everything alright inside?"

"Yeah, I'm looking through the windows right now. Everything is normal. Nothing to see."

I listen with my heart in my throat. "Nobody is in the backyard?"

"No, boss, of course not. The only way to get in here is to scale up a cliff or over the neighbors' twelve-foot fence. We're parked in the driveway and are doing perimeter checks every half hour. I'm telling you, everything is fine. Alora's asleep and you should try and relax and get some too."

"Okay." I think for a moment. "Maybe I should come over and stay in the car with you?"

"Then it's just more people to guard. Get some sleep."

"You're right." I nod. "Call me if anything happens."

"Of course."

I hang up and walk out into the deck, I watch the lights of Monaco twinkle in the distance. A deep anxiety swirls deep in my psyche and I feel so unhinged without her by my side. One night without her and I feel like I'm falling apart.

Who even am I?

ALORA.

Swish, swish.... Swish, swish...swish, swish.

Metal clangs in the distance, a hard sound, familiar and yet unknown.

Swish, swish.... Swish, swish...swish, swish.

I doze, somewhere between reality and hell. It's dark but the area appears to be lit by a flashlight, where am I?

My heavy eyelids battle to open and I gag, whatever is in my mouth is so big that I can hardly breathe.

Help me....

I look around as I try to get my bearings. I go to wipe my face only to realize I'm tied down; dragging my eyes up to my wrists I see huge bolts have been drilled into the floorboards and I am spread out and tied down by my hands and ankles.

I pull to try and loosen them but I can't move an inch.

Swish, swish.... Swish, swish...swish, swish.

What the fuck is that noise?

Where the hell am I? My eyes dart around, suddenly panicked. What's going on here?

I look to the side of me and there on the floor is a blue cloth tool kit rolled open and in it a set of stainless-steel hunting knives.

Swish, swish.... Swish, swish... swish, swish.

What the hell is that noise?

I look over to the corner to see a person dressed in black, wearing a black balaclava and some kind of goggles. Sharpening a knife on a honing rod. They swipe it back and forth making the *swish* sound as they stare at me blankly.

Oh my god....

My breath hitches in fear as tears roll down into my ears.

No.

Panic screams through me and I struggle to break free. I try to yell around the gag in my mouth but no sound comes out.

Help me! Help me!

Swish, swish.... Swish, swish...swish, swish.

I screw up my face as I fight and struggle and pull on the ropes and try my hardest to break free.

The person in black calmly kneels down beside me and seemingly studies my face.

I frantically shake my head.

Please don't do this!

They slowly run the tip of the blade down my cheek and then hold it to my neck, they stare at me for a long time. Emotionless and cold.

I shake my head, frantically hoping for a miracle.

Please, God.

Please don't let this happen...help me!

Please help me.

"Prescott will pay." They cup my face in their hand and brush their gloved thumb over my bottom lip. "With your life."

I shake my head frantically as I scream around the gag. I kick and fight with everything I have.

"It's time to die."

CHAPTER THIRTY-EIGHT

EDWARD.

Patience isn't my greatest strength.

I've tossed and turned all night, fought with myself long and hard not to go to Alora and make her believe me. The only thing that's stopped me is the knowledge of her zero tolerance for my controlling ways.

Turning the corner into her street, I glance at the time on my dash: 6:21 a.m.

I couldn't wait a minute longer.

I pull my Bentley into the drive beside Philippe; he's sitting inside the car and another man is sitting on the front porch.

"Hi." Philippe scrambles out of the car. "I wasn't expecting you this early."

"Yeah, I know." I walk past him. "Just wanted to get here." I walk up the stairs and put my key into the door and push but it doesn't open.

"The deadlock's on," Philippe tells me from behind. "We checked for that last night."

"Good." I take out my phone to call her, I really want to surprise her while she's still in bed. "I'll go around to the back door." I make my way around the side of the house and to the set of French doors. I open the door with my key and head upstairs. The room is dark and the blankets are pooled over her body. I lie down beside her and pull the blanket back to see pillows strategically placed under the covers to look like her.

"What?" I jump up and rip the blankets back. "What the fuck?" I turn the lights on. "Alora?" I call. I check the bathroom. "Alora," I call as panic begins to set in. I dial her number and I hear a distant muffled ring downstairs.

I take the stairs two at a time.

Hello, you've reached Alora Sorenson. I'm sorry, I can't take your call right now.

Leave a message and I'll call you back as soon as I can.

Have a nice day.

"The fuck?" I dial her number again. "Alora," I call as I walk through the house, a sense of urgency coursing through my veins. I hear her phone ringing, it's muffled and my eyes dart around as I search for it. "What is going on?"

Hello, you've reached Alora Sorenson. I'm sorry, I can't take your call right now.

Leave a message and I'll call you back as soon as I can.

Have a nice day.

I march to the front door and tear it open. "Where is she?" I yell.

Philippe's eyes widen and he runs up the driveway. "What do you mean?" he stammers.

"She isn't here, there were pillows in her bed."

"What?" He and the other guard glance at each other. "She hasn't left and nobody has been here all night."

I dial her number and once again a muffled ring sounds through the house. "Find. The. Fucking. Phone," I growl.

Ring, ring.... Ring, ring....

They run from room to room as they follow the sound.

"It's in here somewhere," Philippe calls from the kitchen, we all run in and concentrate as we try to listen.

Hello, you've reached Alora Sorenson. I'm sorry, I can't take your call right now.

Leave a message and I'll call you back as soon as I can.

Have a nice day.

"Fuck," I yell. I hang up and immediately call it again.

Ring, ring.... Ring, ring.

"It's low." I listen.

Philippe gets down and puts his ear to the floor. "It's down here somewhere." He crawls along. "It's under the fridge."

My heart begins to hammer. "Why the fuck would it be under the fridge?" He gets a broom handle and slides it under and sure enough her phone comes into view.

He picks it up and we all stare at it, unsure what this means.

I open the fridge to see the two-liter bottles of milk and orange juice are tipped over as if the fridge was tipped. I look around and put two and two together. "There's been a struggle."

"I don't, I have no..." Philippe stammers.

"What the fuck were you idiots doing all night?" I scream so loud the paint nearly peels from the walls. "Alora," I cry. "Where are you?"

"Did she take off?" Philippe says. His fingers are clasped on top of his head; he too is beginning to panic. "You were fighting, perhaps she snuck out."

"Without her phone?" I look around and see her purse on the table. I march over and search through it, her wallet is inside and I check and find all of her credit cards still here. "Without any money?"

Thump.

Thump.

Thump...goes my heart.

"Check her tracker," Philippe snaps as he runs up the stairs.

"Yes, yes." With shaky fingers I try to open the app on my phone, I'm so frazzled I can hardly see the screen. I watch as the little dot comes into view and I press *Track*.

The red dot begins to flash and I zoom in as I try to read it. The satellite view of a street comes into view. I zoom in further...it's.... "Fuck, it's this street."

I zoom again and it gets closer and closer...it's in this house. I frown, confused. "It says she's still here?"

"Is she in her garden?" Philippe calls from upstairs.

I run into the garden and look around, no sign of her. "Check the back cameras," I cry.

They begin running through footage on their phones while I walk around. I go back upstairs and look at the crumpled bed. I go into the bathroom and bend down in the shower, no water. She hasn't showered. The first thing she would have done when she got home last night was shower. I walk around her bedroom, my eyes search every inch of the walls, the floors, the bed linen.... Anything, as I try to pick up a scent, a semblance of a clue to her whereabouts.

"Alora," I call. "Are you here?" I get down on the floor and look under her bed, I search the wardrobe and go through her clothes. No empty hangers, did she pack anything? I run down to the level below and check where she keeps her suitcases, everything is still here.

"Where the fuck are you? Alora," I call, I listen....

Nothing.

I check the tracker again, the dot flashes right here. I frown, this doesn't make any sense.

She took it off....

Fuck.

My god, I should have told her it was a tracker and then she would have kept it on. But she never took it off anyway so.... Where is it?

I look in the bathroom and in her bedside drawers, I walk from room to room trying to locate it. My eyes scan every nook and cranny and still I can't find the diamond bracelet. I walk back to the kitchen and get on my hands and knees and look around, did I miss anything down here?

Thump.

Thump.

Thump...goes my heart.

"Babe, where are you?" I whisper in a panic. "Are you okay?" I get up and take out my phone. I concentrate to try and read the screen, I dial the number.

"Thomas Stone."

"Thomas." I pause, what the fuck even is this conversation? "It's Edward Prescott."

"Oh, hey, Edward."

"Please tell me Alora is with you."

"No. Why?"

I close my eyes.

"We had a disagreement last night and she came home and now she's missing."

"Oh no, that's my fault you had a fight."

"What?"

"I texted her to see if she was okay after the story."

"You fucking idiot," I snap.

"She said she was fine. She texted me on her way home last night to say that you had fought but she was fine and she wanted to stay at home."

"What else did she say?"

"That you and her were going to work it out today at lunch, she thought that maybe she was being naïve but her gut told her that the woman had set you up."

"I thought that too."

"Have you called her?"

"Her phone is here, her purse with all her cards is here."

"Check her phone, see if anyone else called her."

"Good thinking." I grab her phone, put in the passcode, and scroll through her texts. "I last texted her yesterday morning and then only yours and hers," I reply as I search. "Let me check the call register." I scroll through and see her calls to me and my office yesterday that I didn't answer and my gut twists in disgust, why didn't I call her back? "It shows my missed calls to her last night but nothing else."

"Oh my god," he whispers. "You don't think...that fucking weirdo ex of hers. I knew he was fucking off."

"I've had people trailing him since Sunday, he was home all night. I've had people on Isadora too, just to be safe." I think out loud. "She was home all night as well. I get notified if either of them leaves their house."

Hermione....

No....

"Have you tried calling her?" he asks.

"I just told you her phone is here, her purse with all her cards is inside."

"Shit. That's fucking weird, nobody leaves the house without a phone and money."

"Right?"

"Call her dad."

"I don't want to worry them."

"She's fucking missing, Prescott. They need to be worried."

I drag my hand down my face. "This is my worst fucking nightmare."

"Did you call her workers from the store? Helene, try Helene."

"No."

"Do that. I'm on my way."

I nod, cortisol stealing my ability to reply.

"It's okay, Edward. We'll find her."

"What if something has happened?"

"How? She's guarded like a fucking treasure." He thinks for a moment. "Look, I think maybe she's just pissed and has taken off to cool down."

I nod, hoping that's true.

"I'll see you soon."

I hang up and go back to walking around the yard. "Anything?" I call.

"Nothing came in or out all night," Philippe calls as he stares at his phone.

"Check again, she didn't just vanish."

They keep searching and I go to the side fence and look up at the top, nobody could get up there. I walk to the back of the garden to the cliff and that's when I see it, a set of footprints leading to the cliff, and I kneel down beside them. "Down here," I cry.

They come running out and fall to the ground beside me. "Are these your footprints?" I ask. "Were either of you at this cliff overnight?"

They exchange glances and both shake their heads. "No."

"That's a man-sized shoe," I murmur as I stare at it in the dirt, adrenaline is surging though my bloodstream. "Call the police."

"And what happened then?" the policeman asks as he sits opposite me on the couch.

"I...." I pause. "She was going to bed so I did too." I throw up my hands. "I had men out the front...." I shrug as I struggle to push words past my lips.

"Has she ever taken off before?" he asks.

"She hasn't taken off," I snap. "She's been taken. There are fucking male footprints in the back garden."

He gives me a condescending smile. "With all due respect, Mr. Prescott. There has been no indication that this is the scene of a crime, they could be a gardener's or anyone's. She hasn't even been gone for twenty-four hours; she may have just left under the cloak of privacy to get away from your guards."

"She wouldn't do that." I shake my head. "And if this isn't the scene of a crime, why was her phone under the fridge?"

His eyes hold mine.

"Why were things knocked over in the fridge as if there was a struggle?"

"We have forensics checking everything now and I'm sure she's going to turn up fine."

I glance into the kitchen to see them combing the space with dusting powder.

Thomas is out the front with the guards, they are calling everyone in search of her.

"Is there anyone who may know where she is?" he asks. "Anyone who may have a grudge against her?" He is scribbling down notes. "Anyone that may have an idea of what has happened here?"

"I don't think—" I cut myself off.

"Who?"

"Um...." My hands are shaking, my mind is fried. "I'm...."

"I know who you can ask," Thomas says from behind me.

"Who's that?" the policeman asks.

"Edward's ex-girlfriend, Princess Hermione of Switzerland."

The policeman's eyes come to me. "Anybody else?"

"Her father, King Volter."

Three days, seventy-two hours, 4,320 minutes....

It's a long time to hold your breath, to pray with every cell in your body for a miracle. To miss someone so much that it physically hurts.

Alora hasn't accessed any bank accounts; my worst fear is coming true.

I stare through the window and out over the marina down below.

Where are you, my love?

We've exhausted every lead possible, every person who's ever hated me. Every business deal gone bad. Pascal, Hermione, and Isadora.... Checked the video footage from their homes.

Nothing.

Not even a scent of a lead. Every one of them can be accounted for.

Alora's father and brother are downstairs, along with my brother and father. Theodore, Sinclair, and Thomas. It's all hands on deck and even with all our resources pooled, we still have no idea how she just vanished without a trace.

The marina blurs and I swallow the lump in my throat. As the hours tick by, my dread grows. A twisted dark vine taking over my soul.

Where is she?

I haven't slept, I haven't eaten.... I'm barely able to function. Clinging to hope is the only thing keeping me sane.

"Alora," I whisper into the silence, her name an ethereal prayer.

From the corner of my eye I see the post delivery truck, he pulls up at the marina and begins to walk along the yachts as he hands out the mail.

"You okay, man?" Thomas says softly from behind me.

I nod, unable to push a lie through my lips.

I'm as far from okay as physically possible but I won't rest until I bring her home.

Where are you, Doe?

"Thank you," I hear someone say from down below.

"Can I get you anything?" Thomas asks.

"No."

"I'm worried about you," he replies.

"I'm worried about me," I murmur, my gaze still out the window.

"Mr. Prescott." I hear someone walking up the stairs. "You have a delivery from the casino, sir."

"Put it in my office."

"It's marked urgent."

"Just leave it here," Thomas tells him. He puts it on the table and disappears down the stairs. "Do you want me to open this?" Thomas asks.

I keep staring out the window, battling to find the will to breathe.

I hear packaging unwrap. "Huh?" Thomas frowns. "What *is* this?"

I turn and see him unwrapping a box, inside it another box and inside that another box.

The hairs on the back of my neck stand to attention and I walk over to the table and take over from him. I open the final box and plastic wrap sits on top, I peel it back to see a lump of meat covered in blood, there's a vine wrapped around it.

"What the fuck?" There's a laminated card sitting within it and I pick it up, blood drops off it onto the floor.

THE HEART YOU KEPT

"Oh my god," Thomas gasps. "No."

"I don't understand," I whisper. "What...is this...."

"It's a human heart." He cuts me off. My eyes flick up to him. Thomas is a doctor, he would know this.

I stare at it as I connect the dots.

My eyes widen, dear god.

The heart I kept was Alora's....

The earth moves beneath me as I stare at the card, my hand covered in blood...her blood, and I grab the table to stop myself from falling.

She's dead.

CHAPTER THIRTY-NINE

THOMAS.

Edward sways and I reach out to steady him on his feet. "It's okay," I whisper, but it's not. It's as far from okay as it can possibly get. "William," I call.

Silence.

Edward looks down at the blood dripping off his hand and sways again.

Our eyes both float to the heart in the box and I too become unstable.

Dear god.

"William," I scream. "Philippe, somebody get up here." I hold Edward up with all of my strength. "I've got you."

The sound of footsteps comes running up the stairs, the room spins hard.

A million dark thoughts race through my mind at speed.

Who would do such a thing?

William appears first, his eyes immediately drop to the blood on the floor. "What happened? Are you injured?"

"I...." Edward's eyes flutter as he fights shock.

"What's wrong?" William's eyes dart between us in question.

"Somebody sent that," I whisper. I point at the box as I step back from it.

He peers into the box. "I don't understand, what is it?"

"A human heart."

His horrified eyes flick up to meet mine. "What the...." He pulls the plastic back and he steps back from it as if seeing a ghost. "Are you sure?"

"I...." I grip the table, feeling woozy too. "I don't know."

"What's going on?" Philippe asks from behind him.

"Somebody sent something...." William shakes his head in disbelief. "Call the police."

Whispers in the hallways, police interviewing people, fingerprints, and bodyguards everywhere you look.

A morbid cloud hangs over Monte Carlo.

Edward hasn't said a word to anyone since the package arrived yesterday. He walked into his room, locked the door, and hasn't come out.

I guess, what else is there to say?

Edward's closest friends are with his and Alora's family inside. DNA testing was carried out yesterday, but no results or leads so far.

I sit on the deck alone, an outsider. As we were looking for Alora, Edward asked me to be here, but now.... I'm not sure if I should go or stay.... Or if I'm intruding or what the hell to do.

Helene is at the store trying to hold Alora's world together and her sister can't stop crying.

My mind trolls every possibility of who could do such a thing, of what to do next.

How can I help?

I know I only just met Alora and our friendship was young, but she's had such a profound effect on everyone she knows.

Deeply loved for the caring, sweet person she was.

Was....

The lump in my throat hurts again, a reminder of the tears I cannot cry.

God...I can't even imagine what Edward is going through right now.

I glance at my watch: 7 p.m.

I've hung around all afternoon waiting for the DNA results to come in but the lab closed two hours ago, so one can only assume they mustn't be coming today. My phone vibrates in my pocket, Helene.

"Hi," I answer softly.

"Any word?"

"No." I stare out over the sea.

"I'm still praying."

"Same...but." I stop myself from saying my worst fears out loud, because if I say them out into the universe then they might come true.

"What?"

"They confirmed it was a human heart."

"I know."

"You don't just find human hearts lying around," I murmur. "You definitely don't send them to random people if there isn't a connection of some sort."

"I know," she sniffles through tears.

We hang on the line for a while, both lost in our own thoughts.

"I'm going to get going home, I feel like I'm in the way here," I whisper.

"Okay," she replies softly. "Thomas."

"Yeah."

"Thanks for being there, it would mean a lot to Alora."

My nostrils flare as I try to keep it together, I need to get off the phone before I have my own meltdown. "Keep me posted?"

"Of course." I hang up and walk to the door and wave over William, he gets up and comes to the door.

"I'm going to get going."

"Okay." He shakes my hand. "Thanks for being here."

"How is he?"

"Still hasn't said a word."

I nod, unsure what to say next. "Can you let me know if there are any developments?"

"Of course." He pulls me into a hug and damn it, I wish to god this wasn't real. I turn and walk off the yacht and as I walk up the marina I glance back at the superyacht.

Five stories of hell.

EDWARD.

With my hands in my pockets, I stand at the window and stare out over the sea.

I watched the sun rise and go down, cemented to this spot.

Alora's words swirl around in my psyche, over and over like a spell cast.

I'm not going to dim my light to feed your shadows.

She knew.... And deep down, I knew.

My shadows were always going to catch up with me. There is a darkness that follows my soul.

Steals everything from me that I love.

My vision blurs and I angrily wipe my eyes with my forearm.

I can't do this, I'm not strong enough.

As soon as the results come in....

I go to my drawer and take out my Glock, I check it's loaded and hide it in my bathroom laundry basket because I know they will take it from me when the time comes.

"Edward," my father's voice says urgently from the other side of the door. "Open up. The results are here."

I close my eyes. I don't want to know.

"It's not hers."

I glance to the door. "What?"

"Open the fucking door."

I tear the door open to see my and Alora's fathers, standing side by side in the hallway. "There's no DNA match. They don't know whose heart that is, but it's not hers."

My body screams with adrenaline as I hear my pulse beat hard.

"Don't you see," my father stammers. "If they killed her, it *would* have been hers."

My eyes search theirs as my breath hitches in my throat.

"She's still alive."

THE END

THE SOUL YOU OWN

Revenge is a double-edged sword. He'll set fire to the world for his one true love …. But who gets burned alive in the process?

Blackmail, Darkness, and a missing person.

When Edward Prescott's luxurious world comes crashing down around him, he has to fight his every demon and move heaven and earth in a race against time.

Haunted by his past, present and future…. Can he find his beloved Alora before it's too late?

If you enjoyed *The Heart You Kept*, continue reading the Kings of the Riviera series with book two, *The Soul You Own*. To guarantee a copy of the deluxe first-print edition that includes sprayed-edges and all the front-cover embellishments, pre-order your copy now.

READ THE MR. SERIES - AVAILABLE NOW

Before Edward Prescott, there were the Misters...

Three men. Three forbidden stories.
Each one grumpy, bossy, and far too irresistible for his own good.
From a brooding judge, to a notorious playboy, to a dangerously charming politician—every book in T L Swan's *Mr. Series* is passionate, powerful and heartbreakingly real.
Start reading, and discover the world where it all began...

Find *Mr. Masters, Mr. Spencer* and *Mr. Garcia*
in your favourite bookstores today!

NOTE FROM THE AUTHOR

Thank you so much for reading and for your ongoing support. I have the most beautiful readers in the whole world!

Keep up to date with all the latest news and online discussions by joining the Swan Squad VIP Facebook group and discuss your favourite books with other readers.

Visit my website, subscribe to my newsletter and follow me on my socials for all updates and new-release information.

www.tlswanauthor.com
www.tlswanauthor.com/newsletter/

facebook.com/tlswanauthor

Instagram.com/tlswanauthor

tiktok.com/tlswanauthor

ACKNOWLEDGEMENTS

It takes an army to write a book and I undoubtedly have the best army in the world.

To my beautiful mum, who reads chapter by chapter on the day that I write it. I love you so much and thank you for everything you do for me.

To my incredible publishing team from Arndell - Keeperton. The care, attention to detail, preparation and work you put in behind the scenes for every book just blows me away. It's a privilege to get to work alongside you. You're my teachers, my mentors, my cheerleaders, and there's no doubt about it that you are the hardest-working and most caring publishing team in the business. Thank you for sharing my vision so vividly, you're a dream come true.

To my beta readers, Lisa and Rena, you make me better. Thank you so much for your patience while I rewrite every book a gazillion times.

To my editing team, Lindsey, Imogen and Claudette. You are the dream team and I don't know how I was lucky enough that you took me on, but you did.... and amazing things happen when we work together.

To our incredible cover designer Alex Ross. I'm so in love with the Kings Of The Riviera Series and I needed a cover I love just as much. Thank you for the perfect covers, they are everything I dreamt they would be.

To our Romance Community, the book bloggers, the Instagrammers, the TikTokers, the Facebookers, and the reviewers. I couldn't do this job without your never-ending support. Thank you so very much, I can't always reply to everything I see online that you do for me (though I try). Please know how much I appreciate everything you do.

Every post, every reel, every Tiktok, every little detail in the things that you do …. change an author's life. My life… Please know that. We are so, so grateful.

To my family, thank you for supporting me through what has been the hardest health year I have ever had. Breaking my back was not on my bingo card but you held me up, helped me walk again… Quite literally. And breathed life back into me when I thought I was broken forever. You will never know how much your love, patience, and support healed me back to health. I love you so, so much.

And last but not least, you.

My beautiful reader friends, you have made my dreams come true.

Thank you for always showing up for me, for reading my books, for believing in me when I forget to believe in myself and for waiting for what seems like forever for my next release. It's because of you that I get to write books and do my dream job. The words *thank you* never seem enough, but I'll say them again anyway.

Thank you. Thank you. Thank you.

From the bottom of my heart, thank you.

ABOUT THE AUTHOR

T L Swan (aka Tee) is a *USA Today*, *Wall Street Journal*, and #1 Amazon bestselling author from the South Coast of New South Wales, Australia. Best known for her addictive, heart-pounding romances, she's built a devoted global readership who can't get enough of her witty banter, emotional depth, and swoon-worthy heroes.

With millions of books sold worldwide, her stories have been translated into twenty languages and have regularly hit #1 on Amazon in the USA, UK, Canada, Australia, and Germany. Known for her bestselling billionaire romance series *The Miles High Club*, Tee writes stories filled with irresistible chemistry and heart-melting emotion. Her books are known for their unforgettable characters, laugh-out-loud moments, heartfelt romance, and sizzling heat.

A hopeless romantic, Tee started writing to escape into worlds where love, wit, and happily-ever-afters always win.

When she's not writing in coffee shops, soaking up the atmosphere while crafting her next brooding hero or fiery heroine, you'll find her at her favourite place, home with her husband and three children, living her own happily ever after with her first true love, her family, and friends.

A word lover, bookworm, and margarita addict, Tee aims to bring the same joy, humour, and heart to her life as she does to each one of her stories.

Connect with Arndell

Love this book? Discover your next romance book obsession and stay up to date with the latest releases, exclusive content, and behind-the-scenes news!

Explore More Books

Visit our homepage: keeperton.com/arndell

Follow Us on Social Media

Instagram: @arndellbooks
Facebook: Arndell
TikTok: @arndellbooks

Stay in the Loop

Join our newsletter: keeperton.com/subscribe

Join the Conversation

Use **#Arndell** or **#ArndellBooks** to share your thoughts and connect with fellow romance readers!

Thank you for being part of our book-loving community. We can't wait to share more unforgettable stories with you!